Head IN THE Clouds

Books by
Karen Witemeyer

A Tailor-Made Bride

Head in the Clouds

Head IN THE Clouds

KAREN WITEMEYER

MINNEAPOLIS, MINNESOTA

Head in the Clouds
Copyright © 2010
Karen Witemeyer

Cover design by Dan Thornberg, Design Source Creative Services

Scripture quotations are from the King James Version of the Bible.

Published by Bethany House Publishers
11400 Hampshire Avenue South
Bloomington, Minnesota 55438

Bethany House Publishers is a division of
Baker Publishing Group, Grand Rapids, Michigan.

Printed in the United States of America

Library of Congress Cataloging-in-Publication Data

Witemeyer, Karen.
    Head in the clouds / Karen Witemeyer.
        p.   cm.
    ISBN 978-0-7642-0756-3 (pbk.)
    1. Governesses—Fiction. 2. Ranches—Texas—Fiction. 3. Texas—History—1846–1950—Fiction. I. Title.
    PS3623.I864H43   2010
    813'.6—dc22

                                                                            2010016353

To my mom.
We've shared so many dreams.
I pray you will share my joy as this one comes true.

And to my second mom, Hilda.
You shared your son with me and believed in my abilities
while I floundered in uncertainty.
You're welcome to raid my book closet anytime!

A man's heart deviseth his way:
but the Lord directeth his steps.

PROVERBS 16:9

Prologue

CISCO, TEXAS—APRIL 1883

Tonight is the night. She could feel it.

Adelaide Proctor stared at the man across from her, so many flutters dancing in her stomach she couldn't possibly eat a bite of the apple pie he'd just ordered for her. The secret smiles he'd sent her that morning over breakfast at the boardinghouse, his request to dine with her so they might discuss the future . . .

The future! How could it be anything else? Henry Belcher was finally going to propose.

"Is the pie not to your liking, my dear?" He set his fork down and glanced up at her. Always solicitous, that was her Henry.

"I'm sure it's delicious," Adelaide said, looking down at her lap and fiddling with the hem of the white tablecloth. "It's just that you mentioned you wished to discuss something with me this evening, and I'm afraid my curiosity has stolen my appetite."

"Of course. How thoughtless of me." He pushed his plate of half-eaten pie to the side and reached across the table, holding his hand palm up. "I should not have kept you in suspense all through dinner."

With a hitch in her breath, Adelaide drew one arm from her lap and eased her fingers into his. His thumb rubbed the back of her hand—an intimate gesture that infused her with hope. And if it didn't stir her deeper emotions . . . well, what did that matter? Not all marriages were based on a grand passion. She and Henry shared something much more likely to last: common interests and mutual respect. If carefully cultivated, she had no doubt such attributes would bloom into love.

"You have come to mean so very much to me over this last year," Henry said, his tone oozing sincerity. "Every month when I start my route anew, I long for the day the train brings me to Cisco so that I might see you again. You've been so loyal to me, ordering books for your classroom or yourself. I can't tell you how much your generosity has stirred my heart."

Adelaide met his gaze, her own heart stirring. "I love to read, and I . . . I try to instill a similar value in my students." She gently squeezed Henry's fingers and watched as his mouth curved into a warm, masculine smile. "You always go out of your way to find just the right books for us. Other peddlers try to foist only their most expensive volumes. But not you. You care about your customers. I could tell that right from the start."

"I care about *you*, my dear."

Adelaide's pulse hummed through her like a whirligig picking up speed. Before the T&P brought Henry to town, she had despaired of ever finding a husband. She'd signed a two-year teaching contract that precluded her from marrying within that time frame. The few suitors who had demonstrated interest when she first arrived lost patience and married elsewhere. But all her waiting was about to pay off.

Henry reached across the table with his other arm and cocooned her hand within both of his. "I care about you a great deal, Adelaide.

That is why I've been reluctant to spoil our dinner with the news I must share with you."

"Spoil our dinner?" Unease slithered through her. "What do you mean?"

"I received word from the home office. I'm to be promoted from salesman to regional manager."

Relief so keen it nearly hurt washed over Adelaide. "Henry," she scolded, "shame on you. You had me thinking the news was going to be dreadful. A promotion is cause for celebration. I'm so proud of you."

Henry patted her hand in a way that felt less like reassurance and more like sympathy. "You don't understand, darling. I'll be working in Fort Worth permanently. I won't be traveling the rail lines any longer. There will be no more visits to Cisco."

Adelaide didn't care if she left Cisco. Didn't he realize that? She'd gladly resign from her teaching position and move to Fort Worth if it meant having a husband and family of her own. She'd yearned for such a blessing since the day her father died.

"It breaks my heart to think that I'll not see you again." Henry's expression was so somber it frightened her. Was he not going to propose? Could he be so unsure of her answer that he'd not risk asking her to choose him over her students?

Yes. That must be it.

How could she embolden him without being too brazen? Adelaide nibbled on her lip and leaned forward in her chair. "With all the tales you've told me about Fort Worth's burgeoning society—the concerts, the fancy hotel dining rooms, the parties of the wealthy cattle barons—I would think you'd be pleased to settle in such a town." She lowered her lashes. "*I* would be happy to call such a place home."

Adelaide peeked at Henry to judge his response. His sad smile remained fixed, his eyes unchanged. After a year of acquaintance she should have been able to decipher his mood better, but in truth, if she tallied all the days she'd actually spent in his company, they would barely add up to a couple of weeks. That's what came from stepping out with a traveling book salesman. Riding the rails was his business. She'd only seen him once or twice a month. Yet, in those few days, she'd come to believe that Providence had brought him to her.

Henry released a heavy sigh and then slid his hands away from hers as he sat back. "I wish I could take you with me."

Why can't you? Adelaide withdrew her hand and fisted it around the dinner napkin in her lap. *He's leaving me?*

Before the panic could fully claim her, Henry smiled—a beatific expression void of all worry and disappointment. "Who knows?" he said. "Fate may bring us together again."

Adelaide loosened her grip on the napkin and successfully inhaled a full breath. Everything would be fine. It would. Something was holding Henry back, but he still cared for her. He wouldn't have hinted at a future together otherwise. Perhaps this was simply the Lord's way of testing her commitment.

As she looked across the table at Henry, she straightened her spine and nodded. They would meet again one day. She'd see to it. It didn't matter what obstacle kept him from offering for her tonight. They would overcome it. The happy ending she'd longed for was within her grasp. She'd not let a little distance or a hesitant suitor steal it from her.

Chapter 1

ONE MONTH LATER . . .

The grandest adventure of her life waited on the other side of these tracks. That or the most humiliating debacle she'd ever created. Either way, there was no going back.

Adelaide Proctor drew in a deep, hope-filled breath . . . and nearly choked on the pungent odor of cattle dung wafting up from the stock pens farther down the rail line. She sputtered and wrinkled her nose but stepped forward nonetheless. It was of little consequence that Fort Worth smelled like manure or that gray clouds darkened the afternoon sky. She had traveled there to capture her dream, and nothing would deter her.

Adelaide waded across the depot platform through a sea of people who bustled about with energetic purpose. Returning travelers hurried to greet loved ones. Station attendants unloaded mailbags and other cargo. Hotel drummers plied newcomers with solicitations, each representative promising finer accommodations than the last. Adelaide drifted through them all, uncertainty dimming her excitement.

A gust of wind swirled around her and tugged at her straw

bonnet. She smashed it back down on her head and stopped for a moment to adjust her hatpin. As she wiggled the pin into place, the locomotive behind her let out a burst of steam, its loud hiss startling her into motion. At a loss over which way to go and already missing the simplicity of small town life, Adelaide allowed herself to be swept along with the crowd.

It certainly hadn't taken long for the first pangs of homesickness to hit. She'd only left Cisco a few hours ago. Aunt Louise would be *tsk*ing up a storm if she could see her. One would think that a young woman who had spent four years in Boston furthering her education and polishing her social graces would be right at home in a place the size of Fort Worth. Yet Adelaide remained a country girl at heart. No amount of social polish or book learning had been able to change that. Much to Aunt Louise's everlasting consternation.

"Pardon, ma'am." A boy no older than fifteen wheeled a cart loaded with trunks and leather bags into her path. She sidestepped to let him by. He nodded his thanks but didn't pause in his work and soon disappeared into the crowd.

The image of his young face stayed with her, reminding her of her former charges. Boys with McGuffey's readers on their desks and lizards in their pockets. She bit back the wistful sigh that rose in her throat, surprised to find that it tasted suspiciously like regret.

Adelaide straightened her spine and lengthened her stride. Regret? This was no time for second thoughts. It was time to chase her dreams. Henry was somewhere in this city, and she aimed to find him. She would teach again someday, if not in a schoolhouse, then with her own children. Hers and Henry's. Her heart gave a little leap at the idea. Today was once-upon-a-time for her. The first page in a story that promised to lead to happily-ever-after.

"Have a place to stay, miss?" A man wearing a green uniform approached her with a salesman's smile. "Clark House is the nearest hotel to the depot," he said, his discourse well rehearsed. "It's only a few steps away on Main Street. Guaranteed clean rooms. Fine dining. Respectable lodging for a young woman like yourself. I can even cart your luggage for you."

Clark House. Something about that name sounded familiar. Adelaide tipped her chin up to get a good look at the drummer. Her father had taught her to take a man's measure by looking him straight in the eye. Unfortunately, few men were short enough to make that task as simple as it sounded, so she had to settle for assessing him at an angle. The cap he wore bore the words *Clark House* etched into a brass oval above the brim. He looked legitimate.

"Is there a livery stable near your establishment?"

Before he could answer, a man in blue appeared at her elbow. "Afternoon, miss. If a livery is what you need, the Day Hotel is the place for you. Freighter's Wagon Yard is around the corner and Turner's Livery is right across the street. Plenty of options to help a lady like yourself get around town."

"Thank you, but I—"

"Turner's Livery is actually closer to Clark House, miss," the man in green insisted as he shot a glare at the interloper. "I'd be happy to show—"

"Ack. Don't believe a word either of these fellas is tellin' ya, lady."

Gracious. Now there was one in red vying for her attention. Adelaide turned from one to the next. They were like park pigeons, pecking at each other in hopes of winning her crumb. And the longer she put off her decision the hungrier they became, edging closer and closer. Adelaide retreated a step.

"What you need is a room at the Clayton," the red one said. "Our rates are much lower than these other rackets. We got good food, too."

The men jostled each other as they tried to sell her on their establishments, their words running together. Adelaide's gaze darted back and forth. Her breaths grew shallow and came a touch too fast, making her dizzy. Then one statement rose above the rest to grab her attention.

"I assure you that Clark House's restaurant offers the finest fare in town. All of Fort Worth's elite dine there."

Now she knew where she had heard that name before—from Henry. When the boardinghouse fare was not to his liking in Cisco, he would rave about the sophisticated dishes he ate in Fort Worth, his favorite being the beefsteak at Clark House. So tender it would dissolve on a man's tongue before he could chew it.

Adelaide made her decision. If Henry frequented the restaurant at Clark House, that's where she'd stay. Who knew, the staff might even be able to provide his address.

"I'll be staying at Clark House, gentlemen."

The man in green smirked at his competitors, then tugged his vest over his waistband and straightened his face before turning his attention back to her. He nodded with a regal air. "Excellent. I'll make the arrangements."

The other men grumbled under their breath but ceded the victory, fading back into the crowd to hunt some other unsuspecting traveler. Adelaide snapped open the ball clasp on her handbag, feeling better now that the pigeons had fluttered off, and dug out two baggage tickets. She handed them to the Clark House drummer along with a couple of coins. "If you would be so kind as to fetch my trunks, I'll collect my mare."

"Very good, miss." He pocketed the coins and pulled out a small writing tablet. "Your name, please?"

"Adelaide Proctor."

His pencil moved across the paper. "I'll see to it that your room is prepared and that a key is waiting for you at the front desk." He flipped a page and scribbled some more. "If you take this note to Turner's Livery, they'll give you a discount on boarding fees." He tore off the page and extended it to her. "Just go a block past Clark House. It'll be on your right."

"Thank you."

The drummer headed toward the baggage car, leaving Adelaide to find her way to the stock area. Now that the crowd had thinned, she had a clearer view of the railcars. Plotting a path toward the rear of the train, Adelaide crossed the wooden platform to where a rail worker was unloading horses from a ventilated boxcar. She recognized Sheba's glossy black tail and haunches as the mare skittishly backed down the ramp. The livery owner in Cisco had urged her to sell Sheba to him before she left town, but she couldn't bear to do it. Her father had given her that filly the summer she turned sixteen. The same year he died. Sheba connected her to the only parent she'd ever known. She couldn't possibly sever that tie.

Reaching the edge of the platform, she lifted the hem of her mustard-colored traveling dress just enough to safely descend the steps to the hard-packed dirt near the tracks. The handler led Sheba to a trough, and Adelaide let her drink her fill before walking her down to the livery.

In an effort to apologize for stuffing her into a smelly stockcar for the last several hours, Adelaide borrowed a curry comb from the stableboy and gave Sheba a thorough brush down.

"What do you think, girl? Is this a good place to make a new start?" Dust billowed out of Sheba's ebony coat as Adelaide applied the comb in long strokes.

"I know Henry's not the romantic hero I'd always hoped would sweep me off my feet, but he'll be a good provider."

Sheba snorted, unimpressed.

"Oh, hush." Adelaide pulled up a wooden stool and stood on it to reach Sheba's mane.

Even if Henry was not as passionate as Charlotte Brontë's Mr. Rochester or as chivalrous as Jane Austen's Mr. Darcy, he had his charms.

It was high time she let go of her girlish fancies anyway. She'd waited years for a hero to walk out of the well-worn pages of the books she read by lantern light and capture her heart. But he never came. He always seemed to find someone prettier, or more biddable, or with better bloodlines. Well, she was tired of waiting. Tired of being passed over. She would shape her own destiny. She might not have found Mr. Heroic, but Mr. Satisfactory would do just fine.

After checking in to her room at Clark House and rinsing off the travel dirt, Adelaide changed into a lemon gingham dress that lightened her mood with its cheerful hue and headed down to the hotel dining room for supper.

No tables were available when she arrived, so she took a seat in the adjoining sitting room. A young girl perched on the edge of a red plush settee in the center of the room, blushing prettily as her swain wooed her with clumsy compliments. A more sophisticated couple stood conversing in the far corner, apparently discussing the merits of the landscape painting that dominated the wall beside them. Adelaide couldn't help but notice how the woman's gloved hand rested securely in the crook of the gentleman's arm, and how he smiled at her with comfortable intimacy.

Envy flared within her. She turned away. Tucking her ankles beneath the base of her chair, she directed her gaze to the floor. There was nothing so awkward as being the only unattached female in a room of couples.

A discarded newspaper lay on the parlor table near her elbow. She snatched it up, hoping for a distraction. Her eyes roved back and forth across the page, but the words didn't penetrate her mind. *Oh well.* Pretending to read served her purposes, too. She'd just hide behind the *Gazette* until her table was ready or the lovers left. Whichever came first.

Her chair was positioned in such a way that she could view the entrance to the dining area through the sitting-room doorway if she twisted her head to the side just a bit. And leaned back several inches. And hooked her foot around a chair leg so she didn't lose her balance while she teetered on the edge of her seat.

The headwaiter rarely looked in her direction, but she planned to be ready with the most pitiful, pleading, puppy-dog expression she could muster if he did. She wanted nothing more than to slink off to her room, but the ham sandwich she had packed for the train ride had long since disappeared from her stomach. If she were to wrangle an early table, she'd be able to gulp down a quick meal and make her escape. After all, the sooner this day ended, the sooner she could set about the task of finding Henry. Then *she* would be the one whose hand rested on a gentleman's arm and who swam in a flood of adoring glances. Yep. As soon as she found Henry, everything would be better.

"Have a good evening, Mr. Belcher," the headwaiter intoned from the restaurant's entrance. "I hope the food was to your liking tonight."

Mr. Belcher? Adelaide's heart pounded. *Henry?* She shoved the paper into her lap. The crinkling sound deafened her to the man's response. She leaned to the side and craned her neck to see his face, but two patrons blocked her view. Willing the woman and young boy to get out of the way, Adelaide leaned farther, needing to see him. He was the right height, and his pomaded hair glistened just like Henry's. . . .

The oak chair leg bruised her foot as she pulled farther away from her support. If he would just turn around . . .

Plop.

Adelaide fell onto the floor in a graceless heap. Face aflame, she shot up as fast as possible, ignoring the gasps and titters from others in the room.

"Oh my. Are you all right, dear?"

The woman from the dining room left the boy's side and came to assist her. Adelaide waved off her concern, the crumpled newspaper rustling in her hand.

"I'm fine, really. Thank you."

"Well, if you're sure . . ."

She began to nod, but the mystery man turned around at that very moment, and she froze with her chin tipped at an odd angle.

At the sight of his familiar features, happiness burst inside her. "Henry! It *is* you." She had found him on her very first day in town. God had led him right to her. How marvelous!

She moved toward him, but her steps slowed as the color drained from his face. Somehow she had expected a flush of pleasure, not deathly pallor. It must've been the shock of seeing her outside their usual setting.

"Miss Proctor, how delightful to see you again. Are you taking a holiday?"

His voice sounded odd, rather squeaky and pinched. Dots of perspiration stood out on his forehead. Adelaide struggled to make sense of his reaction. He had always been confident and controlled. Had she really flustered him so badly? Before she could think of a way to politely ask what on earth was the matter with him, the kind woman who had come to her aid edged around her to stand next to Henry.

"You know this young woman, dear?"

Did she call everyone *dear*?

Henry took a handkerchief from his coat pocket and dabbed his brow. "Yes. Miss Proctor teaches school in Cisco, one of the stops along my old route. She was one of my best customers. Has a hankering for novels, as I recall."

He gave a forced little laugh that did nothing to make Adelaide feel better. In fact, a sick feeling settled in the pit of her stomach.

"I see." The woman smiled with guarded warmth. She reached out to clasp the hand of the boy who stood watching the adults with wide eyes, and drew him to her side. Then she placed her other hand in the crook of Henry's arm. Just like the elegant woman in the sitting room.

An unseen weight pressed down on Adelaide's chest until she could scarcely breathe. *No. Please, God. It can't be.*

"It's a pleasure to meet you, Miss Proctor." The woman flexed her fingers slightly, tightening her grip on Henry's arm. "I'm Caroline Belcher. Henry's wife."

Chapter 2

The Bible taught that truth set a person free, but Adelaide had never felt more trapped. She wanted to slap Henry's face and spit on his shoe. She wanted to strike out at the woman who held the arm of the man who was supposed to be hers. She wanted to weep over her shattered dreams. Yet she did none of those things. After all, the woman had been kind to her, and the boy with the wide eyes didn't deserve to have his illusions destroyed. One disaster stemming from this meeting was more than enough.

Choking down the bile that burned the back of her throat, Adelaide nudged her lips into a shape she hoped resembled a smile. "It is an honor to meet you, Mrs. Belcher."

The woman dipped her head in acknowledgment. "Will you be in town long?"

"No. My business concluded earlier than I anticipated. I'll be taking my leave shortly."

She wanted to take her leave right then—saddle Sheba and ride off, far and fast. But courtesy demanded she stand her ground and pretend there wasn't a volcano of emotions erupting inside her.

"We really must be going, Caroline. You know how much clerical work waits for me at home." The source of her trouble became her rescuer as Henry tugged his family toward the door. Undoubtedly he cared more about protecting himself than her, but she was too glad to see them go to care about his motives.

"Good evening, Miss Proctor." He failed to meet her eye.

"Good-*bye*, Mr. Belcher."

The instant the family exited onto the street, Adelaide hoisted her skirts and ran for the stairs. Her empty stomach didn't matter. The curious hotel guests didn't matter. The fact that she was still gripping the mangled newspaper in her hand didn't matter. All she cared about was escape.

When the door to her room clicked shut behind her, she threw herself onto the bed and sobbed. She smothered her anguished moans in the white feather pillow that the hotel maid had plumped so beautifully and cried until it became a soggy mess. Once she ran out of tears, anger took over. First she got mad at the pillow for being so wet and clammy and hurled it across the room. Then she turned her ire onto the unsuspecting mattress, pummeling the ticking with her fists.

How could he abuse her trust like that? He intentionally led her to believe he was unmarried. The cad! She had given up everything for him. Her job. Her friends. Her self-respect. The scoundrel probably had a woman at every train stop between Longview and Abilene. Women to divert him during those long, taxing business trips. Widows. Spinsters. Lonely women who were overly susceptible to his charms. Women easily led astray. Women . . . like her.

A sorrowful groan vibrated in her chest. How could she have been so foolish? She should have suspected something was amiss when he never spoke of their future in any detail and offered only vague promises that really were no promises at all. Now here she was, nose running, eyes puffy, arms sore from tenderizing a hotel mattress, all over a man she'd never really loved in the first place.

To be honest, she didn't mourn losing *Henry*. She mourned the loss of the dreams he represented. Romance. Family. An arm to lean on and a warm, masculine smile that belonged to her alone. She had bought into his snake oil, believing it to be the cure for what ailed her heart. Yet his restorative turned out to be plain old sugar water—sweet at first but worthless in the end.

Wrung out, she slid off the side of the bed into a limp pile of self-pity. She rested her head against the badly wrinkled coverlet that hung askew over the edge of the bed and turned her recriminations in one final direction.

"Why did you let this happen, Lord?" Her voice, scratchy and weak, wobbled over the question. "You let a man of deceit prey on one of your children. Why didn't you protect me from him instead of leaving me to flounder around by myself?"

Stung by the injustice of it all, Adelaide hit the mattress a final time, then jabbed her finger at the ceiling. "I prayed about this, God. You know I did. For weeks I asked you to show me what to do about Henry. I petitioned you for wisdom. I pled for guidance. And all I got was silence. How is that supposed to help?"

No answer echoed through the rafters or even whispered to her heart. God didn't seem to be on speaking terms with her at the moment, and she had no idea why. Yelling at him probably didn't help matters, but David had ranted often enough in his psalms, so it must be allowable in times of extreme distress. Still, her tirade felt a tad irreverent.

Looking up out of the corners of her eyes, she mumbled a quick apology, then turned around and leaned her back against the bed frame. She exhaled a heavy sigh and drew her knees to her chest, hugging them tight. Her head fell forward as she curled into herself. *Why has God abandoned me?* She knew he never promised his followers a trouble-free life, but he did promise to always be there for them. So why wasn't he? Why was he silent?

Too weary to ponder the mind of God any longer, Adelaide

wrapped her fingers around the bedpost and hoisted herself to her feet. She hobbled over to her trunk and pulled out a clean cotton nightgown and held it to her breast as she wandered toward the window that overlooked the street.

The sky had cleared considerably since her arrival, but one large cloud lingered. White and rimmed with gray, it hovered directly above the saloon across the street, bringing to mind a Bible story she used to teach her students. Of course in the Bible, God's cloud had hovered over the tabernacle, not a saloon, but still, it was a symbol of his guidance. A tiny flutter stirred in her heart. Could God be trying to tell her that he *was* with her?

Adelaide stared at the cloud, waiting for . . . something. Some kind of message explaining what her next step should be. But the cloud just hung there, as if suspended on an unseen thread. Hazy, undefined, and completely unhelpful. Adelaide sighed and turned away from the window. She tossed her nightgown onto the bed and sank into the upholstered armchair in the corner, tucking her feet under her the way she used to do as a little girl in her father's study.

If only she could go back to Cisco and pretend none of this had ever happened. But that was impossible. The school board had already hired her replacement. She would have no means to support herself. Besides, the humiliation would be unbearable. Whispers about her shameful man-chasing behavior would circulate through town, destroying her reputation. No. She couldn't go back.

Adelaide opened her eyes and stared straight ahead, focused on nothing but the blank slate that was now her future. Willing herself not to panic, she took a deep breath and dug out the logic that had always served her well when handling problems in the classroom. Granted, solving the mystery of where Beth Hansen's lunch bucket disappeared to every day after recess wasn't quite on the same level as her current dilemma, but maybe a similar thought process would produce at least a modicum of insight.

All right. She knew where she wasn't going—back to Cisco. That narrowed her options down to only a few thousand other possibilities. So how was she supposed to choose one?

She glanced over her shoulder at the window. The cloud still lingered outside. Why did she get the feeling it was there for her benefit? The flutter in her heart returned, stronger this time. God had used clouds to guide his people in the past. Perhaps he meant to do so again.

But a cloud? Adelaide huffed out a breath and crossed her arms over her chest. Could there be a more ambiguous symbol? A fiery beacon in the night sky would be much better. No mistaking that message. Clear. Affirming. Definitive.

Clouds obscured things. They blocked out the sun and made everything gloomy. She wouldn't be able to see more than a foot in front of her with that in her path.

"Walk by faith, not by sight."

The verse popped into her mind, halting her mental tirade. Maybe God was speaking to her after all. Just not in the way she'd expected.

The more she thought about Moses and the Israelites wandering in the desert, the more she remembered the role of that cloud. Not only did it lead them, but it contained the very presence of God. Through it he spoke to Moses and filled the tabernacle with his glory. The people never journeyed to a new place until the cloud first moved away from the tabernacle. They waited on that cloud and made no move without it.

Adelaide squirmed in her chair, the tapestry cushions no longer comfortable as a new conviction settled over her. She had moved without the cloud. Folding her arms beneath her breast, she bowed her head.

"God, forgive me for my impatience. I saw what I thought I wanted, and when you made no move to give it to me, I took matters into my own hands. I wasn't content, and I didn't trust you enough to wait."

She inhaled a shaky breath. "I've really made a mess of things, haven't I? I need you more than ever, now. Show me where to go, what to do. And please give me enough faith to follow you even when I can't see where the path is leading. In the name of Jesus, amen."

Feeling calmer but somewhat numb, Adelaide relied on habit to steer her through the process of readying herself for bed. A splash of water from the pitcher on the dresser top soothed her face, and the cool cotton nightgown refreshed her body. She picked up the pillow from where it lay in a pathetic wad beside the bureau and fluffed it out as best she could. Then on wooden legs, she straggled over to the bed, arranged the pillow soggy side down, and crawled into the sheets. Half-sitting, she reached for the coverlet, but when she tugged it toward her, something crinkled.

She lifted the blanket and rescued the crushed newspaper that she had pilfered from the hotel sitting room. Stretching it across her lap, she smoothed out the wrinkles with the flat of her hand. The poor thing had been in the wrong place at the wrong time, and look how it had suffered. Between the paper, the mattress, and the pillow, she was accruing quite a list of casualties.

As she straightened the interior section, an advertisement seized her attention.

Wanted: Governess for Ranch Owner's Daughter
Experience and References Required
Apply in person to James Bevin, Esq.
Corner of S. Houston and W. 13th Streets

A giddy sensation vibrated through her middle and sent tingles down her arms. Her cloud was on the move.

The next morning, Adelaide skittered around her room in a dither, wearing nothing but her corset and drawers. Every dress she owned had been flung over the furniture for her inspection. There were three on the bed, two draped across the armchair, and one hanging from the dresser mirror. Why was it that she could make huge decisions like resigning her teaching position in order to chase a man in the blink of an eye, but when it came time to select something to wear, she had the hardest time making up her mind? A frustrated growl rumbled in her throat. *This is crazy. I just need to pick something and be done with it.*

The mustard traveling dress was still crushed and stained from the train ride, and the lemon gingham she had worn last night was worse for wear after all the trauma she had put it through, so those two could be excluded. Her butter-cream riding habit wasn't appropriate for the occasion, either. That left the saffron calico, the pale gold wool, or the sunshine yellow muslin. The wool would probably be too warm now that spring was easing its way into summer. She adored the tiny floral print on the calico, but the solid-colored muslin might appear more professional. She debated for a minute, then grabbed the muslin.

Half an hour later, her credentials tucked away in her handbag and directions from the hotel clerk fresh in her mind, Adelaide set out to find Mr. Bevin.

His building appeared rather dull and nondescript on the outside, but once she walked through the door, a welcoming warmth infused her. The office was decorated in masculine tones, and the scent of pipe tobacco lingered in the air. Burgundy leather chairs formed a seating area beneath a painting that depicted an English fox hunt. She stepped closer to get a better look. A smile curved her lips. She could practically hear the barking of the hounds.

"May I help you?"

Adelaide jumped and knocked the picture off center. Hurrying to set the crooked artwork to rights, she nudged the frame back into a straight line and then spun around. A studious young man sitting behind a polished mahogany desk regarded her through circular lenses.

She cleared her throat. "I'm here to see Mr. Bevin."

"Do you have an appointment?" He lifted his brows in a haughty manner that put her in mind of the arrogant young men she had met in Boston.

She stiffened her spine and turned her gaze to the side, as if the clerk were beneath her notice. "Kindly inform Mr. Bevin that Miss Adelaide Proctor has arrived as per his invitation. He did not specify an appointment time when he requested my appearance, so naturally I presumed he would see me at my convenience. Now, if you would be so good, sir . . ." She motioned for him to rise, like a queen commanding her subject.

Just as the man began to stand, a quiet chuckle from off to her right ruined the effect. An older man, probably in his early forties, stood in the doorway that appeared to lead to an inner office.

Drat! That had to be Mr. Bevin, and here she was trying to win some kind of snobbery contest with his clerk. That couldn't be good. He smiled at her, though, and nodded.

"Come into my office, Miss Proctor. I'm afraid you'll have to excuse me for the misunderstanding. I seem to have forgotten all about our plans to meet today and therefore neglected to inform my assistant." His cultured tones soothed instead of insulted. Due to the grin that continued to dance across his face, no doubt.

Holding high her head, which still only reached to his chin, she swept past him and took a seat in a leather chair. He closed the door and went around the side of the desk, seating himself behind it.

"You'll have to excuse Mr. Lyons. He's a bit high in the instep, but his father is a friend of mine and asked me to take him on."

Some of the starch went out of her. "I shouldn't have let him rile me. I apologize for my rudeness, and for imposing on you."

His chair creaked as he leaned back, resting his weight on one elbow. "I actually thought you handled him quite well. A person needs to be able to stand his ground without letting others intimidate him, especially out here. Texas abounds with ruffians who will run over you given half a chance. Now . . . tell me about this invitation that has slipped my mind in such discourteous fashion."

Adelaide felt a blush heat her cheeks. "Well . . . it was more of a general invitation, not one addressed to me in particular. I've come about the advertisement in the *Gazette*. I wish to apply for the governess position."

"Cleverly evasive, yet honest. An admirable combination."

His manner put her at ease. In fact, the paternal smile he favored her with, combined with the silver at his temples, reminded her of her father. Of course Daddy would be dressed in broadcloth and denims, not a distinguished black frock coat and vest, but it was a nice feeling all the same.

"Are you qualified for this position, Miss Proctor?"

"Yes, sir." She retrieved her credentials from her bag and pushed them across the desk for him to examine. "I graduated from Boston Normal School in 1880 and have taught in Cisco, Texas, for the last two years."

She clutched her purse so firmly, the brass closure bit into the pads of her fingers. By the time Mr. Bevin finished reading through her letters of recommendation, precious little feeling remained in them.

"Your colleagues and board members speak highly of you, both personally and professionally." He set the papers down and peered at her from across the desk. "It sounds as if they wished you to stay on. If I may ask, why did you leave?"

"I thought I was getting married."

As soon as the words burst out of her mouth, she wanted them back. The tension of waiting for him to peruse her letters must have rattled her brain. Any intelligent person would have simply stated "personal reasons" and left it at that. Why couldn't she have taken two seconds to come up with an appropriate response instead of spouting off the first thing that came to mind?

"I take it things didn't work out?" His tone was mildly curious, but not laden with pity, and for that she was grateful.

"God seems to have other plans for me," she said, hoping that the tremor in her voice conveyed anticipation and not fear.

"Ah. So you are a believer. Mr. Westcott prefers hiring people of faith. That will work in your favor." He placed his palms on the desk top and pushed to his feet. "There are two other candidates whom I have deemed qualified. However, Mr. Westcott insists on conducting the final interviews himself—after he sees how each of you interacts with the child. We leave on the eight o'clock train tomorrow morning. If you are interested, I will procure a ticket for you."

He held out his hand and helped her to her feet. After struggling with patience when the Lord refused to move as fast as she expected, she was left feeling a bit dizzy with the blistering pace he was setting now.

"I'll need to secure passage for Sheba, as well," she said, still trying to sort things out in her mind.

Mr. Bevin raised a disapproving brow. "Don't tell me you have a child, Miss Proctor?"

Dazed, she tried to make sense of his question. "A child? No, sir. I have a horse."

After a stunned moment, he let out a guffaw that shook the walls. "A horse, she says. Ha! Well, Miss Proctor, I would advise you either to sell the horse or board it until Mr. Westcott makes his decision. He—"

"I'll pay the stock fare." She rummaged in her bag for the necessary money. "Sheba comes with me."

She held out the coins and watched for his response. He cocked his head to the side, contemplated her for a moment, and accepted the money.

"Very well. I'll see to it." He moved past her and placed his hand on the doorknob. "The train will only take us halfway. We will be traveling overland for a few days after that. Having an extra animal along could prove beneficial, I suppose."

"Thank you, Mr. Bevin."

He opened the door, and she stepped into the outer office, taking her first full breath in several minutes.

"Oh, Miss Proctor? There's one more thing."

She pivoted to face him. "Yes?"

"Should Mr. Westcott hire you, be prepared for a challenge."

Maybe his daughter was a hellion who terrorized governesses with snakes and lizards in their beds. Well, Adelaide had been raised on a ranch, too. She'd pulled her own share of stunts on the ranch hands and the cook her father paid extra to tend his little girl.

"I think I can handle a few pranks," she stated with confidence.

"It's not pranks you have to worry about. It's communication."

She waited for him to elaborate.

"The child is barely five years of age and has yet to learn her letters."

"I don't see how that will be a problem. I've taught numerous students—" She stopped when he started shaking his head.

"Miss Proctor, the child is mute."

Chapter 3

MENARD COUNTY, TEXAS

"A telegram has arrived, sir."

Gideon Westcott, youngest son of Baron Mansfield, formerly of Leicestershire, England, lifted the linen napkin from his lap and dabbed at his mouth before turning to address his butler.

"Thank you, Chalmers." He accepted the message from the servant's white-gloved hand and dismissed him with a slight nod of his head.

After spending the last two years learning the sheep business from the ground up, subsisting for weeks on end with only bleating ewes for conversation, beans and bacon for food, and gnarled mesquite branches for shelter, the strict English formality he'd been raised with seemed at odds with the man he'd become. However, his mother had insisted that he bring Chalmers and Mrs. Chalmers with him to set up house after his last visit home, and he knew better than to gainsay her. She maintained that since he was now to be a landowner backed by his father's finances and not a mere herder, it was his duty as an Englishman to help civilize Texas.

And, of course, nothing provided civilization more effectively than proper household staff.

Gideon scanned the telegram from his man Bevin. He and the three women had disembarked the train at the terminus in Lampasas and were to have started their overland journey this morning. Taking into account the slower pace necessary for a wagon and genteel ladies, they should arrive sometime the day after tomorrow, barring any unexpected complications.

They couldn't arrive soon enough, as far as Gideon was concerned. The spring shearing had been postponed longer than wisdom dictated. This time last year, teamsters had already hauled the wool clip from the other ranchers in the area off to the warehouses in San Antonio. It had only been through the grace of God and his own nimble negotiation that the Mexican crew he'd hired this year for the shearing agreed to return to his ranch after completing their northern route.

The late shipment would hurt his competitiveness in the market; however, he hoped the superior quality of his wool would add to the value. But even if he had to accept a low price, he did not regret his decision. Isabella needed someone whose sole responsibility was seeing to her care. During the shearing, he would be consumed with overseeing the crew's progress from dawn till dark. And the rest of his staff would have increased responsibilities, as well. Bella would get lost in the shuffle. And that was unacceptable.

Gideon bit back a sigh. All those months spent carefully outlining his business strategy and meticulously calculating risks like prairie fires, predators, disease, and anything else that could harm his flocks, he had failed to factor in personal issues. But then, how was he to anticipate becoming a parent overnight without benefit of the normally requisite wife?

He pushed aside his unfinished dish of bread pudding and slid his gaze down the table to where Isabella sat, her sad, soulful eyes fixed on the telegram in his hand. It was hard to reconcile this silent, somber creature with the vibrant, carefree child he had first met aboard ship four months ago. Her radiance had died with her mother three hours before they reached American soil. Lady Petchey, frantic to protect her daughter in the hours before her death, extracted a vow from a man she barely knew, having him claim Isabella as his own.

He hadn't regretted that vow for a single moment, for the tiny blond beauty had stolen his heart the day she'd braved the cold January air to trounce him in a game of tiddlywinks on the steamer's deck. Recalling that day, he found it easier to smile in the face of her melancholia.

"Good news, Bella." Gideon injected as much cheer into his voice as he could manage. "Mr. Bevin is on his way. Soon you'll have a new governess to teach you your lessons and play all sorts of games. Won't that be fun?"

The girl didn't even meet his eye. She just shrugged her shoulders and picked at her food.

Not easily deterred, however, Gideon plunged ahead. "We will have three ladies to choose from, and I'm depending on you to let me know which one you like best."

Her eyebrows lifted a touch, and she tilted her chin a shade to the right. Such a small change in most children wouldn't signify a thing, but for Isabella, it was a rare indication of interest. Slowly she turned her gaze on him and brought her finger up to point at her chest.

Gideon winked at her, hoping to uncover a hint of the jolly child he remembered from beneath the layers of apathy she'd insulated herself in. "I thought you should have some say in the process since you will be the one spending so much time with her. Do you think you can handle such an important decision?"

She thought for a moment, then nodded.

"Excellent."

Isabella lifted the edge of her dish off the table and sent him a questioning glance, her way of asking to be excused. Gideon hid his disappointment.

"Yes, love. You can go play. I'll be up to read you a story in a few minutes."

She glided out of the room without leaving a single ripple in her wake. Her golden curls didn't bounce. Her shoes didn't squeak. Nothing. Children weren't supposed to glide. They were supposed to skip and run and frolic. He would give anything to see her smile again. Grief was supposed to fade over time, but with Isabella, it locked her away. And so far, he'd been helpless to find the key.

When they'd first arrived at the ranch, his work had kept him close to the house, so he encouraged her to follow him around, hoping that once she became comfortable with her surroundings, she would open up, but she only withdrew further. Then lambing season hit and he'd been forced to leave her behind, trusting the staff to care for her. Mrs. Chalmers assured him she was no trouble. She always sat quietly in a corner, flipping through the pages of a picture book or playing with her doll. But that was the problem. She was easy to ignore. He needed someone looking after her who wasn't distracted by other duties. Someone who would draw Isabella out of her silence and bring joy back into her life. He needed a miracle.

Miracles had been in short supply in her life, but if she managed to land this job, all the credit would certainly go to the Almighty. Adelaide held on to the side of the wagon bed as the vehicle rocked over yet another rut. Traveling had been much easier the previous two days when she had ridden Sheba, but since this was the final leg of their journey, she had chosen propriety over practicality. The other two women applying for the position were refined ladies reared back east who had only recently come to Texas. They had looked at her askance the first day she'd appeared in her split skirt astride Sheba. Astride. Oh, the horror.

True, most women in these parts still rode sidesaddle, if they even had a saddle, but being raised on a ranch full of accomplished horsemen, Adelaide had never seen the use in it. Her split skirt properly covered her ankles, yet she could tell the other women thought her scandalous. It wouldn't do for her to make the same impression on the man who had the power to hire her.

"Mr. Bevin, I thought you said we would reach Mr. Westcott's property before noon." Mrs. Carmichael's shrill voice grated across Adelaide's nerves. "My timepiece indicates that it is well after twelve thirty, and I see no sign of the ranch. You cannot expect us to swelter away in this intolerable heat another day, sir. I must insist that you pick up the pace at once."

Adelaide stifled a groan. The day was lovely. Blue sky. Sunshine. A light breeze. If Mrs. Carmichael thought this was sweltering, what would she do in August when the heat could melt the hide off a buffalo?

"Actually, madam, we've been on Mr. Westcott's property for the last twenty minutes. The ranch house will be in view soon."

She marveled at the man's restraint. He didn't grind his teeth or raise his voice or condescend to her in even the slightest degree. After three days of her harping from the seat beside him, it was a wonder he hadn't stuffed his handkerchief in her mouth. Or his own ears.

"I didn't realize he resided so far from town," Miss Oliver observed. "I haven't seen more than two buildings since we left Menardville. Are you quite certain it is safe out here?"

This time a small sigh escaped the heretofore unflappable Mr. Bevin. "You're as safe here as anywhere else. Westcott's ranch lies halfway between Menardville and Fort McKavett, and the cavalry units stationed there drove out the Comanche from this area years ago. You don't have to worry about Indians, miss."

He had given Miss Oliver the same assurances last night at the hotel. Adelaide smiled and shook her head. It was probably a good thing she rode in the back of the wagon with the trunks and supplies. If she had been squished in between the women, she would've probably said something unforgivably rude by now. No. It was better to watch the dust swirl out behind the wagon wheels and wave at Sheba plodding along behind them. She'd get herself into less trouble that way. Unfortunately, not participating in the conversation gave her plenty of time to ponder her hazy future.

She had been sure that her combined ranch and teaching experience would win her the position, but now that she knew more about her competition, her confidence waned.

Though Mrs. Carmichael was a stern, pinched-face woman who put one in mind of a grape that had hung on the vine too long, she had twenty years of experience. Not just teaching experience, either. She'd served as governess to some of the finest families in New York. Adelaide had hoped that Mrs. Carmichael might not be so anxious to take the job once she saw how primitive the conditions were, but the old gal had proven tough. She complained about everything under the sun, but she never once asked to go back.

Miss Oliver, on the other hand, seemed afraid of her own shadow. She rarely spoke above a whisper, and although she was securely sandwiched between Mr. Bevin and Mrs. Carmichael, she jumped at every sound, gulping and gasping each time a hawk cried or the wind rustled the brush near their wagon. When they were indoors, however, it was a different story. She became the essence of serenity and feminine dignity the minute four sturdy walls surrounded her. A plank of wood wouldn't stop anyone bent on doing her harm, of course, but Adelaide decided not to mention that fact to her. Miss Oliver's last position had been headmistress of a girls' school in Virginia. She would be the obvious choice if Mr. Westcott valued poise and deportment. As long as she stayed inside.

And then there was Mr. Westcott. It turned out he wasn't the wealthy cattle baron she imagined him to be when she first came across the ad in the *Gazette*. Mr. Bevin informed them last night that he was an Englishman. The son of a baron, no less. He was probably the stodgy type who wore a monocle and drank tea out of fancy china cups while waiting for his Texas investment to turn a profit without him having to dirty his hands with actual work. A proper English gentleman would most likely be drawn to what the other women had to offer.

To top it all off, he ran sheep. Sheep, for pity's sake. Daddy would disown her if he were still around. His passion had been horses, but he had run several hundred head of cattle, too. There wasn't a cattleman in Texas who didn't get his dander up at the thought of a sheepman running his flock over rangeland that God created for longhorns. It felt as if she were conspiring with the enemy. Yet her cloud was leading her. Was it possible for God to take a wrong turn?

"There you go, ladies," Mr. Bevin called out. "Your first glimpse of Westcott Cottage."

Adelaide clambered atop one of the trunks, balancing precariously on her knees, in order to see over the heads in front of her. As the wagon crested the hill, the house came into view. Her jaw hung slack. Only an English nobleman would call that mansion a cottage.

The ivory two-and-a-half-story Queen Anne home sat elegantly atop a rise, a fairy-tale vision contrasting sharply with the rustic Texas landscape. A dreamy sigh escaped her. It was the most romantic house she'd ever seen. It boasted a wraparound porch that encircled the entire lower floor, gabled roofs, large bay windows, and even a turret. All it needed was a handsome prince to fulfill every girlish fantasy she'd ever had.

The wagon dipped, and Adelaide tumbled off the trunk, banging her elbow against the wooden slats at her side. The throbbing pain in her arm brought with it a dose of reality. She wasn't a princess in a gilded carriage journeying to find her prince. She was Adelaide Proctor, unemployed teacher, journeying to find a job.

The harness jangled as Mr. Bevin pulled the wagon to a stop. Instead of waiting for him to come around for her after assisting the other two women, Adelaide climbed over the rail and used the spokes of the wheel like a ladder to take her to the ground.

"You know, you really should allow the gentleman of the party to help you alight." The suppressed laughter in Mr. Bevin's voice drew an answering smile from her.

"You seemed to have your hands full." Adelaide brushed off her skirts and bent to untie the lead line that tethered Sheba to the buckboard.

Placing one hand on the edge of the wagon, Mr. Bevin leaned close to her ear. "Just between you and me," he murmured, "I don't think I could last another minute with those two. I have a terrible feeling that Westcott is going to hire you and stick me with the wilting violet and tart persimmon all the way back to Fort Worth."

Adelaide giggled. "Shame on you, Mr. Bevin." Then she rose up on her tiptoes to whisper back to him. "I'll make you a deal. If I don't get the position, I'll spell you by driving the rig half of each day and letting you ride Sheba."

He put his hand over his heart and gazed at her with overdone adoration. "You are an angel, Miss Proctor. Truly an angel." Then his adoration shifted to a look of pure mischief. "You realize, of course, that I now have no motivation to put in a good word for you."

She grinned up at him, not afraid of his threat in the slightest.

"Must you leave us standing out here all day, sir?" Mrs. Carmichael rasped. "Escort us to the house."

Mr. Bevin pulled a woebegone expression for Adelaide's amusement and then set his polite mask back in place. "Coming, ladies." He offered her his arm, but she shook her head.

"I'm going to see to Sheba first."

"Abandoning me already?" He winked. "The stables are just beyond the house to the west."

Adelaide led Sheba in the direction Mr. Bevin had indicated. Once she moved past the house, her surroundings looked much more like a ranch. Several outbuildings stretched across the yard. A bunkhouse, barn, stables, and what looked like smaller storage sheds dotted the area. As she headed for the stables, she noticed several large fenced-off pastures covering the land beyond. A handful of sheep grazed dispassionately in the closest pen, most with lambs hopping playfully nearby. The young ones danced around their sedentary mothers with a glee Adelaide found impossible to resist. Maybe sheep weren't so bad after all.

Sheba snorted as she caught the scent of other horses and nudged Adelaide from behind.

"All right. I'm going."

They entered the stable, but no one arrived to offer assistance. Deciding it would be easier to locate an empty stall herself than wait for someone to find them, Adelaide led Sheba down the alleyway. The mare's hooves clicked against the planked floor, drawing the attention of the other residents. Numerous heads bobbed over stall doors to inspect the intruders. Adelaide's experienced eye noted two saddle horses of Thoroughbred quality mixed in with quarter horses, a draft animal or two, and even a pony—which surely belonged to the young princess of the castle. Mr. Westcott had quite an eclectic collection of horseflesh.

"Here we go, girl." Adelaide found a tie stall near the rear of the stable and hitched Sheba in. She checked the hay in the feedbox and picked up an overturned bucket from the ground. "I'll get you some fresh water and see if I can't rustle up some oats for you."

The bucket handle creased her palm as she headed back to the stable entrance. A feed bin along the wall drew her attention. She veered to the side to investigate and caught the sound of approaching male voices.

"Esmeralda finally dropped her lambs, Miguel. Twins."

"Ah. *Muy bien, señor.*"

"Keep a close eye on her, though. She didn't seem too fond of the little tykes. You'll probably need to tie her up and force her to nurse them for a while."

"*Sí.* I watch her, *patrón.* You go clean up for your guests."

Patrón? The first man *had* spoken with a British accent. Was she about to meet Mr. Westcott? Her pulse raced in alarm. She hadn't had the chance to freshen up yet. Adelaide retreated until her rear bumped into the feed bin. She clutched the bucket tightly against her chest and held her breath. Just her luck. The proper ladies were up at the house awaiting him in the parlor, and she was off cavorting in the stable. She could only hope she hadn't stepped in horse droppings. Nothing like the smell of manure on a person to win over a potential employer. Her hair was probably a wreck, too. Why hadn't she gone inside with Mr. Bevin when she'd had the chance?

She stood utterly still and trained her ears on the noises outside the stable. The pad of footsteps moving away from the building buoyed her spirits. Maybe she'd get out of this unscathed. She continued to listen, not sure if one man or both had left. When everything remained quiet, she inhaled deeply and let her muscles relax. Determined to get Sheba taken care of as quickly as possible so she could skedaddle up to the house, she took a nose bag down from the wall and heaved open the heavy, wooden hinged lid of the bin, leaning it against the wall.

Drat. It held oats all right, but the bin was nearly empty. She bent over the side, the worn edge digging into her stomach as she reached for the large tin scoop. Pushing up on her toes, she stretched her arms down as far as she could and managed to get a fingertip grip on the scoop handle. The scoop scraped against the bottom of the wooden box as she cornered the grain. It would have to be enough. All she needed was for someone to come in and see her dangling over the side of the feed bin, bottom up.

"Might I be of assistance?"

The rich, masculine, and very British voice startled her so badly that she flung herself backward too fast. She lost her footing and knocked her knees against the bin. As she swung her arms out in a desperate bid to regain her balance, the oats sailed out in a powdery arc and splattered all over the front of the man who could only be Gideon Westcott.

His blue chambray shirt must have been damp from his exertions with the laboring ewe, for the oats stuck to him. Dread settled into the pit of her stomach.

"I'm so sorry, sir." She rushed forward and began swiping at the front of his shirt, but after the first contact, her hands became as oats-covered as his clothes. Not knowing what else to do, she stepped back and tried to explain.

"I wanted to get my mare some grain, but the bin was nearly empty, and I'm so short I couldn't reach . . . had to lean over the edge, then you came in and startled me . . . the oats flew . . . I . . . I'm sorry."

The poor man just stood there, stunned. He wore ordinary work clothes like any other Texas rancher and had a strong, capable stance that communicated experienced stockman, not arrogant dandy. He was nothing like she had expected. Consumed with the need to get away before he could chastise her, she thrust the bucket at him.

"If you'll just see that she gets some water . . . ?"

Then she fled, praying his shock would keep him from recognizing her when next they met. Westcott Cottage did have a handsome prince as it turned out, and she'd just floured him like a drumstick headed for the frying pan.

Chapter 4

Gideon shrugged into his morning coat and tugged his shirt cuffs beyond the end of the charcoal coat sleeves as fashion dictated. While he straightened his silk Windsor tie, his mind traipsed back to the stable. He couldn't get the image of frothy petticoats and yellow calico out of his mind. It wasn't every day a man found a woman draped over the edge of his oat bin.

She'd been a tiny slip of a thing with thick sable hair that threatened to burst out of its pins and hazel eyes that danced with life . . . and a healthy dose of panic. He chuckled softly. No doubt she was one of the candidates Bevin had brought down from Fort Worth, and if her eagerness to make amends was any indication, she'd probably deduced his identity the moment she showered him with grain. He couldn't wait to see her reaction when he joined the group in the parlor.

He hoped the other candidates were a bit more seasoned. The girl from the stable looked barely out of the schoolroom. What kind of experience could she possibly have acquired in her short life? Isabella didn't need a playmate; she needed someone who had dealt with a wide variety of children and issues. Someone capable, dedicated, patient. The girl in yellow might be chipper, and no doubt would prove fun to tease, but judging by the impetuous display earlier, patience didn't seem to be one of her virtues.

Before descending the stairs, Gideon stopped by Isabella's room. She sat on the light-colored Brussels carpet, a village of wooden blocks encircling her. Painted iron men and women, horses and dogs, carts and wagons went about their business in the miniature town. Two of the figurines faced each other, leaning in and out at Bella's direction. She shifted them back and forth, a single finger atop each head. Her face portrayed alternating personalities and emotions as the characters took turns in a conversation only she could hear.

He stepped into the room and hunkered down in front of her, careful not to disturb the building blocks. She looked up at him, the hint of a smile playing across her lips. His heart constricted. Thankfully, his presence still brought her a small measure of happiness, but he wouldn't be satisfied until she returned to full-faced toothy grins and girlish giggles. *God, grant me the wisdom to choose the right person to help accomplish that feat.*

"I'm on my way to the parlor to meet the women Mr. Bevin brought. Will you join me?"

She shrank back, but Gideon held out his hand.

"Remember, I'm counting on you to help me select the best candidate."

She laid her fingers tentatively in his palm, and he helped her to her feet. She used his arm for balance as she maneuvered over her blocks, but when they came to the doorway, she faltered. Letting go of his hand, she darted back to her bed and snatched up the doll that lay across the white lace bedspread. A gift from her mother, its golden hair and blue eyes matched Bella's own. He knew she drew comfort and security from it, so he made no protest when she went back for it.

"Ready?" he asked when she returned to his side.

She nodded. Together they moved down the hall and descended the stairs. The door to the parlor stood open. Gideon led Bella in without slowing his step. He feared any hesitation on his part would simply allow her insecurities time to resurge. Like loading sheep up the chute, once you got them started it was best to keep them moving until the job was done. Otherwise, you left your gate open for all kinds of trouble.

"Westcott! It's about time you got here." James Bevin pushed himself away from the hearth and approached Gideon with a warm grin. "These ladies have been subjected to my inferior conversation long enough, old boy. I fear they've grown weary of my company."

"Don't be silly, Mr. Bevin." A graceful blond woman rose from the sofa and floated toward them, her face serene. "You have been a delightful companion."

"Gideon Westcott, may I present Miss Lillian Oliver?"

"Miss Oliver." Gideon bowed toward her, and she answered with a deep curtsy elegant enough for any London drawing room. By the time she rose, the other two women had come to stand behind her, waiting for their introduction—one a rather severe-looking female with streaks of silver in her tightly pulled-back hair, and the other a petite young woman with a delightful blush staining her cheeks. The elder of the two stepped forward first.

"Mrs. Esther Carmichael," Bevin announced.

Gideon dutifully sketched a bow and noted a distinctive medicinal odor emanating from the older woman. It reminded him of one of his own childhood nurses. She had rubbed liniment into her joints every day and preferred the comfort of the schoolroom over outdoor excursions that required chasing after him and his brothers. Would Mrs. Carmichael be the same?

Finally, the brunette in yellow calico took her place in front of him. Bevin opened his mouth to introduce her, but she beat him to it.

"Mr. Westcott and I met briefly in the stable earlier today."

Bevin's brow arched. "Oh?"

Gideon dipped his head in agreement. "Quite true. But I'm afraid she left before I learned her name."

The rose in her cheeks deepened from a dusky pink to a vivid scarlet.

"Well then," Bevin said, "allow me to present Miss Adelaide Proctor."

The energetic Miss Proctor bobbed a quick curtsy and then thrust her hand out to him before he could complete his bow. She didn't offer him dainty fingertips or the back of her hand for him to kiss. No, she offered a straight-out, flat-palmed, thumb-up handshake, which until now he had only associated with other men. Not wanting to offend or embarrass her, he took hold, surprised at the strength of her grip. And when he glanced up, he got the distinct impression that she was taking his measure. For some odd reason, he found himself hoping that he passed her test.

She released his hand after a second and stepped back, her gaze dropping from his face to somewhere beyond his right hip.

"Hello." Genuine warmth lit her face.

His mind jerked back into motion. *Isabella.*

He cleared his throat. "Ladies? My daughter, Isabella."

Gideon placed his hand between the girl's shoulder blades and steered her forward. She resisted slightly and smothered her doll against her chest, but she came around to face the three women.

"Make your curtsy, child." Mrs. Carmichael spoke with authority yet not unkindly, and Bella hurried to obey. The older woman nodded her approval to the girl and faced Gideon with satisfaction, having demonstrated her proficiency.

"She's a lovely girl, Mr. Westcott. A true beauty. You must be very proud." Miss Oliver smiled up at him like a debutante. He almost expected her to start batting her eyelashes. It bothered him a bit that she addressed her comments to him instead of speaking directly to Isabella, but he pushed the feeling aside, for she spoke the truth. He was proud of his daughter.

"Thank you." Gideon cupped his palm around the upper part of Isabella's right arm and gave her an affectionate squeeze. "She's the sunshine in my day."

The sound of an indrawn breath brought Gideon's attention back to Miss Proctor. Her eyes glowed with quiet intensity, and he felt as if he were stealing a glimpse into the private recesses of her heart. A film of moisture appeared, which dulled the effect and left him wanting to clear it away so he could look deeper. She blinked the wetness away, but before he could delve into the mystery behind her eyes again, she lowered herself to face Isabella.

"Did you hear that?" She spoke intimately to the child, as if there were no one else in the room. "You're the sunshine in your papa's life. That's just about the highest compliment a girl can get. My own father used to say much the same thing to me. In fact, he once told me that yellow was his favorite color and that whenever I wore it, it was like having his own personal sunshine whether indoors or out, clear sky or gray. And do you know what?"

Isabella slowly shook her head from side to side, entranced. Gideon felt entranced, too. Not so much by the story, though, as by the effect it was having on his daughter.

"Now that my father's gone," she continued, "yellow is the only color I ever wear. It reminds me of him and makes me happy to think that maybe if he looks down on me from heaven, he will see his little sunshine and smile."

Isabella loosened her grip on the doll and reached out to pat Miss Proctor's cheek. The woman covered the girl's hand with her own and leaned into the touch. Gideon stared, his eyes burning. All these months, he had tried to comfort Bella in her grief, and now, with a single story, this woman had bonded with his daughter in a way he had been unable to. They had connected through the shared loss of a parent, and for the first time in ages, Bella was reaching out to another instead of withdrawing into herself. The Lord had brought him a miracle after all. A miracle wrapped in yellow calico.

Later that evening, Gideon sat alone in his study. He had read every recommendation letter, scrutinized each diploma, and weighed the prospective candidates on an imaginary credential scale. Miss Proctor didn't have the experience of Mrs. Carmichael or the refined social graces evident in Miss Oliver, but what she did have was tipping the balance decidedly in her favor—Isabella's vote.

Yet it wouldn't be responsible of him to rely solely on a child's first impression in making such a decision. All Bella knew was that she and Miss Proctor shared a common grief. She didn't understand the qualifications a governess should posses or the ramifications of this decision on her future. That was his obligation.

He'd come to Texas to prove to his father that he could be responsible, to establish and perpetuate a profitable business, to rise above his desultory ways and make something of himself. No more rounds of parties, meaningless flirtations, and a fly-by-night existence. So how exactly did turning a vital decision over to a child demonstrate his competency?

Gideon closed his eyes and pinched the bridge of his nose in an effort to alleviate the dull ache throbbing between his brows. A knock sounded on the door. Gideon dropped his hand and looked up from the papers strewn across his walnut pedestal desk.

"Enter."

James Bevin sauntered into the room, closing the door behind him. "So is there anything you'd like to know about these ladies before you make your decision? Say . . . the fact that Miss Oliver is afraid to venture out of doors for fear of Indian attack or that

Mrs. Carmichael likely drove Mr. Carmichael to his grave with her sharp tongue."

He wandered nonchalantly up to Gideon's desk and lifted one of the documents by the corner, pretending to examine it. "Or perhaps you'd care to learn that Miss Proctor sits a horse better than most men, has a keen wit, and can travel days at a time without uttering a single complaint."

"Do I sense a touch of partiality in your comments, James?" Gideon smirked at his friend.

"Come now, Gid. You'd be a fool not to hire Miss Proctor, and you know it. Tell me I'm wrong."

Gideon braced his elbow on the edge of his desk and rubbed his jaw. The slight stubble there abraded his thumb and forefinger. "It's just so illogical. Based on her credentials, I never would have considered her for the position. To be honest, I'm surprised you did."

"She was a last minute addition."

"Ah." Gideon leaned back in his chair, the leather creaking as he shifted his weight. "I wondered why you brought three candidates out here when the plan was for me to interview the top two."

James grabbed an armchair by the seat and dragged it over to the desk. He sat down, stretching his long legs out in front of him. "I tell you, Gid, it was as if a divine hand brought her to my door. We ran that ad for two weeks and I sorted through a dozen or more applicants, narrowing it down to the most experienced two, just like we discussed. I purchased their rail passes, and we were all set to go. Then, the day before we were to leave, Miss Proctor shows up at my office, tames Mr. Lyons, and ropes me in, as well. I can't explain it, but somehow I knew in my gut that she was meant for this job."

Gideon said nothing. After watching Miss Proctor interact with Bella, he couldn't deny that there was something special about the way she related to the child. His instincts resonated with what James said. But could he trust his instincts? He'd never been a father before, had no idea what would be best for a girl like Bella. Wouldn't it be wiser to set aside gut feelings and concentrate on facts?

Sitting forward, he shuffled the papers on his desk until he located the one he sought. "It says here that she taught school in Cisco up until about a month ago. How did she even hear about this position?"

"Providence, I guess," James said. "She'd only been in town a day, apparently on business of a . . . um . . . personal nature, when she got hold of a week-old copy of the *Gazette*. I don't think she even noticed the date."

James's hedging about her business in town didn't escape Gideon's notice. He was obviously keeping a confidence of some kind. Gideon peered closely at his friend. The man had integrity, and Gideon trusted him. He wouldn't have recommended Miss Proctor for the position if there was something scandalous in her past. Yet the seed of curiosity had been planted and was already taking root. What was the woman running from?

"You should hire her, Gid." James's features lost all traces of amusement. "Trust your instincts. Shoot, trust *my* instincts. If she doesn't work out, I'll take the blame." A spark of humor reappeared. "Of course, I also get to claim the credit when she surpasses all your expectations."

Gideon shook his head in surrender. "Well, I did tell Isabella that she could help me decide. And with you voting for Miss Proctor, as well, I'm already outnumbered."

"You weren't really going to choose one of the others, were you?"

"Truth is, I wasn't sure what I was going to do." Gideon pressed his palms into his thighs, bracing his arms. "All right. I'll give her a try. But keep tabs on Mrs. Carmichael and Miss Oliver. I may need a replacement if Miss Proctor proves unsatisfactory."

Gideon gathered the strewn documents and tapped the edges

against the desk until they formed a straight pile. Setting them aside, he turned back to James. "Now, about that other matter you were taking care of for me. Has that been resolved?"

James pulled a packet of papers out of his coat pocket and tossed them onto the desk. "Yes, finally. The court ruled in our favor. Isabella will remain with you."

"Thank God." Gideon hadn't really doubted the outcome. He knew they were in the right and stood on solid legal ground. Nevertheless, the result flooded him with relief. "And what of our investigations?"

"Your man in London turned up enough dirt on Lord Petchey to make me want to take a bath after I read his report. The scoundrel is in debt up to his ears, gambles in the seediest clubs, frequents brothels, and even ran his horse to death once trying to win a bet during one of his fox hunts.

"I had wondered why Lady Petchey named you Isabella's ward when the girl had family back in England, but now I understand. Her husband, the late viscount, even wrote his brother out of the family will for the most part. Reginald inherited the title and a tidy sum that would have kept him in style had he curbed his wastrel habits and invested it wisely, but of course he didn't. Lady Petchey retained control of the rest. No doubt he expected to regain access to the family funds once Lady Petchey fell ill. It must have come as quite a shock to learn she put all the money into a trust for Isabella and named you executor as well as guardian. Contesting the will was his only option."

Gideon recalled the last hours he had spent with Bella's mother onboard ship. Lucinda Petchey had demanded that he send for the captain to witness her will. The ship's surgeon had assured him she was dying, and all he could think to do was make her as comfortable as possible. Her emaciated body had looked so forlorn lying in that narrow berth, her skin paper thin, her flesh wasted away by whatever sickness had ravaged her.

He sent for the captain right away, unable to deny her anything that might bring her ease. In the end, she had hung on to life long enough to have her will properly signed and witnessed, as well as to give strict instructions on how to deliver it to her solicitor in London while leaving a copy with him. Once everything had been put in order and she had hugged her daughter one last time, she slipped away, accepting the peace death offered.

Clearing his throat, Gideon ran a shaky hand through his hair. "I knew Lucinda feared for Isabella's future. I can only imagine what kind of life the child would have been subjected to once her uncle ran through her fortune. The bounder would have probably tried to marry her off to some rich blueblood before she was out of the schoolroom. He would have sold her off to the highest bidder, no doubt, not caring a whit about how the fellow treated her. Makes me want to tear him apart just thinking about it." Gideon took several measured breaths in an effort to cool his temper.

"Yes, well, Lady Petchey was wise to have Captain Harris witness everything." James's own expression had turned rather dour. "His testimony to her soundness of mind—along with that of the ship's doctor—is what swung the court in our favor. Petchey had painted her as a mentally unstable, paranoid woman who had run away from her only family for no reason whatsoever. He nearly succeeded in convincing the court that a sane woman would never have given her only child into the care of a stranger. If not for their testimony, you might have been forced to hand Isabella over to Petchey."

"God forbid."

Gideon slouched in his chair, glad for the first time since settling in Texas that several thousand miles and one very large ocean stood between him and England. The distance might separate him from everything that was familiar and the family he loved, but it also kept Isabella out of her uncle's greedy grasp, and that was worth any sacrifice.

Chapter 5

LONDON

Reginald Petchey stormed into his solicitor's office and slammed the door.

"This better be good, Farnsworth." He took a seat in front of the thin man's desk and glared his displeasure. "You've turned up nothing of importance in the fortnight since the court ruled against us, and now you have the nerve to summon me away from my club? I ought to dismiss you out of hand for such impertinence. You—"

"I found Westcott."

Reginald halted his tirade and pierced his solicitor with a contemptuous glance designed to put him in his place. Farnsworth looked decidedly pasty-faced, and no doubt his knees were knocking together behind his desk, miserable milksop that he was, but he held steady. For the moment. Perhaps he wasn't a complete invertebrate after all.

"Go on."

Farnsworth managed to hold his gaze for a second or two before his mouth started quivering. Then his attention dropped to somewhere in the middle of Reginald's chest. Satisfied at the man's reaction, Reginald turned over his hand and began examining his manicured fingernails, sliding a dark look out of the corner of his eye every few seconds for good measure. He admired Farnsworth's unusual display of mettle, but it wouldn't do for the man to suddenly grow a backbone. There was too much at stake.

"Yes, my lord." The little toad coughed and shuffled his papers. "I dispatched a man to Leicestershire last week to bribe Baron Westcott's servants into divulging his son's location. Unfortunately, the staff turned out to be quite loyal. We made little headway until I changed tactics."

"You're rambling, Farnsworth."

The solicitor twitched and squirmed in his chair, then apparently dredged up what remained of his spine and looked Reginald in the eye again.

"Blackmail, my lord. The Westcotts insist upon morality from those who work for them, so we started searching for blemishes among the lambs, if you will. One loose-lipped fellow at the local tavern let it slip that an upstairs maid was rumored to have had a child out of wedlock a couple years back. My man traveled to her home village to investigate and found the girl's parents raising the brat and claiming him as their own in an effort to preserve her reputation. However, he dug up several fine citizens who eagerly verified the rumor once they saw coin was involved. When we threatened to reveal her secret, the maid intercepted a letter her mistress intended to post to America and turned it over to us."

Impatient with the long-winded explanation, Reginald gritted his teeth. "We already know he's in America."

"Yes, but until now we didn't know where."

Farnsworth paused for effect, but Reginald was fed up with the theatrics. He pushed up out of his chair, planted his palms on the solicitor's desk, and leaned across the surface. His face lowered an inch closer to Farnsworth's with each word he forced through his clenched jaw.

"Where . . . is . . . he?"

Farnsworth swallowed and pulled back, his round eyes emitting a delightful quantity of distress.

"H-h-he's in the state of Texas. On a sheep ranch in a region called Menard County."

Triumph surged through Reginald's veins, but he masked his pleasure. He was having too much fun watching Farnsworth sweat.

"I assume you've booked passage for me on a steamer, then?" His nose nearly touched the man's cheek as he rumbled the question.

"N-n-no, sir. But I'll go as soon as we've concluded our business."

"You'll go now."

Farnsworth sprung backward out of his chair, like a hare evading a hound. "I'll go now." Never taking his wary eyes off Reginald, he stumbled toward the door, plucked his hat off the rack, and fumbled with the latch. After several unsuccessful attempts, the cornered hare finally found his rabbit hole and escaped down the corridor.

Reginald paced over to the window and watched Farnsworth scurry down the street. Then his gaze blurred as his focus turned inward, his lips twisting into a feral smile. Lucinda's attempt at revenge had failed. Why had he ever doubted it? No mere woman could outmaneuver him. Stuart might have surrendered to her wiles, but his brother had gone soft, letting her virtuous manner and religious drivel turn his insides to mush. Reginald would never fall for such tripe, and Lucinda knew it. She had thought herself so clever by fleeing England. Yet she hadn't been able to outrun death, had she? He brushed his thumb and forefinger over the thick mustache that sat atop his lip. No. He always won in the end. Always.

Too bad that fact was harder to prove to his creditors than it had been to his sister-in-law. The impatient leeches. He had bought some time when Lucinda died, assuring them the Petchey fortune would revert to him. However, now that news of the will had spread, they would be back, and more demanding than ever. Reginald's hands bent into fists. Ruin. Disgrace. Sour contemplations. It was his duty to protect the Petchey name. His ancestors fought and died to bring honor to this house. He wouldn't allow it to be stripped away just because his brother had abdicated family loyalty in order to please his delusional wife.

Sunlight streamed through the window and glinted off the ring on his right hand. Reginald lifted it up to take a closer look and frowned as dark memories assaulted him. The black onyx stone overlaid with a gold P had been handed down to first sons for generations. Now it belonged to him, ever since the day a hunting accident had taken Stuart's life.

Ah, Stuart. He wished things could have worked out differently. The two of them had been close once upon a time. Before Lucinda. Reginald tapped the ring against the glass, his agitation building. The taps grew more forceful until he finally willed himself to stop. With mechanical precision, he lowered his hand to his side. The past could not be changed. He must focus on the future.

Stuart's daughter *was* the future. Petchey blood ran through her veins, and it was his duty to restore her to her rightful family. Westcott couldn't give her that heritage. Only he could. And with his niece under his protection, he'd have the blunt he needed to settle his debts and rebuild the Petchey fortune. All he had to do was remove Gideon Westcott from the equation.

Chapter 6

Adelaide leaned against the spindled porch railing and waved farewell to her traveling companions. Mrs. Carmichael sat stiff in her seat, but Miss Oliver returned the gesture, her genteel expression unruffled. Mr. Westcott said a few final words to his friend, shaking his hand and thumping him on the back before Mr. Bevin climbed aboard the wagon. With a snap of the reins, Mr. Bevin set the horses in motion, leaving her behind. The new governess. Her. Adelaide Proctor. The truth struggled to settle into her brain.

Mr. Westcott stood in the yard watching the wagon depart, and Adelaide watched him. The man seemed to be two people. By day he was a rancher wearing cotton shirts and denim trousers, wrestling pregnant ewes, and watering strange women's horses. But in the evening, he became an elegant nobleman in silk ties and fine coats with fancy manners and cultured charm. The hardworking rancher earned her respect, but the English gentleman made her heart flutter, embodying every storybook hero she'd ever fallen in love with.

He was well formed and tall, but not overly tall. He kept his dark hair trimmed short, and his eyes were the color of melted chocolate. But it was his smile that did her in. He had dimples. Amazingly, the boyish creases did nothing to hinder his masculinity. Instead, they enhanced it and gave him a cheerful mien that was impossible to resist.

When he'd entered the parlor last night and met her gaze for the first time since their encounter in the stable, his eyes had teased her, bringing a blush to her cheeks and even greater warmth to her heart. It was as if she were Jane Eyre arriving at Thornfield to begin her position as governess to the young Adèle, but instead of finding the house without its master, her Mr. Rochester was in residence. A sigh bubbled inside her as the daydream played out in her mind, but the sound of Mr. Westcott's approaching footsteps banished the fantasy.

Adelaide spun around and pressed her back to the railing to avoid looking at him. Her heart pounded in time with the rhythm of her guilty conscience. The last thing she needed was for her employer to find her mooning over him. Hadn't her romantic inclinations gotten her into enough trouble already? Mr. Westcott smiled too much to play the role of a dark and brooding Rochester anyway. And her impulsive nature and chatterbox personality couldn't possibly be more unlike the staid, proper Jane, who spoke more with her eyes than with her mouth.

She was at Westcott Cottage to do a job, not to reenact her favorite novel. Isabella deserved the very best she could give. God brought her here to minister to a child, not swoon over a man. She'd best not forget that.

"If you would be so good as to accompany me to the study, Miss Proctor, I'd like to go over your duties with you."

She forced herself to meet his gaze. He grinned, setting loose those dimples to wreak havoc on her already quivery nerves. Those things were deadly to a woman's concentration. She clasped her hands together at her waist and squeezed her fingers until the pain dislodged the breathless feeling from her chest.

"Of course," she said, pleased that her voice sounded normal.

He ushered her inside and past the front parlor to a doorway near the foot of the stairs. Dark walnut furniture dominated the room, including an entire wall of built-in bookshelves. Soft olive and ivory fabrics in the upholstery, carpet, and draperies offset the heaviness of the dark wood, however. Cream-colored paper on the walls sported gilt-embossed designs that reflected what little sunlight penetrated the room. Some of the tension drained out of her. It was certainly a masculine space but not unwelcoming, which was a blessing. Meeting with her new employer was intimidating enough without having the walls press in on her.

"Please have a seat, Miss Proctor."

A settee and two chairs were arranged along the wall opposite the bookshelves. Mr. Westcott touched the back of one of the chairs and motioned for her to sit. Once she did, he took the place across from her, their knees separated by a varnished table topped with two small leather-bound books. The covers showed a great deal of wear, not the pristine display one would expect.

Curiosity pushed all worries about the interview from Adelaide's mind. The cracked leather spine of the first volume indicated a collection of Shakespeare's works, while the other read *Holy Bible*.

"I keep them out to remind me that success requires sacrifice."

Her hand twitched, and she nearly reached out to lay hold of the books, but at the last second, good sense suppressed the impulse. She primly folded her hands in her lap, hoping he didn't notice that her grip was tight enough to cut off the circulation to her fingertips.

"I can understand how the Bible might bring sacrifice to mind," she ruminated aloud, "but Shakespeare? I'm afraid I don't see the connection."

He answered with a self-deprecating laugh.

"You caught me. The truth is not nearly as noble as I tried to make it sound. The reminder is actually more physical than philosophical."

"How so?"

"Those two books were my bosom companions for the two years I trailed sheep from California to Texas."

"*You* trailed sheep?"

"Hard to believe, isn't it?"

Shock must have stolen her manners. She fumbled to repair the damage. "I didn't . . . mean to imply . . ."

He waved off her sputtering apology, his eyes dancing with humor. "Sometimes it's hard for me to believe, too, and I'm the one who lived through it. Barely."

Heat crept up the back of her neck. Why did she never think before she opened her mouth? She bit her tongue before it could cause any more trouble. Unfortunately, her hesitation bogged the conversation down in awkward silence, leaving her employer to wade into the mire to rescue her.

"I am the youngest of three sons, and I'd always been something of a gadabout."

He picked up the Bible and thumbed through the pages, the thin paper crinkling. "My mother hoped I would follow in her father's footsteps and join the clergy. I considered it for a time, but something held me back."

"How did you end up in Texas?"

"Propaganda."

She waited for more, but he just sat there with a smug look on his face. The rascal. He was going to make her ask, wasn't he? She'd bet in his childhood he was one of those boys who pestered his brothers to the precise point where they would retaliate so that he could escape punishment while they received a scolding for beating on him. He probably had a full arsenal of crocodile tears to go along with those devastating dimples.

"You gave your brothers fits growing up, didn't you?"

Belatedly, Adelaide realized her comment made no sense in the context of their discussion. At this rate, she was going to talk herself out of a position before she ever truly started. However, Gideon seemed to follow without difficulty. He exhibited no blank stare or puzzled frown the way most people did when she made a radical mental shift. Instead, his eyes danced with mischief.

"Every chance I got."

She grinned, and he steered them back on course without a single bump.

"Word had it that any man with money to invest could earn vast profits with little to no effort in the American West. Buy a half-dozen sections of land, fill it with stock, and let the money roll in while you hunt big game and host parties."

"Don't tell me you believed that nonsense?"

He shrugged. "Well, I was intelligent enough to know there would be some work involved, but it sounded too good to pass up. My father, bless his wise soul, gave me a condition. He would provide the capital for me to invest in land, build a house, and purchase stock if I agreed to learn the wool business through firsthand experience. I consented, never imagining what a hard teacher experience could be. But everything worked out. The *pastores* I hired on in California had me trained right and proper by the time we arrived in Texas, and several of them stayed on to work the ranch with me."

He laid the Bible back on the table, leaving it open. Adelaide couldn't read the tiny print from where she sat, but she recognized the number 23 and figured it must be Psalms.

"I never realized how many verses there are about sheep and shepherds until I spent two years of my life outside with the silly creatures. Gave me a whole new appreciation for the Lord as the Good Shepherd and for how much grief his flock must put him through."

Gideon Westcott might be a rascal, but he had depth.

"What about you, Miss Proctor? What circumstances led to your coming here?"

She couldn't exactly say she followed a cloud, now could she? He'd think her deranged. Instead she opted for the bland version of the truth. "I came across the advertisement Mr. Bevin ran in the *Gazette* and decided to apply."

Her employer shook his head at her and clicked his tongue, the frown lines in his brow at odds with the twinkle in his eye. "For shame, Miss Proctor. Surely there's more to the story than that dull explanation." He leaned on the chair arm nearest her and winked. Her heart stuttered. A lock of dark hair fell across his forehead just as she imagined any true rake's would, tempting her to reach out and comb it back into place with her fingers.

"The chairman of the Cisco school board wrote you a glowing recommendation. Obviously they would have preferred you to stay. So what made you leave? Wanderlust? An overzealous suitor? A sick friend?"

Panic knotted her stomach. Not even the little-boy grin he was favoring her with could ease the tightness. Had Mr. Bevin told him of her marriage fiasco? She hadn't revealed the details to him and he hadn't pressed her for them, but if he had said something to Mr. Westcott . . . No. She shouldn't borrow trouble. She'd learned her lesson about saying too much during her interview in Fort Worth. She'd not make the same mistake here. A woman was due some privacy after all, and a true gentleman would never pry.

"My reasons for leaving were of a personal nature. I'm sure you understand." Adelaide smiled, hoping her words didn't sound as prudish to him as they did to her.

"Of course." He splayed his hands before her, palms up, as if accepting her vague response. Then he touched her. His index finger pressed lightly on the back of her hand, and shivers danced up her arm. "But it doesn't seem fair for me to reveal a piece of my personal story without you doing the same. I promise to hold whatever you tell me in the strictest confidence."

Adelaide bit her lip. He *had* opened up to her. She wanted to reciprocate, especially when he looked at her as he did now, as if she alone held the key to his future happiness. He wasn't asking for much, just an answer to his question. But that answer could jeopardize her position.

"I'm sorry, Mr. Westcott." She glanced down, her eyes glued to where his hand touched hers. "I'd rather not go into specifics. I can assure you, however, that the situation that led me to Fort Worth will in no way affect my ability to carry out the duties you hired me to perform."

He sighed. "Very well."

Gideon withdrew his hand, and his demeanor subtly changed. He shifted away from her in his seat. His smile faded to a polite curve. No dimples. No twinkle in his eye. No flirtatious wink. He once again became lord of the manor.

Another shiver ran through Adelaide—only this time it held foreboding instead of delight. Henry Belcher had charmed her with sweet words and false promises in order to get what he wanted—a female companion to toy with while he was away from his wife . . . and promotion-worthy book sales. Was Gideon Westcott cut from the same cloth?

He didn't strike her as the type to lure her into a tawdry affair under the same roof as his daughter, but he had certainly been working his wiles to try to get her to divulge her secret. And she had nearly done so. If she had learned nothing else from her experience with Henry, she'd learned charm could not be trusted.

"So, Miss Proctor . . . about your duties."

Relieved that her employer had assumed a more professional mien, Adelaide sat up straight and nodded. "Yes, sir."

"Isabella is a very quiet child, and not just because she chooses not to speak. Ever since—"

"Excuse me. Did you say she *chooses* not to speak?" Adelaide's mind spun. If the child wasn't truly mute, then why didn't she speak? Was she afraid? Obstinate? Unstable?

Gideon's voice cut into her thoughts.

"She used to prattle on about everything under the sun." Regret tightened the corners of his mouth. "I think it is somehow tied to her mother's death. She hasn't spoken a word since."

Adelaide pressed her lips together to keep them from trembling. It had been years since her father's passing, but she recalled the heartrending pain of the loss. She'd never really known her mother as anything more than a pretty woman in a picture on the parlor mantel. Anna Proctor had died trying to birth a stillborn son when Adelaide was two. But she remembered everything about the day her father passed, as well as the anger and resentment that flooded through her when Aunt Louise whisked her away to Boston, forcing her to leave everything familiar behind.

Well, except for Sheba. Adelaide had refused to leave without her filly. She'd slept in her horse's stall every night until Aunt Louise finally agreed to bring the animal along. The sale of the ranch paid for Sheba's boarding as well as Adelaide's schooling, leaving her a small portion on account at the bank that could tide her over in an emergency. But even if her father had left her an inheritance equal to that of a British nobleman, she would have traded it all to have him back.

Was that what Isabella was going through? If Gideon had been trailing sheep the last two years, he surely would have left his wife and child back in England. Out of necessity he would have been absent from them for most of that time, becoming a near stranger to the child. Isabella lost her mother—not the only parent who loved her, surely, but the only one she truly knew. And on top of that she'd been pulled from everything familiar, from friends and grandparents and the house she thought of as home. No wonder the child was detached.

"Miss Proctor, I need your help." The muscles in Gideon's jaw clenched, and his dark eyes pleaded with her. "She's slipping away from me, and I worry that the melancholia won't let go. I tried to give her time to grieve, but this can't be healthy for her. She withdraws more and more. I don't want you just teaching her reading and arithmetic. I want you to teach her joy."

Moved by his genuine love for the child and by the pain of one so young, Adelaide arose from her chair and went to him. He quickly gained his feet but seemed to have difficulty looking at her. She knew she had no right to offer him comfort, yet her heart demanded that she try. Putting her hand on his arm, she drew his attention and peered up into eyes that brimmed with desperation.

"I don't know if I am capable of the task," she said, "but I will give everything I have to the effort. If the Lord wills it, we will find a way."

He held her gaze for several seconds, then nodded. "Thank you."

Gideon stepped back and cleared his throat. When he looked at her again, all evidence of vulnerability had vanished. He motioned for her to walk with him to the door.

"I purchased a selection of schoolbooks several weeks ago. I wasn't sure what you would require, so if an area is lacking, let me know and I will order whatever materials you need." He occasionally glanced her way, but for the most part kept his head angled toward the floor as they made their way across the room. "You'll find the books stored on the third floor, along with various other supplies. Set up the schoolroom however you see fit."

They slowed as they reached the doorway. He clasped his hands behind his back and rocked on the balls of his feet. "Explore the house. Get to know Isabella. Ride that horse of yours all over the countryside. This is to be your home now. I want you to be comfortable."

"Thank you, Mr. Westcott."

"Keep me informed of—"

A high-pitched scream rent the air. The tormented sound tore away all pretense of formality, leaving nothing but raw emotion visible on Gideon Westcott's face.

"Bella."

He sprinted out of the room toward the sound. Adelaide followed close at his heels.

Chapter 7

It took only a minute to reach the kitchen, but Gideon felt as if he'd aged ten years by the time he burst into the room. The screaming continued, piercing his ears as well as his heart. He expected to find Bella crumpled in pain, wounded in some way, but she stood hale and hearty before him, not a wrinkle on her dress or scuff on her shoe. He rushed up to her and fell to his knees. He scrutinized her from head to toe, yet he saw no visible injury. Panic mingled with helplessness and caused him to grip her arms tighter than he intended.

"Bella. What is it? What's wrong?"

All at once the screaming stopped, but the anguish didn't. Isabella's pain-filled eyes stared past him as if he weren't there. Chills speared through him.

"Bella." He shook her gently. "Bella!"

"*Señor.*" Miss Proctor's voice. "*Quitarse su camisa.* Take off your shirt."

What was she talking about? And why was she addressing him in

Spanish? But then she moved into his line of sight, and he realized she wasn't talking to him at all.

His foreman, Miguel, stood directly across from Bella, his features frozen in shock. Gideon looked back to Bella. Then to Miguel. Then Bella. His daughter's eyes were locked on the *vaquero*. More specifically, on his bloodstained shirt.

"Please, señor. If she sees that you are unharmed, it might calm her."

The governess's instruction roused Miguel from his stupor. He started yanking the shirttails out of his waistband, then hesitated when Miss Proctor spun around, turning her back to him.

"*¿Patrón?*"

Miguel waited for permission. Gideon wavered. A man never disrobed in front of a lady, let alone a young girl. However, Miss Proctor seemed to think it would help, and right now he would do anything to break Bella free from her torture.

"Do it."

Miguel complied. A feminine squeak emanated from somewhere off to Gideon's right. Only then did he realize that Bella's screams had brought the rest of his staff to the kitchen, as well. Mabel Garrett, his cook, turned the color of a ripe tomato and disappeared through the door connecting to the dining room. A calmer Mrs. Chalmers followed Miss Proctor's example and turned her back while her husband slipped his arms out of his morning coat and handed it to the herdsman. The butler then collected the soiled shirt and took his wife's arm.

"We'll launder this and have it returned to Mr. Ruíz." The two quietly exited into the hall.

Gideon turned his attention back to Bella. She stared blankly at Miguel. He wanted to shake her and force her to wake up from her nightmare, but what if that made it worse? His palms grew moist where he held her arms. *God, help me.* He knew nothing about healing little girls with wounded souls. Then again, he knew next to nothing about anything having to do with little girls.

Miguel approached them, holding the edges of the borrowed coat together. Gideon stood and stepped aside, but he grasped Bella's limp hand, unwilling to sever his connection to her. He hated being helpless. Where was Miss Proctor? Wasn't she supposed to be an expert on dealing with children?

Then he heard her voice, and some of his tension eased.

"Show her, Señor Ruíz. Talk to her." Her soft voice projected patience and confidence, diluting the panic in the room.

The herdsman tentatively lowered himself down on one knee in front of Bella. "Is all right, *chica. Estoy bien.* See?" He took Bella's other hand and lifted it to his chest where the blood had stained his shirt—directly over his heart.

Gideon felt Miss Proctor's warm breath near his neck. "Did her mother die violently?" she whispered. "From some kind of wound that would cause a great deal of blood?"

Their thoughts obviously ran along the same lines—a past trauma had elicited Bella's panic. However, it couldn't have been her mother's death. There were no similarities to this situation at all.

"No," he whispered back, careful to turn his head away from Isabella. "She died in her bed, from an illness."

She frowned a bit at that. Her confusion mimicked his own. He knew so little about Bella's life before he met her. What had she seen that a bloody shirt should trigger such a horrific reaction?

Just then, Bella tugged free of Gideon's grip and began scraping at Miguel's shoulder with both hands. Her movements grew more and more frenzied, as if she were trying to unearth something. The truth?

"Open your coat, Miguel."

His foreman shot him an uncertain glance, but complied. Bella immediately shoved the fabric to the side and patted his chest with her hand. Once she convinced herself there was no injury, she turned back to Gideon with tears welling in her eyes—eyes that were once again cognizant of her surroundings.

"Papa." The rusty sound broke his heart the instant before she buried her face in his stomach and sobbed.

Gideon lifted her into his arms and hugged her close, his breath catching as her small arms tightened about his neck. She had spoken. Only one word . . . but, oh, what a word. She'd called him Papa.

Bella cried herself out and fell asleep thirty minutes later. Miss Proctor promised to watch over her until she woke, so Gideon changed his soaked shirt and headed outside, thanking God that she had been there. The fear he had felt in those moments before Miss Proctor took control of the situation haunted him still.

He searched out his foreman and found him by the smokehouse skinning a deer strung up by its hind feet. Chalmers's coat dangled from a nail protruding from the side of the smokehouse, well away from the butchering.

"Well, that explains how the blood got on your shirt."

Miguel, bare from the waist up, whirled around to face him. "Señor Westcott." He wiped his knife across his trousers and slid it into the small sheath attached to his belt. Remorse creased his face as he moved toward Gideon.

"*Lo siento, patrón.* I'm so sorry. I only went to *la cocina* to ask Señora Garrett if she want a fresh venison roast. Then the little *señorita,* she walk in and start screaming. I . . . I not know what to do." His shoulders arched upward and his hands followed, palms out. Gideon recognized his helplessness. Bella's screams had debilitated him, as well.

"Forgive me, señor. I not come to the big house dirty again."

Gideon laid his hand on the man's shoulder. "You are welcome in my house at all times, Miguel. The state of your attire is immaterial."

Miguel hung his head. "*Gracías*, but I not make the same mistake again. The little señorita, she is too tender for my rough ways." He paused for a moment. "She reminds me of my little Rosa."

"Rosa?" Gideon took a step back. When he'd hired Miguel to herd with him back in California, the man had given no indication that he'd be leaving family behind.

"Sí, my niece. Only she's not so little anymore." He lifted his face and gazed off to the west, a touch of a smile on his lips. "One of the young vaqueros from the *rancho* where I used to herd had his eye on her. He is a good man. Maybe they are wed by now, eh?"

Miguel met Gideon's gaze finally, and for a brief moment their friendship seemed to supersede their business relationship. How could he have worked side-by-side with this man for two years and not known about his family in California? Perhaps Miguel had his reasons for not sharing, but most likely he took his cues from his gringo employer, who never saw fit to ask.

Gideon understood how difficult it was to be apart from one's family. He looked forward to the newsy letters his mother sent twice a month, chronicling the lives of his brothers and their wives, the neighbors, and the latest social buzz. Yet Gideon couldn't recall a time when a letter for Miguel had arrived in the post. "Have you not heard from them since you left?"

The herder shrugged. "My sister, she no read so much. And Rosa is young. Her mind is filled with other things. But *no es importante*. How is the little señorita?"

"Better." Gideon leaned his back against the smokehouse wall, bracing the heel of his boot on a protruding board. "Sleeping, I think."

"*Bueno.*"

Gideon nodded. "It's odd, though. Bella has seen blood before and not made a fuss. Remember when I sliced my finger open on that broken window glass? She held my hand and watched you stitch me up like an experienced nurse."

His foreman's eyes lit with a thoughtful gleam. "Sí. That is true."

"Miss Proctor believes there was something specific about the stain on your shirt that triggered her reaction."

Gideon turned back toward the house, imagining Miss Proctor sitting at his daughter's bedside. In actuality, they'd not discussed it much further than the brief exchange in the kitchen, but knowing her supposition matched his brought assurance and, with it, control. Odd that it had stemmed from a woman.

His experience with the fairer sex had been derived predominantly from the social sphere. He'd never witnessed a female, outside of his mother, deal with any crisis more serious than a torn ball gown or an impertinent servant. And even his mother depended heavily on his father when difficulties arose. As was only right. After all, it was a gentleman's duty to protect women from hardship. The man should bear the burden as the stronger vessel. Yet his new governess had not recoiled from adversity. She'd waded right in, her feminine shoulder proving quite capable of sharing his load.

She had also proved immune to his charm. Well, perhaps not immune. He had felt the tremors in her when he touched her hand in the study, but she'd held fast to the information he sought. And in the process, her earnestness had left him feeling like the serpent in the garden, tempting Eve to sacrifice her principles. Not a complimentary comparison.

"There is more I need to tell you, patrón." Miguel's voice broke into his thoughts. "When I rode out this morning to check on the *borregos* in the north pasture, I found the fence cut."

Gideon frowned and pushed away from the smokehouse. "Deliberate?"

"Sí." Miguel nodded, his swarthy face grim.

Many of the ranchers in the area had warned Gideon that fencing off the rangeland might anger some of the old-school cattlemen. They were accustomed to free range where they could herd their animals wherever the grass grew thickest. However loath they were to admit it, though, the time of free range was coming to an end. More and more people were moving into west central Texas now that the Indian threat had passed, which meant farms and ranches competed for the same resources. In order to protect their water and land, owners turned to barbed wire, and those who opposed it turned to wire cutters.

"Juan say a man came through the fence after dark and shot his rifle in the air many times to scatter the borregos. The night hid his face, but he rode a painted horse with white markings that glowed in the moonlight."

Gideon filed away that piece of information, but his anger would not be pushed aside so easily. No one had the right to trespass on his land and harass his sheep. It was illegal, unethical. This flock represented his chance to prove to his father that his trust in his youngest son had not been misplaced. For two years, he'd trailed these animals from California, enduring filth, solitude, and unsympathetic weather in order to furnish his ranch with the finest Rambouillet stock available. And now some disgruntled cowboy thought he could waltz onto his land and try to intimidate him? Not a chance.

Instinct urged him to mount up and confront his neighbors about the incident, to uncover the truth. Yet a more rational, spiritual voice penetrated the haze of his indignation. Turn the other cheek, Jesus had taught. Vengeance belongs to the Lord. If Gideon allowed the aggression of this unknown man to beget more aggression through his response, he might inadvertently provoke a range war, putting Bella and all the others on this ranch in danger. Such a consequence was unacceptable.

Taking a moment to gather himself, Gideon kicked at the corner of the smokehouse with the tip of his boot. The rhythmic thuds and repetitive motion calmed him somewhat.

"How many head did we lose?"

"Maybe a dozen. *No más.*" Miguel tugged his hunting knife free and went back to work removing the deer's hide. "Juan worked all night to gather the borregos. Most were only frightened. A few lambs were trampled, and a handful of ewes fell into an arroyo. Juan, he treat the cuts and scrapes on the rest. I returned to get wire for mending the fence, but this buck crossed my path, and I could not refuse such a gift."

Miguel looked over his shoulder, a roguish grin exposing the gap in his teeth that Gideon had come to associate with the man who had been more mentor to him than employee.

"No, I guess you couldn't." Gideon shook his head and smiled back. "I'll take care of the wire and check in with Juan. When you finish here, notify the other pastores that they can start bringing in their sheep. The shearers are due next week, and we'll be able to keep a better eye on things with everyone close to home."

"Sí, Señor Westcott. I take care of it."

Pulling his leather work gloves out of his hip pocket, Gideon headed to the shed to collect a coil of barbed wire along with a wire stretcher. He'd repair the damage done last night, and pray there would be no further altercations.

The door to the shed creaked as he pulled it open, and the darkness inside seeped into him, bringing with it a new fear. What if doing nothing emboldened the man who had paid them a visit? Would he return and inflict more damage?

Am I making the right decision, Lord? Guide me and protect those in my care.

His mind immediately centered on Isabella and how she had clung to him and called him Papa. His mouth flattened into a determined line. He would do everything in his power to ensure her safety and happiness—which included setting aside his pride and allowing a petite brunette to help shoulder his load. Although if Isabella should decide to speak again, the load would be a good deal lighter.

Chapter 8

The child hadn't said a word. She'd been awake for an hour, helping Adelaide collect books and other items that might be put to use in the schoolroom, yet she remained as mute as before. Adelaide followed Isabella up the narrow stairway to the third floor, her arms burgeoning with alphabet blocks and art supplies. Had she dreamt that moment in the kitchen? No. The look of awe on Gideon's face when his daughter spoke had been too real to be a figment of her imagination. Maybe Isabella's nap had erased the incident from her mind. It would be a blessing if the young girl had indeed forgotten the painful memories evoked by Miguel's bloodstained shirt, but did she have to forget her success in breaking through her wall of silence, too? It seemed unfair somehow.

When Isabella had awakened, Adelaide set aside the copy of Jane Austen's *Emma* she'd been reading and posed dozens of questions to the girl. But to her dismay, Isabella pantomimed each answer without uttering a solitary syllable. After about thirty minutes Adelaide had admitted defeat.

Her charge now held the door wide as Adelaide moved into the large storage area at the top of the stairs. It was really more of an attic than a third story, since the back of the room sloped downward with the roof line. A couple of gabled windows cut into the slanted ceiling, however, letting in a good deal of sunlight.

The alphabet blocks plinked and plonked against the hardwood floor as Adelaide clumsily deposited her load in the corner where they had chosen to stash their treasures. She pulled herself upright and swiveled from side to side to stretch her muscles as she examined the room. The dust dragons must have scared off the furnishings, for the only things brave enough to inhabit the space were the crates of books Gideon had told her about and two large trunks shoved against the side wall. The cobwebs curtaining the recessed windows looked fierce, as well, but she was ready to do battle. A good sweep, some soap and water, and this storage area would make a fine classroom.

Adelaide wandered around the room, planning where to place her desk and Isabella's to best exploit the light. They would probably need a lamp for cloudy days, and she would have to talk to Gideon about putting in a stove for when the temperature grew cool. She ran her fingertips across the sloped ceiling a few inches from her head as ideas continued to percolate in her mind. For once in her life, her lack of height came in handy—she managed to roam through the majority of the room without having to stoop, but a taller person would have had much less freedom.

Out of the corner of her eye, Adelaide glimpsed Isabella climbing into one of the window niches. The squared opening was the perfect size for a young girl to curl up in for a daydream or two on a sunny afternoon. Unfortunately, judging by the somber expression on her face, Isabella had lost not only her voice but also her ability to dream.

Well, as her teacher, Adelaide had no choice but to remedy the situation as soon as possible. No happy girlhood could be sustained without a healthy dose of castles in the air and daring heroes who slew dragons to rescue fair maidens. Or even fair maidens who outwitted dull princes to rescue friendly dragons. A smile curved Adelaide's lips. How many times had she imagined her pony to be a mighty dragon flying over the land with her on its back, breathing fire with every snort that passed through its nostrils?

Of course, as she grew older, she became less enamored with the dragon and more enchanted by the handsome prince on his stately steed, but that was neither here nor there. The point was that Isabella needed to pretend. Life had treated her harshly of late, and while Adelaide would never condone a full escape into an imaginary world to avoid reality altogether, learning how to visit such a place upon occasion might remind the girl how to smile.

"Front and center, Private Izzy!" Adelaide thumped her heel into the floor with military precision and stood at attention.

Isabella startled at the abrupt sound. She turned to look at her governess, her brows raised in bewilderment. Adelaide broke her pose long enough to wink at her charge, hoping to reassure her that she still possessed all her faculties, and then immediately returned to character.

"The third floor of Westcott Cottage is under attack, and I need every available soldier at my disposal. Are you with me, Private Izzy?"

Adelaide held her breath as Isabella regarded her as if she were a curiosity at a sideshow. The poor child probably couldn't figure out if it was better to humor her crazy governess or run for her father. Oh well. In for a penny, in for a pound.

"Come on, Private." She stamped her foot again and motioned for Isabella to join her. "There's no place for dillydalliers in this militia. If we don't defend our position from the dust balls and spider-web snares fired at us, all of Westcott Cottage will fall into enemy hands. We are the last line of defense. Your country needs you. Your family needs you. Your schoolbooks need you."

Finally, a corner of her mouth quirked. One leg swung out

of the window seat, then the other. Adelaide fought to keep her expression screwed into the stern visage of her commanding-officer persona while her heart gamboled about in her chest. Isabella slowly made her way to the center of the room, her wary face infused with a glimmer of interest. Adelaide hid her pleasure by marching a circle around the girl as if inspecting her fitness for battle. When she completed her circle, she clicked her heels and addressed her recruit.

"Stand tall, Private. That's it. Shoulders back. Chin up. Good." Isabella looked like a young rooster learning to crow with her shoulders near her ears and her neck stretched up to the sky, but Adelaide found it charming. Isabella had agreed to join the game.

"This is no duty for the faint of heart," Adelaide cautioned. "Only the bravest soldiers are chosen to serve with me. You must be willing to venture into dark corners and arid flatlands with only a broom rifle and a bucket of soapy ammunition. If you think you can handle this assignment, salute."

Adelaide demonstrated the motion as she said the word, then waited. A second or two ticked by, but Isabella's flat hand eventually crept up to her temple before falling back to her side. Though not the crispest or most confident salute ever executed, it would do.

"Excellent. Now, off to the armory. We need to be outfitted with uniforms and collect our weapons. We can't wade into this battle unprepared. Follow me, Soldier."

Adelaide marched out of the room and started down the two flights of stairs, her ears straining to catch the sound of light footfalls behind her. They raided Mrs. Chalmers's broom closet and armed themselves with tied-kerchief helmets, apron shields, two broom rifles, and two wooden ammunition bins that bore a striking resemblance to ordinary wash buckets. Isabella took charge of the dry rounds, dutifully holding her bucket of clean rags, while Adelaide commandeered a cake of soap and pumped liquid firepower into her bucket from the hand pump by the sink. She had just begun dipping warm water from the stove reservoir into her bucket when Mrs. Chalmers walked in.

"What's going on in here?" she asked in a voice that held more inquisitiveness than accusation.

Isabella shrank back toward the wall as if she'd been caught doing something naughty. Not wanting to retreat after making valuable headway with the girl, Adelaide brazenly pressed forward.

"We are battling to retake the third floor, ma'am. In order to protect Westcott Cottage from falling into enemy hands, we plan to clear out the dust mines and web snares and set up our base camp there. Then we can educate the troops from our position on the front line and fight off any future invasions at the same time."

Mrs. Chalmers eyed Adelaide askance. "If something needs cleaning, miss, I'll see to it. There's no need to put the child to work."

Adelaide finished dipping out the heated water and turned to face the housekeeper, keeping her back to Isabella. "That's a very courageous offer, but this business is too dangerous for civilians." She tipped her head ever so slightly in Isabella's direction and mouthed the words *play along*. "It'd be safer to leave this job to us military types. Isn't that right, Private Izzy?"

Isabella stepped out of the shadows and signaled her agreement with a salute. It was even a tad snappier than her last attempt. A little thrill ran through Adelaide. They were making progress.

"Well . . ." The housekeeper's gaze softened as she looked at Isabella. "If you're going off to war, the least I can do is pack you some provisions."

In a blink, she halved a pair of biscuits, slathered peach jam on them, folded them back together, and wrapped them in a linen napkin. She laid the bundle in Isabella's bucket and pulled an oatmeal cookie from a jar sitting atop the jelly cupboard. Mrs. Chalmers placed the treat in Isabella's hand.

"To keep your strength up, young soldier. We're all depending on you."

The girl nodded and began to salute but stopped when she realized her hand was full of cookie. Then, toting her bucket of munitions, she fell in line behind Adelaide, who slung two brooms over her shoulder and gathered up her sloshing pail before leading the short procession to the battleground.

Afternoon faded into evening as Gideon rode into the yard, tired, hungry, and anxious to check on his girl. The whole time he'd been stringing wire and helping Juan herd the stragglers up in the north pasture, he'd worried that leaving her alone with the new governess had been a mistake. He didn't doubt Miss Proctor's ability, but after the frightening episode in the kitchen, Bella might have needed her papa.

Papa. Just the memory of that word made his pulse jump.

Gideon dismounted and walked his bay to the stable. As he rubbed the gelding down, his concerns melted into anticipation. Would Bella greet him by name tonight? She must have stored away quite a few words during the last four months. He couldn't wait to be swept up in her rush of chatter.

With a newfound lightness to his step, he crossed the yard to the side of the house and cleaned up in the washroom. Delicious smells wafted to him from the kitchen. The savory aroma of Mrs. Garrett's beef stew mingled with the sweetness of what Gideon hoped was an apple pie. His stomach rumbled in response.

Avoiding the temptation of the kitchen, Gideon walked through the door that led directly to the hall. Bella often helped Mrs. Chalmers set the table at suppertime, so he stuck his head into the dining room. He found Mrs. Chalmers exacting her usual meticulous standards on the placement of the china, but tonight she was doing it without his daughter's assistance.

The housekeeper glanced up from her work and favored him with a polite smile. "Good evening, Mr. Westcott. Dinner will be served in twenty minutes."

"Excellent." Gideon stepped into the room. "Do you know where I might find Bella?"

The housekeeper's grin broadened for an instant, but she ducked her head before he could examine it too closely. Instead, she fussed over an already perfectly rectangular napkin.

"I believe she and Miss Proctor are waging war up in the attic, sir. They've been at it most of the afternoon."

Gideon's heart sank. They were at odds? He'd never known Bella to be belligerent, and Miss Proctor didn't strike him as overly combative, either. Yet if Mrs. Chalmers described them as being at war, things must have seriously deteriorated since that morning.

"I see." He tried to hide his concern behind a placid expression, but his efforts didn't matter since his housekeeper refused to look at him. The blasted dinner napkin concerned her more than the state of affairs under his roof. Well, let her amuse herself with lining up cloth corners. He had more important duties to see to—namely, his daughter's welfare.

"If you'll excuse me?"

Without waiting for a response, he stiffened and turned away. He took the stairs two at a time but slowed as he neared the attic. A strange one-sided conversation floated down to him.

"All clear on your side, Private Izzy?"

Two taps sounded in answer.

"Good. Our campaign is almost over. The enemy has been routed, our supplies are organized, and our camp is in order according to military regulations. You've performed admirably, Private. I'm proud to have you in my regiment."

Gideon frowned as he topped the stairs. They were certainly war words, yet not the kind he'd expected. No anger or petulance. No tantrums. It sounded more like collaboration. On silent feet, he approached the gaping door and peered inside. His eyes widened. A newly scrubbed floor shined up at him around the edges of a large tapestry rug he last remembered seeing in the guest room that Miss Proctor occupied. On top of the rug stood a ladies' writing desk, also from Miss Proctor's room, and a child-sized table and chair set from Bella's. Two library tables flanked either side of a large bookcase. One held the globe from his study while the other was bare except for a decorative glass lamp whose twin resided in the parlor. The bookcase boasted a wide assortment of books, but the bottom shelf held pyramids of wooden alphabet blocks, school slates, and Bella's collection of farm animals that could be drawn about the room by a string attached to wheeled platforms.

He didn't know how she'd managed the feat, but Miss Proctor had transformed a neglected storage area into a cozy schoolroom. He stretched his neck to get a better view and spied Bella sitting in a window seat. She held a broomstick at her side, and as he watched, she hoisted it to her shoulder and leaned her head to the side as if sighting down a rifle barrel. She aimed it out the window for a moment, then lowered the pretend weapon and tapped twice on the glass. The all-clear signal. He nearly laughed aloud.

"I think we're done here, Private." Miss Proctor came into view, wiping her hands on her apron. She ran her sleeve across her forehead, obviously weary from her afternoon's work. Strands of chestnut hair hung around her face where the kerchief had failed to contain them, and delightful smudges of dirt painted her cheeks. He had the oddest impulse to rub them away for her.

"Let's head down to din— Aaaaah! Izzy! One of the prisoners is escaping. Come quick!"

Miss Proctor danced around on her tiptoes and pointed to the floor. Bella bounded out of the window seat like a seasoned warrior, swinging her weapon around in a single motion to position the straw end in front of her. She pounded the floor beside the governess but must have missed, for she swung again and again, moving across the room in a random zigzag pattern. Gideon caught sight of the frenzied prisoner as he tried to dodge another bullet. The poor spider didn't stand a chance against his Bella.

Miss Proctor took up her own broom but stood back to let Bella have her chance at glory. And glory came. After chasing the eight-legged creature to a spot along the near wall, Bella whacked the floor with three successive and apparently deadly strikes. She lifted her broom in victory and jumped up and down. Miss Proctor squealed in glee and rushed to her side.

"You did it, Izzy!"

As the girls celebrated, Gideon moved toward them, drawn to their joy. The sound of Bella's laughter filled his ears like an angel's song of good tidings. He was so mesmerized by it, he failed to see the blow coming until pain crashed into his jaw.

Chapter 9

"Hoorah!"

Adelaide thrust her weapon firmly into the air in celebration of Isabella's triumph. Only she hit more than air. Vibrations from the collision skittered down the broom handle and into her arm. A muffled masculine groan tolled like a death knell in her ears. She squeezed her eyes shut, not wanting to face what she'd done. But there was no escape. Her stomach sick with dread, she turned.

Gideon stood at her side, slightly hunched as he cradled his jaw in his hand. He worked the injured bone back and forth, as if assuring himself that it wasn't broken. When he glanced over at her, she cringed, expecting to be flayed by an angry glare, but his chocolate-brown eyes twinkled with humor.

"One of these days, I'm going to learn not to sneak up on you."

The fiasco in the barn flashed through her mind. Yesterday she'd showered him with oats and today she'd pummeled him with a broom. At this rate, he'd be dead by the end of the week.

"Mr. Westcott, I'm so sorry. I had no idea you were there."

Adelaide dropped the broom as if distancing herself from the weapon could remove some of her guilt.

He wiggled his jaw one final time and then lowered his hand. "I don't think you did any permanent damage." The red welt rising on the left side of his face looked ready to argue.

"Besides," Gideon said, "we can't let an accident spoil the celebration. I haven't had the chance to congratulate my brave little soldier yet." He peered around Adelaide. "Come here, Bella."

The giggles had subsided, but a residual smile lingered on her face. She trotted over to him, and he scooped her into his arms. "I'm impressed with all the work you two did up here. It looks like you had some fun, as well."

Isabella nodded with enthusiasm.

"What was your favorite part?"

The girl answered by putting her hands together and wiggling her fingers. Then she placed one fist on top of the other as if holding a broom handle and made quick forward thrusts.

Adelaide watched Gideon closely during the silent explanation. Impressively, his smile never faltered, but the glimmer in his eyes dimmed. As disappointed as she had been this afternoon over Isabella's lack of speech, his regret must have been ten times stronger.

"So you liked smashing enemy spiders, did you?"

Isabella nodded, but added nothing further. Gideon also seemed at a loss for words. Adelaide waded into the fray, hoping to alleviate the awkwardness of the faltering conversation.

"Tell your father how many spiders you killed."

Isabella preened and held up seven fingers.

"Seven? My little Bella? I can't believe it."

The girl raised her chin and pointed to her chest, verifying the claim.

"I dubbed her Spider Slayer." Adelaide grinned up at her charge but found her gaze wandering to her employer, as well. His eyes met hers, and for a moment she forgot what they'd been discussing.

Gideon cleared his throat and turned his attention back to his daughter, bouncing her in his arms once more before setting her down. "Well, Miss Slayer, dinner is about ready, so why don't you wash up and see if Mrs. Chalmers needs any help."

Isabella gave a final salute and disappeared down the stairs.

"I should follow those orders, as well," Adelaide said, overly conscious of her grimy apron and the perspiration that glued her dress to her back. She moved toward the door, but Gideon's voice stopped her.

"I'd like to speak with you for a moment, Miss Proctor. If you don't mind."

"Certainly, sir." Adelaide tucked a wayward strand of hair behind her ear, refraining from scratching the itchy spot under her kerchief. She wished she looked more presentable for this interview. No fair maiden wanted to converse privately with a handsome prince while resembling a bedraggled scullery maid. Then again, no fair maiden would slam a broomstick into her prince's jaw, either. She stifled a sigh and tried not to stare at the bruise forming on his cheek. After that mishap, she guessed her appearance was the least of her worries.

She waited for him to speak his mind, but all he did was stare at his shoes and shift his weight from one leg to the other. A slight frown disrupted the charm that usually flowed from him, tarnishing his storybook-hero shine a bit. Yet instead of being disappointed by the loss, Adelaide felt compelled to peek beneath his veneer to find the real man behind the winsome manners. She stepped closer and angled her head to peer into his face. He opened his mouth as if to say something, but when their eyes met, he froze.

In that instant she saw his vulnerability, his doubt, his determination. Then, with a blink of his lashes, it disappeared. His smile returned in all its devastating glory. His dimples winked at her and almost succeeded in their distraction attempt. As always, her stomach fluttered under their influence, but for the first time she found herself wondering how often Gideon used them to shield his true feelings.

"You have accomplished quite a feat this afternoon, Miss Proctor." His light comment seemed at odds with his initial reluctance.

Adelaide considered him a moment longer, then decided to set her investigation aside for the time being. "Thank you, sir. I hope you don't mind my borrowing a few household furnishings to set up the classroom."

"Not at all. I'm glad you found what you needed."

He turned to examine the area again, his smile firmly in place, but Adelaide wasn't fooled. Unasked questions hung heavily in the air around him.

"Isabella hasn't spoken since she awakened."

Gideon pivoted to face her, his dimples gone and his gaze filled with gratitude along with a hunger for more information. Adelaide's heart stirred in response.

"I prompted her repeatedly, but she acted as if the events of this morning never happened. Maybe it's best that she not remember . . . at least for now." Adelaide laid her hand on his arm for a brief second, then pulled back. "I'm sorry, Mr. Westcott."

"I had hoped . . ." He shook his head. "It doesn't matter. It will come in God's time. I should not be so greedy."

She quirked a brow. "Greedy?"

The dimples returned, accompanied by a genuine sparkle in his eyes. "I have no reason to lament Bella's small reverse step when you helped her leap forward in such dramatic fashion today."

"I only reminded her how to pretend. I don't think—"

"Miss Proctor."

The rest of her words dissolved in her mouth.

"You accomplished a feat in a single afternoon that I have been attempting for months." Gideon paused, and Adelaide nearly melted from the warmth in his eyes. "Bella laughed."

The following morning, just after dawn, Gideon crept out of the house and down to the stable to saddle his horse. He still preferred the lightweight English saddle he was raised on for pleasure rides even though he had adopted the Western saddle for ranch work. The bulky thing was unwieldy, but he couldn't dispute its practicality.

Like most aspects of his life since coming to this country, he had learned to blend tradition with utility. That blend was reflected in his stables, as well. He kept a Thoroughbred or two for prestige and the occasional country race, but his mount of choice for the range was Solomon. The bay gelding was surefooted in the rough terrain and as wise as his namesake, although there was something humorously ironic about a gelding being named after a man with seven hundred wives. But the horse's intelligence couldn't be denied. Solomon's instincts had spared Gideon trouble on more than one occasion when predators or foul weather had caught him unaware. At times, he would even swear the horse could sniff out sheep that had gone missing from the flock.

Gideon finished buckling the girth and swung up into the saddle. He patted the horse's neck with a firm hand and bent forward to place his mouth close to the animal's ear.

"Ready to run, boy?"

Solomon answered by dancing around in a circle. Gideon grinned in anticipation and tightened his grip on the reins. He touched his heels to the bay's flanks and Solomon lunged forward. Moving as one, man and horse raced toward the river.

Fading pink clouds stretched across the sky as Gideon galloped over rolling grassland, skirting the shadows cast by occasional oak trees. Cool wind rushed past his face, invigorating him and raising his spirits. It had been too long since he'd last taken the time to privately commune with the Lord. His habit of reading Scripture daily during those long months on the trail had slipped into disuse as he'd busied himself with setting up a new household. However, when Miss Proctor noted the old Bible in his study yesterday, it had awakened a thirst in him to reestablish the pattern.

Gideon reined Solomon in as he neared the top of the knoll that overlooked the San Saba River. He loved this spot. The water streamed by at a gentle pace, pecan trees lined the bank, and across the river his land extended for miles in waves of beauty that only an owner full of dreams for the future could appreciate.

A flash of pale yellow off to his right dragged his attention away from the vista before him to a woman's skirt quivering on the breeze. He turned. Now, there was a beauty any man could appreciate. Delicate features, thick chestnut hair, and eyes that reminded him of the river on a spring day, blue-green with a sun-kissed sparkle.

What am I thinking? He spun away from her and focused in the opposite direction. The woman was his daughter's governess, not some society miss ripe for a flirtation.

Gideon stood up a bit in the stirrups, stretching his legs and considering his options. Should he leave? He stole a glance back toward the river. Miss Proctor sat a few feet away, propped against the trunk of a pecan tree with her legs drawn up to her chest. A book lay balanced precariously atop her knees while she gazed into the distance. She didn't seem to have noticed him. He might still escape without detection. Yet if she noticed him as he was riding away, he'd look like a tactless boor.

And a gentleman never acted the part of a boor. No matter how tempted.

Blowing out a resigned breath, Gideon dismounted and left Solomon to graze. "Good morning, Miss Proctor."

She swiveled toward him, the book on her knees tumbling into the folds of her skirt

He favored her with one of the famous Westcott smiles. "I hadn't expected to encounter you out here this morning."

"Mr. Westcott!" Her eyes widened, as if she'd been caught nabbing the silver. "Mrs. Garrett said she would see to Isabella's breakfast if she awakened before I returned, but if you'd prefer I be there, I'll certainly . . ." Her sentence faded away as she grabbed her book and began to push to her feet.

"Don't get up, Miss Proctor." He waved her back down. "I won't begrudge you your bit of morning freedom. Not when I was seeking some of the same."

She complied, although uncertainty lingered in her expression. After resettling herself on the grass and tucking her legs around beside her, she tipped her chin up to him. A tentative smile graced her lips. "You're welcome to share my tree, if you like. The view is splendid, and I promise not to make a nuisance of myself."

"Why, thank you, ma'am," he drawled in his best imitation of Texas twang. "Don't mind if I do."

Her gentle laughter put him at ease as she slid over to make room for him. He sat with one leg bent upon the ground while the other tented up to give his arm a place to rest. A touch of pink colored her cheeks when he smiled at her, but she dutifully resumed her reading, reminding him of why he had come out here in the first place.

Reaching into his coat, he drew out his pocket Bible. He thumbed through the pages for several minutes but had a devil of a time concentrating on anything. He lowered his head to block the sight of yellow fabric and managed to read a handful of verses from a passage in Isaiah. Then a puff of breeze wafted something his way—a clean, sunshiny, and very feminine scent. He drew it in for a moment, enjoying the pleasant fragrance until he realized he couldn't recall a single word he'd just read.

Readjusting his position, he turned his back slightly to her and bent over his Bible once again. Then he noticed her breathing, the brush of fabric as she moved, the soft crackle of the page as she flipped it.

Botheration! Gideon pushed to his feet, scrunching twigs and pebbles noisily beneath his boots. Miss Proctor started.

"Forgive me." Gideon took a couple of steps toward the river. "I'm having trouble concentrating."

"That's all right," she said from behind him. "I'm sure you have a lot on your mind."

He latched on to the excuse. "You're right. I do. Shearing is around the corner and we have to get everything in readiness before the crew arrives. Bella's situation is never far from my mind. And if that weren't enough to worry about, I've got a fence cutter on the prowl."

A rustle of skirts or grass or both teased him as Miss Proctor stirred, but Gideon kept his gaze forward.

"Do you know who the culprit was?"

"No. Probably some unprincipled cowhand trying to make a point about free range."

"Unprincipled cowhand?" Something in her voice changed. It tightened.

Gideon turned and found her advancing on him.

"I'm sorry that someone cut your fence, Mr. Westcott, but there's no need for you to jump to unsavory conclusions. It could have been anyone. A drifter. A boy bent on mischief. A hungry thief in the mood for mutton. No cattleman of my acquaintance would ever cut another man's fence or behave in any other *unprincipled* manner."

"And are you acquainted with many cattlemen, Miss Proctor?" Gideon asked with no small dose of sarcasm. For once he felt no compulsion to diffuse the rising conflict with an artful dodge or a bit of flattering repartee. The woman had been making him itch since the moment he caught sight of her blasted yellow skirt flapping in the breeze, and he was ready to scratch.

She slapped her hands on her hips. "As a matter of fact, I am. My father was a cattle rancher for twenty-three years, and you'd be hard-pressed to find a man of greater integrity. And the men who worked for him shared his values."

"I'm sure your father was above reproach, but not all cowhands share his scruples. Even in England, we heard tales of the range wars that have afflicted your country in the last decade."

"And most of those were due to migratory sheep ranchers letting their flocks graze on land that belonged to cattlemen." Miss Proctor thrust out her jaw, her loyalty unwavering.

"You're forgetting the instances of cowboys driving their cattle to market across pastureland that belonged to sheepmen. Devouring grass, draining water holes, trampling earth."

"So there was guilt on both sides. That doesn't mean you can automatically accuse cattlemen for your fence-cutting problems without proof."

Gideon closed what little gap remained between them and glared down at her. She made no move to back down, just tipped her head farther back to hold his stare.

"You know," he said, "it's not too late to bring Miss Oliver back. I'm sure she'd make a much more biddable governess."

The instant the words left his tongue, he tasted regret. The stricken look on Miss Proctor's face only twisted the guilt knife deeper into his chest.

He immediately stepped back and held out a conciliatory hand. "I didn't mean that—"

"No, no. You're absolutely right." She wagged her head vigorously as she backed away from him, her gaze dropping to the grass. "I overstepped my bounds and spoke without thinking. I have a tendency to do that, I'm afraid. It was disrespectful and presumptuous of me, and I can only beg your forgiveness." She hesitated, as if searching for the strength to face him. Finally, she dragged her chin up. Tears had pooled in her eyes.

If Gideon were the type of horseman to carry a whip, he would have turned it on himself in that moment.

"I'm the one who should be begging forgiveness, not you." He wanted to eliminate the distance between them, but he held back. "I never should have made such a threat. It was hurtful, not to mention completely idle. After what you achieved with Bella yesterday, I wouldn't let you leave, even if you wanted to."

Miss Proctor blinked. That was all. She didn't say a word.

Gideon grabbed the hair at the nape of his neck and tightened his fist until it hurt. Then with a sigh, he let go. His hand slapped against the side of his leg.

"You were right about the fence cutting. I don't know for sure who did it or why. I'm surrounded by cattle ranchers, so I made an assumption. Whether or not the assumption is true doesn't really matter at this point." He looked up at the sky. "I lost eleven sheep. A handful of ewes fell into an arroyo. Some even trampled their own lambs in the panic. That's probably why I was so cross."

Gideon bit down on his tongue for a moment, then turned back to Miss Proctor. "When you defended the cattlemen, I felt as if you were siding against me, justifying the actions of the man who cut my fence and scattered my animals."

"That's horrible. I would never defend such actions. I—"

Gideon held up his hand. "Of course you wouldn't. Now . . ." A small cluster of white fleabane near Miss Proctor's boot drew his attention. He grinned and bent to pluck the tiny daisy-like flowers. Making a deep bow, he held the miniature bouquet out to her. "Will you accept my apology, dear lady, and erase this entire conversation from your memory?"

To his great relief, she returned his smile and even dipped into a curtsy as she accepted the flowers. "Thank you, kind sir. All is forgiven."

Her eyes no longer glimmered with tears but with playfulness. Gideon found it difficult to look away. A horse nickered off to his right, breaking the spell. A small black mare was nuzzling up to Solomon.

"That's my cue," Miss Proctor said as she tucked his flowers into a buttonhole below her collar. "Sheba always lets me know when it's time to get back to work."

"Sheba?" Gideon couldn't keep the laughter out of his voice.

"Are you mocking my horse?" Miss Proctor crossed her arms and scowled at him in a teasing fashion. "I'll have you know she was sired from some of the finest stock in Texas. My daddy named her himself before giving her to me for my sixteenth birthday."

"It's a fine name," Gideon appeased. "In fact, I couldn't think of a finer name for your horse, seeing as how my gelding's named Solomon."

Her mouth fell open. Then all at once, laughter spilled forth. The bell-like sound washed over him in delightful waves.

"Well, I'm sure with a name like that your steed must be smart, but can he run?"

Before he could defend Solomon's honor, Miss Proctor dashed off and bounded onto the back of her mare with astounding agility. He admired her form for a moment before realizing he was being left in her dust. The fire of competition sparked, and he leapt into his own saddle and raced after her.

Solomon's hooves pounded into the ground, gradually eating up the distance separating him from the mare. Blood pumping through his veins, Gideon thrilled to the chase, not caring to examine why pursuing this woman felt so right.

Chapter 10

Over the next two weeks, Gideon busied himself with preparations for the shearing. He made a point to return to the house for mid-day meals in order to spend time with Bella, as well as to continue mending fences with Miss Proctor. Thankfully, the governess was not one to hold a grudge. In fact, her sunny disposition and lively conversation at meals never failed to energize him after hours of herding sheep and repairing holding pens and chutes. There had even been a couple of nights where he'd climbed the stairs to Bella's room to kiss her good-night when he'd caught the end of one of Miss Proctor's Bible stories.

She had a way of telling the old familiar tales with such enthu-siasm and drama that from his vantage point just outside the room, Gideon found himself as delighted as his daughter. Not only did Miss Proctor give each character a distinct voice, but she acted out the roles, as well.

One evening, she had stood on a stool as the towering Goliath and flopped across Bella's bed, bouncing the mattress in her death scene as the giant fell to the ground in defeat. Bella had giggled and clapped while Miss Proctor smoothed out the mussed covers.

"Why you smile, patrón?" Miguel plodded into the shed, a grim look on his face. Gideon stopped the downward motion of his hammer to give his vaquero his full attention.

"What do you mean, Miguel?"

"The crew is ten days late, no? The sheep, they grow restless, and the men are on edge."

"Including you, it would seem." Gideon turned back to his task and pounded the half-driven nail into the shearing platform with a quick swing of his forearm.

"Sí." Miguel let out a hearty sigh.

"Patience, my friend. Ramirez wired that the river was swollen at Eagle Ford. We knew they would be delayed."

"Sí, patrón, but that was a week past. They should be here by now."

Gideon sympathized with his foreman's frustration. They'd been ready for days. The holding pens had been built and the dipping trough had been set up, and he must have gone over this platform a hundred times, repairing any board that didn't lay perfectly flush. The truth was, if Bella and Miss Proctor hadn't been around to distract him, he probably would have been even more irritated than Miguel. Already the first week of June, and he had yet to send his wool clip to market. Not the most sterling of starts for his ranch.

Setting aside his hammer, Gideon strode over to Miguel and clasped his shoulder. "You know how bad the roads get after a rain. If they encountered wet weather, the crew would be hard-pressed to get their wagons through the mud. We must wait."

Miguel nodded his assent, but before he could comment further, a shout rang out across the yard. Excited voices called to each other in rapid Spanish that Gideon had trouble deciphering. Miguel's head shot up, though, and a hopeful smile stretched across his face.

"Riders come, patrón! They say there is enough dust for two, maybe three, wagons." He waggled his eyebrows. "Enough for a shearing crew, eh?"

" 'The Lord is good unto them that wait for him,' " Gideon quoted, unable to quell the grin that demanded release.

Miguel clapped his hands together and gave a little jig-like hop before rushing out of the shed to join Juan and the other pastores. Gideon chuckled at the man's antics before leaving the shed at a more sedate pace. Turning toward the house, he left the herders to celebrate in the yard while he warned his household staff of the imminent invasion.

He entered through the kitchen and found Mrs. Garrett shaping bread dough into balls for the evening's dinner rolls. She glanced up as he pulled the door closed.

"Mr. Westcott. You're a mite early for supper."

Gideon winked at his cook. "Want to know a secret? All the setting up I've been doing for the shearing is just a ruse. My true reason for lingering about the house is to snitch treats from your cupboards when you're not looking." He grinned and strode past her to the crockery jar that held the cookies. He removed the lid with one hand and delved inside with the other. Drawing one out, he popped the entire thing into his mouth.

"Ack! Get out of my cookies, you oversized pup, or I'll have your head." She threw a wad of dough at him.

Ducking his head, he plucked the ball out of the air. "Now, now, Mrs. Garrett, no petty theft is worth ruining a fine yeast roll." He set the dough ball on her tray and wiped the stickiness from his hands with a towel. "I was looking for Chalmers. I need to inform him that the shearing crew has arrived."

"He and the missus is polishing the silver in the dining room."

"Thank you, Mrs. Garrett. And thank you for the cookie, as well."

"Bah." She shooed him out, but not before he caught the hint of a smile twitching at the corner of her mouth.

He entered the dining room and discussed the shearers' arrival with his butler, but when their business was concluded, he found himself loath to leave the house. He told himself he simply wanted to see his daughter, but he couldn't deny a hidden longing to encounter Miss Proctor, as well.

"Is Bella in the schoolroom?" Gideon forced a heavy dose of nonchalance into his voice. "I thought to check in on her before I headed out to greet the crew."

Mrs. Chalmers shook her head. "No. I believe she's still napping. The child didn't sleep well last night, and Miss Proctor thought the rest would do her good."

Bella was occasionally troubled by nightmares, so this news didn't surprise him. He wished he'd been told of it, though. A father should know such things.

"Is Miss Proctor with her?" If not, perhaps now would be a good time to discuss the matter.

"I believe she took a book out to the porch, sir," Chalmers replied.

Gideon nodded and headed for the front of the house. When he opened the door, however, all thoughts of the impending discussion left his mind. Miss Proctor was sitting not on the wicker chair that backed up against the wall, but on the railing, where sunbeams kissed her cheeks and the afternoon breeze tugged wisps from the hair loosely tied at her neck. One silky strand blew across her face and clung to the fullness of her lower lip. Absently, she raised her hand to brush it away, her eyes never leaving the book she held.

Footsteps sounded from the far side of the wraparound porch, startling him back to his senses.

"You better head inside, missy. The shearing crew's here." Gideon recognized Mrs. Garrett's voice, but the woman retreated without ever rounding the corner.

"All right." Miss Proctor answered distractedly, her gaze focused on her book as she flipped a page. She did slide down from the railing, though, and Gideon tried not to notice the flash of trim ankle exposed by the movement.

Instead of moving toward him, as he expected, she stepped in the direction from which the cook's voice had come. She staggered slightly, her gait uneven as her attention remained fixed on the book.

Gideon smiled. The little damsel was so lost in her story, she might require a guide to lead her back out.

She teetered to the right, precariously close to the stairs that led down to the yard. Gideon's smile faded.

Another step. She wobbled but continued on, unconcerned. Which only concerned Gideon more. He moved across the porch, opening his mouth to call out a warning. But before he could form the words, she stepped again and lost her balance as her right foot hit nothing but air.

He lunged forward and wrapped an arm about her waist, tugging her back against his chest. "Whoa, there."

Miss Proctor gasped and pulled away from him, craning her neck to discover his identity. "M-Mr. Westcott. Sir."

Crimson stained her cheeks. Gideon released her, surprised at the reluctance that surged inside him as he did so. "You nearly took a tumble. Are you all right?"

"Yes. I'm fine." She glanced at the stairs and then at the book dangling from her hand. "I guess I should pay more attention to where I'm going. I'll . . . um . . . just go check on Isabella."

She dashed past him and disappeared into the house. Gideon rubbed the spot on his chest where her head had briefly rested and watched her go.

Adelaide awoke at dawn the following morning, but instead of donning her riding habit as had become her custom, she pulled her oldest gown over her head. The lemon gingham, once her favorite, had fallen out of favor with her. It was still serviceable enough, but her fondness for the garment had plummeted since wearing it on that horrible night in Fort Worth when she'd discovered Henry was married. Now, whenever her gaze rested on it in the wardrobe, bad memories stirred. It was as if she were looking at an old friend who had betrayed her. Yet today it would be welcome. She had never attended a shearing before, but she had no doubt it would be a day full of dirt, sweat, and greasy fleeces—a fitting penance for the unfaithful scrap of cloth.

She quickly arranged her hair into a simple knot and tugged on a sunbonnet, leaving the strings to drape over her shoulders. On quiet feet, she padded down the hall to Isabella's room and eased the door open.

"Time to wake up, my sleeping beauty."

A small hand poked out from under the lacy coverlet as Isabella rolled onto her back. She rubbed the sleep out of her eyes and forced her lids open, blinking several times. Adelaide slid into the room and sat on the edge of the bed, accidentally squashing the girl's foot. The child's face puckered into a pout. Murmuring an apology, Adelaide scooted down.

"It's shearing day, Izzy."

Isabella sat up, her eyes suddenly focused. The pout disappeared.

"Today we will both be students."

Adelaide had decided to forgo their regular lessons for a few days in favor of some experiential education. If Isabella was going to be a sheepman's daughter, she needed to understand her father's trade. And if Adelaide was going to teach her, she needed to gain some firsthand knowledge herself. She could think of no better way to accomplish those goals than to observe and possibly participate in the sheep shearing.

After helping Isabella dress, Adelaide slipped into the kitchen and snitched a few biscuits and several slices of bacon. She fashioned her pilfered goods into sandwiches, secreted them in a linen napkin, and stole away to meet her accomplice on the front porch. Isabella had already climbed into one of the white wicker chairs that adorned the veranda, so Adelaide settled into a matching seat and handed her charge a biscuit. She cast a glance at the stairs, memories flashing through her of a knightly rescue—a strong arm around her waist, a muscular chest sheltering her from harm. But now was not the time for silly romantic fantasies. Mr. Westcott had kept her from falling. That was all. *I'd be a fool to read anything more into his actions.*

As she and Isabella nibbled their breakfast, the sun cleared the horizon and brightened the sky enough to reveal all the changes that had come over the ranch since the previous evening.

Thousands of sheep had been moved from the pasture into two large corrals. The flocks hadn't seemed so big when they were spread out over the hillside, but now that all the animals were crammed together into a confining space, they appeared too numerous to count. Adelaide couldn't tell which head belonged to which body or even where one woolly back stopped and another started. An occasional bell clanged as one of the lead sheep adjusted positions, but the overall melody was a plaintive ballad of bleating that almost made Adelaide feel sorry for the silly creatures. She had to remind herself they were only losing their coats, not their lives.

After dusting the biscuit crumbs from her lap, Adelaide stood and held her hand out to Isabella.

"Ready?"

The little girl shoved the last bite into her mouth and nodded, her cheeks bulging. She squirmed out of her chair and grasped Adelaide's hand. Together, they stepped off the porch and ambled toward the corrals. A thrill of anticipation bubbled up in Adelaide, tempting her to dash about so that she could see everything at once. But she swallowed the urge and kept a modest pace. She couldn't very well teach Isabella decorum and propriety if she failed to enact those virtues herself. Sometimes it was just no fun being an adult.

As they neared the edge of the first corral, Adelaide noticed a smaller pen extending toward the shearing shed. One of Gideon's men stood at the inner gate separating the sheep in the small holding area from the masses in the main corral. Thinking to ask him what his duties were, she led Isabella around the perimeter of the fence toward the pen. Before she could call out to him, however, a small dark-skinned man she didn't recognize strode up to the pen and hopped over the fence.

Intent on his work, he gave no indication that he was aware of her presence. He simply inspected the wool of several ewes and made his selection. Grabbing one unsuspecting female by a single hind leg, he dragged her toward the edge of the pen. The poor old gal bleated in protest and hopped backward in an attempt to keep up. The shearer turned a deaf ear to her complaints, however, and forced her to endure the indignity of a graceless exit before her watching peers. After he maneuvered her through the gate, he disappeared with her into the shed.

Adelaide suppressed a shudder. She knew the animal was not being carried away to a calamitous fate, but somehow the scene made her uneasy anyway. Hoping she would feel better once she witnessed what actually went on inside the shed, she led Isabella toward the busy building.

Over a dozen men were bustling around in the shed, most of them strangers to her. Wariness tinged her curiosity, and her footsteps slowed. Isabella grabbed hold of Adelaide's skirt but gamely leaned forward to observe the goings-on. The scene before her resembled a bawdy tavern more than a workshop. Perhaps it had been a mistake to bring a young girl out here. The men laughed and bantered with one another, trading insults that she understood more by their facial expressions than by her rudimentary grasp of their language. Some of the more colorful words she managed to make out over the incessant clicking of the shears brought heat to her face and left her grateful for Isabella's ignorance.

The girl tugged on her dress, and Adelaide looked down, afraid of what she might see in her charge's eyes. However, a glittering smile engulfed Isabella's face as she pointed toward the opposite side of the platform. Adelaide followed her gaze.

Gideon stood talking to one of the shearers, the leader of the crew by the looks of him. Relief poured through her. With Gideon in the building, she need not worry about the men.

Taking Isabella by the hand, she skirted the edge of the platform. The boisterous conversation waned, and Adelaide felt uncomfortably conspicuous. She lifted her head and smiled politely at the men on the platform. Most nodded their heads in a mannerly fashion before returning to their work, but one fellow on the end held her gaze and smiled back in a way that caused her to discreetly check her bodice to make sure her buttons were done up.

Gideon caught sight of them and rushed forward. "Miss Proctor. What are you doing here?"

She couldn't decide if there was censure in his voice or not. Perhaps it was just her own regret echoing in her ears. Regardless, the smile he turned on his daughter was genuine. He lifted Isabella into his arms and ushered both females to the far side of the building while she explained.

"Since neither Isabella nor I have experienced a shearing before, I thought this a good opportunity to expand our education on the matter. I hope our presence isn't too disruptive."

Gideon's brow wrinkled a bit. "Well, the two of you probably shouldn't linger overlong in the shed, but I don't think it would hurt anything for you to watch for a while."

"Thank you, Mr. Westcott." Adelaide easily agreed with his assessment. She was accustomed to being around working men, having grown up the only female on her father's ranch, but the atmosphere in this room full of strangers was different. She didn't have the security of her father's protection. Here she was just an employee. And while certain that Gideon would not allow any harm to befall her in his presence, she worried about what could happen if he wasn't around. Borrowing trouble never accomplished anything more than giving her a headache, though, so Adelaide pushed her anxiety aside and resumed her role of educator.

"Would you explain the process to us?"

Pride glowed in Gideon's eyes. "Certainly."

Adelaide could still feel the stare of the impertinent shearer on her. She turned her back to the platform and stepped closer to Gideon. His familiar accent soothed her as she listened, and soon her quest for knowledge obliterated all other thoughts from her mind.

"The shearers work on the platform in order to keep the fleeces as clean as possible," he was saying.

Adelaide wrinkled her nose as she looked at the sheep that had just been brought in from the pen. The man she had seen outside knelt with a knee on his ewe's hindquarters and held her head up with one hand as he worked the shears with the other. She had always thought of sheep as white, fluffy creatures, but after being on the range for months at a time, they more closely resembled dark gray storm clouds than the cheerful white ones dotting the sky on a sunny summer day.

"Why does cleanliness matter when they are so greasy and dirty already?"

Gideon winked at her. "It's not the top we care about but the underside."

He pointed to the second man on the line. A mass of snowy fibers hung down from his sheep like an elegant coat the lady was allowing him to remove.

"When he's finished, he'll fold the fleece white side out and hand it off to the *lanero*, the boy whose job it is to carry the fleeces to the bag." Gideon tipped his head away from the platform, and Adelaide twisted her neck to look behind her. She expected to see a pile of bags the size of large flour sacks, but the giant tube that hung suspended from a tall wooden frame several feet away dwarfed every man in the room.

"My word . . ." Adelaide moved closer, angling her chin up as she went. "Izzy, look at this. You'd have to stand on your papa's shoulders to reach the top." She placed her back against the canvas to measure herself against it, but something poked her. She squealed and hurried back to Gideon's side.

He chuckled.

Feeling foolish, she glanced back at the bag. It stood perfectly still. Then all at once it undulated and a sharp angle protruded.

"Mr. Westcott! I think an animal has somehow fallen into your wool sack."

Laughter rang throughout the shed, and Adelaide realized she had spoken much too loudly.

"No, Miss Proctor." Gideon shook his head, his lips twitching. "That's the packer. It's his responsibility to tramp down the fleeces so that each bag holds the maximum amount of wool."

"There's a man in there?"

"Yes." His eyes danced with mirth.

She strove to cover her embarrassment by babbling on. "It must get dreadfully hot in there by the end of the day."

Gideon just grinned.

"*Tecolero!*"

One of the shearers shouted out the word, causing Adelaide's heart to jump. A young boy rushed to the platform with a can containing a black tarlike substance and began to carefully daub it on each little cut on the now scrawny, naked sheep. Her father used to do the same for their horses and cattle when they acquired open wounds from barbed wire or other sharp objects.

"That's to keep out the blowflies, right?"

Gideon nodded. "It is, indeed. We don't want any worms causing trouble later for our little ladies."

Isabella shivered and made a face. She wiggled her forefinger in the air and curled her lip in disgust.

"I agree." Adelaide screwed her features into a similar expression. "I don't like worms, either. Let's get rid of this one, too, shall we?" She grabbed hold of Isabella's finger and pretended to pull it off. She threw the imaginary appendage to the floor and ground it into the earth with her boot. Isabella giggled, and Gideon gave Adelaide one of those smiles that sent tingles through her.

The boy finished with the tar, and pushed the ewe through a chute that Adelaide assumed led to another corral. The man she had seen talking to Gideon when she first came in approached the platform and handed the shearer a small metal disc.

"What is that he's giving him?" she asked.

"It's like currency," Gideon explained. "Every fleece shorn earns a disc that can be traded in for cash when the job is done. They make about five cents a fleece, so the men work as fast as possible. Most of the top men can shear about a hundred sheep a day."

"Impressive."

As if he thought she had cued him, the rude shearer on the end stood up, drawing Adelaide's unwilling attention. He waved the medicine boy over and jangled the discs in his trouser pocket, gazing at Adelaide all the while. She tried to ignore him, but he pulled out a red bandanna to wipe his forehead, and the bright color danced in her line of vision, taunting her. Then, without a scrap of modesty, he cooled himself further by stripping out of his loose cotton shirt. A small gasp escaped her, and Gideon immediately stepped between them to shield her from the sight.

"Let me show you the branding station," Gideon said, his voice tight with disapproval. She didn't dare look up, but she hoped her employer was glaring the miscreant into submission.

Chapter 11

The warmth of Gideon's hand pressing into the small of her back eased some of Adelaide's tension as he escorted her out of the shed and into the sunshine. Taking a deep breath, she gathered her wits while Gideon set Isabella on her feet and led her a short distance away to where Miguel and another herder waited for the next sheep to amble down the chute. Gideon called for her to follow, but the branding iron in the foreman's hand made her reluctant.

She had never cared for branding. It seemed cruel to burn an animal just to prove a person's ownership. Bad enough for a tough-hided steer, but a delicate ewe without even her wool for protection? Adelaide wasn't sure she could stomach such an act.

A sheep came through the chute just then, looking somewhat traumatized from her recent ordeal. Her hooves thudded into the ground sporadically as her uneven, hopping gait led her toward her next travail. Her dull-witted, teary eyes seemed to plead for help as she tripped past Adelaide. Unable to offer rescue, Adelaide watched helplessly as the herder deftly caught the ewe at the end of the chute and held her still while Miguel pressed the red iron to her flesh.

Adelaide squeezed her eyes shut, waiting for the scream of pain and the smell of singed skin, but neither came. When she found the courage to peek, she found Miguel dipping the iron into a bucket at his feet while Gideon held the sheep's head so Isabella could run her fingers over the shorn wool. That's when Adelaide finally noticed the lack of a fire. No hot coals to heat the iron. Curious, she sidled up to Miguel and peered into the bucket.

"Paint."

"Sí, señorita. We use a red circle W." Miguel lifted up the iron for her to inspect. Red paint dripped off the brand.

Consoled by the gentler process, Adelaide's interest burgeoned. "Won't it be hard to see once the wool grows out?"

"Sometimes it gets obscured," Gideon confirmed from where he knelt with his daughter, "but the other ranchers in the area use blue or green for their flocks, so even if you can't see the W, you can tell it's one of ours by the color."

Another ewe headed down the chute, sparking an impulse.

"May I try?" Adelaide asked.

Miguel handed her the iron and helped her press it flat against the animal's hip. In an instant, Isabella was at her side demanding a turn, as well. By the time the next sheep came along, she wielded the heavy iron with two hands, and with Miguel's aid, produced a beautiful, lopsided W that had her beaming with pride.

Adelaide met Gideon's eye after he closed the corral gate behind the last sheep.

"I had hoped we would find a way to help today," she said. "With your permission, Isabella and I would like to stay here a while and assist with the branding."

Isabella ran over to her father and nodded vigorously.

Gideon rubbed his chin for a moment, then shrugged. "You'll have to ask Miguel."

His daughter didn't hesitate. She scurried over to the foreman and pleaded with the biggest, dewiest blue eyes she could muster. Miguel didn't stand a chance.

The vaquero held his hands up in surrender. "Sí, sí. You can help. But you must listen to Miguel, eh?"

The child nodded, and everything was settled. Adelaide and Isabella worked with Miguel most of the day, taking breaks at noon and several times in the afternoon as weariness set in. By supper-time, exhaustion finally demanded they stop. Nevertheless, Miguel's praise sent them to the house with smiles on their faces and satisfaction in their hearts.

Dirty as they were, Adelaide decided it best for them to eat in the kitchen before heading up to bed. Mrs. Chalmers set them each a place and dished up bowls of chicken stew with dumplings. The food was delicious, but Adelaide had trouble summoning the strength to eat it. Isabella fared even worse. After she had dozed off, spoon in hand, for the third time, Adelaide decided getting the child into bed was more pressing than getting her to finish her meal.

"The poor dear is tuckered out," Mrs. Chalmers said from the doorway.

"She worked hard today." Adelaide pushed slowly to her feet, her muscles aching with each movement. "I think I'll take her up to her room."

The housekeeper laid a gentle hand on her shoulder. "You're too tired to carry anything heavier than a candlestick up those stairs. I'll see to her." She pushed forward and gathered Isabella into her arms. The girl's head immediately flopped onto the woman's shoulder.

"I really should be the one to—"

"Pish, posh." Mrs. Chalmers breezed past. "I'll brook no argument, miss. You take care of your own needs tonight."

Adelaide hesitated for only a moment before accepting the offer. "Thank you."

Mrs. Chalmers gave her a brief nod and headed for the staircase.

Wanting to return the kindness in some small way, Adelaide cleared the table and washed the cups and bowls in the tub of lukewarm dishwater sitting on the cabinet by the stove. She dried them and put them away in the hutch. As she closed the glass door on the cupboard, something orange peeked out at her from under the bottom shelf. A carrot. It must have fallen while Mrs. Garrett prepared supper. Adelaide bent to retrieve it and dusted it off on one of the few clean spots she could find on her skirt.

Sheba had been cooped up in the stables all day since they had forgone their usual morning ride. Gideon's men would have seen to her food and water, but Adelaide felt guilty about neglecting her dear friend. Perhaps a tasty carrot would make up for her lack of attention.

Clutching her peace offering, Adelaide exited the house through the kitchen door and headed for the stable. Daylight was fading, so she forced her sore muscles to a quick pace. The yard looked deserted, but raucous noise drifted to her from the shearers' camp on the far side of the corrals. Gideon had warned her not to venture in that direction in the evenings since the men usually spent the night drinking and gambling with their hard-earned discs. She'd just pay a quick visit to Sheba and be back in the house before full darkness set in.

Enough light drifted in through the wide stable door to allow her to see without a lantern. Shadows lurked in the back by Sheba's stall, but that didn't bother her. She knew exactly where she was going. Sheba nickered a greeting, and Adelaide patted her cheek.

"Did you miss me today, girl?"

Sheba nuzzled her neck.

"I brought you a treat." She held out the carrot and smiled as Sheba greedily chomped it to bits. "I thought you'd like that."

All at once, Sheba yanked her head away from Adelaide and pricked her ears. She neighed and stomped nervously in her stall.

"What is it?" Adelaide stroked her horse's neck in an effort to calm her. "Do you smell an animal or something?"

"*Hola, señorita.*"

Adelaide gasped and spun around, her heart pounding. The lecherous shearer stood as bold as brass in the stable alley, his shirt hanging open to expose his chest to her view. He leaned insolently against the neighboring stall door and winked at her.

"I knew you'd come to me, *bonita*. After teasing me in the shed today, you want to finish what you started."

The dumplings she had eaten such a short time ago turned to rocks in her stomach, and her legs threatened to buckle under her. Her mouth was so dry she couldn't even voice the denial her mind was screaming.

Sheba kicked at the stall, and a memory jarred. "*You're too small to overpower a man who wants to hurt you, sunshine,*" her father had said. "*You've got to outthink him.*" Outthink him. Buy herself time to find a weapon or summon help.

Adelaide inhaled a tremulous breath and tried to stem the terror that spiraled through her like a cyclone. His cocksure manner didn't bode well. He probably wouldn't accept a simple refusal. She'd have to try to keep him talking long enough to come up with a plan.

"I'm sorry, señor." She forced her lips into a polite smile, praying he couldn't smell her fear. "I'm afraid there's been a misunderstanding. I came out here to see to my horse, not to meet anyone."

Her eyes desperately scanned the barn for something she could use to defend herself. A pitchfork stood against the far wall a couple yards away. If she could just take a few steps past him . . .

He pushed away from the stall he'd been leaning on and moved closer. Adelaide pressed her back into the wood of Sheba's door. The man clicked his tongue at her and wagged his head.

"Ah, señorita. You should not lie to José. I know what you want."

He licked his lips and his gaze raked over her from head to toe. As his eyes slowly worked their way back up her form, they lingered at the line of her breasts. Adelaide twisted her head to the side and leaned away from him, feeling sullied by his visual caress.

The wood support behind her began to shake. She floundered for a moment but then realized Sheba was kicking at the door again. *Sheba.* Her ally. As surreptitiously as possible, Adelaide slid her hand along the edge of the door.

"No, señor." She mustered all the bravado she could manage, hoping to distract him from her purpose. "I am a respectable woman, a teacher. I do not participate in clandestine meetings with men I hardly know." Her fingers brushed the edge of the latch. "I must insist that you return to your camp. Mr. Westcott would not want you snooping around in his stables or pestering his staff."

His frown grew deeper as she spoke. Did he not understand her? Perhaps "clandestine meetings" had not been the best choice of words.

"You need to go. Now." She pointed toward the entrance as her hidden hand closed over the sliding bar that held the lock in place.

His scowl darkened, and all hints of charm disappeared. He lashed out and gripped her chin with biting force. She fumbled to hold onto the latch while he forced her face up.

"So, you are just like all the other *gringas* who swish their skirts at us like it's some kind of game. You make us hungry for you then send us away. You cannot steal a man's pride like that and not pay."

His eyes glowed with fury. Fury borne from pain.

"What was her name?"

The shearer jerked her neck around, his fingers digging even harder into her jaw. He bent his head over her and placed his face so close to hers that she could smell the whiskey on his breath. Her stomach roiled, but she fought down the urge to gag.

"The woman who hurt you," she gritted out. "What was her

name?" If she could get him to focus his anger on someone else, maybe he would release her.

José smiled with an unholy delight, and all hope of release died.

"It does not matter, bonita, for today you *are* her."

His lips crushed hers in a bruising kiss designed to punish. She squirmed in protest, but he held her fast. Praying for strength, Adelaide threw the latch on the stall door and stomped José's foot with the heel of her boot. He loosened his grip for just a second, and she took full advantage. She brought both arms down hard where he held her chin and tore free. Dashing around the edge of the stall door, she slammed it forward into her attacker with all her might. He stumbled back.

Sheba bucked, nervous from all the commotion. Adelaide grabbed her mane and dragged her out. She wanted nothing more than to jump onto the mare and gallop away with her, but she'd never be able to mount bareback without her split skirt. Remembering the pitchfork, Adelaide opted for a distraction instead. She slapped Sheba's rump and yelled, causing the already skittish mare to rear up. While José dodged Sheba's flailing hooves, Adelaide ran for the weapon.

It didn't take long for José to get past her horse. Adelaide faced him, brandishing the pitchfork in front of her. Sheba's fleeing hoofbeats echoed dishearteningly through the stable.

"Put it down, bonita. You can't hurt me."

She feared he was right but refused to admit it. "I don't want to, but I will if you don't leave me alone." She jabbed the prongs at him to accent her words, but he laughed at her efforts.

Adelaide gathered her gumption and lunged toward him, cutting off his laughter. He hopped backward and knocked the metal tines aside with his forearm. He nearly grabbed the weapon away from her, but she snatched it out of his reach at the last second. Not wanting to make that mistake again, Adelaide shifted her hold.

Before he could guess her intent, she hoisted the handle up to her shoulder and with a mighty grunt, swung the pitchfork like a stickball bat. Doubting she could reach his head without his blocking her, and not wishing to kill him if he didn't, she aimed for his knees. The handle connected with a thud, and José dropped to the ground.

Abandoning the weapon, she ran for the door. His roar of pain filled the air like a demon's cry. Halfway to the door, she heard his pounding footsteps closing the gap behind her.

Panic surged. Her legs flew. The door drew near. Escape.

But before she could gain her freedom, he tackled her from behind. She crashed to the floor. Pain shot through her elbow and hip. She screamed and clawed for the door. He dragged her back. Her nails scraped against the wooden planks, searching for something to grasp. They found nothing.

Then he hefted her up, encircling her middle with an unforgiving arm that bent her in two. His dirty hand closed over her mouth, cutting off her screams. She kicked and hit at him with her fists, but the awkward blows had no effect. He cursed and carried her back to the depths of the stable.

"It's time to pay, bonita."

She fought for breath under his violent grip. He kicked open a vacant stall and threw her roughly onto a thin pile of straw. She gasped for air and found her voice.

"Let me go!"

He slapped her hard across the face.

"Not till I'm done with you."

Her head spun from the blow, and her heart lurched at his words. She turned onto her belly and tried to crawl away from him, but there was nowhere to go. He flipped her onto her back and slapped her again, slamming her head into the floor. Tears ran down her cheeks. She begged for mercy, her pleas coming out in tiny, broken whimpers. He leered at her, grabbed the collar of her dress, and yanked. Buttons popped off and disappeared into the hay. She bucked and scratched at his face, shrieking at him to stop. But he pinned her arms to the ground and pushed his weight on top of her, once again stealing her breath.

"Ready for your lesson, teacher?"

God, save me!

He raised himself a bit in order to grab her skirts, inadvertently allowing her to inhale a lungful of air. Before he could hit her again, she concentrated all of her energy into one final scream. And this time she screamed a name.

"Gideon!"

Chapter 12

Cool water sluiced over Gideon's head as he bent under the pump. Rivulets ran down his neck, pushing aside the dust and grime of a long day. His stomach clamored for supper and his back ached for a soak in the tub, but he welcomed the discomfort. It was a good feeling—the feeling of productivity, of knowing at the end of the day that what you chose to occupy yourself with had merit and value. His old school chums no doubt scoffed at him from across the ocean for trading his pampered, idle life for sore muscles and dirt-encrusted skin. Yet he couldn't imagine going back. He felt more alive and authentic here than he ever had in the drawing rooms of London.

Gideon blindly reached for a strip of toweling he had hung on a nearby fencepost and began rubbing the wetness from his hair. A distant screech caught his attention. He stilled. Cocking his head, he listened but didn't hear it again. Cougars were rare in this area, but if one were around, its cry would sound much like a woman's scream. Perhaps he should instruct Miguel to post a guard on the sheep tonight. He resumed drying his hair at a slower pace, not wanting the towel to muffle the sound of another cry if it came.

Unease wrapped around him as he listened. He attempted to rationalize away the disquieting sensation with logical explanations of the sound—like a prowling cougar or a high-pitched shout from the shearers' camp—but it wouldn't abate. His shoulders grew taut with trepidation, and he scanned the darkening yard for clues to what he had heard.

"Gideon!"

The cry shot through his heart like an arrow. *Adelaide.*

Urgency pumped through his veins. He took off at a dead run, praying he was going in the right direction. He instinctively veered toward the house, but the sight of Sheba stamping and snorting in the middle of the yard changed his mind. The stables.

He pounded through the entrance and halted, letting his eyes adjust to the dimmer light. Something whimpered at the back of the building.

"Miss Proctor?"

The whimper cut off. Gideon moved forward.

"Miss Proctor, are you in here?"

A masculine hiss of pain answered, followed by a short series of smothered cries and boot leather scraping against wooden floorboards.

Gideon sprinted down to Sheba's stall. Empty.

Desperation nearly drove Gideon mad as silence once again hid her from him.

"Miss Proctor!"

He ran from one vacant stall to the next, peering over the half doors, straining to see. All he could make out were straw-covered floors and dark shadows. Then at the third gate, fading twilight glistened upon a swatch of yellow gingham. Never had he been so thankful for her choice of bright attire. He had only a second, however, to take in her hiked-up skirts, torn bodice, and unnaturally still form before a fist slammed into his jaw, sprawling him out on the floor.

Gideon scrambled to his feet in time to see a man rush at him. Rage like he had never known surged through him, and he lunged forward to meet Adelaide's attacker head on. Gideon smashed his fist into his opponent's side again and again, ignoring the blows to his own torso. Wanting to end things quickly so he could see to Adelaide, Gideon took a risk and raised his arms to grab his opponent's head, leaving his side vulnerable to the man's brutal punches. Gideon braced himself for the pain, and as soon as the next blow came, he jerked the man's head down and jabbed his own knee upward to crash into his forehead. Dazed, the man staggered back and Gideon got his first good look at him.

One of the shearers. A man he had paid to come onto his land.

A vision of Adelaide's prone form swam in Gideon's mind. He exploded. Growling, he threw himself at the man. Blow after blow, Gideon punished him. He pummeled his midsection and head until the man could barely stand. The shearer's open shirt waved like a flag of surrender as he fell to his knees. The brute deserved no mercy. Gideon grabbed a handful of the loose fabric and lifted the man off the ground. He drew back his fist, ready to finish it. But a soft voice reached him through the haze of his wrath.

"Enough, Gideon."

She was clutching one of the support beams, clearly unsteady on her feet, yet he was so relieved to see her conscious he nearly dropped his opponent. Securing his grip, he slowly lowered his fist. Hooves clicking behind him turned his attention away from Adelaide and back toward the entrance. A familiar whistle accompanied the percussive hoofbeats.

"Miguel!" Gideon called out to his foreman.

"Patrón?"

Miguel approached, leading Sheba. "I found the young teacher's horse wandering the yard. You want me to . . ." His words died off as he came close enough to take in the scene.

Adelaide moaned. Gideon swiveled to find her clutching at her torn bodice and trying to hide behind the post. Her undeserved shame rekindled his anger. He yanked the shearer to his feet and bent his arms behind his back. Motioning Miguel forward, he kept his voice low in an effort to save Adelaide further upset.

"I need to see to Miss Proctor. Deliver this piece of refuse to the nearest authorities." Gideon thrust the man at his foreman, and Miguel easily took charge of him.

"Sí, patrón. I'll take him to town to wait for the marshal. But I will also talk to Ramirez." Miguel tightened his hold on the man until he winced. "After I tell what happened, *el capitán* will see that this scum is cast out of the crew. Even after the law is done with him, no one will hire him."

"Good."

Miguel hauled the man out of the stable, threatening him with a host of atrocities in Spanish, only half of which Gideon understood.

After Miguel exited the stable, Gideon turned to look for Adelaide. She was no longer standing behind the post where he had last seen her. Sheba was missing, too. He found them in Sheba's stall, Adelaide's face buried in the mare's flank. Quiet sobs shuddered through her and tore at his heart.

No woman should endure such betrayal, and the fact that it had been Adelaide—a woman who exuded joy and sunshine—made the outcome that much darker. Gideon clenched his jaw in an attempt to suppress his lingering rage. He needed control. Anger would only frighten her. Closing his eyes for a moment, he released a quiet breath and forced his muscles to relax.

Lord, help me.

Gideon opened his eyes and stepped softly into the stall. His hand shook as he lifted it to her shoulder. Too many emotions still throbbed within him. Something had cracked the moment he saw her crumpled form lying motionless in that stall, exposing an inner depth of feeling he hadn't known existed. He wasn't sure what to make of it, but now wasn't the time to sort out his confusion. This tiny lady with her big smile and vivid imagination had suffered an atrocity, and for today he would set aside the boundaries of their professional relationship to bind up her soul's wounds as best he could. Tomorrow would be soon enough to worry about propriety.

"Miss Proctor?" Gideon gently squeezed her shoulder. "Adelaide?"

She stiffened under his touch. Lifting her head, she swallowed her sobs and rubbed the tears from her cheeks with the back of one hand. She turned to face him but kept her eyes downcast, holding the collar of her dress modestly together, as if she were clinging to the last shreds of her dignity.

Compassion welled in him. He tilted her chin up. Red welts covered both sides of her face and blood oozed from a cut at the corner of her bottom lip. He wanted to roar his outrage, but he held back for her sake, allowing his features to convey nothing but concern. Her body trembled from her suppressed grief, her breath hitching each time she inhaled.

"Miguel is carting him away. He won't bother you again." Why did the promise sound so hollow?

Adelaide bit her lip and dropped her gaze to the small piece of straw-covered ground between them.

Gideon released Adelaide's chin and fisted his hand behind his back until his short nails dug painfully into his palm. What did one say in a situation like this? He wanted to help her, to ease her anguish, but a simple apology or pat on the back seemed horrendously inadequate. Not knowing what else to do, he let instinct guide him and placed a chaste kiss on her forehead. Her eyes rose to search his, full of doubt, fear, and a touch of hope.

Gideon opened his arms to her. She hesitated. Then with a weepy hiccup, she leaned into his embrace, her arms still folded protectively in front of her. Laying his chin upon her head, he rocked her back and forth, committed to staying with her as long as necessary.

Gradually her sobs subsided and she pulled away. He cupped her face in his hands and wiped her cheeks dry with the pads of his thumbs.

"Thank you," she said between sniffs. "Thank you for everything."

"Can you tell me what happened?" Gideon didn't want to cause her more pain, but he feared if she held the poison from these events inside her, it would fester and eventually kill her joyous spirit.

Adelaide stared at him for a long moment, then gave a tentative nod.

Sheba shifted restlessly, no doubt weary of having them in her bedroom. Gideon swept Adelaide up into his arms and carried her out of the stall. He headed toward the entrance, thinking to take her back to the house, but she moaned a denial.

"No. Please. I'm not ready yet." Her voice cracked. "The others will see . . . I don't . . ." She buried her face in his neck. "Can't we just stay out here for a few minutes?"

"Of course." Her request made little sense to him, but it didn't matter. Right now, he would grant her the moon if she asked it of him.

He set her down by the far wall and reached to the shelf above, where he could make out the shadowy outline of a barn lantern. Darkness had descended, and while his eyes had adjusted to the lack of light, the warm glow of a lamp might ease the telling of Adelaide's tale. He lit the burner and, after lowering the globe, placed it on the floor.

"I know it sounds silly," she said, "but when I exit this stable, I want to leave all of this behind me." Shivers wracked her body.

Whether from the chill in the air or from the aftermath of her attack, he didn't know. "If I'm going to tell you what happened, I want to do it here. That way, when I walk through those doors, I never have to think of it again."

Gideon knew it would be a long time before her mind completely banished thoughts of the attack, but he would do whatever he could to make the healing easier for her.

First things first, though. He needed to find something to cover her with to restore her sense of modesty and stop her shivering. All he had to offer was a sweat-stained work shirt, and it would probably scare her half to death if he took it off. He rummaged around for a horse blanket instead. Finding one, he shook out the worst of the hair and draped the thick felt square around Adelaide's shoulders. He rubbed her arms until he could feel her shivers subsiding, then sat down with his back braced against the wall.

She gathered the blanket around her like a cloak and sank to the floor next to him.

"None of this was your fault," Gideon assured her

He waited for her to speak, but she said nothing. Accustomed to her cheerful, rambling conversations, the silence ate at him. Finally, unable to bear the quiet any longer, he gave voice to the question in the forefront of his mind.

"Did he . . . um . . . compromise you?"

"No."

Sweet relief poured through him at her muted answer. *Thank you, God!*

Then, as if that single word had pulled the plug, all the details drained out of her in a gush.

"I came to the stables to feed Sheba a carrot I found in the kitchen. José snuck up behind me."

Gideon tucked away the name.

"He moved like a coyote. I never heard him approach until he spoke. Oh, Gideon, I was so frightened. He acted like I had been toying with him all day, but I hadn't. Truly. After he looked at me in the shed, I avoided him as much as possible."

"I believe you." Did she realize she had called him by his given name? Whether it was unconscious or not, he couldn't deny the pleasure that shot through him at hearing his name on her lips. He plucked a piece of straw out of her hair and smoothed the tresses with his hand. "Go on."

"I apologized and told him it was all a misunderstanding, but he didn't believe me, or didn't want to accept it, or . . . who knows what the crazy man thought." She sat up straighter, a spark of indignation finally evident in her stricken eyes. "I tried to be civil, but he wouldn't leave, so I finally demanded that he go. That set him off. He turned ugly and started ranting about how I was like all the other gringas who flirt and tease yet think they are too good for a Mexican shearer. I tried to reason with him, to tell him I wasn't like that at all, that he had misread the situation. But he didn't care. Some white woman in his past had spurned him, and he sought to redeem his pride by taking me."

"But he didn't." He waited for her to look at him and repeated the statement, reminding himself as much as her. "He didn't."

A tiny smile curved her lips, and Gideon felt as if the sun were coming out from behind a cloud.

"You're right. He didn't." The small curve widened into a satisfied grin. "Between me plowing him with a pitchfork and you beating the stuffing out of him, his pride is probably more tattered than my dress."

"You plowed him with a pitchfork?"

"I sure did. My daddy didn't raise no hothouse flower, you know."

Gideon had a feeling he would have liked her daddy.

"I managed to get Sheba out," she explained, "and she distracted José long enough for me to grab the pitchfork. I slammed the handle into his knees and ran for the door. I almost made it, too, before he dragged me back."

Adelaide's burst of vim and vigor dissipated. She sagged against the barn wall and looked away. Gideon wanted to hold her again but didn't know if she would welcome his touch. Would it be better to give her some space, or would she think he was disgusted by her if he made no further move to comfort her as he had before she told him what happened? Indecision warred within him. Biting the inside of his cheek, he scooted closer to her. Watching her carefully for any sign that he was causing her distress, he slowly reached out and covered her hand with his. She grasped his fingers, and his doubt disappeared.

When Adelaide finally spoke, her voice quivered. "I screamed whenever I could find the breath and prayed for someone to come. I prayed for you." She tilted her face up to his. "And you came."

It was crazy, but at that moment, with Adelaide looking up at him with eyes brimming with admiration, he wanted to vow that he would *always* be there for her. Yet he could make no such promise. She was an employee, not family. Even if she stayed with Bella until the child was grown, she would still leave one day.

Gideon tore his gaze away from Adelaide and pressed his back more firmly into the stable wall. The notion of her leaving didn't sit well. Not at all.

"When I heard you call my name," she continued, drawing his attention back to her face, "I tried to make a sound—anything to lead you to us—but he was too strong for me." Her hazel eyes pooled with tears again. "He muzzled me so tightly with his hand, I couldn't breathe. I must've passed out. When I revived, I found you pummeling him. No hero has ever shone more brightly."

She raised the hand that held hers to her lips, and placed a tender kiss onto each of his bruising knuckles. Suddenly he was the one who couldn't breathe.

"Thank you, Gideon. Thank you for saving me."

Uncomfortable with her praise, Gideon didn't answer beyond a silent squeeze of her fingers. His mind still swirled with the sensation of her lips pressed to his skin. Was it just an act of gratitude, or did a deeper affection linger behind it?

"I think I'm ready to go back to the house now."

Saved from trying to answer his own question, Gideon snuffed out the lantern and helped her up. Adelaide clung to the horse blanket but appeared steady on her feet as he led her to the entrance. When they reached the yard, moonlight illuminated the snags and tears in the fabric of her skirt. She stopped for a minute to examine the damage and then, with surprising resiliency, shrugged her shoulders and started walking again.

"At least he ruined a dress I no longer care for. I think this gown must have a secret longing for the rag bin. First, it leads me into that fiasco with Henry and now this. Maybe I'll just burn it so I won't accidentally catch a glimpse of it braided into a rug somewhere. It's brought me enough bad memories."

Gideon halted abruptly in the middle of the yard, a new emotion assaulting him. "Who is Henry?"

Chapter 13

Now she'd done it. When would she ever learn to guard her tongue? Adelaide briefly considered ignoring Gideon's question and continuing up to the house, but her conscience wouldn't let her. He had just acted the hero on her behalf, slaying her dragon and consoling her with a level of tenderness she hadn't experienced since her father died. She should be willing to sacrifice anything for this man—even her pride.

She stumbled to a stop, but couldn't face him. Not yet. What if he thought her a shameless hussy for chasing after a married man, even if she didn't know he was married at the time she was doing the chasing? Would he then accuse her of enticing the shearer? Her heart would shatter to see scorn replace the compassion in his eyes.

Courage, Adelaide. Courage. Gideon had treated her with nothing but respect and kindness since she arrived. He wasn't going to shift roles from charming prince to slimy ogre in this story of hers. Not in a single page, anyway.

"Is he your brother?" Gideon's voice had a forced lightness to it that worried her. He was obviously trying to give her the benefit of the doubt. She hated to disappoint him, but she could no longer delay telling him the truth.

Adelaide turned around and made a valiant attempt to look him in the eye. She made it to about his chin.

"No. I have no brothers. Sisters either—although I don't guess that relates to your question, does it?" She sighed. "It's a rather embarrassing tale, but I suppose you should know."

She paused, giving him a chance to stop her, to tell her that she didn't have to explain, but he didn't. He just gazed at her with an intensity that warmed her and unsettled her at the same time.

"My father died when I was sixteen, and ever since then, I've longed to replace the family I lost. That's what led me to teaching. I discovered a passion for children, and working with them seemed to fill part of the emptiness inside. But I yearned for more."

Adelaide couldn't read Gideon's expression as he took her elbow and steered her toward the front porch. That worried her. He usually smiled so easily, but not now. If she could just make him understand her motivation for getting tangled up with Henry, maybe it would soften the effect of her foolishness.

"When the town of Cisco contracted me to teach for two years on the condition that I not marry during that time, I set aside my own dreams of family and focused on nurturing the dreams of my students."

They reached the steps, and Gideon led her to one of the wicker chairs where she had begun her day with Isabella. Morning seemed days ago. He leaned against the banister across from her, patiently enduring her long-winded answer to his simple question.

"But you still longed for a husband and children of your own," he said.

"Yes. My two years were nearly complete when I met Henry."

Gideon sat up a little straighter at the mention of the man's name.

"He was a traveling book salesman who rode the T&P Railroad line peddling his goods. He stayed in the same boardinghouse where I roomed when he was in town, and we spent many a pleasant evening in the parlor discussing literature and the latest novels. I was probably his best customer. I ordered something every time he came to town. Maybe that's why he decided to pay court to me—to increase his commission." Adelaide's brow creased at the depressing thought.

"What happened?" There was a bit of an edge to his voice now. Adelaide's mouth went dry.

"I only saw him about once every three or four weeks, but it was enough. He made sweet promises and spouted romantic non-sense that made me giggle. He could be a bit condescending, and the quality of his spiritual life was questionable, but I was willing to look past that. No man is perfect, after all."

Adelaide gazed at Gideon's shadowy form. Well, maybe for her one man could have been. No use pining over the impossible, though.

"A couple of months ago," she continued, "Henry received a promotion and told me that he wouldn't be riding the rails any lon-ger. He acted so devastated about not seeing me again that I made a rash plan. I resigned my teaching position and followed him to Fort Worth. Providence intervened, and I ran into him at the hotel restaurant my first night in town. I also had the honor of meeting his wife and child. Not quite the reunion I had envisioned."

"He was married?" The question sounded like it had been forced out through clenched teeth. Not a good sign.

"A fact he failed to mention during the course of our acquaintance."

Gideon mumbled something quite ferocious under his breath, but Adelaide couldn't make it out. Perhaps that was for the best. Bracing herself for his response, she prayed he wouldn't send her away on the spot. She rather liked her cloud resting over Westcott Cottage. She wasn't ready for God to move her on just yet.

"Are you still in love with him?"

The terse question caught her off guard. Not sure how to answer, she blurted the first thing that came to mind.

"I don't think I ever really was." The rest of the words poured out before she could stop them. "The shameful truth is, I was so desperate to make my dream of family a reality that I chased the first thing in pants that showed some interest in me."

Adelaide stared at her lap. Until that moment, she hadn't realized just how pathetic she truly was. He would certainly send her packing after this. Tears spilled over her eyes. At least she could spare him the discomfort of having to discharge her.

"I'm sorry, Mr. Westcott. I should have told you from the first. I'll pack my things and ride out in the morning. Your daughter deserves better than me."

She jumped to her feet and tried to flee into the house, but Gideon lunged away from the railing to block her path.

"Adelaide, wait." Gideon reached out but let his hand fall back to his side without touching her. "As far as Bella is concerned, there is no one better than you."

"But you know different now, don't you?" She moved to sidestep him, but he wouldn't let her pass.

"No. I don't know. In fact, I agree with her."

Adelaide looked into his face, searching for clues as to his meaning. "What?"

"Bella has improved more under your care in the short time you've been here than I dared hope. We need you."

"But my past . . ."

Something rumbled in Gideon's throat.

"There's nothing wrong with your past! That Henry fellow was an unscrupulous lout that toyed with your affections to serve his own ends. He's the one with the shameful past, not you."

She heard his words, yet she couldn't quite believe what he was saying. He couldn't really be excusing her actions, could he? He had seemed so upset earlier.

"I never should have gone to Fort Worth," Adelaide ventured, testing the waters of his reaction. "It was a stupid thing to do."

Gideon did take hold of her arm then, his gentle grip comforting through the felt blanket still draped over her. "Not stupid. Impulsive, perhaps. But I can't really hold that against you when that same impulse eventually led you here, can I?"

"But I could sense your anger when I told you about Henry. I thought—"

"I know what you thought, but you were wrong." Gideon released her and shoved his fingers through his hair, expelling a loud breath in the process. "Yes, I was angry, but not at you. At Henry for abusing your trust and at myself for making you rehash painful memories after you had already been through so much tonight." He cupped both of his hands around her upper arms and bent his face close to hers. "I let my own selfishness get in the way of what was best for you. Forgive me, Adelaide."

He was apologizing to *her*? If he hadn't been holding her arms, she probably would have fallen over.

Not trusting her voice, she nodded.

"Let's get you into the house." Gideon moved to her side and slipped his arm around her waist.

Too tired to ponder the ramifications of their conversation and too relieved over not being sent away to care, Adelaide hobbled numbly along, hoping that everything would make more sense in the morning.

Full daylight poured through her window when Adelaide finally awoke the next day. She squinted against the light and stretched, flinching at the soreness in her muscles. Memories assailed her as consciousness returned. She ignored the ugly ones, unwilling to succumb to the fear and despair she knew they would evoke. Instead, she settled back onto her pillow, closed her eyes, and savored the good ones. Gideon holding her. Gideon defending her. Gideon's patience and understanding. *Gideon. Gideon. Gideon.*

Smiling to herself, she opened her eyes. No doubt about it. She was sappier than a sugar maple. Her Rochester was turning out to be even better than Jane Eyre's. No excessive moodiness, no flirtations with other women, and as far as she could tell, no mad first wife secreted away in the attic.

Hmmm . . . There was a first wife, though, and her memory might still hold sway over his heart. The thought cast an unwanted shadow on Adelaide's romantic daydream. The woman had only been dead for, what, five months? Gideon never spoke of his wife, so it was hard to know if he still pined for her.

Adelaide yanked the spare pillow from the mattress beside her and plopped it over her face. She flattened the ticking against her mouth and released the groan that had been building inside her. She needed to take her head out of the clouds and focus on what God had led her here to do—teach Isabella. Heroes in castles lived in storybooks, not real life. And even if by some miracle Gideon one day came to view her as something more than his daughter's governess, it would be unfair to measure him against a fictional standard that he could never possibly achieve.

Yet something stirred in her heart whenever she thought of him, whenever she found herself in his presence, whenever he smiled at her. It was more than the silly fluttering of a schoolgirl crush. It was deeper than the hope of family that had drawn her to Henry, and she feared it would not simply vanish at her command. She'd have to bury it. At least for now. Maybe after an appropriate mourning period had expired . . .

Adelaide removed the pillow from her face and stared up at the ceiling. What had Gideon's first wife been like? Beautiful? Elegant?

Courtly? Had she complained about leaving her home in England or eagerly boarded the vessel to join her beloved on the grand adventure he had plotted for them in America? Had she been tall and fair, poised and proper—everything that Adelaide was not?

A tiny cramp pulled Adelaide's brows together. Strange. Now that she though about it, there were no pictures of her. Anywhere. A portrait of Gideon's parents hung in the parlor, and the mantel sported a photograph of Gideon with his brothers as young adults. There were miniatures of Isabella, too, but only at the age she was now. None from her toddler years. Had Gideon banished all evidence of his dead wife because he couldn't bear to see the reminders, or had the two been so estranged that they'd had no pictures made? Arranged marriages often occurred among the English aristocracy. Maybe theirs had not turned out well. But surely he would have kept at least a wedding photograph. And another thing . . . whenever he did mention the woman, he always designated her as Isabella's mother, never as his wife. . . .

Crazy, ridiculous hope clawed past her newly installed barriers. Jane and Edward had overcome their obstacles. It was possible that she and Gideon could do the same. She just prayed her hero wouldn't have to be blinded and maimed to accomplish the deed.

Adelaide savored her resurrected dreams for a moment longer. She would pack them away again in a few minutes, but for now, in the privacy of her bedchamber, she'd let them spin their delicate webs where they may.

Gideon had been so solicitous last night after their awkward conversation. He had bustled her into the house and turned her over to the care of Mrs. Chalmers. Miguel must have said something to the housekeeper, for she'd lingered in the kitchen, darning socks by lamplight with two full pails of heated water plus a kettle waiting on the stove. Gideon filled the tub in the washroom and ordered Adelaide to soak until the steamy water turned tepid.

Mrs. Chalmers had shooed him away after that, but not before he gruffly demanded that Adelaide sleep until noon.

She had given it her best effort, too, but the porcelain clock sitting atop her chest of drawers indicated only half past ten. As much as she enjoyed her dreams, even they could not keep her abed when there was work to be done. She packed them away as one would a set of fine china, lingering over each piece, until with a final sigh, she closed the lid. Then with a toss of the coverlet, she slid from her dreamy cocoon to face the day.

After washing her face, braiding her hair, and getting dressed, Adelaide contemplated her reflection in the oval mirror above the washstand. The swelling in her face had gone down, thank goodness. Nevertheless, Isabella was bound to notice the bruising around her cheekbones and jaw. Adelaide winced as she pressed a finger against the puffy corner of her bottom lip where a tiny scab had formed overnight. She practiced a reassuring smile in the glass, ignoring the tenderness as the flesh around her mouth stretched. A bit lopsided, but hopefully it would convince Isabella that all was well.

If Mrs. Chalmers had abided by her wishes, Isabella had been told a very watered-down version of the truth this morning. Adelaide had asked the housekeeper to inform the girl that she had had a mishap in the barn last night, but that she was fine. For the first time, Isabella's lack of speech would be a blessing. She wouldn't be able to ask questions. Adelaide didn't want her to worry, though, so she planned to seek her out straightaway.

She nearly tripped over the girl as she exited her room.

Isabella was sitting against the wall by the bedchamber door, clutching her doll to her chest. When Adelaide stepped into the hall, Isabella scrambled to her feet, distress etched into her young face.

"Oh, sweetheart! Have you been waiting here all morning?" Adelaide crouched down in front of her charge and brushed a hand over her blond curls. "I'm sorry I slept so late."

Blue eyes raked Adelaide's face. Disregarding the child's concern would certainly not help her. Best to deal with the situation in a more direct manner.

Adelaide patted her cheeks with her fingertips. "Oh dear. Does it really look that bad?"

Isabella nodded.

"Well, don't let it frighten you. I hardly feel it any longer. My lip is a little tender, but that's all. I think I ache more from all the hard work we did with Miguel yesterday than from anything that happened in the stables." Adelaide stood up, took Isabella's hand, and began leading her down to the kitchen. Her stomach growled in eagerness. Adelaide covered it with her hand and winked down at her charge.

"That wasn't very ladylike, was it?"

Isabella smiled, and Adelaide breathed easier. Now, if she could just keep the child distracted until she grew accustomed to the bruises. She needed a project of some kind. Something big.

When they reached the staircase, Adelaide maneuvered Isabella toward the railing so she could hold on with her free hand.

"Since I'm not feeling well today, how about we let the men handle the shearing without us?" Even knowing José would be gone, Adelaide had no desire to encounter any other members of the crew. However, Isabella had enjoyed herself so much yesterday she might want to join her father again today. "Would you mind?" Adelaide held her breath.

Isabella shrugged an answer, not looking too dejected by the prospect of staying in. Adelaide exhaled in relief.

"I thought we might start a new project," she ruminated aloud. "Something educational, but a wee bit frivolous. Something feminine. Something . . . I've got it!"

Adelaide tugged Isabella to a halt one step shy of the bottom. Letting go of her hand, Adelaide hopped down to the floor and turned around, excitement thrumming through her. Not caring that her wide grin pulled painfully against her scabbed lip, she clapped her hands to her knees and leaned over until her eyes were level with those of her charge.

"Izzy! We're going to have a party. And you will be our hostess!"

Chapter 14

The rocking of the rail car unsettled Reginald Petchey's stomach. First the steamer passage across the Atlantic with its sloshing to and fro and now this infernal jostling. It was a crime for a country to grow so wide a man couldn't ride a horse across it in decent order. The colonies should have stayed huddled together on the eastern seaboard and let the heathens keep the rest. Most of the scenery speeding by his window looked godforsaken anyway.

Farnsworth had managed to secure a private compartment on a Pullman car, but the quarters were still much too close. Reginald escaped to the smoking room as often as possible for a cigar or a game of cards with whomever happened to be handy. He made sure not to win too heavily, though. Wouldn't do to leave too memorable an impression on anyone.

Just then the door opened, letting in the clatter from the public section along with his not-so-esteemed companion. "I have the soda crackers you requested, Lord Petchey."

Reginald bounded to his feet and threw the door closed. "Have a care, man." He snatched the biscuit tin out of Farnsworth's hand

and glared down at the man. "How many times do I have to tell you that for the purposes of this trip I am *not* Lord Petchey. You are to address me as Mr. Edward Church. Do you think you can wrap your feeble brain around that particular instruction?"

"My apologies, my lor— I mean, sir. My apologies, *sir*." Farnsworth's neck reddened as he tripped over his tongue.

Reginald gritted his teeth. If the fellow weren't so talented at doctoring his ledgers he'd have turned him out ages ago. The man had the social intelligence of a gnat.

Farnsworth turned his back and hung his hat on one of the wall-mounted hooks. "I don't see why we must keep up the pretense in private. In fact, I don't really see why there's need for a pretense at all. Our best chance to convince Westcott to relinquish guardianship of the girl is to reveal your familial connection. An assumed name serves no purpose."

"That is why you will never be a great man, Farnsworth. You only consider what is expected. It is by anticipating the unexpected and preparing in advance to meet that challenge that success is achieved." Reginald opened the tin and extracted a single square. His companion didn't yet fully grasp his intentions toward Westcott, and if Reginald could continue manipulating the cards in this game to suit his pleasure, he never would.

"We don't know what kind of hand Westcott is holding or how much he is willing to drive up the wager. Traveling under an assumed name protects me should anything . . . inauspicious occur. It wouldn't do for scandal to follow us across the sea once dear Isabella is returned to me. My niece has suffered enough."

Taking a bite of the salty biscuit, Reginald returned to his cushioned bench, brushing away the crumbs that fell upon the dark wool of his coat. Farnsworth lowered himself into the seat opposite him. Reginald raised an affronted brow as he swallowed, but the fellow was too busy staring at his boots to notice. Truly, he didn't know which was making him more ill—the ceaseless rocking of the rail car or having to stare at Farnsworth's pasty face throughout the journey.

Reginald popped the rest of the soda cracker into his mouth and turned his attention to the window. He'd heard tales from some of his countrymen about how in years past a man could pay for the privilege of hunting big game from a rail car. Buffalo, wasn't it? Now, that would be a welcome diversion. Nothing like a good hunt to take a man's mind from the dreariness of travel. Considering his prowess with rifles, he'd probably fell dozens before the herd could stampede out of range.

A cluster of rock outcroppings came into view, and Reginald imagined pressing his Remington to his shoulder as the rocks took on the shape of fierce, horned beasts. They'd be in range soon. Slowing his breathing, he mentally loaded a cartridge and selected a target. *Sight down the barrel. Finger the trigger. Wait for the perfect moment.*

Patience.

Just a bit closer.

"Why am I not using an assumed name?"

The intrusion of Farnsworth's whiny voice scattered Reginald's fictitious herd and obliterated his good humor. "Because you're a servant," Reginald snapped. "No one remembers servants."

A knock sounded on the door, sparing Farnsworth a further dressing down.

"Enter," Reginald called, taking pains to erase all annoyance from his voice.

A dark-skinned porter stepped through the opening. "I brung your shoes, Mr. Church, sir. All polished up real fine they are. Real fine."

Reginald smiled at the man. "Thank you. You may place them in the wardrobe."

"Yes, sir, Mr. Church, sir."

Mr. Church. He liked the sound of that. Had a lovely, ironic ring. Lucinda put such store in the institution, after all, it seemed only fitting that he use it to cleanse his palate of the last dregs of her influence.

Soon he would be in Texas. He'd deal with Westcott and return to his estate with Isabella in tow. Rescuing his niece from the wilds of America and raising her as a Petchey on Petchey land was the least he could do to honor his brother's memory. Of course, seeing to the girl's upbringing would necessitate solidifying the family finances. Thankfully, her trust fund would make quick work of that little detail.

"I'll be back in a couple of hours to make down the berths for the night, sir," the porter said, pausing beside Reginald's seat.

"Excellent." He pulled a coin from his vest pocket and slid it into the man's palm. "For I plan to have supremely pleasant dreams this evening."

Golden dreams.

Chapter 15

It had been just over a week since Adelaide hatched the party scheme, and Isabella had taken to the plan with relish. The two of them spent hours huddled together in the schoolroom plotting the perfect event. No detail escaped their attention. Guest list, invitations, location, entertainment, and menu all received comprehensive study and discussion. Adelaide dispensed advice on how easily an idea could be implemented and how each choice would affect the guests, but Isabella made the final decisions.

Adelaide glanced up from her desk to check her student's progress. Isabella's mouth twisted in concentration as she splashed her brush into a puddle of blue watercolor paint before returning it to the half-finished sky on the paper in front of her. Three similar paintings sat drying in the windowsill. Each depicted two sheep—one fat and fluffy, one shorn and skinny with a red W on its hip. A bright summer sky streaked across the top of the page, but the bottom remained void of color. Adelaide would pen the invitation message in that space once the pictures were dry. If all went according to plan, Isabella should be able to deliver her unique offerings to those on her guest list after supper.

Adelaide turned back to her own work, rereading the latest version of that all-important message. She had written the thing three times and still found it lacking. How did one compose an invitation formal enough for an English nobleman yet colloquial enough for a sheep herder? Her etiquette classes hadn't prepared her for this scenario.

The crinkle of paper waving against air saved her from further mental deliberation. Glad for the distraction, Adelaide rose to meet Isabella as she carried her final piece of artwork to the window.

"These look wonderful, Izzy."

Isabella grinned up at her teacher.

"One for Chalmers and Mrs. Chalmers, one for Mrs. Garrett, one for Miguel, and of course, one for your father. Excellent."

"Shhh!"

It wasn't speaking, exactly, but the sound warmed Adelaide's heart anyway. Isabella had begun bending her own rules. She'd laughed, grunted, and even whined a time or two. Now she shushed. No decipherable words, yet each verbalization raised Adelaide's hopes that speech would follow someday soon.

Doing her best to act as if nothing momentous had occurred, Adelaide patted the child's shoulder. "Don't worry. The door is closed. Our secret is safe. Mrs. Garrett is the only one who knows of our party plans, since we gave her our menu yesterday, but I doubt she expects to receive an invitation. All of your guests are sure to be surprised."

Isabella pointed at her shearing pictures and then waved her hand behind her, which usually meant *finished*. Then she looked at Adelaide with raised brows, indicating a question. Usually Adelaide understood her signals quite well, but this one stumped her.

"Are you asking if you can take a break since you finished your painting?"

Her charge shook her head and frowned. She repeated the motions and Adelaide searched for another possible meaning.

"Are you asking if the shearing is over?"

The girl didn't nod, but she jutted out her chin and found a way to arch her brows even higher. Adelaide figured she was on the right track.

"Yes, the crew left on Monday, remember? The freighters carted the wool off yesterday to the warehouse in San Antonio."

Isabella stamped her foot and a low growl reverberated in her throat. She stabbed a finger at the invitations again.

"Something about the party?"

That got a nod. And a rather exasperated glare. No doubt Isabella thought her as dim-witted as her father's sheep. *Her... father's... sheep*. An idea sprouted.

"Will your father finish with the sheep in time for the party tomorrow?"

Isabella's arm flopped to her side and she nodded with a large, exaggerated motion, chiding her teacher for taking so long. Adelaide nearly let loose a triumphant whoop at her successful deduction, but she tamped it down. This wasn't a game of charades after all. That would come tomorrow. This was communication, and she didn't want to trivialize it. Moving to Isabella's side, she tucked the girl under her arm and gave her a squeeze.

"I spoke to your father after you went to bed last night. He expects to finish the dipping today and to drive the sheep back out to the upper pasture tomorrow. They should be done in plenty of time to attend your party, and I'm sure they'll be thrilled by our celebration surprise."

Some of the stiffness relaxed from Isabella's shoulders, and Adelaide led her toward the door.

"Now. Even though we are hosting an informal dinner party, it is still important for a hostess to look her best. In this way, she honors her guests and lends an air of sophistication and elegance to the gathering. So, while we wait for your paint to dry, why don't we go down to your room and choose a dress for you to wear. I've laid out my yellow muslin. Maybe you could— Where are you going?"

Isabella had pulled free and darted back into the schoolroom. She dropped to her knees in front of one of the trunks stored along the side wall and unlatched it. Adelaide hurried over to help her lift the lid.

"Do you wish to wear something of your mother's?" Adelaide peered over the girl's head as she dug through the contents. "It's a lovely idea. Maybe a shawl or a special necklace?"

Anticipating a small piece of frippery, Adelaide had to blink several times to make sure her eyes were working properly when Isabella carefully extracted a mound of satin and lace. The child held it out to her, and Adelaide felt the air rush from her lungs. A ball gown. A romantic, fit-for-a-princess, *yellow* ball gown. The delicate, straw-colored bodice beckoned her closer. Unable to resist, Adelaide ran her fingertips across the ribbon leaves and silk rosettes that trimmed the over-the-shoulder neckline.

The weight of the fabric grew too heavy for Isabella, and the dress began to slide to the floor. Adelaide leapt to the rescue, grabbing hold of the bodice with both hands and hoisting it high. A slender sheath of ivory lace cascaded before her. Clusters of golden roses set against olive leaves decorated the waist and peeked out beneath the draped layers that fell near the hem. If dreams could be sewn into a dress, hers would look like this.

"Oh, Izzy. It's exquisite. Was this one of your mother's party gowns?"

Isabella nodded, her eyes alight. She thrust a pair of long ivory gloves at Adelaide.

"Do you want to wear those?" Adelaide winked at her charge. "You could probably pull them up to your shoulders. Why don't you pick a pretty ribbon I can plait into your hair instead?"

Adelaide set the gloves on top of the trunk lid, and with a stern lecture to her heart about not wishing for things beyond her grasp, she gathered the skirt of the dress and began to fold the lacy fabric. It seemed a shame to pack such loveliness away, but it had to be done. Perhaps one day Isabella would wear it to a grand ball and meet her own dashing hero. Just as the image of a grown-up Isabella waltzed across her mind in the arms of a faceless gentleman, the not-so-grown-up version yanked the dress out of her hands.

"What are you do—" Adelaide's voice cut off as two small hands crashed into her ribcage. The pounding temporarily stole her breath, but when she saw that Isabella held the gown up to her body like a miniature dressmaker ready to commence a fitting, her breath faltered for an entirely different reason.

"You want *me* to wear your mother's dress?"

Isabella's head bobbed up and down, and Adelaide's heart tripped over itself. Wearing that dress would be like living out her own fairy tale, but it was too extravagant for their simple party and too sentimental for Isabella to loan out on a whim.

What if she spilled something on it or ripped the fragile lace on the heel of her shoe? No. She couldn't accept. Besides, it was at least three inches too long for her.

"It's a very kind gesture, Izzy, but I couldn't. I—"

The girl slammed the dress into her chest again, her pink lips puckered in a scowl. Adelaide couldn't find the strength to refuse a second time.

"All right." She collected the dress from Isabella and arranged it in her arms so it wouldn't crease. Then she waved the girl back toward the trunk. "But only if you find something equally lovely to wear. Tomorrow is your night to shine as a true Texas princess."

Later that evening, after the invitations had been distributed and the princess had been put to bed, Adelaide sat at the kitchen table sipping tea with Mrs. Chalmers. Ever since surrendering to the impulse that led her to agree to Isabella's demand, a growing sense of misgiving had built inside her. What had she been thinking?

Well . . . she knew what she'd been thinking. She'd been thinking how much she wanted to wear that dress. To go to a ball and dance with a handsome prince. Or the son of a baron, as the case may be.

What she *hadn't* been thinking was how she would appear to be grasping at things above her station. Or worse, how her careless whim could wound Gideon. The dress belonged to his first wife. His recently deceased first wife. If she came traipsing down the stairs in his wife's dress, it would surely spawn a flood of painful memories. Would he fly into a rage? Or hide his pain behind those marvelous dimples, all while dying inside?

Would he compare her to the woman he'd lost and find her wanting?

Adelaide sighed. Circling the rim of her teacup with the tip of her finger, she stared into the brown depths, searching for a way out of the bind she'd placed herself in.

"Tired, dear?" Mrs. Chalmers smiled sympathetically over the edge of her cup.

"Yes, but that's not what has me fretting."

Mrs. Chalmers set her tea aside. "Can I help?"

Adelaide looked up at the kind woman, the urge to unload her burden nearly overwhelming. "I made a promise to Isabella without thinking things through, and now I'm stuck."

The housekeeper's face remained blessedly placid. "Go on."

"We were looking through the trunks in the attic, searching for something that had belonged to Isabella's mother that she could wear to the party. She pulled out a lovely ball gown and shoved it at me like she wanted me to wear it. I tried to refuse, but she insisted until I gave in."

"I don't see any harm in that. Those things belong to Isabella now. If she wants you to wear the dress, there shouldn't be a problem."

"But what about Mr. Westcott?" Adelaide propped her elbow on the table and shielded her face with her hand. "Surely he would think me presumptuous or even cruel to wear his late wife's things without asking his permission. I can't risk causing him pain or earning his wrath after he has welcomed me into his home and treated me with such consideration."

Suddenly Adelaide knew what she had to do. The only reason it had taken her so long to see the truth was because her own desire had blocked her view. Dropping her hand, she straightened and met the housekeeper's eye. The poor woman looked quite taken aback. "I'm sorry, Mrs. Chalmers. I shouldn't have bothered you. I know what I need to do. I'll just explain to Isabella that I can't—"

"Wait, dear." Mrs. Chalmers squinted at her through her spectacles. "What is this about a wife? Mr. Westcott's never been married."

Lightheadedness assailed her. Adelaide blinked, trying to steady her thoughts. Never been married? "But his daughter . . ."

All at once the wrinkles on Mrs. Chalmers's forehead smoothed away. "Ah, now I see. Isabella is Mr. Westcott's ward. A child of his heart, not of his blood. I thought you'd seen the picture of Isabella's parents that she keeps at her bedside."

She'd noticed the photograph, and the resemblance between Isabella and the man and woman. But she'd been so certain Gideon was the girl's natural father, she'd assumed the couple were more distant kin. An aunt and uncle, perhaps.

"So, Mr. Westcott has never been married." Adelaide repeated the words, trying to absorb their meaning.

"That's right." Mrs. Chalmers picked her tea back up, hiding her burgeoning smile behind the rim of her cup. "So there's no reason not to wear that lovely dress."

Adelaide's pulse began to accelerate. Gideon had never been married. There was no ghost hanging about who still held claim to his heart. No necessary mourning period. No reason not to wear the dress of her dreams for the man of her dreams.

Her cheeks stretched in a grin that could not be contained. She tried biting her lower lip, but it did no good. Pushing away from the table, Adelaide bounded to her feet.

"If you'll excuse me, Mrs. Chalmers? I have a dress to hem."

Chapter 16

You are cordially invited
to the parlor of Westcott Cottage
for dinner and entertainment
in celebration of a successful spring shearing.
Festivities will begin at six o'clock on Friday evening,
the fifteenth of June, 1883.

Gideon eyed the card that stood propped against his dresser mirror as he folded his white necktie. The stick-legged creatures in the picture smiled their approval of his attire. He hadn't worn formal evening dress since leaving England, yet when Bella presented him with an invitation to her party, he knew he had to look his best.

My girls have gone to a lot of trouble.

My girls.

The thought hit him hard, causing him to fumble the end of his tie and lose the tension in the knot. When had he started thinking of Adelaide as his?

The first time she made Bella laugh? During their confrontation by the river, when she showed her mettle by standing up to him? Or in the barn last week when she wept in his arms? When had it happened?

He frowned at his reflection. Yanking the ends of the tie free, he began again.

When it had happened wasn't as important as what he was going to do about it. And the answer to the second question was much easier to ascertain.

Nothing. He would do nothing about it.

Adelaide Proctor was a lovely woman with a cheerful disposition and a more than capable hand with children. But that was all she was—all she could be.

His parents had always encouraged their sons to marry where their heart led, but that didn't mean there weren't certain unspoken expectations in place. A woman of good family. Refined. Elegant. Upstanding moral character.

Adelaide clearly fulfilled the last requirement. But she was too exuberant to be considered elegant, too whimsical to be refined. And though she was schooled in Boston, her family had no connections to society, no common background that the people in his world would appreciate.

No. She was his daughter's governess. Perhaps even a friend. To think of her as anything more would bring on a host of complications he could ill afford.

Finished with the tie, he tugged his black vest until it lay flat over his waist and adjusted his gold cuff links. Tonight was Bella's night. He'd seen precious little of his daughter over the last few days. The shearing and dipping had consumed his daylight hours, while updating the business accounts monopolized his evenings. And thanks to his worry over how Miss Proctor was faring following the attack in the barn, he hadn't had a full night's sleep in days.

Adelaide hadn't made an appearance at the branding station or anywhere else outdoors since the incident with José. Not that he blamed her, of course. After Ramirez and his crew left, he thought she might venture out again—for a ride on Sheba, if nothing else. But she had cloistered herself in the house.

At least he now had the reassurance that she'd been working with Bella on this party instead of hiding away in a corner somewhere. He'd feel better, however, once he saw her riding again. Perhaps after the celebration tonight he would ask her to join him on a morning gallop down to the river. He could even challenge her to a race. She never turned down an opportunity to show off Sheba's prowess. A fond smile crept onto his face. Adelaide was like a proud mother when it came to that horse. With Bella, too. He couldn't stop himself from wondering if the same loyalty extended to him.

Gideon picked up his black swallowtail coat from where it lay on the bed and pushed his arms through the sleeves. Once it settled comfortably on his shoulders, he smoothed his hair a final time and made his way downstairs.

Miguel sat on a bench in the front hall rubbing his palms along his pant legs. The way his knees jounced up and down, he looked like a skittish horse ready to bolt the instant the reins slackened.

"Steady, man," Gideon said, his voice low. "It's not as bad as all that."

The vaquero lurched to his feet. "Señor Westcott, I no should be here."

Gideon clapped him on the back. "Why not? You're an invited guest."

"But grand parties in the big house? They're for fine gentlemen and fancy ladies. Not hired men who stink of sheep."

Bending close, Gideon sniffed loud and long. "I don't smell anything. Besides, under all these fashionable trappings, I'm nothing more than a sheepman myself. If my daughter invited the two of us, she must not care that we're a couple of herders. Now, stand up straight." Gideon acted as valet and tidied Miguel's clothes. The black frock coat he had lent the smaller man hung loose, but he looked presentable. He evened out the foreman's tie and brushed some lint off his shoulder. "There. Tonight you are in appearance what you have always been in truth—a gentleman rancher."

"*Gracias, patrón.*"

Over Miguel's head, Gideon caught sight of his cook entering from the kitchen. "Mrs. Garrett! How fetching you look."

The woman marched in wearing a green dress that had probably been in fashion more than a dozen years ago, but she blushed like a schoolgirl at Gideon's flattery.

"Craziest thing I ever heard of," she said, pulling off her bonnet. "Inviting servants to a party and not even letting them set out the food. That girl of yours is gonna end up with some backward notions."

Gideon took her hat and hung it on the hall tree, not fooled for a moment by her disgruntled manner. "I rather like the idea. Perhaps this will become a tradition at Westcott Cottage. Once a year, the people who work so hard on this ranch will be rewarded by switching roles for an evening with their employers. Only next time, I'll be joining my daughter in serving you."

A vision of Adelaide serving at his side flashed across his mind. He quickly banished it.

"I tell you, that Miss Proctor sure is a wonder," Mrs. Garrett continued. "She had me fix up a mess of picnic food ahead of time, anything that could be served cold. Roast beef sandwiches, potato salad, coleslaw, boiled eggs and cheese, two kinds of pie, and a chocolate cake."

Gideon smiled. "It sounds as if we are in for quite a feast."

"I spent the last day and a half getting everything together— then she up and tells me to take the afternoon off. She'll set it all out, she says. I should relax and get ready for the party." Mrs. Garrett planted a fist on her hip. "Well, when is *she* supposed to get ready for the party if she's off doing my job as well as hers, I'd like to know?"

Gideon frowned. It sounded as if Adelaide had taken too much upon herself. He should be helping her instead of idly passing time with the rest of the guests.

A throat cleared behind him. "I believe our hostess has arrived," his butler announced.

Chalmers stood at the foot of the stairs, dapper as always in his formal wear. His wife's hand was tucked into the crook of his arm, but her gaze was locked on the small form hovering on the landing.

"She's an angel," the housekeeper declared, and Gideon readily agreed.

His daughter ran her hand along the railing and descended the last few steps as regal as any queen. Her pleated pink satin dress looked familiar, but he didn't recall it having a beaded neckline or a large lacy bow at the side. Bella's curls, usually a bit unruly, were perfectly turned out with twists of pink and white ribbons threaded throughout and gathered at the back of her head with a pretty pink bow. He strode forward to meet her, smiling all the way. When she smiled back at him, his shoulders suddenly felt a little broader, his arms a little stronger. Which was probably a good thing, for in a few years, every young buck in the county would be calling at his door.

Before she reached the bottom of the stairs, Gideon bowed over her hand and pressed a kiss to her knuckles. She giggled and blushed but bowed her head in return. Then, as every good hostess must, she left his side to welcome the rest of her guests. She curtsied to each one in turn and motioned for them to follow her into the parlor. Gideon hung back, content to watch her take charge. He fell in line behind the others. From what he could see through the doorway, the larger furniture had been moved to the walls, leaving a few chairs to rim a large area covered in quilts. An indoor picnic.

The sideboard had been moved in from the dining room and was laden with all the food Mrs. Garrett had described, artfully arranged on silver platters and in crystal bowls. China plates and glass tumblers stood ready to be filled. Adelaide had certainly set an elaborate table. But where was she? She should be here to enjoy the guests' reactions.

A creak on the staircase drew his attention. He backed out of the parlor doorway and turned, expecting to see Miss Proctor in her bright yellow Sunday-best dress—the one that never failed to put a smile on his face when they attended services at the small church in Menardville. However, when his gaze finally found her, the smile on his face slipped. And as he stared at the riveting sight before him, he could neither move nor breathe.

Adelaide in sunshine calico was temptation enough, but Adelaide in starlight and lace devastated his senses. No elegant lady in London could compare.

Her dark chestnut hair had been piled in waves atop her head and decorated with a pearl comb that matched the string at her throat. Slippered toes peeked out from beneath her gossamer skirts as she descended, each delicate step bringing her closer to him. When she gained the floor, he couldn't stop his eyes from traveling over the rest of her as she approached. The dress accentuated her slender waist and feminine curves in a way that inspired very husbandish ideas. He jerked his eyes back to her face and brusquely reminded himself he was a gentleman.

She halted an arm's length away from him, her hazel eyes shuttered by shy lashes. He yearned to close the distance and gather her to him, but he remained rooted in his spot. Just when he managed to get his pulse under control, she tilted her face up and melted her gaze into his.

"Good evening, Gideon."

Good? He doubted any could be better.

Chapter 17

Adelaide's palms grew clammy inside her gloves. When she'd first noticed Gideon watching her, all of her feminine instincts heightened, sure of the appreciation in his gaze. Yet the nearer she came to him, the more her confidence wavered. A gentleman enamored of a lady would hurry to her side, wouldn't he? Gideon never moved. She searched him for a smile as she crossed the floor, hoping to find some evidence of his pleasure. His face offered only a penetrating stare. Now she stood before him, her stomach fluttering, and waited for him to return her greeting. He said nothing.

What if he hadn't been mesmerized by her appearance as she had so arrogantly concluded at first? What if he was appalled by her dressing in a manner so far above her station? What if he was searching for a polite way to ask that she change?

"Isabella insisted that I wear this dress," she rushed to explain, shifting her gaze away from his. "It belonged to her mother. I know I shouldn't have worn ... but it was so pretty ... and yellow ... and she was adamant." Adelaide sighed. What a muddle.

She couldn't slink away and change, though. The party had

begun and Isabella needed her. Adelaide mentally added some starch to her spine. Gideon would just have to ignore her gown if he didn't like it. If he killed her fantasy in the process, well, she'd get over it. She'd worn this dress for Isabella anyway, not Gideon.

Right. Just like she'd gone to Fort Worth to hunt a new teaching position, not a husband.

Doubts continued to spiral in her head, like a whirlwind kicking up dust on the prairie. Then Gideon's strong hand clasped hers. His thumb caressed the back of the fine silk glove she wore, sending delectable little shivers up her arm. He bowed deep and raised himself slowly, capturing her gaze as he did so.

"Miss Proctor, you are truly stunning. I've never been happier for Bella to have her way."

Wanting to disguise the giddy delight that effervesced in her at his words, she tried to affect the sophisticated mien of one accustomed to such gallant compliments but failed miserably. Unable to suppress it for more than a second, she released the jubilant smile that pressed against her lips, not caring if it made her look like a naïve bumpkin. Her hero had just rescued her again. He slew her fears and restored her romantic dreams in a single breath. If that didn't deserve a grin as wide as the Brazos, nothing did.

Gideon released her hand and offered his arm in exchange. "May I escort you in?"

"That would be lovely. Thank you."

Adelaide curled her fingers around his bicep and allowed him to lead. She stepped cautiously, not wanting to catch her toe on the newly basted hem that tucked away the bottom flounce of her dress. However, when they entered the parlor, all thought of the lacy skirt flew out of her head. She and Gideon were the focus of everyone's attention.

Heat crept into her cheeks, yet Adelaide held her head high. She'd never been more proud to be on a man's arm. Gideon was dashing and handsome, considerate and kind—and British, for goodness' sake. All those adolescent years spent sighing over Jane Austen novels, and now she was living one. What could be more delicious than that?

She drank in the moment as long as she could, then released Gideon's arm—and with it, her sentimental fancies. The time had come to grasp her role as hostess instead. She dared not disappoint the young girl who depended on her.

Sweeping into the depths of the parlor, Adelaide smiled at each of their guests and took her place at Isabella's side.

"Ladies and gentlemen, welcome. We are honored to have you join us for our shearing celebration. A wide variety of foods awaits your pleasure. Please fill a plate and have a seat. Or you might prefer to recline alfresco under our imaginary trees." She winked and spread her arms up and out as far as the fabric of her dress would allow. Isabella took her cue and lay down on her side under Adelaide's branches, propping herself up on one elbow.

High-pitched titters and muted masculine chuckles permeated the room. Isabella beamed. When she hopped back to her feet, Adelaide bent to whisper in her ear.

"Why don't you take your father to the sideboard to get things started? I'll direct the rest. Just remember not to help yourself to anything until all of the guests have been served."

Her charge gave a tiny salute, reminiscent of their imaginary army days, and marched up to Gideon. She took his hand and yanked, setting him clumsily in motion toward the food. Adelaide bit her lip to keep her smile under control. What the child lacked in finesse, she more than made up for in enthusiasm. Gideon's twinkling eyes met Adelaide's from across the room, and the two shared a silent laugh. Isabella's party was off to an auspicious beginning.

The lighthearted tone continued throughout the evening. Gideon and Miguel joined Isabella on the picnic blankets while the others perched in chairs nearby. Adelaide longed to join the alfresco crowd, but preserving her borrowed gown took precedence.

So she inquired after Mabel Garrett's coleslaw recipe and smiled at the childhood anecdotes Mrs. Chalmers told on the Westcott boys. Meanwhile, Miguel finally showed signs of relaxing as he and Gideon romped with Isabella. In less than an hour, the stiff formality that had hung over the group disappeared into a hum of friendly banter. Adelaide could not have been more pleased.

They played several rounds of charades, Isabella being by far the most accomplished actor of the bunch. In keeping with their theme, all of the words were things that could be found on the ranch. Isabella's pecking chicken was deduced at once, thanks to her flapping elbows and telescoping neck. However, Mabel's pitchfork proved more difficult. She stood stiff and straight with three fingers poking out from the top her head, but no one could decipher her clues. The group guessed everything from a fence post to a yucca tree. Huffing in frustration, she finally stomped over to her chair, grabbed her icing-encrusted fork from where it balanced on her plate, and held it out until someone named the utensil. Then she pitched it right at Miguel—who dodged the flying prongs yet, at the same time, successfully identified the elusive farm implement.

The only worry came when Chalmers incorrectly concluded that his wife was imitating a whale when in fact she was a delicate little trout. After hurling a decorative pillow at his head, she pouted for several minutes, muttering about his insulting speculation. Adelaide considered halting the game for fear that the housekeeper's feelings had been truly injured, but Mrs. Chalmers avenged herself when her husband took his turn. The minute he lowered himself to his hands and knees to imitate an animal of some sort, his wife gleefully called him every foul name she could think of under the guise of playing the game. *Toad. Skunk. Rat.* Even *louse* made her list until Gideon correctly surmised that Chalmers was nothing more threatening than a barn cat. Fortunately, the butler took it all in stride and laughed along with everyone else, restoring the group's good humor.

For the final entertainment of the night, the ladies folded up the picnic blankets and stacked the dishes while the gentlemen pushed the remaining chairs against the wall, thereby clearing the floor in preparation for blindman's bluff. Amid squeals, shrieks, and shuffling feet, the blindfolded guest had to catch someone and then guess the captive's identity. Adelaide assigned everyone a number so that Isabella could name her hostage by a show of fingers when it was her turn.

Thanks to the small group, everyone had multiple opportunities to wear the blindfold. Chalmers always managed to snag his wife, and after the third time of doing so, she accused him of peeking. He readily admitted to it and whispered something in her ear that set her to blushing. She stopped complaining after that.

Isabella was the easiest to identify, due to her size, but the hardest to catch. Miguel finally wrangled her near the end of the game. She, in turn, latched on to her father. Gideon must have spied her yawn as she removed the handkerchief from her face, however, for he quickly proclaimed that he would be the last blindman.

He groped about for several minutes, growling like a bear and stamping his feet at anyone who ventured too close. Isabella rushed at him and retreated several times, giggling each time he missed. Then before Adelaide quite knew what had happened, the little mischief-maker shoved her from behind and launched her directly into Gideon's path.

Adelaide trod on his foot and banged into his chest, but Gideon wrapped his arms about her and somehow kept them upright.

"Well, who do I have here?"

His voice remained jovial, but she could feel his heartbeat accelerate under her palm. Did he know?

Gideon's hand moved up her back and lingered at the base of her neck. "Definitely feels like a member of the female persuasion." His fingers toyed with the loose tendrils at her nape. Adelaide closed her eyes against the sensations assaulting her.

His touch traveled to her shoulder, and she forced her eyes open. If he knew it was her, why was he taking so long to claim his victory?

"Let me see . . ." He traced one of the rosettes on the edge of her sleeve. "I don't recall Mrs. Chalmers wearing a flower like this." Warmth from his hand shocked her momentarily as he quickly passed over the small section of her arm covered by neither gown nor glove. Calluses grazed her skin, leaving tingles in their wake. "Too tall to be Bella." He explored her elbow, her wrist, and finally clasped her hand where it lay pressed against his shirtfront. "Mrs. Garrett's dress had long sleeves, I believe, so this gloved arm must belong to . . ." His thumb drew a small circle against her palm. "Miss Proctor."

He'd known all along, the scoundrel.

She pushed away from him, afraid they'd made a terrible scene. Gideon let her go. She stumbled back and looked around. No scowls of disapproval or eyebrows raised in offense. She noted a few suspiciously bright smiles but decided it would be better for her peace of mind not to analyze those too closely.

Adelaide checked the clock on the mantel, surprised to see how late the hour had grown. No wonder Isabella couldn't hide her yawns. Adelaide had to stifle one of her own just thinking about it. Once again, her hero came to the rescue.

"Thank you, ladies, for a wonderful evening. I can't remember the last time I had such fun." Gideon bowed to Isabella, who curtsied in return. "I'm afraid I must take my leave, Miss Petchey, but know that the memory of your smile will brighten my days."

Petchey. So that was Isabella's family name. Since learning Gideon was Isabella's guardian and not her natural father, a host of questions had arisen in Adelaide's mind regarding Izzy's parents and how she had come to be in Gideon's care. Now she'd received her first clue.

"And Miss Proctor." Gideon turned to face her, his eyes sparkling with deviltry. "I will always carry with me the memory of your . . . arm."

Isabella snickered. Adelaide snuffed out her sparking curiosity and gave Gideon a playful push. "Get out of here, you rogue."

He backed away, and the others guests moved forward to bid their hostesses farewell, each claiming the party to be a smashing success.

Isabella danced all the way up to her room and pirouetted right into bed. Her sleepy smile never wavered. Adelaide helped her into a nightdress and brushed out her hair, carefully removing the pink and white ribbons as she went. She whispered a prayer over the child, whose eyelids had grown heavy, kissed her forehead, and left her to dream of indoor picnics, boisterous games, and the people who loved her.

Adelaide slipped down the hall to her own room and changed out of the lacy gown. Romantic reveries had their place, but she had responsibilities to attend to now. The party dishes wouldn't wash themselves, and the food would attract ants if left out. She could push most of the parlor furniture back into place, as well, although the sideboard would have to wait until she could enlist some masculine muscle in the morning.

Doing up the final buttons on her calico, Adelaide moved toward the door. The faster she cleaned up the mess downstairs, the sooner she could crawl into bed herself. And like Isabella, she planned to dream of love, laughter, and a handsome man with dark hair and warm chocolate eyes.

With that thought spurring her on, she made her way down to the parlor, rolling up her sleeves as she went. However, when she stepped into the party room, she froze, her thumb still tucked into the folds of fabric at her elbow. The dishes had washed themselves after all. And the food fairies had cleared away every last crumb. The chairs and settees had walked on their own legs back to their proper locations, and even the sideboard had sprouted wings and flown to its home in the dining room. All her work was done.

Adelaide smiled and let her arms fall to her sides. She roamed the room, shaking her head at the evidence before her. Those warmhearted rebels. The servants had offered to help clean up as they made their good-byes, but Adelaide had insisted they not interfere. It was their night off. She would take care of it. But in the short time she'd been upstairs putting Isabella to bed and changing out of her gown, those disobedient dears had put everything to rights.

Including the master of the house, it would seem. Adelaide bent to pick up a white necktie that had fallen along the wall where the sideboard had stood. She held it against her cheek and inhaled the faint scent of Gideon that lingered on the cloth. This place, these people were becoming home to her. Family.

She tucked the necktie into her pocket and climbed the stairs to her room. There might not be any work left for her to do in the parlor, but there was at least one chore she could complete before retiring for the night. Adelaide turned up the lamp on her bedside table and carried her sewing box over to the borrowed gown. With meticulous care, she snipped and removed the basting threads from the lacy hem and used her hand to flatten the hidden flounce back down to its original position. That done, she folded the dress and carried it up to the schoolroom.

Feeling her way in the dark, Adelaide followed the path of the wall until her toe struck the first of the trunks. She laid the dress upon the lid and turned toward the center of the room. Enough moonlight filtered through the windows to outline the furniture. She reached her desk and fumbled in the top drawer for the matchbox. Once she managed to grab hold of one of the tiny wooden sticks that lay inside, she struck the phosphorus tip and lit the lamp. Soon the room glowed with mellow light.

Adelaide returned to the trunks and opened the second one. She sat back on her heels and grimaced. The contents were a mess.

Apparently yesterday's hunt for pretty treasures had been a mite too vigorous. She would probably have to unpack the entire thing to reestablish order. Pushing back up to her knees, Adelaide got to work.

As she refolded the gowns and accessories, she discovered a stationery set and a leather-bound journal. Adelaide set those aside, thinking Isabella might wish to see them. Later, when she closed the lid on the straight-as-a-pin trunk, she carried the paper items back to her desk. Settling into her chair, she contemplated the journal. Perhaps she should place it back in the trunk. If Isabella's mother had recorded confidential thoughts in the book, Adelaide had no right to pry. Yet the words might bring Isabella comfort and give her a way to reconnect with the parent she'd lost. Did privacy really matter when the author was dead?

Adelaide toyed with the ribbon that protruded from the bottom of the book, marking a page near the end. When her father had died, she would have given anything to hear his voice one more time, even through an old letter. Sheba had filled that need for her in many ways, a physical reminder of her father's love. What did Isabella have? If Adelaide could find a kind thought penned in the deceased woman's hand, it could ease Izzy's grief. Wouldn't her mother want that for her?

Nibbling on her bottom lip, Adelaide pulled on the ribbon and opened the book. Only two lines had been scrawled across the top of the marked page, the handwriting so scratchy and weak Adelaide struggled to decipher it. She squinted as she focused on the nearly illegible script. As it began to make sense, her throat tightened in an effort to keep her racing heart from escaping her chest.

If Reginald ever finds Isabella, he will destroy her. Protect her, Lord God, for I know he will come after us.

Chapter 18

Adelaide didn't climb into bed until well past midnight. Even then sleep eluded her. She was too disturbed by what she'd read in Lucinda Petchey's journal. After stumbling upon that final entry, she knew she had to read it all. Forewarned was forearmed, and she was determined to learn every scrap of information she could in order to defend Isabella from whatever danger her mother believed threatened her. Adelaide had read straight through from the first page to the last, not moving from her desk until she had reached the end.

Now she huddled in her bed, trying to recover from the shock of her discovery. Such vile treachery was difficult to take in. Yet once it penetrated, a devastating ache crept through her body. She hugged her pillow to her chest and rolled to her side, drawing her knees toward her stomach. But comfort eluded her. She wept for Lucinda and the evil she'd been forced to endure and whispered prayers on behalf of her soul and that of her beloved Stuart. But most of all, she prayed for Isabella, for protection from the danger that stalked her.

How could God allow such tragedy to befall his people? It was wrong! Oh, she knew he didn't *cause* the death of Isabella's parents. A heart hardened by envy and greed accomplished that feat. Still, God held the power to intervene, to prevent this kind of suffering. So why didn't he?

Adelaide shivered beneath the coverlet, unable to get warm. Every time her eyes drifted closed, she saw the journal pages fan before her and watched Lucinda's elegant, flowing script deteriorate into an illegible scrawl. She hadn't deserved such an end.

Lucinda had started off so happy—a blushing bride with an adoring husband she had affectionately dubbed her reformed rake. Stuart had apparently been quite a rogue in his youth. When he first proposed, she turned him down, telling him she could never marry a man who didn't share her Christian convictions. She expected him to vanish from her life. Instead, he showed up at the chapel she attended every Sunday morning.

At first, she suspected that he only came in order to woo her into accepting his proposal, so she waited for him to tire of the effort. He never did. Weeks later, she discovered that he was meeting privately with the minister. That's when she knew his faith was more than pretense. They married the following summer.

The journal had been full of happy anecdotes and loving sentimentality for dozens of pages. The only dark spot was Lucinda's concern over Stuart's relationship with his brother. Reginald resented the changes in Stuart and blamed Lucinda. Her husband had tried on numerous occasions to explain to his brother about how coming to know Christ had been the true catalyst for his transformation. Yet Reginald refused to listen. He flaunted his wild way of living and began accruing substantial gaming debts. Stuart excused his behavior in the beginning, telling Lucinda that Reginald felt betrayed and was just lashing out. However, when Isabella was born, Stuart stopped paying off his brother's debts. The money wasn't just his anymore. It represented his daughter's future.

For several years, things were better. Reginald seemed to learn restraint, and an awkward peace fell over the family. Then he started gambling again—heavily—and his losses greatly outnumbered his wins. He used guilt, family obligation, and even the argument of Christian charity to wheedle money out of Stuart. His brother had no choice but to cut him off before he ran the family into the ground. He rewrote his will. Reginald would remain the heir and inherit the family title and entailed estates, but all the money would go to Lucinda and Isabella. Stuart bequeathed his brother a generous monthly stipend, but Reginald refused to be mollified. He raged when he learned what Stuart had done. The hunting accident occurred less than a month later.

Adelaide opened her eyes and stared at the darkness. She didn't want to think about such a dreadful thing, but images spawned from Lucinda's terse description played over and over in her mind.

Stuart staggered out of the forest into the clearing where the women were playing croquet. Blood stained the left side of his shirt. I screamed. He reached for me, then fell to the ground. I ran to him. Reginald got there first.

The entry had not been recorded until two months after the event, once the fog of grief had begun to clear, and it marked a decided shift in tone for the rest of the journal. From this point on, the writings consisted of facts and questions and deductive reasoning. Lucinda was no longer keeping a diary of precious memories. She was documenting evidence. Evidence condemning her brother-in-law of murder.

He raced out of the woods, leapt off his horse, and cradled Stuart's limp body in his arms. I remember that when I finally came upon them, the first thing I did was press my hand over Stuart's wound. Which means Reginald had done nothing to staunch the flow of blood before my arrival. Then, every time Stuart tried to rasp out a word, Reginald told him not to talk, to save his strength. It seemed like a caring gesture at the time, but now I wonder if he was afraid of what Stuart might reveal.

There was so much blood, and his chest rattled like the chains of death each time he took a breath. I knew my beloved Stuart wouldn't survive, so I whispered words of heaven in his ear as tears coursed down my face. He closed his eyes and seemed to find a measure of peace amid his pain. Then Reginald gained his attention with a loud promise to take care of me and Isabella. Stuart's eyes shot open, the terror in them unmistakable. My only concern was calming him again, so I didn't dwell on his reaction. However, I have thought of little else lately. Stuart feared for me and our daughter. Even with the rift between the two brothers, my husband would have no reason to fear for our safety unless something had convinced him that Reginald posed a dire threat.

What would be more convincing than a bullet fired into his chest from the barrel of his brother's rifle?

Adelaide moaned and curled into a tighter ball. Cain and Abel. That's what this was. Cain and Abel. She'd known the Bible story since she was a child and understood that jealousy could twist love into hate, even between brothers, but she'd never personally been exposed to such venom. It made her ill. She didn't want to believe it.

If only the journal had been full of emotional rants and wild accusations. Then she could have rationalized that Lucinda's grief had led her to misinterpret the situation. However, the woman's cool logic seemed irrefutable. Even so, Lucinda had no proof, only speculation, and Adelaide considered dismissing the woman's theories for her own peace of mind if nothing else. But she couldn't. Because what the journal revealed next only solidified Lady Petchey's hypotheses.

Lucinda remained at their country home after the funeral, knowing Reginald wouldn't forfeit the excitements of London for long. After he left she and Isabella slowly began to recover from their loss.

Then Reginald returned, claiming his brother's death had

changed him. He charmed the servants, the neighbors, and even the local vicar with his solicitous attitude toward her. They all remarked on how fortunate she was to have such a caring relative to see to her needs. What truly surprised her, though, was that he kept up the pretense in private. So much so that she began to doubt her own conviction that it was all a ploy. Then he started offering to take over her financial responsibilities in an effort to relieve her of the tiresome duty. That's when she knew her first instinct had been correct. He was after the money.

She refused his offer of assistance three times before he finally stopped asking. However, his kindness did not abate, further confounding her. And when she became violently ill a week later, he stayed by her side. Reluctant though she was to accept any favors from him, she found herself relying on his strength more and more as her body turned traitor on her. She vomited off and on for weeks, the cramping fierce and debilitating. Unable to keep any food down, she grew steadily weaker. Her physician diagnosed an inflammation of the stomach and intestines and left her several packets of medicinal powders. The medicine left a bitter taste in her mouth but alleviated her symptoms to the point that she was able to eat again. Yet when the packets were gone, her illness returned.

Lucinda requested her maid see about replenishing her supply of powders, but the maid insisted that she was still mixing medicine into her lady's tea every morning and evening, just as the doctor had instructed her. Lucinda trusted the maid's honesty yet couldn't shake the feeling that something wasn't right. She no longer tasted the bitterness of the doctor's remedy. That's when the maid explained that, according to the viscount, the doctor had recommended returning to the previous treatment. Therefore she had gone back to using the white powders that Lucinda had taken before the physician visited her. According to the maid, the viscount was so worried about his sister-in-law's condition, he had instructed her to increase the dosage every week if there was no evidence of improvement.

Lucinda questioned her maid further and discovered that Reginald had started her treatment roughly the same time as her symptoms first appeared. There could be only one possible conclusion.

Poison.

Lucinda was smart enough not to voice any accusations. If Reginald guessed she had found him out, there was no telling what he might do. Protecting Isabella outweighed all else, and until Lucinda regained a measure of strength, she was at his mercy. Therefore, she kept her mouth shut and simply stopped drinking her tea. She poured it into a potted plant near her bed when she believed no one watched. However, Reginald must have learned of her deceit, for the sickness continued to worsen. She stopped eating altogether then, fearing he had begun adding the poison to her meals. She sneaked down to the kitchens to pilfer food during the night, and occasionally Isabella would smuggle her a treat. But she couldn't stave off the effects.

Arsenic. It had to be. The white powder fit the maid's description. Colorless. Tasteless. It would explain the lack of bitterness she'd noted after the doctor's packets had been depleted. Decades before, arsenic had even been known as the *inheritance powder* by heirs who wished to speed along the arrival of their share of a relative's estate. It was exactly the type of weapon her scheming brother-in-law would choose.

Reginald had murdered her husband and was now killing her. She had to get Isabella away from him. Lucinda had no family with whom to take refuge, no one to protect her daughter when the poison finally won. So she plotted and planned until nearly every contingency was accounted for. God would have to take care of the last detail—to provide a guardian for Isabella before Lucinda breathed her last. She trusted, and the Lord proved faithful. He sent Gideon.

The blackness outside Adelaide's window lightened to a charcoal gray as the early morning sky prepared to greet the sun. The household would soon begin its routine, unaware of the staggering truths she had uncovered while everyone slept. The others would still be delighting in the sweetness of last night's party, and she didn't want to dim their pleasure. But Isabella was in danger. Something must be done.

She might not understand why God had allowed such an atrocity to take place in Isabella's family, but Adelaide grudgingly admitted to herself that he had not abandoned them, either. The hand of the Lord had been at work through it all, fashioning good out of the devastation the enemy had wrought. He helped Lucinda piece together the truth about her brother-in-law and gave her the strength to escape. He provided an able protector in Gideon and a place of refuge where Isabella could find sanctuary far away from Reginald's grasp. And though Adelaide had a tendency to rail at him for being unfair when life didn't work out the way her precious fairy tales had led her to expect, God managed to use her, as well. He led her to the journal and placed an urgency in her soul that didn't diminish even when the hope of a new day crested the horizon.

Exhausted from her sleepless night and heartsore from reading Lucinda's tale, Adelaide pulled the blankets over her head and blocked out the predawn light that filtered through her window, wishing to postpone the inevitable. But her paltry attempt to forestall her responsibility proved about as effective as her blanket at holding back the sun.

Why couldn't she have had another day or two to enjoy the closeness that had sprung up between her and Gideon last night? She could still see the admiration in his gaze and feel his touch on her arm as he teased her during blindman's bluff. Such feelings were meant to be savored, not shoved under the rug after only a few hours. Yet pouting would do no good. The Lord's timing was perfect, and she had to have faith that there was purpose behind it. The cloud that had led her to Westcott Cottage was still hovering nearby. Only now it had darkened to an ominous gray. A storm was approaching, and Isabella was standing directly in its path.

Adelaide pushed herself up and dragged her legs over the side of the bed. She sat slumped for several minutes, her shoulders curled forward and her spine wilted as a prayer tumbled out of her spirit.

"Lord, your ways don't always make sense, but I believe you brought Isabella to Gideon and me for protection. Whatever comes, give us the wisdom and courage to see it through. And if we fail, please intervene on her behalf. Don't allow evil to triumph over her already wounded soul."

With a heavy heart and equally heavy limbs, Adelaide peeled off her white cotton nightdress and slipped into a clean set of undergarments and a loose-fitting ivory wrapper. During their conversations at the party the previous evening, Gideon had hinted that he would be amenable to having her join him for a morning ride down to the river. She had planned to meet him in the stables. Now it seemed better to meet him in the hall. He would need privacy and time to digest the passages she had marked.

Adelaide splashed some water on her face and fashioned her hair into a simple plait. She knew she looked limper than a wrung-out dishrag, but she was just too tired to exert any significant effort on her appearance.

Feeling as if she were walking to the gallows, Adelaide picked up Lucinda's journal, opened the door, and trudged down the long hallway to Gideon's chamber.

Chapter 19

Gideon whistled softly as he buttoned his tan riding trousers. Stepping over to the washstand, he caught a glimpse of himself in the shaving mirror. He shook his head. Twenty-eight years old and he was grinning over a woman like an inexperienced pup. Although, he guessed he *was* inexperienced. The feelings Adelaide inspired in him were stronger than anything he had encountered before. Even now, a thrill vibrated through his bones as he anticipated the two of them galloping over the countryside together. After their ride, she would sit beside him in the grass and they would talk. Perhaps he'd even find a way to hold her hand or stroke the line of her cheek. His smile widened as he reached for his shaving mug and lathered his whiskers.

Visions of Adelaide filled his mind as he scraped the razor along his jaw. She had been so beautiful last night. It was a shame that his servants had been the only ones to see her on his arm. He'd been so proud of her; he would have gladly escorted her to the finest soirees in London.

Gideon toweled away the residual soap lines from his cheeks, chin, and neck and examined his jaw for any places he missed. Satisfied, he fetched his white linen shirt from where it lay draped over the back of a chair, and slid it over his head. He'd just turned down the collar when a quiet rap sounded on his door.

Adelaide. He would have recognized Chalmers's brisk knock, had it been his butler.

"Just a moment."

He quickly fastened the three buttons down his chest and shoved the tail of his shirt into his trousers. Walking toward the door, he snapped his suspenders onto his shoulders and tossed his morning coat over his arm. He didn't want to keep his lady waiting.

The hinges squeaked as Gideon pulled the door open.

There she stood, his little brown-haired pixie. He smiled down at the top of her head for a few seconds before it hit him. Something was wrong.

Instead of her customary split riding skirt and matching jacket, she wore a flowing housedress that hung unbelted and shapeless on her petite form. A single braid reached forward over her right shoulder, its tasseled end caught between her arm and a book that she was clutching to her chest. Bare toes poked out from under her gown.

Her silence worried him the most, combined with the fact that she hadn't looked up at him yet.

"Adelaide?"

She tilted her chin up and his heart skipped a beat. Dark circles shadowed her red-rimmed eyes, and the pallor of her skin drove a dagger of fear into him. He dropped his coat and took hold of her arms.

"You're ill." Not waiting for her to confirm his conclusion, he lifted a hand to her forehead and felt for fever. "I'll send Chalmers for the doctor."

He moved past her, intending to see to the task at once, but her free hand latched on to his forearm and brought him to a halt.

"I'm not sick, Gideon. I'm grieved."

What was that supposed to mean? Had someone died?

"Danger's coming," she said. "We have to protect Isabella." After making that cryptic pronouncement, she shoved the book into his hands.

He frowned down at the slim volume. "I don't understand."

She let out a sigh. "I'm sorry, Gideon. I didn't sleep last night, and I fear I'm not making any sense. Read the passages I marked. Then you'll grasp what I'm trying to tell you."

He held up the book. "Is this what kept you up all night?"

"Yes. I found it in Lady Petchey's trunk when I returned her dress." Her eyes met his. "I can't explain it, but I believe God wanted me to find this journal. You may already know some of what is written there, but I doubt you know all of it. We must prepare, Gideon. He'll come for her."

He was having the hardest time following her jagged thoughts, but her fear communicated itself to him quite clearly. Whatever she'd read had shaken her badly.

"Who will come?"

"Reginald."

Viscount Petchey. Relief flooded him. This he could handle. She didn't know about the court decision and how his guardianship of Isabella was secure. He tucked the book under his arm and placed his hand at her waist. Adelaide looked as if she were about to fall over. He wanted to carry her to the sofa in his room, but that wouldn't be proper. The study would have to do. She needed reassurance, and he planned to give it to her before her worrying made her truly ill.

"Let's go down to my study. I think I can alleviate your mind about this."

She resisted, her feet firmly rooted to the floor. "You should read the journal before we discuss it."

Gideon didn't think there was much need, and she probably wouldn't think so either once she heard what he had to say, but if he didn't give her his word regarding the journal, she probably wouldn't allow him to take care of her. Right now, getting her into a chair was his first priority.

"I promise to read it when we get downstairs, all right?" He nudged her forward, satisfied when she complied.

He'd explain about Petchey first, of course. Then, if she still wasn't convinced of Bella's safety, he would read the journal to placate her. Once he'd assuaged her fears, he'd see that she got the rest she needed.

They navigated the stairs together, Gideon keeping a firm grip on her as she wobbled along. Then he ushered her into his study and directed her to the settee. He slid in beside her, not caring if one of the servants spied him cozying up to the governess. Comforting her was more important to him than his staff's opinions. He wished he could wrap his arm around her and pull her into his side, but he wouldn't flaunt propriety so much as to cause her embarrassment should someone stumble upon them.

"I know about Lord Petchey."

She grabbed his hand, and her hazel eyes searched his. "You do?"

"Yes." He rubbed his thumb over the back of her hand, trying to erase some of her tension. "He contested Lucinda's will and my guardianship, but the courts ruled in our favor. Bella is safe. He can't take her away."

"Maybe not legally, but that's not stopped him before." In the blink of an eye, the soft woman who had leaned against him for strength vanished. Adelaide yanked her hand out of his grasp and lurched to her feet. "He wants the money, Gideon. He's already killed twice to get it. He won't let a court decision stand in his way."

"What do you mean . . . he's already killed twice?" Gideon stood and reached for her, but she backed away.

"I had him fully investigated prior to the trial," he said in a soothing tone. "He's a scoundrel to be sure, but the only crime he's guilty of is trying to cheat at the card table. If he was involved in murder, there'd be rumors circulating. Not even a whisper of such a foul deed was linked to his name."

"That's because he manipulates everything into looking like an accident or illness!"

Accusation flared in her eyes as she turned on him. Why, she was glaring at him as if he were in league with the villain! He didn't know what to make of it. She acted like a scared rabbit one minute and a defiant tigress the next. He blew out a breath. The only thing he knew for sure was that his efforts to comfort her had fallen far short of the mark.

Before he could figure out what to do, she snatched up the book from where he had left it on the cushion of the settee and thrust it at his chest.

"Read the journal, Gideon." She flopped into one of the armchairs with a huff. "I folded the corners down on the most pertinent pages."

He cracked open the cover and began scanning the entries as he sank back down onto the settee. His eyes skimmed over the sentences quickly until his mind caught up and finally recognized what he was reading. After that, he went back and studied each word, absorbing the implications.

A deadly rifle shot with no one to witness the shooting. Arsenic disguised as medicine. No proof to offer the authorities, only the coincidental timing of events and a grieving widow's supposition.

Gideon lost track of time as he pored over the journal. He'd met Lucinda Petchey. She hadn't struck him as one prone to bouts of paranoia or vindictiveness. She'd certainly been frail and desperate to find a protector for her daughter, but everyone on the ship had agreed she was of sound mind.

He set the book down and leaned against the cushioned back of the settee. Staring at the ceiling, he fought against the tremors that rocked through him. If Lucinda's conclusions were true . . . God have mercy.

Adelaide was right. No court dictate would fetter Reginald Petchey. An ocean might not even be big enough to keep him away. Gideon hoped the Lord had a plan, because his gut told him Petchey wouldn't challenge him directly. No, the snake would continue his subversive methods and strike while hidden in the grass. Only God would be able to see him coming, and Gideon would need all the warning he could get.

A soft purring sound arose across from him, drawing Gideon's attention. Adelaide had curled up like a kitten with her head pillowed on the chair arm. A delicate snore rumbled out of her open mouth. His little tigress had succumbed to her exhaustion. Perhaps seeing him read the journal finally gave her the comfort she needed.

He walked over to where she lay and dropped a whisper-soft kiss on her forehead. She trusted him—trusted him enough to let go of her burden once he had a solid grip on it. Warmth spread through his veins. He wouldn't disappoint her.

After tucking the journal away in his desk drawer, he returned to Adelaide's side. She really did need her rest, but she'd end up with an awful crick in her neck if he left her in the chair for very long. A slow smile stretched across his face. He *had* hoped to get her in his arms this morning. Surely nothing could be nobler than carrying a weary woman up to her bed so she could get some proper sleep. He would simply be performing a good deed. His duty, even. And if he happened to derive a great deal of pleasure from that duty . . . ? Well, that was no one's concern but his.

Gideon carefully gathered her into his arms. She moaned and her eyes cracked open for a moment, but she almost immediately cuddled her cheek against his chest and resumed her deep breathing. He could get used to that sound.

When he reached the top of the stairs, he readjusted his hold and carried her the rest of the way to her room. Her door stood ajar, so he pushed it open with his foot and moved inside. Her chamber was a bit disorderly, but a delightful reflection of the woman in his arms—someone more concerned with people than things. The dress she had worn prior to the party lay hurriedly discarded atop a chest in the corner, while school papers littered the top of her bureau. A collection of Bella's artwork sat propped against the mirror on proud display amid a bird's nest of ribbons and bits of lace.

Gideon lowered her onto the bed, thankful that he'd felt no evidence of stays through her gown as he carried her. As soon as he slid his arms out from under her, she rolled over onto her side and grabbed the second pillow. She snuggled the downy square to her bosom and mumbled a few unintelligible words before settling herself. An unexpected tenderness rose within him as he watched her sleep.

Could there be more to his feelings than simple attraction? Something deeper and more lasting? He'd escorted countless debutantes about London in the past, beautiful women who inspired ample appreciation within him for their feminine charms. But none of those women had created the tug of possessiveness he felt when he gazed at Adelaide. None of them stirred this desire to cherish and protect. And no matter how suitable their background and manner, none of them made him smile like his Addie.

Addie. The name fit. Fanciful, whimsical—just like the woman herself. Yet there was strength in it, too. Simple, straightforward strength. He'd known she cared for Bella, yet until her relentless plea this morning, he hadn't realized how deep her affections ran. Gideon couldn't help hoping that some of those affections extended to him, as well.

The blankets were tangled up in a clump at the foot of the bed, so he straightened them and held them aloft. He hesitated to lower the covers, admiring her a second or two longer. But as he did so, his admiration became concern. Perhaps it was the nearly colorless hue of her gown, but she seemed to blend in with the sheets, her face still pale from her upset. She had lost her vibrancy, her zest. A pattern of small golden flowers dotted the ivory fabric of her housedress, but it wasn't enough. He wanted the cheerful, full-blown yellow he associated with her personality. This faded version made his heart ache.

He would fix this. He would. Bella and Adelaide depended on him. Whatever it took, he would see to their protection and ensure their future happiness.

His jaw clenched in conviction as he finally let the covers float down over Adelaide's sleeping form. Gideon pulled the curtains closed against the daylight and turned to leave but came up short. Bella was standing in the doorway, her eyes huge in her tiny face as they darted from him to her teacher and back again.

Gideon held a finger up to his lips and tiptoed to where Bella stood. It wasn't until after he had closed the bedroom door behind them that he recognized the irony of shushing his mute daughter.

She pointed toward the door, jabbing her finger over and over as her eyes pled with him for answers.

"Miss Proctor is fine, sweetheart." He hunkered down in front of her and rubbed her arm. "She had trouble sleeping last night after the party and is very tired. I talked with her in the study this morning, and she fell asleep in one of the chairs. So I carried her up here and put her to bed. Like I do with you when you fall asleep in the wagon during the long ride back from town."

It took a while for her to accept his words. Her reaction reminded him of the day she found Miguel wearing that bloody shirt in the kitchen, only this time, thankfully, it was less severe. That memory triggered another thought: the blood on Stuart Petchey's shirt when he came staggering out from the forest.

Bella hadn't been speaking to him at all when she'd said the word *Papa* in the kitchen that day. She'd been remembering her father's fatal injury. Lord help her. She watched her papa die.

Chapter 20

That same morning, two hundred miles northeast of Westcott Cottage, Reginald Petchey sat tapping his cane against the floor of the Fort Worth Land Office, waiting for Farnsworth to stop blabbing with the squinty-eyed clerk and bring him the documents he'd requested.

The letter Lady Westcott's maid had so kindly supplied them was addressed to *General Delivery, Menardville, Texas*. It would have been easy enough to ask for directions to Westcott's residence from the people in that small town, but he preferred to keep his presence—and purpose—hidden. A British gentleman would stand out like a Thoroughbred among mules in a backward little mudhole like Menardville. And if Westcott should happen to suffer a fatal accident following the esteemed Mr. Edward Church's arrival, it could generate unwelcome suspicion.

Reginald preferred to hedge his bets. With access to the deed and property surveys, he could plot his own course while maintaining a low profile.

"Farnsworth," he called out through clenched teeth, "I'm waiting."

"Coming, sir." His assistant turned, a smattering of documents in his hand and a long paper roll tucked under his arm. As he scurried across the floor, a bell sounded above the door. A well-dressed gentleman entered the office, satchel in hand.

"I have another lien for you to file, Dan."

The clerk waved him forward. "Bring it in, James."

The man nodded to Farnsworth as he passed, then headed to the counter. Reginald ignored him after that, concentrating instead on the survey map his assistant unrolled upon the tabletop. He pushed to his feet for a better view.

"The deed indicates that the Westcott ranch lies 9.65 miles west of Menardville, along the San Saba River," Farnsworth said. "So that would place it about . . ."

"Here." Reginald thumped his cane over the spot. "Make a sketch, Farnsworth."

"Perhaps I can be of assistance?"

Reginald jerked his head around to find the newcomer standing behind him. He bit back an oath and twisted his mouth into a smile. "Thank you, sir. But that won't be necessary. We have all we need."

The man smiled back yet made no move to depart. He had a steady gaze. Friendly, but there was something behind it that bothered Reginald, something firm that indicated this man would not be easily duped or deterred.

"Dan told me you were looking for information on a piece of property owned by Gideon Westcott. I brokered that particular sale and thought I might be able to aid you in your search. James Bevin at your service."

The man extended his hand, leaving Reginald no choice but to shake it. "Edward Church." Bevin looked past him to the table, a question in his eyes. "Oh, and my assistant, Mr. Farnsworth."

"A pleasure." Bevin stared at Farnsworth for a moment, a thoughtful look on his face, then stepped up to the table to examine the map. "So, how do you know Mr. Westcott?"

Reginald mentally scrambled. Refusing to be open would only breed distrust. He had to tell the fellow something. Something reasonable yet neutral enough to discourage further questions.

The letter!

"Westcott's mother is a friend to mine," Reginald said, lacing his voice with an appropriate level of resignation. "When she learned I was soon to be making the journey to America, she prevailed upon me to deliver a letter to her son in person. She expects me to give a full account of his well-being upon my return." Reginald extracted the worn envelope from his interior coat pocket and held it out to Bevin. "You know how women are. Apparently her son has not written with enough frequency to put her mind at ease."

"Ah." Bevin fingered the letter, then returned it. "Well, it's good of you to pay him a call. I hope it's not taking you too far out of your way."

"I don't mind the side trip. I've been enjoying my tour of the American West." About as much as he enjoyed a toothache. The place smelled of cattle dung, and his lungs were full of the dust that hung thick in the air. Yet he grinned like a vacuous tourist, not wanting to give Bevin a hint of his true feelings.

"If you need a hotel recommendation, there is a new one in Menardville called the Australian Hotel. A fellow by the name of William Saunders built it a couple years back. Brought his wife here from Australia, as you might guess from the name."

Wonderful. As if the American colonies weren't bad enough, now the penal colonies of Australia were adding their inferiority to the mix. But the topic of Menardville did give him an opportunity to pursue a line of questioning that might prove helpful.

"I'll keep the place in mind." Reginald drew a circle around the Westcott ranch property with the tip of his cane and tapped it a couple of times as if cogitating a new concern. "I noticed on the map that Mr. Westcott's ranch lies nearly halfway between Menardville and Fort McKavett. Do you know if he conducts his business more in one town than the other?" He shrugged then, as if the answer was of no great importance. "I thought to bring as many details as possible home to his mother. What merchandise the local shops carry, how many churches are in town, the level of refinement, etc. . . ."

Bevin smiled his understanding. "The military fort is practically deserted, although there is a small civilian contingent that has put down roots there. Menardville is the larger community. I happen to know Westcott carries a line of credit at their general store."

"Excellent. I'll make a point to visit there."

Actually, Reginald would make a point to avoid the place like he did his creditors. If Westcott had friends in Menardville, he would go directly to Fort McKavett. He needed to recruit a couple of men who were willing to get their hands dirty, and the fewer in town who knew Westcott, the better his chances of buying loyalty. If he were very fortunate, he might even stumble across someone who disliked the man as much as he did.

His smile widened.

Gideon Westcott wouldn't stand in his way much longer.

Bevin bent over the chart again, his brow furrowing. "This map is not very detailed. I traveled through this area several times while I finalized the sale of Mr. Westcott's property. Would you like me to sketch out a route for you?"

"How generous of you, sir. Thank you." Reginald snapped at his assistant. "Farnsworth, give the man some paper and your fountain pen."

As Bevin began to draw, triumph surged through Reginald, just as it did whenever a respected card player fell prey to one of his bluffs. He'd noted the intelligence in the American's eyes and the confidence in his stance when he approached, but it was the nobility in his manner that Reginald exploited with expert precision. A man like Bevin would assume other gentlemen subscribed to similar values as he himself did. Integrity. Honesty. He wouldn't expect deceit, so he wouldn't see deceit. Not until it was too late.

"Here you are." Bevin handed over a remarkably detailed map, including numerous landmarks. Reginald's satisfaction grew. Little did the man know, he was only making it easier for Reginald to destroy his associate.

"This will be a tremendous help. Thank you."

"My pleasure, Mr. Church. When do you plan to leave?"

"Tomorrow." Reginald's pulse accelerated in anticipation.

Bevin frowned a bit and shook his head. "You'll never manage to acquire decent rail accommodations. I have a contact at the railroad office. Let me make arrangements for your travel. I can have a private car set up for you on the Gulf, Colorado, and Santa Fe Railway in a day's time. You can depart in comfort the day after tomorrow. The train will take you as far as Lampasas, and then you can rent a carriage for the remainder of the trip."

Reginald massaged the side of his head to alleviate an imaginary headache while he weighed his options. The sooner he could get to Westcott, the sooner he could return home with his niece. On the other hand, a private car would go a long way to soothe his nerves and his stomach while on the train. He could afford an extra day.

"You are a man of great insight, Mr. Bevin. A private car is exactly what I need. We are staying at Clark House. You may leave the information at the desk. Once again, I am in your debt."

"Think nothing of it." Bevin dipped his chin in a subtle bow. "I'm afraid I must be off. I have some other business to attend to. You will have the details within the hour. I wish you and Mr. Farnsworth a pleasant journey."

Reginald heard Farnsworth mumble his thanks from somewhere behind him as Bevin collected his satchel and exited the office.

What a fortuitous meeting. He'd been given a map, a private rail car, and key information regarding Westcott's habits. His luck was finally turning. And why not? He held a hand that couldn't lose. All he had to do now was eliminate the other player at the table and collect the pot. Isabella and her trust were as good as his.

Chapter 21

Over the next two days, Adelaide hid her concerns from Isabella and endeavored to go on as if nothing had changed. She didn't want Isabella to sense her alarm. Adelaide feared that if she did, the child would withdraw again and undo all the progress they had made. The poor girl had been through enough already. She was too young to do anything about the situation, so Adelaide reestablished their educational routine and concentrated on helping Isabella master her letters and numbers while secretly trying to master her own apprehension.

Taking a seat behind her desk, Adelaide eased the top drawer open and removed the small pocket Bible she kept there. Searching for something to anchor her, she flipped through Psalms until a line in the fifty-fifth caught her eye. *Fearfulness and trembling are come upon me, and horror hath overwhelmed me.* The verse reflected her personal turmoil so completely that she knew she had to read the entire passage. Adelaide went back to the beginning and drank in the words. The author faced a deadly foe, as well, one whom he had previously considered a friend. Even so, he had confidence in the

Lord's salvation and called out to him in full trust. And at the end, he seemed to reach through time to speak directly to Adelaide's heart. *Cast thy burden upon the Lord, and he shall sustain thee: he shall never suffer the righteous to be moved.*

God was worthy of her trust. Adelaide believed that with all her heart. But at the same time, she couldn't completely dispel her worry. She couldn't ignore the fact that the same God who rescued Daniel from the lions allowed Stephen to be stoned. The God who shielded the infant Moses did nothing to spare the lives of hundreds of other Hebrew babies murdered by the Egyptians. What if Isabella was one of those other babies?

Her parents had been righteous, godly people, and they had died at Reginald Petchey's hand. So far, the Lord had provided escape for Isabella, but who could say that would continue? Christ never promised that his people wouldn't suffer. In fact he warned them to expect it. What he did promise was to be with them, giving them strength and courage to overcome. But what if she didn't want to overcome? What if she just wanted Isabella to be safe?

I know I have to leave this in your hands, Adelaide prayed, *but I beg you to protect this child. Please.*

Adelaide glanced up and studied Isabella as she counted out her sums with a pile of dried beans. Surely no natural mother could love a child more deeply than Adelaide did Isabella. Only God could love her more. And that was what she had to trust in. That and the fact that Reginald Petchey was far away in London. She hated to admit it, but at the moment, Adelaide took more comfort in that bit of geography than anything else.

Needing to be close to her charge, Adelaide got up from her desk and circled around behind Isabella. She watched her take a handful of pinto beans from the Mason jar on her tabletop, and just as Adelaide had shown her earlier, she counted out the number of beans for each numeral in the simple addition problem, then pushed the beans together and counted the total.

Adelaide quickly scanned the previous answers written in child-ish scrawl next to the appropriate piles of beans.

"Good work, Izzy," Adelaide praised. "You answered all of them correctly."

The girl's smile lit up the dim room, pushing back the after-noon shadows. Adelaide grinned in return and patted her pupil on the shoulder.

"As a reward for such excellent problem-solving," Adelaide announced, "you may either choose a story for me to read or we can play with the alphabet blocks."

Isabella dashed off to make her selection while Adelaide fun-neled the counting beans through her fingers and back into their jar. After cleaning the slate and putting the items away on the shelf, she joined Isabella in the center of the rug, alongside a jumble of wooden blocks.

"Let's see . . ." Adelaide lowered herself to the floor and exam-ined several cubes, turning each over in her hand until she found the letters she wanted. "How about U-N?" She placed the blocks together on the carpet. "U and N make the sound *uhn*, like in the word *sun*. What letter should you use with U-N to make the word *sun*?" She emphasized the first consonant, hissing as she pronounced the word.

Isabella began digging through the blocks, setting aside the C and the S as she found them. Her gaze bounced between the green S and the yellow C while her face screwed up in concentration. Adelaide could guess her dilemma. The yellow C looked more like a sun, but the green S was the better choice for the sound. Finally, Isabella reached for the S and pushed that block next to the other two.

"Perfect!" Adelaide clapped her hands. "Can you make the word *run*?" She removed the S block and sat back to give Isabella plenty of space.

They continued the process for *bun* and *fun*, but when they got to *gun*, the sound of pounding hooves approaching the house caused both teacher and student to look up.

"You continue working, Izzy. I'll see what it is." Adelaide pushed to her feet and strode over to the window.

A single rider dismounted in the yard near the stable. He seemed familiar. Miguel rounded the corner of the barn, rifle in hand, but once he saw who it was, he set his weapon aside, propping it against one of the corral posts. He held out his hand to the man, and the two shook a hearty greeting.

The visitor gestured toward the house as he spoke and turned just enough to give Adelaide a good view of his face. Mr. Bevin! Happiness bubbled inside her. She'd only known him a few days as they traveled from Fort Worth, but he'd been kind to her. It would be a pleasure to have his company again.

"I believe we'll be having a guest for dinner." Adelaide turned back to her charge and smiled. "Why don't you straighten the schoolroom while I inform Mrs. Chalmers about the new arrangements?"

Isabella nodded, and Adelaide glanced out the window again in time to see Miguel pick up his rifle and bolt into the stable. *Odd.* He should have seen to Mr. Bevin's horse first. Even from inside the house she could see the animal's heaving sides and the lather on its chest and neck. Her throat tightened. Mr. Bevin had ridden awfully hard. What had driven him to such haste?

Before she could begin to speculate, Miguel burst out of the stable astride a sorrel gelding. He galloped out of sight, heading north—the same direction Gideon had taken after lunch when he left to inspect his flock.

Good news could wait. It was the bad that demanded to be imparted right away.

Adelaide reminded herself not to jump to conclusions. She calmly sauntered out of the room, ignoring the hoydenish compulsion to pick up her skirts and sprint down the stairs. Her pulse raced ahead as she forced her feet to maintain their painfully decorous pace. Once she'd located the housekeeper, she asked her to set an additional place for supper and then strolled outside to greet their guest.

Mr. Bevin was no longer standing in the yard by the time she stepped off the porch. Most likely he was giving his horse a good rubdown in the stable. Adelaide crossed the expanse of packed dirt separating the house from the horse barn and paused at the large double-door entrance. Disturbing memories sent shivers down her arms. She rubbed her hands over her sleeves to dispel the unwelcome feeling.

This wasn't the same. It might be early evening, as it had been the last time she'd walked into the stables alone, but this wasn't the same situation at all. Her hands didn't recognize the difference, though. They trembled something fierce as she tried to secure several stray hairs the wind had blown free from her pins.

Mr. Bevin wouldn't hurt her. The very idea was ludicrous. She had nothing to fear by going in there. The shearing crew had departed long ago. The only men around belonged to Gideon, and she trusted them. So why was it so hard to step across the threshold?

Adelaide stamped her foot against the dusty ground. There were bigger issues at stake than her skittishness. She didn't know what was wrong, but she cared too much about the people here to let a little thing like bad memories keep her from finding out.

With her chin jutted out at a defiant angle, Adelaide surged into the stable and let the familiar scents of horse, hay, and leather envelop her—smells that had comforted her since her childhood. Breathing deeply, she gathered her courage and moved forward. About halfway down the alley, she spotted a sawhorse pushed against the outer partition of one of the stalls. A saddle she didn't recognize sat atop it.

She peeked around the corner. "Mr. Bevin?"

The towel he'd been rubbing along the horse's flank stilled. He straightened and turned to greet her, a smile of welcome spreading across his face.

"Miss Proctor! How lovely to see you again. You're looking well."

"Thank you, sir." She bowed her head to acknowledge the compliment. "And what a delightful surprise to have you pay us a visit. Have you come to check up on me?"

He chuckled softly. "No, my dear. I don't doubt for a moment that you are exactly what Gideon needs." He winked at her and turned back to his horse.

Had he meant that the way it sounded, or was she reading more into the innocent comment than was warranted? A little flutter of pleasure wobbled through her at the thought of him approving a match between her and Gideon. Of course, he might simply have been referring to her fulfilling Gideon's need for a governess. Adelaide decided not to press him for clarification. She'd rather preserve the possibility that her initial interpretation was valid than to be disappointed should he not confirm it for her.

Flustered by her mental digression onto the unmarked path of romantic potentiality, it took her a moment to regain her bearings.

"I apologize for not being better prepared for your arrival. Mr. Westcott neglected to mention your visit. I do hope you'll be staying for a while."

An enigmatic look passed over his face, and he seemed to speak more to himself than to her. "I'll stay as long as Gideon needs me." He gave his horse a firm pat and moved out of the stall. His facial muscles eased as his charm returned in full force. Mr. Bevin tossed the rubdown rag aside and offered her his arm. "I apologize for catching you unaware," he said as he led her back to the entrance. "Gideon didn't know of my plans, either, but it couldn't be helped. An urgent matter has come up that requires his attention. I could not delay."

Adelaide hated tiptoeing around in conversations, but it really wasn't her place to ask for more information. Gideon deserved to hear the news first. Yet the unsettled feeling that gripped her earlier only intensified as they walked through the doorway.

Once in the yard, Mr. Bevin swung his gaze north. Adelaide followed the direction of his eyes and spied a small cloud of dust moving toward them. Gideon would be here soon.

"You must be thirsty after your long ride," Adelaide interjected into the silence. "Mrs. Garrett set out a jug of apple cider for supper this evening. I'm sure I could convince her to sacrifice a glassful on your behalf."

He brought his attention back to her face. "Thank you. That would be refreshing."

She nodded and made her way to the kitchen. Mabel grumbled about not having enough cider to go around after serving it to men who lacked sufficient manners to wire ahead that they were coming, but she eventually handed over the jug. Adelaide purposely dawdled, keeping an eye on the yard through the window as she took a glass from the cabinet and dribbled liquid into it. She waited until Gideon rode up and dismounted before pushing the cork back into the cider jug. If she timed it just right, she might pick up a clue as to what the problem was before the men disappeared into Gideon's study to discuss their business.

Walking as quietly as she could manage, she crept up behind Gideon as he clasped his friend's hand. Mr. Bevin never glanced her way, his gaze focused solely on her employer. The charming gallant man had been replaced by one on a mission. A distinctly unpleasant mission, judging by his expression. Adelaide felt the glass of cider in her hand begin to quiver.

"Miguel told me there was trouble," Gideon said without preamble. "What's happened?"

"Reginald Petchey is in Texas, Gid. He's probably no more than a day or two behind me."

The glass slipped from Adelaide's grasp and shattered upon the unforgiving ground.

Chapter 22

Gideon spun around at the sound of glass breaking behind him. Adelaide stood there, eyes wide, jaw slack. She'd obviously heard James's comment. She rallied quickly, though.

"How clumsy of me. I'm so sorry, Mr. Bevin. I'll fetch you another glass."

"That's not necessary," James assured her.

Adelaide waved her hand in the air, undeterred. "Nonsense. You've ridden a long distance. You must be parched. Let me clean this up, and I'll be back in a trice."

She bent down and began picking up the fragments of glass. The jagged edge of a larger piece pricked her palm, and a drop of blood oozed out. The red blared against her fair skin.

Gideon crouched down beside her and dumped the offending shards from her hand. He dug in his vest pocket for a handkerchief, which thankfully he'd not yet had reason to use, and pressed the clean white square against her wound.

"I'll take care of it, Adelaide. Go back to the house and tend your cut."

"It's just a scratch. I'm fine." Her voice resonated barely above a whisper, yet it was laced with iron. She shoved the handkerchief back at him and reached for the bits of glass.

Stubborn woman. He scowled at her, then unfolded the handkerchief, draped the cotton over his cupped hand, and silently demanded a compromise. If she insisted on clearing away the glass, he would at least make sure she didn't cut herself again. She glared at him but complied.

When all the pieces had been gathered, he set the handkerchief on the ground and tied the corners together. As he finished the knot, she laid her hand atop his and grasped his fingers.

"I want to hear what Mr. Bevin has to say, Gideon." Desperation and determination reflected equally in her eyes.

He swallowed hard. She wasn't going to like his answer. He didn't even like his answer.

"I know you do, but your place is with Bella now."

She shuttered her gaze and averted her face, favoring the ground more than him at the moment. He could feel her disappointment in him, and it stung. But she wasn't his only concern right now.

"James and I will be closeted in the study for a long while sorting out this predicament, and if you aren't there to distract Bella and help her understand what is going on, she'll become frightened. She can't tell us what she's feeling or ask questions, and I'm afraid she will bottle everything up inside her again, like she did when her mother died. I need you to guard her spirit for me. Can you do that?"

Gideon dipped his head, searching out her eyes. When he finally found them, tears were glistening in their depths. Adelaide bit her lip. He could only guess what it cost her to nod agreement.

At her acquiescence, he started to stand, but all at once, her grip on his hand tightened. "Don't leave me in the dark, Gideon. Please. I have to know what's going on or the worry will drive me mad." Her whispered plea cut at his heart.

He glanced at James. The man had turned his back and taken up an avid interest in the barn swallows nesting in the eaves of the stable. Thankful for the pseudo-privacy of the moment, Gideon returned his attention to Adelaide. He cradled her face with his free hand and rubbed away a teardrop that hung suspended from her dark lashes. "You're my partner in caring for Bella. I won't shut you out. I promise." He locked his gaze with hers and repeated his vow, willing her to believe in him. "I promise, Adelaide. I'll show James the journal and get his opinion, but I'll discuss everything with you, too. Trust me?"

"Yes."

He stared at the lips that formed that sweet word and nearly bent forward for a taste. Unfortunately, sanity prevailed. Taking hold of her, he rose to his feet and brought her along with him.

"Everything will be all right. You'll see." Gideon squeezed her arm and watched her go, the makeshift pouch of glass shards dangling from her hand. He prayed his prediction would prove true.

"Sorry." James threw the apology out into the silence left in Adelaide's wake. "I didn't see her there. I should have waited until we were assured privacy before I said anything."

Gideon turned to his friend and clapped him on the back. "It doesn't matter. I'd end up telling her about it anyway."

James raised an eyebrow. "A servant? I know she's your daughter's tutor, but surely you don't intend to confide such personal information with one of your staff."

"Miss Proctor is more than a servant around here, and I'll thank you to speak of her with respect." Indignation heated Gideon's temper until he noticed the twinkle in his friend's eye. "You old goat. You're baiting me, aren't you?"

James grinned.

Gideon grinned back, not caring how much his friend read into that smile. Ever since the night of the party, he'd been slowly losing his grip on his resolution to ignore his attraction to Adelaide. Her passionate concern for Bella only expedited the process. He was beginning to think elegance and refinement were overrated. Who wanted staid and proper when they could have warm and spirited?

Adelaide's imaginative nature and uninhibited cheerfulness filled his house with laughter and sunshine. And he'd been affected by it as surely as his daughter. A man would be a fool to forfeit such a treasure.

"I'm thinking about asking her to be my wife once this mess with Petchey is over and we get the chance to spend more time together." Gideon waited for shock to register on James's face, seeing as how even in America class distinctions were rarely breached in such a manner, but the man simply crossed his arms over his chest and gave him a glance that looked downright smug.

"You don't seem surprised."

"I'm not." He winked. "You can thank me later."

"Thank you? What for?"

"For bringing you two together, of course."

Gideon gave James a shove. "You're worse than an old woman. Don't you have anything better to do than to sit around matchmaking?"

James shoved him back. "You complaining?"

Gideon shook his head and a slow smile stretched across his face. "No."

"Good. Ungrateful cur."

The two men shared a chuckle. Then Gideon's smile faded.

"Come into the study, James. I have something you need to see. Then I want to hear everything you know about Petchey and his plans."

James nodded, and the two headed into the house.

An hour later, James set Lucinda's journal on the desk and leaned back in his chair, his mouth pulled down in a grim expression.

"What do you make of it?" Gideon asked.

James stared at the ceiling and blew out a long breath. "I don't want to credit it, but I've met the man, and I have to admit her accusations fit my impressions of him. He's a scaly fellow who knows how to sprinkle enough charm over his lies to make them palatable." He jabbed his index finger against the cover of the journal. "If he wanted to commit murder, this is precisely the underhanded way he would go about it."

"So what do you think his goal is in coming here?" Gideon rubbed his forehead, the ache inside his skull building. "Lucinda's will has been ratified. The man can't just snatch Bella and run off with her. No court would acknowledge his claim, and the bankers are fully apprised of the guardianship stipulation. They won't release funds just because Petchey is a relative."

"I hate to say it, Gid, but . . ." His voice faded away as if he couldn't bring himself to form the necessary words.

"What?" An ominous weight pressed against Gideon's chest.

James finally met his eye. "As the closest relative, it stands to reason Petchey would inherit the money should Isabella die."

"No!" Gideon surged to his feet. "She's a child, an innocent. Surely you don't think . . ."

But after reading Lucinda's journal, he knew the idea was not so farfetched. The viscount had already killed his own brother and sister-in-law. What was to stop him from murdering his niece, as well?

James came near and gripped his shoulder in silent support. In that moment, Gideon's fear hardened into steely determination. A predator was threatening his family. He had to prepare.

"Tell me everything you can about him, James."

The two men sat. James scratched a spot behind his ear and stared at the wall as he recalled the encounter. "Petchey called himself Edward Church, and had I run into him anywhere other than at the land office, I probably would have accepted that false identity without question."

"Why didn't you?"

"Well, there were several subtle nuances in his story that raised my suspicions." James leaned forward toward Gideon. "First, when

I arrived, the clerk mentioned that the two men had been asking to see your deed records as well as survey maps of Menard County. He thought I might be able to assist them in whatever quest they were undertaking. When I introduced myself and inquired after their purpose, Petchey was ready with a logical explanation. He claimed his mother was a dear friend to yours, and when Lady Westcott learned of his plans to tour the American West, she requested that he deliver her letter to you personally and then return with a full and detailed account of your situation. Naturally, being a gentleman, he could not refuse such a request and was at the land office to ascertain the best way to travel to your ranch. Showed me the letter and everything."

"He must have intercepted a missive somehow." Gideon tapped his thumb against his knee. "So he knows my location."

"I'm afraid so."

"And you're sure this Edward Church is actually Petchey?" *Please, God. Let it not be him.*

James nodded and Gideon's heart sank.

"There was something about him that struck me as odd," his friend explained. "It wasn't until after I started putting the pieces together that I realized I recognized him from the photographs of Isabella's parents. He bears a striking resemblance to his brother. But even this could have been a coincidence. It was his solicitor who provided the truth."

"His solicitor?"

"Yes. A fellow by the name of Farnsworth. Sound familiar?"

Gideon rifled through the documents in his desk, the documents James had delivered on his last trip out to the ranch. "Farnsworth . . . Farnsworth . . . Aha. George Farnsworth." He stabbed at the signature on the bottom of the fifth page. "He's the barrister who filed Lord Petchey's motion to have Lucinda's will invalidated."

"Exactly."

That couldn't be coincidence. Edward Church and Reginald Petchey had to be one and the same.

"What can you tell me about him as a man?" The more he could learn, the better prepared he would be.

"It appears he's a bit taller and heavier than his brother, Stuart, but not gone to fat as one would expect from a wastrel who spends all his time at the gaming table. Apparently fox hunting has kept him fit."

"Which means riding horseback across three counties won't be a problem for him." Gideon frowned.

"No," James answered, "but I bought us as much time as I could without making him suspicious."

Gideon met his friend's eye, intrigued by the sly smile creasing his face.

"Being the thoughtful gentleman that I am," James explained, "I arranged for a private railroad car on the train that left the day *after* mine and even drew him a map overflowing with detailed landmarks."

"A map? That was a bit too helpful, don't you think?"

"Not when it recommends a rather circuitous route and is littered with markers generic enough to add a great deal of confusion along the way." He winked. "Unless he procures better directions from someone on the trail, we should have as much as two full days before he arrives in the area."

"Good thinking." Gideon rapped his knuckle against the wooden arm of his chair like a metronome clicking out a steady rhythm. "That still doesn't leave us much time before he gets here."

"I'm not sure he'll come here directly."

Gideon stilled. "Where else would he go?"

James rested his elbow on the corner of the desk. "I can't be sure since he was careful not to reveal his intentions, but he left me with the impression that he wanted to gather as much information about you as possible before making his move. He knows that your ranch lies between Menardville and Fort McKavett, and he made a point to ask me which town you conducted the majority of your business in. With his use of a false name, I'm guessing he's not planning to confront you directly."

Gideon mulled over all he knew from their previous investigation and added it to what James had just revealed. He stood and began pacing as he cogitated aloud. "He's been patient with his schemes in the past, but the fact that he traveled all the way from England tells me he's getting desperate. His creditors must be applying pressure after the court ruled against him for guardianship. He has nothing left to put them off with. Time is a luxury he can no longer afford."

Gideon slowed his steps as another possibility took shape in his mind. "Perhaps he actually plans to avoid the town where I am known and make his stand in a place where he can garner support more easily."

"It would fit what we know of the fellow," James said. "Likes to stack the odds in his favor."

"True." Gideon reached the edge of the settee and pivoted to make the return trip across the study floor. Then he paused and glanced up at his friend. "I suppose you told him that I manage my affairs through Menardville."

James shrugged. "I saw no reason to lie. He'd discover the truth himself with a few well-placed questions, so I thought it wise to appear cooperative."

"Manipulating the manipulator, huh?" Gideon grinned at the irony.

"I like to think I have a few tricks up my sleeve."

"We're going to need every advantage we can get." Gideon's hands clenched into fists. He needed a way to anticipate his enemy's moves in order to outmaneuver him. As it stood now, he didn't know how or when Petchey would attack. Only that he was advancing steadily. Such ambiguity made it virtually impossible to launch his own offensive.

That left him with no option but to fortify his defenses and try to plan for every eventuality. If he was lucky, Petchey would make a mistake and leave himself vulnerable. When he did, Gideon would strike.

"I'll bring in as many men from the pasture as I can spare," Gideon said, "and use them as guards around the house and on the roadways. They'll take shifts throughout the night, as well. First thing tomorrow, I'll ride into Menardville and ask some of the local proprietors to keep their eyes open for Petchey."

"Can you trust them?" James asked.

"They are pillars of the community. They won't be swayed by the viscount or his money. They certainly weren't impressed with my title when I purchased the ranch. I've had to prove myself and earn their respect. They'll follow through. If anyone sees or hears anything about Petchey, they'll get a message to me."

"Good. What about Fort McKavett?"

"The people there are hurting economically from the fort's closing, so they might be more susceptible to a bribe." Gideon frowned. "There's no telling how many men we might be up against."

James rose to his feet and crossed to where Gideon stood. "I'll stay as long as you need me," he vowed, gripping Gideon's shoulder. "Everyone will pitch in. You know they will. Your men are loyal, and the household staff will help, too. From what you've told me about Miss Proctor, I have no doubt she'll guard Isabella like a mother bear watching over her cub."

It was true. Adelaide already loved the girl with a mother's devotion. She would likely give her life for Bella. But that was part of the problem. How could he adequately protect those he loved from a threat he wouldn't be able to see until it was upon them?

"God help us, James."

"He will, Gid. He will."

Chapter 23

When Reginald Petchey entered the dingy saloon on the outskirts of Fort McKavett, a hush fell over the dozen or so patróns who graced the establishment. *Graced* being a charitable description. The ragtag bunch looked as filthy as he did after two days in the saddle, only they seemed comfortable with the condition while he silently counted the minutes until his man secured a bathing tub in some rustic chamber so he might remove the grime from his person.

Curious stares followed him as he made his way to the bar. One grizzled fellow with a bulging cheek glared at him from where he stood with his boot propped against the bar's foot rail. Without a word, he let fly a stream of brown juice that missed Reginald's trouser leg by the barest of margins.

"Yer blockin' the spittoon, gent."

Reginald raised a single brow and looked down his nose at the offender. For a brief moment he indulged himself with the image of stuffing the abhorrent wad of goo in the man's jowls down his throat, yet he resisted the impulse. He was there for a reason.

Alienating these men wouldn't serve his purpose, no matter how much pleasure it might afford him at the moment.

"I beg your pardon, sir." Reginald bowed to the man, swiping the black bowler from his head with a flourish. "May I offer you the use of my hat?"

The unshaven man didn't hesitate. With a disdainful gleam in his eye and a well-practiced squeeze of his cheek, he spat a second stream directly into the bowler's crown.

The card players seated at the nearest table guffawed. Reginald joined in, playing up the role of merry old Englishman.

"I say! The chap's got marvelous aim."

"Yeah, Jeb can hit a dime at twenty paces," one of the gamblers boasted.

Reginald offered a buffoonish grin and slid into a vacant seat at the card table. "What a remarkable skill. Is he equally talented with a pistol?"

"Was," Jeb answered for himself, "until a renegade Comanche plugged my shoulder full o' lead back in '78." He tossed the soiled hat onto the floor near Reginald's chair and demonstrated his expectoration prowess by launching another round of spittle across the five feet or so separating the bar from the table. It splatted dead center once again.

The mention of Comanche renegades inspired a round of stories, each bloodier than the last as the men recounted the glory days of Indian wars on the plains. Reginald feigned horrified interest as he deftly shuffled the deck of cards that was passed to him and dealt himself into the game.

Careful to lose frequently enough to preserve the good spirits of the group, he gently probed for information about marksmen in the area who might not have qualms about getting their hands dirty if the price were right.

Thirty minutes later, he hadn't made much progress. His pockets were about twenty dollars heavier, but he was still light on names. He had just drawn a pair of queens when a swarthy Mexican stumbled into the saloon.

"José's back," the man seated across from Reginald observed. A collective moan rose up from the group.

"If you ain't got coin, I ain't servin' you, José." The barkeep called out the warning, but the Mexican continued on.

"I pay." He slapped a silver coin onto the bar and downed his shot of whiskey the instant it was poured.

Reginald eyed the man speculatively. "Why so uncharitable to the hapless fellow? I thought it was a code of the West to buy a man a drink if he is short on funds."

"We did the first time or two." The man seated to his right pushed a pair of cards at the dealer. The dealer replaced them with new ones, and the man arranged them in his hand as he answered. "But we got tired of him going on and on every night 'bout how some fancy English sheep rancher ruined his life over an uptight señorita."

In the midst of exchanging two of his own cards, Reginald nearly dropped the queen of spades the dealer handed him. English sheep rancher? From what information Farnsworth had been able to unearth, Reginald was almost certain that Westcott ran sheep.

"How dreadful." Reginald spoke loud enough to ensure that José overheard. "I'd hate to think a countryman of mine was responsible for this man's misfortune."

In an instant, the dark man appeared at his side waving a wicked-looking blade under Reginald's nose. Chair legs scraped against the hardwood floor as the men at the table separated themselves from the altercation.

"You sound like him. Maybe you bleed like him, too—eh, *hombre*?"

"Settle down, José." The card player closest to Reginald held his hands out, trying to placate the Mexican. Yet it did no good.

José jabbed his knife at the man and then turned his attention back to Reginald.

"Any friend to Westcott is enemy to me."

The knife slashed within an inch of Reginald's cheek, but he didn't flinch. In fact, the corners of his lips twitched as he fought a grin. Too elated to be afraid, he stared at his opponent and sized up his potential. Not only had he found a man willing to use violence to get his way—he had found one who already held a grudge against Westcott. A perfect combination.

Three revolvers cocked simultaneously from across the table. All barrels pointed at José's chest. Gone were the jovial old men who had spun yarns to pass the time. In their place were men with flinty eyes and steady hands. Perhaps their tales of adventure held more truth than Reginald had originally believed.

"Unless you want that whiskey you just threw back to be your last, I suggest you put the knife away," the barkeep called out, brandishing a shotgun of his own.

José's eyes hopped from man to man around the room, and he tightened his grip on the hilt of his blade. Reginald needed to take matters into his own hands before someone did something stupid and put a hole in his new henchman.

"Gentlemen, gentlemen. There's no cause for such a show of weaponry. No harm has been done. The man is simply venting some frustration."

Reginald turned to address José directly. "I'll make you a deal, sir. You put the knife away, and I'll buy you a bottle of whatever liquor you choose. We can share a drink while you explain what happened between you and the English rancher. I know of this Westcott fellow, though I've never met him personally, and if he has wronged you, I believe I can help set things right."

The Mexican wavered, his brow furrowed. "You let me keep the whiskey?"

"Of course, lad."

Finally the man nodded and sheathed his blade. The room released its breath as pistols were uncocked and returned to their holsters. Conversations picked up where they had left off, and the card players scooted their chairs back up to the table.

Reginald nodded to his gambling compatriots. "Thank you for allowing me to join your game this evening, gentlemen. Perhaps I'll be able to continue this another time." He hated abandoning three perfectly good queens, but holding on to José was worth more than a piddling poker pot.

After purchasing a bottle and removing to a back table, Reginald poured two fingers of whiskey for himself and his prospective business partner. He saluted with his glass and dumped the cheap booze down his throat. The liquor tasted like brimstone and felt as if it were burning a hole in his gullet. Reginald forced it down and refilled both glasses before passing the bottle to his companion. Once José tucked a few more shots under his belt, Reginald ventured his first question.

"What did Westcott do to bring you so low, my friend?"

José caressed the neck of the brown bottle with his hand. "Huh?"

Reginald bit back an oath. "Westcott. What did he do to you?"

"What he do?" José turned his head and spat upon the floor. "I was champion shearer of my village." He thumped his chest with his fist. "The crew bosses, they pay me top wage to work for them. I shear a hundred sheep a day and always win prize for most fleeces."

He poured another drink, sloshing some of the liquid onto the table. His eyes narrowed and his mouth grew taut as he lifted the glass to his lips. With a jerk, he downed the contents. "Now no crew hire José. El capitán, he listen to the gringo and believe his lies. He say I attack the woman, but her eyes asked me to come."

"Who was she? A servant? Westcott's wife?" Reginald didn't

think the woman important, but one never knew for sure. Better to hedge all his bets.

"A teacher for his *niña*."

Isabella.

Reginald leaned across the table. "Did you see the child?"

"Sí. A little mouse. She never say a word. But the woman . . ." He rubbed his mouth with the back of his soiled hand. "She say plenty." José let loose with a string of rapid Spanish that Reginald could not understand. However, he had no trouble interpreting the vigorous disdain behind the barrage.

It was only José's rediscovery of the whiskey bottle that slowed him. He hoisted it to his lips, his aim slightly off target, and downed a healthy swig. "She wanted José, but Westcott, he charged in like a bull." José's gaze shifted toward the wall. "His men, they hold me down while he beat me with his fists. Then he locked José up like a criminal. *No es correcto.* I do nothing wrong!"

He started to lift the bottle to his lips again, but his mouth twisted into a satisfied grin as the bottle thunked back onto the table. "Those gringos, they not smart enough to hold José. I pretend to be sick," he said, and then proceeded to demonstrate the horrifying retches and moans he'd apparently used to great effect.

"Quite clever," Reginald interrupted before the shearer managed to spew the contents of his whiskey-logged stomach in actuality.

"Sí. Clever." José tapped the side of his head, missing his target the last time and nearly impaling himself in the eye. Reginald bit back a sigh. The things he had to put up with to keep his hands clean.

"The night deputy, he open the cell to check on me," José continued, "and *bam*! I grab him and throw his head against the wall. He fall, *inconsciente.* I take a horse from the saloon and ride. The dumb gringos know nothing. They think I go back to Mexico, but they're wrong. I been here a week, planning my *venganza.*"

José seemed far more intent on planning how to get his next

drink than plotting vengence, but Reginald kept his opinion to himself.

José slurped down another gulp of whiskey and leveled a pair of bloodshot eyes on Reginald. "That gringo pig stole my work and my honor. I make him pay." He slammed the whiskey bottle onto the table, sending a shower of droplets onto the back of Reginald's hand.

Reginald took his handkerchief and wiped away the splatter, careful to veil his disgust for the man across from him.

"Westcott stole from me, as well," Reginald said as José lifted the bottle again, "and I aim to exact retribution. How would you like the chance to pay him back for all the pain he's caused you?"

José halted the bottle's progress halfway to his lips. Anticipation rushed through Reginald's veins as he waited for his words to sink into the man's sotted brain. When the light finally dawned, it was a beautiful, unholy gleam. Then, all too soon, it dimmed into a glower of frustration.

"You think I not have my own plans?" The bottle fell back to the table. "I don't need you, señor. Westcott will feel the stab of my blade in his back without you."

Reginald stifled a groan. The fool's pride was ridiculous. The man had done nothing since his arrival besides drink himself into a sea of self-pity. Most likely, the closest he'd come to plotting his revenge was dreaming of Westcott's demise while he slept off his liquor. Nevertheless, Reginald had dealt with flunkies like José before. They tried his patience but were easily controlled and expendable—two keys to a successful scheme if one could assure their loyalty.

"I don't doubt your ability for a minute, my good man. But wouldn't you rather gain some coin for your pocket while achieving this vengeance?" Reginald reached inside his vest and extracted a double eagle. With a flip of his wrist, he pitched the twenty-dollar gold piece onto the table.

José's jaw hung slack as the coin spun and wobbled, the spiral vibrations tapping louder and faster with each revolution. The crescendo built in speed and pitch until the coin suddenly stopped. The shearer stared at the gold piece with eyes as large as the coin itself.

"You see, I have a score to settle with Westcott. He has something that belongs to me. Therefore, I propose we join forces. I'll pay you handsomely for your time . . . and devise the perfect strategy to effect our revenge. You, sir, will carry out that strategy and avenge your honor."

José finally looked away from the coin and met Reginald's gaze. His lips curled up in a snarl of a smile that bared both his yellowed teeth and his vengeful soul. Satisfaction flared in Reginald's chest.

"We both get what we want," Reginald purred, "the destruction of Gideon Westcott."

Chapter 24

Adelaide gripped the pony's lead line and walked the animal in a wide circle around the paddock.

"You're doing fine, Izzy."

Her young pupil clung to the saddle horn with both hands and stared intently at the pony's mane, not daring to let her gaze venture farther up than the animal's ears. Nevertheless, her lips curled into a smile at her teacher's praise. Adelaide clucked to the gray pony from her place at the center of the circle and tapped the animal's flanks with the end of the lead to keep her moving.

Mr. Bevin, James, as he had instructed her to call him, looked on from just outside the corral fence, one foot braced on the bottom rail. She couldn't see it from where she stood, but she knew a loaded rifle sat somewhere nearby, probably propped against one of the posts. None of the men moved about the property unarmed of late.

It had been four days since James rode onto the ranch to warn Gideon of Reginald's impending arrival. Adelaide had expected the viscount to show his face before now. After all, he was in a hurry to gain control of Isabella's funds, wasn't he? Yet there had been no word of him. She wanted to believe that the confusing map James had given the man had led him off course and caused the delay, but Gideon seemed to think it more likely that the villain was holed up somewhere plotting his attack.

A hotheaded Petchey would have been bad enough, but a patient, calculating one caused gooseflesh to sprout on her arms despite the warm sun shining down on her. Adelaide rubbed her sleeve with her free hand and tried to erase the chilled feeling. Forcing the fear aside, she concentrated on Isabella.

"Try to relax a little, and let your body move with the pony's gait, sweetheart. It'll make it easier for you."

As she slowly pivoted in the center of the pony's circle, Adelaide met James's eye. He lifted a hand in greeting. She nodded in return. Gideon had ridden out to check on his sheep following the noon meal, and as had become his habit, he insisted that James take over guarding her and Isabella. She was thankful for his protection but felt a bit stifled by her lack of freedom. What she wouldn't have given for a long, hard gallop over the countryside with Sheba. Even for an hour. Constantly pretending to be strong and unafraid was wearing her out. But she didn't want to let Isabella out of her sight. Giving the girl horsemanship lessons was as close as she'd get to riding for a while.

She gazed at the girl and pony, trying to envision a vigorous romp through the countryside. The pair trod by her at a breakneck crawl. Adelaide sighed.

God felt farther away than ever.

It didn't make sense. She hadn't stopped praying. Truth be known, she'd probably prayed more than she'd slept in the last week. Yet the comfort she sought remained out of reach. It was as if her petitions were sticking to the ceiling of her room. Not only couldn't she hear God, she was starting to wonder if he heard her.

Just then, the faint sound of an approaching rider caught her attention. James's, too, apparently—for in an instant, he had his rifle cocked and tucked into his shoulder. Adelaide lunged forward and pulled Isabella off the pony. She masked her alarm as best she could, but the young girl still trembled and clung to her, digging her fingernails into Adelaide's neck.

"You did a fine job with your first lesson, Izzy." Adelaide carried her across the paddock toward James. "I'm so proud of you. Why don't we see if Mrs. Garrett has finished baking that batch of ginger-snaps? Maybe we could bribe her into letting us sample them."

Isabella gave no indication that she heard. Her eyes remained fixed on James and the rifle. Adelaide jostled her a bit and tried again, but the child paid her no mind.

A high-pitched whistle carried toward them on the breeze. Adelaide squinted in the direction of the incoming rider, fighting the distance and the afternoon glare to identify the man. James lowered his weapon. He placed his thumb and forefinger into his mouth and returned the shrill greeting. Isabella covered her ears and hid her face in Adelaide's neck. The loud noise that frightened Isabella had the opposite effect on Adelaide. Relief melted over her. Gideon's men were the only ones who knew to signal ahead with a whistle. Friend, not foe, approached.

"That must be Juan coming in from his shift watching the road. All's well, ladies." James winked at them, obviously trying to break the tension. Adelaide offered him a halfhearted smile, but Isabella kept her head burrowed against Adelaide's shoulder.

"We were just on our way to the kitchen to pilfer some ginger-snaps." Adelaide was pleased with her light tone, although it was about as authentic as James's wink.

"Tell you what," James said. "If you promise to bring me a cookie, I'll put the pony away for you. Sound fair?"

"What do you think, Izzy?"

She refused to look up. Adelaide glanced at James and shrugged. His eyes mirrored her concern.

He reached out and teasingly poked Isabella's ribs. "You're not planning on eating them all, are you?"

She arched away from his touch but managed to shake her head *no* in answer to his question.

"We'll be sure to bring you some," Adelaide promised.

She pried Isabella's hands away from her neck long enough to set her on the top rail of the fence so that she might duck between the slats and gather the girl back into her arms from the other side. Isabella held fast to her until the moment the kitchen door closed behind them. Then she let loose with a tantrum the likes of which Adelaide had never seen.

Isabella writhed and kicked. She pounded Adelaide's back with her fists while grunting and screeching in her ear. The girl's head tossed from side to side until her skull rammed into Adelaide's chin. The force of the blow knocked Adelaide's teeth together, pinching the soft tissue of her tongue. Stunned by the sudden pain, Adelaide dropped the girl. That didn't halt the outburst, though. Isabella scrambled to her feet and began pummeling Adelaide's ribs.

"What on earth . . . ?"

The cook sounded as incredulous as Adelaide felt. Their quiet, timid child had turned into a hellion in the blink of an eye.

Adelaide struggled to pin the girl's arms down without hurting her. Having lost the use of her hands, Isabella struck out with her feet. A particularly sharp kick collided with Adelaide's shin. She winced. At least Isabella was giving rein to her emotions rather than withdrawing again. But it was hard to concentrate on that blessing when her leg, chin, and ribs throbbed from the little imp's abuse.

"Isabella. Stop!" Her tone demanded obedience, yet Adelaide hugged her charge close as she barked the order, trying to convey compassion as well as authority. She knew the incident outside had brought this on, but they couldn't address it until Isabella calmed down.

The struggling abated, so Adelaide loosened her grip. "I know you're upset, sweetheart. Let me explain what hap—"

Isabella pushed away from her and glared. She held up her hand as if it were a puppet, tapping her fingers together like a talking mouth. Her own lips mimicked the movement until she smacked the makeshift puppet down with her opposite hand. Then she shaped her thumbs and forefingers into guns and set about shooting up the kitchen with imaginary bullets. For the finale, she stomped her feet a couple of times, crossed her arms over her middle with enough force to bruise her own ribs, and slouched against the back of the nearest chair with a high-pitched grunt that seemed to put an exclamation point on whatever it was she was trying to say.

Adelaide was pretty sure she'd gotten the gist of it. Isabella didn't want to be soothed with meaningless talk. She wanted to know why the men were carrying guns. Demanded to know, actually.

"Mrs. Garrett?" Adelaide's eyes remained on Isabella as she addressed the cook. "We promised to bring Mr. Bevin a sample of your gingersnaps, but I'm afraid we'll be delayed. Would you mind taking him some while I have a word with Isabella?"

"What? Oh . . . cookies. Yes, well . . . I suppose so." It took the bewildered woman a moment or two to reorient herself. She looked at the wooden spoon in her hand as if she couldn't remember how it had gotten there. Then, with a shake of her head, she set it aside, placed the lid back on the pot of beans she'd been stirring, and gathered a handful of the brittle cookies. She wrapped them in a napkin and headed for the door.

"There's more in the canister if the child wants 'em." She nodded toward the japanned coffee canister on the shelf behind the table and went outside.

Adelaide scooted one of the kitchen chairs out from the table and sat down. She waited for Isabella to follow her example, but the child maintained her petulant stance. The teacher in Adelaide wanted to take her to task for her deplorable behavior, but the mother in her just didn't have the heart for it.

"Sit down, Izzy."

The girl continued to scowl, but she grudgingly unlaced her arms and took a seat. Unshed tears glistened behind the anger in her eyes. Adelaide inhaled slowly. She was going to have to tell Isabella the truth. A child-sized version, of course, but the truth, nonetheless. It was the only way to help her understand what was going on. She released the air from her lungs and breathed a prayer out with it.

Help me not to tell her too much or too little. Give me the right words to lessen her fear.

"Do you remember your uncle Reginald?"

Isabella nodded, her mutinous expression reluctantly giving way to curiosity.

How did one go about explaining to a child that her closest living relative was a scoundrel who was coming after her for the sole purpose of taking control of her money? It would break her heart. He was her uncle. She probably trusted him, a weapon the viscount wouldn't hesitate to turn to his advantage. If he ever managed to sneak past their defenses and get to Isabella when she was alone, he could easily lure her away without her putting up the least resistance.

Adelaide hardened her resolve. Isabella needed to be on her guard.

"The night of the party when I returned your mother's dress to the trunk, I found a book. A book your mother had written her thoughts in."

Isabella's face scrunched up in confusion.

"She wrote about you and your father and about how much she loved you both. She sounded so happy, Izzy. One of these days I'll read that section to you." Adelaide smiled, but Isabella just squinted at her as if she were speaking a foreign language.

"There were other stories in this book, too," Adelaide hurried to explain. "Stories about your uncle Reginald."

Finally, the glazed look in the girl's eyes began to recede. She flopped her elbows onto the table and rested her chin on the heel of her hands.

"Your mother found out that he did some bad things, and she

didn't want him to be your guardian. That's why when she got so sick, she gave you to Gideon. She knew he would be a good father to you. He would love you and protect you and do whatever was necessary to take care of you." Adelaide leaned forward and brushed a wisp of curly hair off Isabella's forehead. "Do you think your mama made the right choice? Has Gideon been a good father to you?"

Isabella dipped her chin in affirmation, but her brow wrinkled. She pointed her fingers like a gun again and shook them at Adelaide.

"I'm getting to that part. Be patient." Adelaide's chair legs scraped the floor as she moved closer to Isabella. She took the girl's hand and patted it.

"The men around here are carrying guns because Gideon told them to. He is protecting you."

Isabella squeezed Adelaide's hand while her eyes asked why.

"Your uncle Reginald has come for you, Izzy. He's in Texas."

The girl gasped softly. Adelaide nodded confirmation.

"Gideon is afraid he might hurt you. That's why he asked the men to carry their guns. He loves you too much to let your uncle steal you away."

Her charge looked stunned, and Adelaide wondered how much she really understood. She was only five years old. Too young to comprehend Lord Petchey's depravity.

Adelaide patted her skirt, then held open her arms. Isabella didn't hesitate. She curled up in Adelaide's lap and nestled her head beneath Adelaide's chin.

"You don't have to be afraid, sweetheart." Adelaide stroked her hair. "Gideon and I are watching over you. We won't let anything bad happen to you. God is watching over you, too."

Isabella sat forward and pointed a finger toward heaven.

"Yes. God." Adelaide grabbed Isabella's finger and kissed the tip. "Do you know what I do when I feel frightened?"

Isabella shook her head.

"I pray. Just like we do before you go to bed, only I do it wherever I happen to be. Sometimes I pray when I'm on Sheba. Or when I'm in the schoolroom. Or even when I'm teaching you to ride your pony."

Adelaide nodded at the question in Isabella's eyes. "Yes, ma'am. I was praying today while you were riding in circles around me." She made a show of leaning back and looking both ways for lurkers who might be eavesdropping.

"Don't tell anyone," she whispered, "but I was a little afraid of the guns, too. That's why I prayed. You can do the same thing. God wants us to share our troubles with him. He loves us and doesn't want us to be afraid. In fact, he'll give us courage if we ask him."

That truth fell out of her mouth without her mind thinking it first. When she heard the words, she realized they were as much for her as for Isabella. She had spent so much time petitioning God to change particular circumstances—to give her a husband, to give her life direction, to protect Isabella from her uncle—she had never once asked for courage. No wonder she was such a mess. She'd been so wrapped up in the physical outcomes she wanted, she'd neglected to ask for the spiritual blessings she needed. That was going to change.

With new conviction in her heart, Adelaide slid out from under Isabella and stood up. "How about some of those gingersnaps?"

Isabella grinned and nodded. Adelaide had just opened the canister when Mrs. Garrett pushed through the door, huffing and puffing.

"Another rider coming in," she said between breaths.

Adelaide stepped out the back door and turned toward the sound. She recognized the horseman. It was Gideon, and he was coming in fast.

Chapter 25

Gideon reined Solomon to a halt and leapt from his back before the dust had a chance to settle.

"Juan!" he called to the man who had just emerged through the bunkhouse doorway. "Grab a fresh mount. I need your help in the upper pasture."

The shepherd jumped to obey.

"What's going on?" James moved alongside him as he strode toward the shed.

"Thirty head of sheep were slaughtered—that's what's going on." Gideon threw the door open with enough force to send it crashing into the wall. Fury burned in his belly at the carnage he had stumbled upon. When his boundary fences had been cut last month, he'd assumed the culprit was just a disgruntled cowman letting off steam. But this was different. This attack was without conscience.

Gideon closed his leather-gloved hand around a large tin of ointment. The surviving sheep would require treatment. He barreled back out of the shed and narrowly missed plowing into James, who had to sidestep to get out of his way.

"Hang on, Gid." James laid a hand on his arm, but Gideon jerked away from him.

"There's only a few hours before sundown. I have to go." Anger clipped his words as he tromped over to his horse and flung open the flap of his saddlebag. He stuffed the ointment inside and yanked the leather flap down into place.

"And what if it's a trap? Have you thought about that?" James shouted at his back. "If this is Petchey's doing, you'll be playing right into his hands by going out there. This could be a ploy to lure you away from Isabella so he can make his move."

Gideon let out a breath and turned to face his friend.

"Yes," he said. "I considered that possibility, but I don't believe Petchey's behind this. We had a similar incident over four weeks ago. Someone cut the fence and harassed the sheep in almost the same location. Most likely the fellow returned, emboldened by his previous success, and things escalated. Last time we lost a dozen ewes when the villain fired several rounds into the air, frightening the flock. This time he perched in the branches of a big oak and shot them for sport. I found spent casings scattered over the ground near the tree trunk closest to the first carcass. He used my stock for target practice."

Gideon clenched his jaw, not trusting himself to say anything more.

"I agree it's despicable," James said, "but what if it's not the same person? Are you willing to take that chance?"

"No. I'm not. That's why I came back to get Juan." As if saying his name had conjured him, the herder exited the stable with a dun mare plodding along behind him. Gideon nodded as Juan gathered the reins and swung awkwardly up into the saddle. Unlike their counterparts who worked the cattle ranches, Juan and the other pastores were more accustomed to being on foot with their flock than on horseback. However, when the situation called for urgency, they could manage with sufficient skill.

Gideon turned back to James. "I already patched up the fence with splices of tie wire, so I'll just stay out long enough to help Juan dispose of the carcasses. I'll leave him with the flock tonight to tend injuries and protect them from further threat. In the meantime, I'm trusting you to watch over my girls. I pray to God I'm not making the wrong decision, but if I am, you'll have to stand between Isabella and her uncle until I return."

"I'll stand with him."

Gideon swiveled at the sound of the feminine voice.

"Adelaide?"

He hadn't heard her approach and had no idea how much she'd heard.

"He won't get past us, Gideon." She stood before him, spine stiff, determination etched into her beautiful face. "Isabella can hide in the schoolroom. She understands some of the danger now, and I'm sure I can convince her to cooperate. I can handle a weapon, too, if need be. My father made sure I could hit what I aimed at."

The thought of her in a gunfight made his throat constrict. He fisted his hands at his sides to hide their shaking. What was wrong with him? He couldn't leave her behind to fight his battles. He'd rather lose his entire flock than risk losing her and Isabella.

Then again, James would protect them, and they would be safe inside the house. His sheep would be out in the open and vulnerable to predators attracted to the bloodied remains of the ewes that had been shot. Juan wouldn't be able to drag off all those dead animals on his own before dark, which would leave him exposed. Juan's jeopardy was guaranteed. Adelaide's was only a possibility.

Besides, he'd done a thorough search of the area when he first happened upon the scene. All evidence indicated that whoever had done the shooting had cleared out. Even if Reginald was behind the massacre—and Gideon still wasn't convinced that he was—the man would need to post a lookout in order to know when Gideon was occupied with cleaning up the mess. Few trees grew large enough in that area to conceal a man, and Gideon had checked each one. He had found no evidence of anyone being there except the shooter who left bullet casings and footprints around the big oak.

"An hour or two is all I need." He wasn't sure if he was trying to reassure Adelaide or himself. "I'll be back for supper." It was the only way he could help both her and Juan.

James continued to frown but accepted Gideon's decision with a sharp nod. He swung his rifle up onto his shoulder and took a step toward the house. "I'll keep watch from the front porch and ask Chalmers to keep an eye on the rear from the kitchen."

"The schoolroom windows offer a fine view from the third floor," Adelaide offered as James walked away. "I'll watch from there."

"Adelaide, I . . ." Gideon didn't know what to say, so he just stared at her. She should have been depending on him—not the other way around. Helplessness churned in his stomach. He needed to be in two places at once. But he couldn't. His hands fisted at his sides as he searched for an adequate excuse. Adelaide didn't seem to require one, though. She looked at him without a hint of censure, as if she understood his predicament and approved his choice. Her trust calmed the storm raging inside him and strengthened his resolve.

Juan's saddle creaked as he leaned forward, drawing Gideon's attention.

"I go check on my ladies, patrón. I meet you by the *arroyo pequeño, sí?*

Gideon waved him on. "Sí." He and Solomon could catch up easily enough, and Gideon knew the herder was anxious to check on the animals. Juan urged his mount into a gentle lope, and Gideon turned back to Adelaide. His chest grew tight.

"I don't want to leave you, Adelaide. Even for a short time. If something were to happen to you or Bella—"

"Hush." She stepped close and laid her fingers over his lips. A shiver coursed through him at the delicate touch.

"Nothing happened yesterday or this afternoon when you left us to see to your sheep, and nothing's going to happen now. You're doing the right thing."

Her belief in him vanquished the doubts lingering in his mind. Her words were exactly what he needed. *She* was exactly what he needed.

He gently covered her hand with his, wishing he could feel her soft skin through the rough leather of his work gloves. He dragged her fingers down from his mouth and cradled them against his chest. His gaze never left her face. Her breath caught in her throat, but she didn't look away. Fingers splayed, her palm pressed against the thin cotton of his shirt, directly over his heart. In that moment, he knew she belonged to him.

Gideon cupped her cheek and pressed a light kiss to her forehead. "Stay safe, Adelaide," he murmured against her hair. "No matter what happens, stay safe."

Not waiting for a response, he set her away from him and mounted Solomon. He nudged the horse into motion and headed north without looking back. His mouth tightened into a grim line. An hour. He'd give Juan an hour. Then he was coming home to take care of his family.

One hour, however, blurred into two as the thirty head of slaughtered sheep he'd originally estimated ended up closer to fifty. Gideon worked beside Juan to drag the remains to a mass grave at the base of a shallow arroyo, but when the sun dipped low in the sky, Gideon sent the herder to gather the stragglers and tend to the injured while he finished the unpleasant task of disposing of the lifeless bodies.

Blood and dust clung to his clothes, mixing with the sweat from his labor. The stench of death clung to him and clogged his nostrils. It was such a waste. Such a senseless waste. He pulled off his hat and wiped his brow with his sleeve as he peered into a western sky that was reddening with the approach of sundown. He needed to get back.

Gideon's purposeful stride ate up the distance between him and his horse. The length of rope he'd been using still hung from Solomon's saddle horn. He picked up the end of rope from the ground and wound it over his hand and elbow to form a loose coil as he walked. When he reached the horse's side, he unknotted the rope from around the horn and was strapping it in place on the saddle when Solomon's ears suddenly pricked. His head swung west, the opposite direction of Juan and the flock. Gideon patted Solomon's neck and slid his rifle out of its sheath. He turned and searched the landscape for danger, but the sun's glare blinded him. If the shooter had returned, he was clever enough to position himself with the sun at his back.

Tugging his hat brim low over his eyes, Gideon scanned the areas that would provide the greatest cover. Off to the left stood an outcropping of rocks. Gideon tightened his grip on the rifle. A movement caught his eye, and he yanked the weapon to his shoulder. He peered down the barrel. The rear half of a dark horse stuck out from behind the rocks, its tail swishing the air. Juan had said the first fence cutter rode a painted horse with white markings. What he could see of this one was solid black. Cold dread sunk like a stone in Gideon's gut.

"Adelaide." The whispered name fell from his lips at the same instant a gunshot echoed off the rocks.

Chapter 26

Searing pain exploded in Gideon's abdomen. He staggered back and instinctively clutched his midsection. Something thick and warm oozed over his wrist. As if in a dream, he pulled his arm away and looked down. A red stain spread across his blue-checked shirt.

Before he could fully grasp what his eyes were telling him, the crack of a second shot jerked him out of his stupor. He ducked and scrambled for what cover he could find. A scraggly mesquite stood ten feet away, and though its trunk was barely the width of his hips, it was better than nothing. A third bullet ricocheted off the ground in front of him as he dashed behind the tree.

Gideon thrust his left shoulder against the mesquite and turned sideways to give his enemy a smaller target while he fought to catch his breath. He swung his rifle into position, gritting his teeth against the stabbing pain that accompanied the movement. Thoughts of Adelaide and Bella drove him as he steadied the barrel on a branch. If he didn't stop the demon here and now, they would be his next targets.

Sweat trickled down his brow, near his eye. He swiped it away.

Gideon blinked several times in an effort to clear his vision as well as the haze in his mind. He felt himself weakening as blood seeped from his body. *God help me. I can't fail my girls.*

The firing ceased, and an unnatural quiet stretched between the combatants. Gideon closed one eye and peered down the barrel of his rifle, praying for the man to step into the open.

"I know my bullet hit your flesh, gringo. Are you dead yet?" Gideon clamped his jaw shut and remained silent, hoping to lure his enemy out from behind the rocks.

"The Englishman, he want you dead. But me? I want you to suffer like you made me suffer." He accented his words with another shot.

Gideon yanked his head back behind the tree trunk. The bullet struck a branch to his left, snapping the narrow limb. Gideon flinched as bark fragments spattered his face. He steeled himself, then returned to his position, his finger poised upon the rifle's trigger.

He recognized the shooter's voice. The shearer who'd attacked Adelaide. But he was supposed to be in jail. Why had no one warned him the man had escaped? Gideon gritted his teeth and forced his anger down. How José escaped didn't matter. He was here now—and had evidently met up with Petchey. Gideon could think of no other Englishman who wanted him dead. But where was the viscount? Had he gone after Bella, or was he waiting for his lackey to report that Gideon had been dispatched in the same manner as his sheep?

At least Gideon could take some comfort in the fact that Petchey had come after him and not Bella. There was a twisted sort of hope in that. Maybe the man was not so depraved that he would kill his own niece for money. However, with Gideon dead, Petchey could claim both Bella and her inheritance.

Unacceptable. There was no way he'd allow Bella to live with the man who'd killed both of her parents. The money didn't matter beyond the fact that it was Bella's inheritance, and he'd vowed to safeguard it for her future. But if it meant keeping his daughter out of Petchey's hands, he'd sign the funds over in a heartbeat.

Gideon shut his eyes and grimaced, fighting a wave of dizziness and self-recrimination. He'd been so sure that Petchey was not behind the slaughter of his sheep, and now look at him. He glanced down at the mess that was his shirt. Abdominal gunshot wounds were nearly always fatal, and this one throbbed like the very devil. Gideon bit back a moan and jerked his chin up, away from the grisly sight. It might be too late to stop Petchey from successfully completing the first stage of his plan, but Gideon was determined that Bella wouldn't pay the price for his stupidity.

He turned his eyes to heaven. *God, I won't argue against your taking me on to glory, but I need you to hold off for a little while. All I ask is for enough time and strength to get home and put things right before you send your angels after me. Please. I need to protect Bella from Petchey. Help me.*

Suddenly eager to end the standoff, Gideon called out to his attacker, hoping to goad him into making a mistake.

"I see you're still a coward, José. Ambushing me just as you ambushed my daughter's governess in the barn. I should have killed you that day."

"You think you're better than me, gringo? Which one of us is bleeding, eh?"

"It's only a scratch. I could still wipe the floor with you. Just like last time. The only creatures you're capable of killing are defenseless sheep."

"Shut your mouth, Englishman," José barked back. "I will have my venganza."

Gideon smiled over the tension in the shearer's voice. He was reaching the edge of his control. All he needed was a final push to topple him over the edge.

"Revenge is big talk for a small man, José," Gideon yelled through the mesquite branches. "Why didn't you challenge me when you first escaped if you were so bent on vengeance? You weren't clever enough to do it on your own, were you? No, you needed an *Englishman* to plan out your attack and line your pockets with enough gold to give you courage. You're nothing but a worthless, cowardly—"

A roar of outrage drowned out Gideon's words. José leaned away from the rocks and fired shot after wild shot in rapid succession. Gideon held his position despite the bullets peppering the tree around him and squeezed the trigger. José crumpled to the ground with a howl.

Gideon flicked the Winchester's finger lever to eject the spent cartridge and cocked the hammer for the next shot as he watched his enemy scramble to his feet. The man's right arm hung limp at his side. Gideon fired again, but his shot ricocheted off the rocks as José dove behind the cover. A moment later, the black horse surged away from the outcropping, José riding low on his back. The report of Gideon's rifle echoed three more times before the man was out of range, but no other shot found its mark. Gideon scowled and clamped his teeth in frustration as he dropped the rifle from his shoulder. At least the fellow wouldn't be able to hold a weapon for a good long while. It wasn't the outcome he'd wanted, but it would have to be good enough.

With the immediate danger past, the pain in Gideon's abdomen magnified, demanding his full attention. He groaned and sagged against the tree. The rough bark scraped at his shirt as he slid slowly to the ground. The landscape blurred. He ground his teeth together and fought the lightheadedness that assailed him. He couldn't pass out. He still had to get back to Adelaide and Bella. His job wasn't done yet.

Gideon grabbed the top of his shirt with both hands and ripped it open. Buttons popped and fabric tore, but he was finally able to assess the damage. Blood oozed from a dark hole above the waistband of his trousers. He tugged a handkerchief from his pants pocket and shoved it firmly against the wound, hissing at the agony the pressure created.

A sound to the east brought his head up. He held the hand-kerchief in place with his left hand and snatched up his rifle in his right. He drew his knee up to support the barrel of the gun and waited.

A rider came into view bouncing all over the saddle. Gideon let the rifle fall at his side. Juan must have heard the shots.

When the herder came abreast of him, he tumbled off his mare and rushed unsteadily to Gideon's side.

"Patrón, you bleed!"

"I know." Gideon's dry response was lost on the hired man.

Juan knelt at his boss's side, his eyes scouring Gideon's midsection. When their eyes finally met, Gideon found very little hope reflected in the other man's face.

"It looks bad, señor."

"It . . . feels bad, too."

Juan tried to smile, but the contortion looked more like a wince. He stripped out of his shirt and fashioned a bandage of sorts. Gideon sat forward as Juan wrapped his middle and tied the ends of the sleeves tightly around the handkerchief he had placed over his wound earlier. The binding was so tight he couldn't take in a full breath, but it hurt too much to breathe deeply anyway, so it was a sacrifice easily made.

Gideon glanced around for Solomon, not surprised to find the beast gone. He undoubtedly took off at the first gunshot. He was a smart horse, after all. Gideon sighed. "Help me to your horse, *amigo*. I need to get home."

He held out his hand. Juan clasped his forearm and leaned back. Fire shot through his middle. Gideon grunted and tried to curl forward to protect his stomach as Juan hefted him to his feet, but it felt as if the jarring motion were tearing him in two. It took all the self-control Gideon possessed not to scream.

Juan supported his weight and allowed Gideon to gulp several breaths before steering him toward the mare.

Gideon reached Juan's horse without collapsing and took encouragement from that accomplishment. He gripped the cantle for balance as Juan slipped out from under his arm and moved behind him.

"You ready, patrón?"

Wishing he had a strip of leather or even a stick to bite down on, Gideon set his jaw and nodded. He lifted his left foot into the stirrup, grabbed hold of the saddle horn, and tried to hoist himself up. Juan's hands pressed into his side and pushed him upward. Weak and exhausted, Gideon's muscles shook, the tremors making it difficult to keep his balance. With a final shove from Juan, Gideon dragged his free leg over the horse and slumped into the saddle, helpless to stop the tortured moan that rose in his throat.

Thankfully, the dun mare was well trained and held fast throughout the ordeal. Sweat clung to his skin, and he trembled worse than a leaf in a windstorm, but he was on. Gideon prayed for God to keep him conscious as the pain tried to pull him down into oblivion.

Juan pulled the stirrup free and mounted behind him. The herder took the reins and hemmed him in with strong arms. Gideon clasped the pommel and slouched forward as Juan nudged the animal into a brisk walk.

"I get you to the house, then ride for the doctor."

Trying to keep the saddle horn from digging into his wound, Gideon swallowed a cry as the mare lumbered down a small hill. "Fetch the minister, too," he gritted out between heavy breaths.

"The minister, patrón?"

"Sí." Gideon turned his neck just far enough to look Juan in the eye. "Promise me you . . . you won't come back without the . . . minister. It's essential."

Juan nodded, his eyes full of pity.

"Sí, señor. I get the minister, too."

Satisfied, Gideon turned forward again and plotted his strategy. He knew what he had to do; he just prayed God would keep him alive long enough to see it accomplished.

Chapter 27

Adelaide sat in the window seat of the schoolroom, scanning the landscape for anything that could be interpreted as a threat. Isabella knelt on the rug several feet away building pyramids with her alphabet blocks. Adelaide was too tense to play. Petchey was out there somewhere, just waiting for the opportunity to strike.

She looked off in the direction Gideon had ridden and whispered another prayer on his behalf. He'd said he'd be back in an hour. It had been nearly three. Closing her eyes for a moment, she felt once again the slight pressure of Gideon's lips on her brow.

Ever since the night of the party, she dared to hope that his feelings for her might be deepening. Their friendship and common devotion for Isabella had formed a bond between them, but Adelaide had longed for more. Even though her head had insisted she remain detached, that she focus solely on caring for Isabella, her heart had not heeded those instructions. Somewhere between their bickering by the river and Gideon's tender response to her concerns about Lucinda's journal, she had fallen utterly in love with the man.

And now he'd given her reason to believe he might share those feelings to some degree. For the first time since the fiasco in Fort Worth, she honestly thanked God that Henry Belcher was a married man. The lukewarm affection she'd felt for him seemed ridiculous in light of the blazing warmth Gideon stirred in her. No other man would ever do.

She opened her eyes and spied something moving far in the distance, teasing the edge of her peripheral vision. She turned to get a better look, rising up out of her seat until she was half standing. When her mind finally made sense of the sight, her heart plummeted like a bird shot out of the sky.

It couldn't be. It just couldn't. She pressed her face against the window, the cold glass sending a shiver through her. Gideon's bay gelding was trotting down the hill toward the stable. Without Gideon.

Panic jolted through her, and she had to cover her mouth to hold back a cry. She spun away from the window, picked up her skirts, and . . . stopped. Wide blue eyes full of questions stared up at her.

"Isabella . . . I . . ."

A suitable explanation for her abrupt departure failed to present itself, and she hadn't the time to think one up.

"I . . . I need to go somewhere for a little while," Adelaide stammered. "Stay here. I'll send Mrs. Chalmers up to sit with you until I return."

Without a second glance at the girl, Adelaide dashed out the door and down to her bedroom. Her heart thudded against her rib cage as she tore off her yellow muslin walking skirt and petticoat and yanked her split riding skirt over her hips. Not caring about the mismatched bodice, she flung open her trunk and reached into its depths. She shoved unwanted items left and right until her hand closed over the thick leather belt she sought.

With an ease of motion that hadn't rusted since the days she rode the range with her father, Adelaide strapped the gun belt around her waist. Remembering Isabella's upset about the men carrying guns, she'd not wanted to frighten the child by wearing hers in the house. But there was no help for it now. Adelaide pulled the revolver from its holster and crammed bullets into the empty chambers. Her fingers shook, but she got the job done and raced down the stairs to find the housekeeper. Fortunately, she didn't have to look far. Mrs. Chalmers was dusting the entryway table when Adelaide flew by.

Eliminating any opportunity for the bewildered housekeeper to ask questions or argue, Adelaide made her proclamation on her way out the back door. "Gideon's in trouble," she called out. "I need you to see to Isabella."

She sprinted toward Solomon. Saddling Sheba would take too long, and she refused to forfeit a single minute.

James must have heard the kitchen door bang, for he came running around the side of the house. Adelaide didn't bother to explain, figuring he was smart enough to reason out what she was doing. She grabbed Solomon's reins and led him back toward James.

"Give me a leg up."

James scowled at her and made no move to help. "Where's Gideon?"

Adelaide's patience unraveled. She glared up at him and huffed. "I don't know, but I'm going to find out. Now give me a boost!"

He searched off in the direction from which Solomon had come, concern etched deeply in his features. Yet he still shook his head at her.

"Gideon wouldn't want you to put yourself in danger. Juan's out there with him. If they don't show up soon, I'll send one of the men after them."

"Who are you going to send? Chalmers? Everyone else is out on patrol, and you have to stand guard over Isabella. I'm the best person to go after him, and you know it."

James wouldn't look at her, but a muscle twitched in his cheek. He obviously didn't want to admit she was right. Well, he would have to physically restrain her if he intended to stop her.

Adelaide gave up on waiting for him to help her mount. Attempting the feat on her own wouldn't be very dignified, but dignity couldn't warm her with kisses or brighten her day with a dimpled smile. Only Gideon could do that.

She turned her back on James and gripped the saddle. Solomon stood a good two hands taller than Sheba, but she'd been mounting horses too big for her since childhood—a benefit of having a father in the horse breeding business. She couldn't quite reach the horn, so she tucked her fingers under the pommel and grasped it tight in her palm. She lifted her knee chest-high and wedged the toe of her left boot into the stirrup. Solomon shifted, obviously unused to such odd mounting methods, and Adelaide hopped on one leg until he stilled. Then she leapt upward and grabbed the saddle horn. Tightening her arms and stomach muscles, she grunted her way onto the horse's back.

"You're a stubborn woman, Adelaide Proctor," James said, shaking his head. A hint of a smile played over his lips, though.

"You can thank me later." She turned Solomon in the direction from which he had come and touched her heels to his flanks. "Yah!"

As she passed the bunkhouse, she began to pray. "Please, God. Please, God. Please, God." The repetitive supplication was all she could manage. What it lacked in eloquence, it made up for in fervor.

Solomon surged up a rise, and when they reached the top, Adelaide tugged him to a halt. She scanned the landscape, desperate for a glimpse of Gideon. The sun had nearly disappeared in the west, and shadows swept over the land, making it difficult to distinguish a man's crumpled body from rocks and fallen trees. She was about to nudge the horse forward again when a movement off to the right caught her eye.

Adelaide stood up in the stirrups and squinted. It was definitely a horse, but from this distance, the shape atop it seemed much too large to be Gideon. What if it was Lord Petchey? She had no idea what Reginald looked like. Lucinda had mentioned he was an avid horseman. However, that didn't mean he wasn't a heavyset man. Adelaide steered Solomon behind a nearby oak and pulled her Colt .38 out of the leather holster at her hip.

She cocked the weapon but kept it aimed toward the sky. Her own breathing echoed in her ears. As the horse approached, the form on its back shifted and sprouted a second head. Adelaide frowned. She squinted, trying to decipher what she was seeing. All at once she gasped. There wasn't one rider, but two. And the man in front was swaying precariously in the saddle.

Gideon.

Using both hands, Adelaide carefully uncocked her Colt and secured it in her holster. With a squeeze of her knees and a flick of the reins, she gave Solomon his head and raced to intercept them. Fear pounded an equally fast rhythm in her chest. When she noticed Juan's head turn her way, she slowed and whistled the all-clear signal. He nodded to her but made no move to stop, so she circled around beside him and slowed Solomon to match the mare's pace. Only then did she notice that the herder wore no shirt. It was wrapped around Gideon's middle.

Her gaze flew to Juan's face. He said nothing, but his eyes swam with grief. Adelaide bit her lower lip and pulled a half length ahead to take a closer look at Gideon.

His shirt flapped open to reveal part of a muscular chest, but what drew her attention was the dark red stain soaking the makeshift bandage over his belly. He'd been gut shot. The slowest, most painful way a bullet could kill a man. A whimper rose in her throat.

"Oh, Gideon."

His body flinched, as if her words had awakened him from a doze.

"Addie?" he rasped.

The pet name pierced her heart. She willed her tears not to fall and fought to keep her voice steady. "I'm here, Gideon."

He twisted his head to the side, grimacing only slightly. Then he smiled at her. The dimple in his cheek nearly undid all her hard-earned control.

"Don't worry . . . sunshine. God's not . . . going to take me . . . yet. We made a deal." He shuddered as he drew in a shallow breath. "You and Bella will be safe. I . . . promise."

As if she and Isabella being safe were all she needed. She needed much more than that. She needed him, and he had no right to sound so resigned, as if he knew he wouldn't survive and had made his peace with it.

Disobedient tears rolled down her face, and tremors coursed through her jaw. He couldn't die. Not now. Her whole body shook as the remains of her composure began to crumble—until his gaze bored into hers and anchored her. She immediately straightened. The crazy man didn't have enough strength to be trying to hold her together when he could barely stay in the saddle himself. There would be plenty of time for her to fall apart later. For now, she'd be strong—for Gideon.

Adelaide wanted nothing more than to stay by his side, but her being at hand wasn't doing anything to help him. In fact, she was probably hurting him, draining what little strength he had as he struggled to put on a brave front for her.

"I expect you to stay conscious until Juan can get you home," Adelaide demanded. He looked like he was going to topple to the ground at any moment, his face devoid of color, his head lifelessly bobbing in rhythm with the mare's gait. "Don't you go falling off that horse, Gideon Westcott. You hear me?"

The smile that had faded reappeared momentarily. "Yes . . . ma'am."

"Good. I'll ride ahead and ready everything for you." She gave a sharp nod and then reined Solomon in a bit so that she was once again even with Juan.

"Take care of him," she ordered.

The herder bent his head. "Sí, señorita."

Having collected his promise, Adelaide urged Solomon into a canter. Gideon might have made a deal with the Lord, but she planned to make one of her own. If God would just show her how to keep the fool man alive, she would love and cherish him for the rest of her days. And while the loving and cherishing would be easy, the keeping him alive part had her worried.

Chapter 28

By the time Juan's mare straggled into the yard with her precious burden, Adelaide had gathered everything she could think of for tending Gideon's wound. She had laid two quilts over the kitchen table for padding and covered them with an oilcloth to prevent stains. Rolled cotton bandages cluttered the counter, along with a bottle of spirits, needle and thread, a pair of shears, and every medicinal ointment and elixir she could find in the house. A pot of steaming water sat on the stove, nearing a boil.

The kitchen door banged open and Juan and James pushed into the room with Gideon's arms draped over their shoulders. They each held tightly to one of his wrists to prevent him from slipping away. His limp body hung between them, and the toes of his boots scraped the floor as they dragged him in. Adelaide's heart ached at the sight. Gideon had always been so strong and vital, a man who took care of those around him and always had a smile at the ready. Now his mouth was twisted in an agonized grimace and his weakened body could not even support its own weight.

Adelaide rushed forward. "Lay him on the table." She grabbed hold of his feet and helped the men lever him onto the flat surface.

"Was it Petchey?" James asked.

Gideon rolled his head slightly from left to right. "No. It was Jo—" His eyes darted to Adelaide, then returned to James. "A hired gunman."

Her brow crinkled in confusion. Why was he trying to hide something from her? He'd been shot, for goodness' sake. She cared more about repairing the damage than learning who did the deed.

"I got a bullet into him, though." Gideon's face contorted with pain as he struggled to speak. "Fled . . . with a wounded arm . . . Won't be back."

"Thank God for one less thing to worry about," James said. "I'll go for the doctor."

He turned to leave, but Gideon caught his arm. "No. Need you . . . here." He gritted the words out between clenched teeth. "Juan will go."

James frowned but nodded.

"Take Sheba," Adelaide called out to Juan as he reached the doorway. "She's well rested and fast. She'll run for miles."

"Gracias."

Another thought gripped her, carving away at her hard-earned control. She needed James's strength to help her tend to Gideon, but that would leave them unguarded. Even if the gunman who shot Gideon was no longer a threat, Petchey still was. What if Reginald had planned the attack on Gideon and was even now stalking Isabella? They needed more protection.

"Juan?" Adelaide called out to the retreating herder.

"Sí?" He caught the door at the last second and stuck his head back into the kitchen.

"If Miguel is still on patrol by the road, send him to the house. He can stand guard here while James helps me with Mr. Westcott."

He nodded, then disappeared.

Adelaide returned her attention to Gideon. The amount of blood saturating the cloth around his middle made her knees shake. She glanced around. James was the only one left in the room, and he was looking to her for instructions.

Mrs. Garrett had taken a dinner tray up to Mrs. Chalmers and Isabella before the men brought Gideon in. The cook had hastily explained that she could butcher a chicken without a qualm, but the sight of human blood made her head spin like a whirligig. Chalmers was out on the porch, assuming James's post, and Juan was on his way to fetch the doctor. That left Gideon's care in Adelaide's sadly inexperienced hands. Until the doctor arrived she was all that stood between him and death. What if she couldn't do what needed to be done?

"God, grant me wisdom and healing hands." She murmured the request under her breath. James added his own quiet amen to the prayer, drawing her eyes to his.

"This is no time to lose your stubborn streak, Adelaide. You can do this."

She stared at him for several seconds, needing to believe him. "All right." She looked back down at her patient. "First, help me get him out of his shirt." A blush warmed her cheeks, but she refused to let embarrassment get in the way of tending his wound in the best way possible.

Adelaide didn't know much about doctoring, but while she lived in Boston, she had often accompanied her aunt on charitable visits to the hospital near their home. She hadn't really done more than hand out baked goods and read aloud to the long-term convalescents, but she remembered how adamant the nurses had been about cleanliness. Everything that touched the patients had to be clean—bandages, bedding, even the room itself. It had something to do with germ theory. They were convinced that such hygienic precautions promoted health and decreased the chance of infection and the spread of disease. Adelaide decided that until the doctor from Menardville arrived, she would clean everything that came near Gideon's wound. And if she could overcome her squeamishness, she'd clean the wound, too.

James lifted Gideon's back off the table, and Adelaide worked quickly to remove the blue-checked shirt. The veins in Gideon's neck bulged as he tried to muffle his groans. As soon as the last sleeve slid over his hand, she helped ease him down and was relieved to see his facial muscles relax, if only a little. Very gently, she lifted the bottom edge of the bandage to check on the bleeding. Gideon hissed in response.

Adelaide winced and instantly dropped the bandage.

"Sorry." She couldn't fathom the agony he must be suffering, and what was worse, she knew she was adding to it. Perhaps she should just leave everything alone and wait for the doctor. But what if she could prevent infection? What if she could increase his odds of survival?

Taking a deep breath, she lifted the edge of the bandage a second time. Gideon clutched the edge of the table so hard his knuckles turned white. Tears pooled in her eyes, but she held to her course. She needed to be sure that the bleeding had stopped. A lot of blood had dried on his skin and clothes, but she didn't see any new seepage. She stopped short of uncovering the actual wound for fear of tearing away a clot. However, she examined enough of the area to convince herself that the bleeding was under control.

"I can't do much about the hole in his stomach, but if he survives the bullet, I don't want infection to take him. We've got to clear away all the dirt and grime."

"Just tell me what to do," James said.

"Take some of that hot water from the stove and pour it in a basin. Mix it with just enough cold that it won't burn you. Then roll up your sleeves and wash to your elbows. I'll do the same after I retrieve a couple sponges."

Adelaide unbuttoned her cuffs and rolled up her sleeves as she rushed over to the broom closet. Facing a view of buckets and rags instead of Gideon's bloody torso, she took a moment to inhale several deep breaths and calm the emotions rioting in her breast.

God would see her through this. He would. She just had to ignore her fear of what might happen and focus on the here and now. Do what she could and let God take care of the rest.

Adelaide lifted her chin and reached into a box on the side shelf. She pulled out two round yellow sponges that felt soft and new. Tucking them into the crook of her arm, she turned around to face what must be done and returned to the table.

"Addie?" Gideon's hoarse voice startled her. He had been so still, she'd thought him unconscious.

She leaned close. "Yes?"

His chocolate eyes peered up at her, full of grim determination.

"Take care . . . of Bella."

"You know I will." A lump of despair clogged her throat momentarily, but she ruthlessly choked it down. "Right now, though, I need to take care of you."

Hope was the only weapon at her disposal, and she wasn't about to surrender it. She smoothed his sweat-dampened hair off his forehead and lightly kissed his brow. His eyelids drifted closed again, and she headed for the basin. Once her hands and arms were clean, she and James set about washing away all the dirt and dried blood from Gideon's chest, neck, face, and arms. Using the shears, Adelaide cut away most of the improvised bandage. She left the handkerchief directly over the wound untouched, but set the rest aside so that she could better bathe Gideon's skin.

"We should probably check for an exit wound," James suggested.

Adelaide glanced up at him. "I hadn't thought of that." She looked at Gideon lying still on the table. "It hurt him so much to sit up last time." She bit her lip in indecision. "Perhaps if we rolled him to the side it wouldn't be as painful."

James nodded. "Let's try it."

Adelaide bent near his face and spoke in a loud, clear voice. "Gideon, are you awake?"

He grunted in response and dipped his chin slightly.

"We're going to roll you over now."

James grabbed hold of Gideon's right shoulder and hip. Gideon clamped his jaw tight in preparation.

"One . . . two . . . three!"

James pulled, and Adelaide helped by pushing on Gideon's shoulder blade. Once James had him propped up at a perpendicular angle, Adelaide retracted her supporting hand. She took up a sponge and wasted no time washing Gideon's back. The loose ends of the cut bandage had fallen free, but some parts were still clinging to his skin. She gently drew the bandage away from his back until it resisted. Blood was clinging to the fabric, and if it was indeed from a secondary wound, she had to be careful not to set it into bleeding again. She cut off the loose ends on either side and then faced the task of removing the rest. She needed to loosen it somehow.

Holding her sponge against his skin directly above the stuck fabric, she drizzled a bit of water over the cloth. After moistening it, she tugged at one corner until it started to pull free. She repeated the procedure until the entire bandage was removed. A hole about the size of the tip of her finger marred Gideon's lower back. Adelaide fought off the queasiness that roiled in her stomach. A trickle of new blood seeped from the opening. Her eyes followed its trail and she began to feel woozy. She quickly rinsed the red line away with a squeeze of her sponge. And thankfully her head cleared.

"Well, the good news is the bullet went through you," Adelaide announced, her voice shaking only slightly. "The bad news is that we're going to have to disinfect two sites instead of one."

"Just . . . get it done," Gideon ground out.

Adelaide's hand closed over the neck of the whiskey bottle. She wiggled the stopper out and held her breath against the sour smell that wafted into her face. Angling her nose away from the bottle, she breathed in through her mouth and returned to Gideon's side. She held her sponge below the wound and positioned the bottle above it. Then, with a whispered apology, she poured the alcohol down his back and over the bullet hole.

All of his muscles went rigid, and his strangled cry echoed in the quiet room. Battling tears, Adelaide stopped pouring and set the bottle aside. She grasped a clean roll of bandages and fashioned a compress. Nodding to James, she held it in place over the wound while he rolled Gideon onto his back once again.

Having done it once didn't make the task any easier as she repeated the procedure in the front. By the time she'd cleared away the old bandage, flushed out all the dirt she could see, and sanitized the wound with another dose of whiskey, she felt like yelling right along with Gideon.

At some point during the ordeal, Miguel must have arrived, for when Adelaide next looked up, Chalmers was standing in the corner, his eyes moist as he regarded his employer's suffering.

Adelaide swiped her rolled sleeve across her forehead as she contemplated the butler. "How long until the doctor arrives, Chalmers?"

He stepped forward and cleared his throat. "At least an hour but maybe more, miss."

More than an hour? It already felt as if an eternity had passed. Suddenly weak, Adelaide gripped the edge of the table.

"That's a long time." She stared at Gideon, taking in the deterioration of his features. His complexion had lost most of its color, and his muscles were knotted in torment. She would have preferred to stand in a nest of rattlers rather than hurt him again, but she had no choice. "I suppose we should bind him up. He can't afford to lose any more blood."

Adelaide sighed and waved Chalmers forward. "We must do this quickly and with as little movement as possible." She grabbed a roll of bandages and positioned herself by Gideon's feet. "You two take his arms, and I'll swing his legs over to the side. His hips should keep him on the table while you sit him partway up. With his legs hanging off, he'll be stretched out so I can get a good wrap on him."

Gideon moaned something that sounded like her name. Adelaide moved up the side of the table to be nearer to him.

"I'm sorry, Gideon." She lightly stroked his jaw, wishing she could take away his pain with her touch. "I promise this will be the last time we move you. Then I'll leave you to rest until the doctor comes."

"Addie . . ." He opened his eyes and peered up at her.

"Yes?"

He blinked very slowly, and Adelaide worried he was slipping from consciousness. He forced his lids up again, though, and licked his dry lips.

"I love you."

Adelaide went very still. Then her hand started trembling and her heart started fluttering. Though she had longed to hear those words for so long, she had a hard time believing they were real. She was tempted to ask him to repeat what he'd said, but his eyelids drooped closed over his earnest gaze.

His declaration thrilled her, but the joy it brought was bittersweet. For if she lost him now, the devastation would be multiplied, knowing what they could have shared had he lived. But she couldn't dwell on the fear of future grief and let it cheapen the gift he had given her. No. He deserved the best she could give him. And she would give him all.

Not sure if he could hear her or not, Adelaide bent close to his ear. "I love you, too, Gideon Westcott." Her lips brushed his cheek.

Chalmers and James both averted their gazes the moment she looked up. They hadn't been fast enough to hide the sympathy in their faces, though. Adelaide straightened. She didn't want their sympathy. She wanted their help to make Gideon well. Clearing her throat, she refocused on the task at hand.

"Ready, gentlemen?"

Adelaide grasped Gideon's legs above his boots and nodded to her helpers. They lifted. Weakened by the unending agony he'd been forced to endure, Gideon no longer had the strength to contain his scream.

Holding the rear compress in place, Adelaide worked as fast as she could. Gideon's scream ended abruptly after she had circled his waist twice. He went limp. Oblivion had claimed him at last. She prayed it would not be permanent.

She finished the wrap, and as she tied off the ends of the bandage, she vaguely registered another noise coming from upstairs. Pounding footsteps. Muffled shouts. But she didn't have the mental wherewithal to concentrate on anything beyond Gideon.

They had just laid him back down on the table and cushioned his head with a stack of dishtowels when a small blur raced into the room and rammed into Adelaide's side.

"No, Papa Gidyon. No!"

Chapter 29

Mrs. Chalmers huffed around the corner and collapsed against the doorframe. "Sorry, miss. When she heard the scream, there was no stopping her."

"That's all right." Adelaide waved off the housekeeper's concerns and stared at the girl beside her.

Had Isabella spoken or had Adelaide's frazzled nerves just sent her over the edge into delirium? The gamut of emotions she had run over the last hour had drained her mental faculties to the extent that she wasn't sure of anything anymore.

Isabella lifted one of Gideon's fingers, then let it go. It flopped lifelessly back to the table. She flinched.

"Is he . . . dead?"

The housekeeper's audible gasp echoed Adelaide's amazement at the sound of Isabella's shaky whisper. However, this was no time for rejoicing. One look at the girl's stoic face served as a haunting reminder of the withdrawn, unsmiling child Adelaide had met upon her arrival at Westcott Cottage—a child willing to forfeit joy in order to escape pain. Only the sacrifice hadn't eliminated the pain. It had simply dulled it until she no longer cared about anything.

Adelaide hunkered down beside Gideon's daughter and turned the girl to face her. She couldn't let her retreat behind that wall again. While her heart delighted in the fact that Isabella's voice had indeed returned, she dared not focus any attention on that development. The youngster would probably revert back to her silent ways in an instant. Besides, that wasn't what was important right now. Izzy needed answers to her questions, not fanfare over her speech.

"No, honey. Your papa's not dead. He's resting. Come here." Adelaide gathered Isabella in her arms and hugged her tight. Then she stood and lifted the child onto her hip.

Taking Isabella's small hand in her own, Adelaide bent over Gideon. She placed the girl's palm on his chest above the white bandages. "Do you feel him breathing?"

Isabella nodded.

"That means he's alive."

Isabella pulled her hand back and looked up at Adelaide. "Will he get better?"

Such a simple question, but Adelaide had no ready answer, only an ache in her heart that intensified as she contemplated the most realistic outcome.

"Why don't you take the child to the parlor?" Mrs. Chalmers urged, saving her from having to answer Isabella's question immediately. "I'll sit with Mr. Westcott until the doctor arrives."

Adelaide hated to leave Gideon's side, but she knew he would want her to take care of Izzy.

"All right, but come get me if he wakes or if there is any change in his condition."

"Of course." The housekeeper patted Adelaide's back. "You did a fine job with him, miss. The rest is in God's hands."

Adelaide's gaze lingered on Gideon's face. She wanted to touch him, to kiss him before she left, afraid she might not have another opportunity. But that was selfish. He'd asked her to take care of his Bella, and that's what she would do.

Once in the parlor, Adelaide snuggled into a cushioned armchair with Isabella securely ensconced in her lap. It amazed her how good it felt to sit down. The emotional strain of tending Gideon had taken a physical toll, as well, one she was only now beginning to recognize.

Isabella raised her head from Adelaide's shoulder and looked at her with wide, soulful eyes. Adelaide fingered back a strand of the girl's hair that had fallen across her brow and patted it into place.

"I haven't forgotten your question, Izzy."

Adelaide was tempted to offer a blanket assurance that everything would be fine, yet she couldn't make such a broad promise with a clear conscience. She wanted to offer hope, but not a false hope that would only destroy Isabella's trust.

"Your Papa Gideon has been hurt. Badly." Adelaide tempered her honesty with as much gentleness as she could muster—in her tone, her touch, her expression. "I have done everything I can to make him better, and the doctor will be here soon. I believe he *will* get well, but even if he doesn't, I know that God will take care of him. And us."

Isabella didn't answer. Not knowing what else to say, Adelaide hugged her tight and began stroking her arm.

How could she instill hope in one who had learned to expect the worst in life? At age five, Izzy was too young to have any measure of control over her situation. Her future depended on the decisions of others, and nothing killed hope faster than the belief that one had no ability to positively affect her own circumstances.

Adelaide stilled as an idea occurred to her. Her hand hovered above Isabella's arm midstroke. What if she could give the girl a bit of control back? Would hope follow? It was worth a try.

"Isabella?"

The girl lifted her chin to meet Adelaide's eyes.

"Would you like to help me take care of your father?"

Her brows arched, and she pointed to her chest.

"If you are willing, I could certainly use the help. Perhaps with two of us watching over him, he'll be more likely to get well. What do you think?"

A look came over Isabella's face that reminded Adelaide of the time they had played soldier together. Serious. Determined. Ready to try. She nodded her agreement.

"Wonderful." Adelaide rewarded her with a smile and a buss on the cheek. "There will be all kinds of things for us to do. I'll change his bandages, and you can put cool cloths on his forehead. We'll tend to his hurt body, but we'll also need to take care of his spirit. That will be your most important job."

"How do I do that?" Isabella asked.

Some of the tension that had coiled in Adelaide's stomach when Isabella reverted back to silent gestures unwound at the child's spoken question. She'd feared Isabella had locked her voice away again. Hearing her speak was like a balm on her ragged nerves.

"When people get very sick," Adelaide explained, "it is easy for them to get discouraged. Doctors and medicine can help them heal, but they have to work at it, too. Sometimes they get tired of hurting and they want to give up. It's our job to make things easier for them, to cheer them and help them want to get well even if it hurts right now."

"Does Papa Gidyon hurt lots?"

Images of his pain-ravaged face thrust into her mind, and the sounds of his moans rang in her ears.

"Yes, love. Papa Gideon hurts a lot." Adelaide blinked the moisture away from her eyes before continuing. "That's why our job is so important. Sometimes he will need us to be quiet so he can rest, but other times we can talk to him and tell him funny stories or even just sit by his bed and hold his hand. Anything to remind him how much we love him and want him to stay with us."

"Can I sing him a song? Mama used to like me to sing to her."

"I can think of nothing he would enjoy more." If the sound of his daughter speaking and singing didn't enliven Gideon's spirit, she didn't know what would.

The two would-be nurses sat silently for a minute. Then Isabella wiggled to the edge of Adelaide's lap.

"Can we start taking care of him now?"

Adelaide grinned at the child's enthusiasm. She was about to explain that this was one of those times when Gideon needed to rest, but thought better of it.

"Yes, Izzy," she said. "We can do one of the best things of all for your papa. We can pray for him."

Isabella's face fell. "I'm not a good pray-er."

"You don't have to use fancy words, sweetheart. God knows what's in your heart."

A fat tear rolled down Isabella's cheek as she shook her head. "No. My prayers don't work."

Of course her prayers worked, Adelaide wanted to argue. She was too innocent to have anything hinder her petitions. However, an inner urging kept her silent.

"My first papa died before I had a chance to pray at all, but when my mama got sick, I prayed every night for her to get well. She didn't. She died just like Papa."

"Oh, Izzy." Adelaide pulled her back into an embrace and rocked her. "It's hard to understand why God says no, isn't it? I felt the same way when my father died. I had prayed for him, too. But just because God doesn't give us what we ask for doesn't mean he doesn't love us or hear us."

Adelaide shifted their positions until she was cradling Isabella like an oversized infant. Her head lay in the crook of Adelaide's arm, supported by the side of the chair, while her knees bunched up on the opposite end.

Perhaps this conversation was too mature for a child to comprehend, but Adelaide didn't want her to grow up thinking that prayer didn't work. Even if all she did today was plant seeds for future understanding, that would be better than nothing. Adelaide took hold of Isabella's fingers and commanded her charge's attention.

"God loves us, Izzy, and wants to give us good gifts, but those gifts aren't always what we expect. Sometimes instead of making a person well, he comforts us and gives us the courage to go on. Sometimes he sends new people into our lives to help us—like when he sent Papa Gideon to take care of you. And sometimes he gives us a new joy that we would not have known otherwise."

A lump of emotion rose in Adelaide's throat as she thought about the unexpected joy God had led her to in the form of a heroic sheep rancher and his darling of a daughter.

"After my daddy died and Aunt Louise took me away," Adelaide tried to explain, "I was so heartsore, I didn't think I would ever be happy again. But I was wrong. Over time, God mended my heart and gave me a new joy—the joy of teaching. If I hadn't gone to Boston, I would never have become a teacher. And if I hadn't become a teacher, I would never have met you and your father."

And fallen in love with you both.

Adelaide pressed her lips together to stop them from quivering. She didn't speak again until she trusted her voice not to crack.

"I don't know what God will decide to do about your father, Izzy, but I plan to ask him to make him well every chance I get. And I'm going to start right now. If you want to pray, too, you can."

Isabella shrugged and climbed out of Adelaide's lap. She knelt on the floor and folded her hands together. Leaning her elbows on the padded bench of the settee that stood kitty-corner to the armchair, she mimicked the posture she used at bedtime. Adelaide crawled down on the floor to join her.

"Dear God," Adelaide prayed, "we know you love us and want what is best for us. And right now what we want more than anything is for you to make Gideon well. Please heal him. We love him and need him with us. Spare his life and restore him to full health. In the name of your Son, who claimed victory over death, amen."

Adelaide stayed on her knees, hoping to hear Isabella add a prayer of her own. Second after second ticked by in silence. Adelaide snuck a sidelong glance at her charge. The girl's eyes were squeezed shut so tightly, the resulting wrinkles extended from her eyelids to her forehead. She opened her mouth but couldn't seem to find the words to get started. At least she was trying. Adelaide bowed her head again, content to wait.

"God," Isabella finally blurted, "I don't know why sometimes you say yes and sometimes you say no, but you gotta say yes this time. You gotta make Papa Gidyon all better. Last time it was only me praying. This time I gots Miss Proctor praying, too. So you might as well go along with us 'cause we already beat you two to one. Amen."

For the first time in hours, instead of biting her lip to keep from crying, Adelaide chomped her teeth down to contain her laughter.

Chapter 30

The pain registered first. Like a hundred knives stabbing his gut. Gideon groaned and instinctively tried to curl around his wounded middle, but the movement only drove the knives deeper. Consciousness slowly tore the veil from his mind, allowing memories to surface. Slaughtered sheep. An ambush. José. A bullet ripping through his belly. Petchey.

He fought to open his eyes, but his lids were locked down tight. He scrabbled his way toward full awareness. If he could feel the pain, he must not be dead yet. But there was no guarantee he would linger for long. He needed to talk to James. Now. Before it was too late. He had to protect Addie and Bella.

By strength of will alone, he wrenched his eyes open and focused on a whitewashed ceiling. As he gingerly twisted his head to the right, a kitchen stove came into view. And if he wasn't mistaken, the dark blue lump in front of it was the backside of his cook.

Mrs. Garrett straightened and pulled a pan out of the oven. She kicked the door closed and grumbled something about stubborn men who ruined perfectly good suppers by getting themselves shot.

She sniffed and dabbed her eyes with the corner of her apron. He never thought to see the old bird reduced to tears. It was rather touching. Of course, her upset might be due more to the blackened roast than to him. The edge of his mouth curved just a touch. He wondered if she'd miss their sparring when he was gone.

"He's stirring, Mr. Bevin."

Gideon recognized his housekeeper's voice, but she wasn't in his line of sight. Wood scraped against wood off to his left, as if someone was pushing a chair back. Clenching his teeth, he turned his head in that direction.

"Welcome back, Gid." James stood over him, the smile on his face at odds with the worry in his eyes.

"Thanks," he rasped.

"I'll go fetch Miss Proctor." The housekeeper's voice again.

"No." Gideon had trouble spitting the word out of his dry mouth, but apparently Mrs. Chalmers heard him. Her head bounced into view beside James's shoulder.

"Whyever not?" She frowned down at him. "That dear girl patched you up practically all by herself and only left your side when Isabella ran into the room. She left me strict instructions to come find her when you woke, and I aim to keep my promise."

He'd never had one of his servants take him to task before, yet he couldn't work up any affront over it. The woman was clearly overwrought. Besides, it reassured him to know that Adelaide had Mrs. Chalmers's support. She would need that in the coming months.

"I want to see Addie, but . . . I need to talk to James first. Alone." Gideon stared at the housekeeper, willing her to understand. "I have to set my affairs in order and make arrangements for Bella before . . ."

He couldn't quite bring himself to say it out loud. He knew he was dying. Men didn't recover from abdominal wounds. But some hidden part of his soul must not have fully accepted his fate, for even though he was prepared to plan for his death, he had trouble speaking of it.

His housekeeper blushed and tears filled her eyes. "Of course, sir." She bobbed a curtsy, then turned to the cook and cleared her throat. "Mabel, I could use some help with the dishes in the dining room."

Mrs. Chalmers disappeared through the connecting door, and Mrs. Garrett followed without the slightest complaint over being thrown out of her own kitchen. Strange how that uncharacteristic bit of docility depressed him. Did no one have the pluck to stand up for him, to offer him a glimmer of hope? Defeat seemed to have settled over Westcott Cottage while he'd been unconscious.

Yet who was he to demand hope from others when he couldn't claim it himself? If it didn't hurt so much to move, he'd have banged his head against the table in frustration.

Had Addie given up on him, too? The very thought brought a moan to his lips that had nothing to do with his injury. But then visions filled his mind of his little spitfire, dressed in yellow with her mouth pulled in a tight line of determination. No. Addie was a fighter. He remembered her laboring over his wound and ordering James around like a general, refusing to surrender. If anyone could bring him back from the brink of death, it would be Addie. However, in the event a miracle did not come his way, he intended to do everything in his power to protect her and Bella.

"Chalmers?" Gideon said.

"Here, sir." The butler stepped up to the table.

He tried to turn toward the man, but pain surged through his middle, stealing his breath and, for a moment, his thoughts. Gideon closed his eyes. He fought through the haze to recapture his plan.

"Sir?"

"Fetch . . . pen and ink from my study . . . and several sheets of writing paper."

"Right away, sir."

James lowered himself into a chair and gripped the edge of the tabletop. "You don't have to do this now, Gid. You need to conserve your strength. The papers can wait."

"No. They can't." Gideon's eyes bored into those of his friend. "You know my chances, James. Slim at best. Petchey . . . is still out there. The moment I'm gone, he'll sweep Bella away. Can't . . . let that happen."

A spasm caught him unaware, and Gideon bit back a cry. He latched onto James's wrist and ground his teeth. When it passed, his jaw relaxed, but he did not let up his grip on his friend's arm.

"I need you to . . . compose a new will for me. Name Adelaide my sole beneficiary and . . . Bella's guardian. Then draft a marriage certificate."

James shrank back, his brow creased. "A what?"

"Marriage certificate."

The lawyer shifted in his seat. "You're serious."

"Yes." Gideon released his friend's wrist and sighed. "It's . . . best solution."

"Look, Gid. I know you've developed feelings for the girl, but this is ridiculous." James pushed to his feet and paced the length of the table, a dark frown attesting to his opinion of the idea. "Just leave her the house, the money, and Isabella. You don't have to put her through a sham of a ceremony. Think of Adelaide. It's cruel to ask a woman to marry you when you'll most likely make her a widow inside of a week."

A look of horror crossed James's face as he realized what he'd said. "I didn't mean . . ."

"It's true." Gideon wasn't insulted. It was almost a relief to have someone speak the words for him. However, he needed James's cooperation. He had to make him understand.

"I am thinking of Addie. She has no father, no brothers to watch out for her. If Petchey was willing to kill me to get to Bella, what's . . . going to stop him from doing the same to Addie when . . . I'm gone?"

James lowered himself back onto the chair. "I would look out for her, Gid. You know that."

"But for how long? You have a life, a business back in Fort Worth. Even without Petchey to deal with . . . I wouldn't want to leave Addie and Bella alone out here. As my widow, she'll have a place in my family's home, the protection of my father and brothers. They can come and . . . and fetch her and Bella back to England. See to their financial needs. Their physical safety."

Gideon clenched his jaw and rolled toward his friend, bracing himself up on one elbow. The authority bred into him since the day of his birth surged to the surface, overriding his pain.

"Write to them, James. Tell them to come. I'll need you to stay on until they arrive, but once they're here, they'll take care of Addie. She told me once that she longed to replace the family she lost. I can give her that, James. I *will* . . . give her that."

"You're set on this?" James asked.

"Yes."

James favored him with a sharp nod. "All right. I'll do it."

"Thank you," Gideon said. "Marriage will strengthen Addie's claim to Bella, tie her to me and therefore to Lady Petchey's original choice of guardian. She and Bella need to stay together. If I die, I don't think Bella could handle losing Adelaide, too."

He swallowed hard and forced his mind away from the grim picture that thought conjured. Instead, he dwelt on memories of childish squeals and feminine laughter as Addie and Bella played one of their silly games of pretend. Addie with her sparkling hazel eyes and sunny disposition. Hair that flew on the wind as she raced her mare over the hills, and a courage that boldly faced whatever danger threatened those she loved.

Gideon could imagine no better way to leave this world than to know that, for a time, Adelaide had been his.

"I have the items you requested, sir." Chalmers shuffled into the room and handed James the paper, pen, and ink. Then he helped ease Gideon down until he lay flat on the table again.

Gideon was glad for the assistance. Now that James stood hunched over the corner cupboard, using its work surface as a makeshift desk while he penned the necessary documents, the drive that had kept Gideon pressing forward deserted him, leaving him weaker than a newborn lamb.

"The doctor should be here soon, sir." Chalmers hovered above him, looking like he desperately wanted another task to complete so he wouldn't be left standing around, wringing his hands. "Can I get you a blanket or some cushions to make you more comfortable?"

Gideon nearly growled at the thought of Chalmers jostling him around, trying to poke pillows beneath him. "Just . . . want to . . . lie still for a while."

The butler's face fell.

Gideon took pity on him. "But might be good to . . . have some on hand."

Just then, a small indrawn breath echoed from the doorway. Gideon stilled.

"It worked, Miss Addie."

His heart skipped a beat at the childish voice. Why hadn't he let Chalmers stuff a batch of cushions behind his head so he could see with his eyes what his ears told him was true? He tried to lift his head, but couldn't get his shoulders off the table. Frustration coursed through him, but the voice came again, soothing his soul with its quiet assurance.

"See? He's better."

Moisture collected at the corners of his eyes.

"Bella?"

Chapter 31

Gideon hadn't heard that cherubic voice in nearly six months, and now that Isabella was finally speaking, he was stuck flat on his back, unable to see her.

"Chalmers, prop me up, man. My daughter's talking." Gideon impatiently wagged a hand at the butler.

Not having anything readily available for propping purposes, Chalmers wedged his arms under Gideon's shoulder blades. Gideon mentally braced himself for the pain, determined not to frighten Bella, and gritted his teeth as Chalmers hefted him a few inches off the table. It wasn't much, but it was enough.

Addie and Bella walked hand-in-hand into the room, like two angels come to welcome him home. They approached his side, and as he watched, Bella's lips formed one sweet word after another.

"We prayed for you, Papa Gidyon, and you waked up." A tentative smile flitted across her face, as if she was still trying to sort things out in her mind. Then her gaze left his face to roam over the bandages at his middle. "Are the hurts all gone?"

"No, sweetie," Gideon said. "But hearing your pretty voice . . . makes them feel much better."

The bud of a smile that lingered on her face blossomed into a full-fledged bloom. "Miss Addie says it's my job to make your insides happy and 'courage you. Am I doing it right?"

A small chuckle escaped Gideon, followed by red-hot pain. He'd have to remember not to do that. He closed his eyes to regain control, inhaled a slow, steadying breath, and looked back at Bella.

"Seeing you smile and hearing you speak is the best medicine I could get. It's been so long, I was afraid I'd forgotten what you sounded like."

"I can sing you a song if you want, like I used to for Mama. Want to hear one now?"

"Why don't we wait until after the doctor comes," Addie suggested. "Maybe you can sing Papa Gideon a lullaby tonight to help him fall asleep." She glanced at him and winked. Gideon found himself enchanted all over again. Her clothes might be a wrinkled, mismatched mess, and strands of her hair might be sticking out at odd angles from the knot at her neck, but when he looked at her, he saw a princess.

Now he just had to convince her to marry him.

At some point during the conversation, Chalmers had lowered him back to the table and left the room without him noticing. No doubt he was searching for those spare pillows and blankets. It couldn't have been too comfortable for the old fellow, squashed under his weight like that. Nevertheless, Gideon wished the man would hurry up. How was he supposed to propose properly if he couldn't hold his head up?

And in front of his daughter.

Gideon sobered a bit. He hated to send Bella away after she had gifted him with so much hope, but swaying Addie was going to be hard enough as it was. An audience would only complicate matters. Plus, he would have to explain his reasons, and that would mean discussing the very real possibility of his demise—a subject much too bleak for one so tender.

Clenching his jaw to combat the knife-sharp stinging in his gut as he moved, he lifted his hand and stroked the outside of Bella's smooth cheek. "I'm looking forward to that song, little one. So much."

His hand started to fall away, his strength too depleted to even hold his arm up for more than a few seconds. Before it slipped completely, though, Adelaide clasped it. She gathered it near her waist and placed Bella's hand on top of theirs. Three united as one. His family. Gideon looked into her eyes, and silent understanding passed between them. Her grip tightened slightly as if in agreement. She felt it, too.

Gideon turned his attention back to his daughter. "Bella . . . I need to talk to Miss Addie about some grown-up things. Why don't you ask Mrs. Chalmers to help you wash your face and get into your nightgown? That way, when the doctor finishes his examination, you can . . . sing me that song we talked about before you go to bed."

Bella's face fell and her bottom lip protruded in the beginnings of a pout, but she nodded. She leaned in close and kissed his cheek as she did every night. Then for the first time, she whispered in his ear, "I love you, Papa Gidyon."

"I love you, too, Bella mine." It was a miracle that he could choke the words past the sudden swelling in the back of his throat, but his daughter didn't seem bothered by the strangled quality of his voice.

She ran her fingertips against his whiskers as she pulled away, and joy radiated through him. Though he was lying on a hard-as-rock table, with a hole in his belly that felt like a burning tunnel of brimstone, he could still say with untarnished certainty that God was good.

Bella waved at him from the entrance to the dining room and closed the door behind her, leaving him alone with Adelaide. A masculine cough echoed off to Gideon's left. Well, not completely alone. He had forgotten about James.

"I'll finish this paperwork in the study, Gid."

The irksome fellow had the nerve to wink at him over a knowing grin as he walked by. Gideon stuffed down his annoyance and twisted his neck to look at Addie. Her back was to him as she poured a cup of water from the pitcher that sat atop the cupboard. He hoped that meant she had missed James's rakish gesture.

Addie pivoted to face him, and her shy smile seduced him with its innocence. His gaze followed those curved lips as she stepped closer. Too bad he didn't feel up to stealing a kiss. What he wouldn't give to linger over a slow, gentle caress—one that would communicate his feelings better than words.

Addie leaned over him, her face inches from his. Had she read his mind? She reached behind his neck and lifted his head. His eyelids began to droop in anticipation. He puckered slightly, craving the feel of her warm lips upon his.

"Just a little bit, now," she murmured.

His eyes slid closed and his lips pressed against cool metal. *Cool metal?*

He opened his eyes at the same time she tipped the tin cup, dribbling a small portion of water into his dry mouth. Regaining his senses fast enough to keep from sputtering, he swallowed her offering along with his disappointment.

After trickling half a cupful down his throat, she set the water aside and pulled a chair up to the table. She settled close to his side, with her hands clasped in her lap. Her eyes seemed to have a hard time meeting his. They flitted over his chest, his forehead, the floor, until finally settling on her hands. Her fidgeting hands. Gideon smiled. She was as nervous as he was.

He took a deep breath. "Addie, I need you to . . . do me a favor."

She straightened in her seat and lifted her chin to look directly at him. "Anything, Gideon."

"Marry me."

She froze mid-nod, a mask of shock slipping over her features. Her mouth hung slightly agape, and three tiny lines appeared between her eyebrows. She blinked several times but made no verbal response.

Gideon clenched his fist. *What an idiot!* That had to be the worst proposal ever uttered. Just blurt it out as if he were asking her to pass the potatoes or something. What had happened to the famous Westcott charm? He hurried to rectify his mistake.

"I didn't mean that the way it sounded."

Her brow creased a little more. "You didn't mean to ask me to marry you?"

"No. Yes." He blew out a frustrated sigh. "Yes, I meant to ask you to marry me, but I didn't intend to be so abrupt about it."

"I see."

"No. I don't think you do." He was making a royal muck of the situation. "I meant what I said to you earlier, when you were . . . tending my wound. I care about you, Addie. Dearly. You and Bella mean more to me than anything. After I was shot, I asked God for only one thing—that he allow me to live long enough to see . . . that you and Bella were safe. Marrying me is the best way to do that."

He went on to explain all his well-rehearsed reasons, but with each rationale he offered, she retreated from him. She didn't move physically, yet he could feel the distance growing between them. Her shoulders drooped. Her mouth dipped slightly at the corners. Her eyes lost some of their sparkle. It was as if he were watching her dreams die one by one, and he was the one wielding the weapon.

"So you want me to marry you in order to ensure our protection."

"Yes. No. Partly." Gideon growled and thumped his head against the table, welcoming the pain that came with his jerky movements. He deserved it.

"Stop it, Gideon. You'll hurt yourself. Stop." She stood over him, her hands framing his face as she struggled to still his thrashing. Tears pooled in her eyes. He wished he knew if they were from his mess of words or from her concern for his health. Either way, he wanted to banish them.

Logic hadn't helped the situation, so he tossed aside all his pragmatic arguments and spoke from his heart. No longer caring if she thought him weak or foolish or desperate, he opened himself to her, letting her see the love in his eyes, praying it wasn't too late.

"Did you mean what you said, Addie? When I told you I loved you, you whispered something in my ear. Did . . . did you mean it?"

Her face flushed pink, and for a moment panic set in. Had he imagined her fervent vow of love? Or worse, had she only said it to placate a dying man?

She tried to look away, but his gaze followed her, not allowing her to escape his question. "Yes," she said, ducking her head. "I meant it."

The fear coiled around his heart dissolved.

"This isn't how I wanted to do this, Addie. I planned to court you properly with flowers . . . and poetry and sunset rides by the river. Not lying flat on my back on a kitchen table. I've known for some time that I wanted to make you my wife, but I thought to wait until the problems with Petchey were resolved before speaking of my feelings. Now I wish I had said something sooner, for I'm afraid you don't believe my love is real."

Gideon held his breath, waiting for her to offer some kind of confirmation. She said nothing. However, she did lift her gaze to meet his. He opened himself to her, letting her search his soul for the truth behind his words.

"Wanting to protect you and Bella is only part of the reason

I'm asking you to marry me. The smaller part. I don't know if I have five hours or fifty years left on this earth, but I want to spend whatever time remains with you. I love you, Adelaide Proctor. With all my heart."

A tear fell on his chin. She moved her thumb across his jaw to wipe it away. It was soon replaced by another, and another. But he didn't care. All he could see was the trembling smile that beamed above him.

"You already own my heart, Gideon Westcott, and it is yours forever. But before I can give you my hand, I need some time—time to think and to pray. I thought to marry once before, but I followed my own instincts instead of waiting on the Lord's guidance, and ended up lost in a hurtful wilderness of my own making. So even though my instincts are shouting at me to answer yes to your proposal, I can't take that step yet. I need to seek the Lord's will."

Humbled by her vow of love as well as her abiding faith, he nodded. If the Lord saw fit to give him this woman, he would cherish her with every breath he had left in his body.

Slowly, she drew her hands away from his face, her fingers leaving quivers of awareness in their wake. He wanted to grab her and keep her at his side, but he let her go. And as she walked out the back door, he prayed that God would send her an answer soon. He feared his time was running out.

Chapter 32

Adelaide staggered out the back door in a daze. Gideon loved her. He loved her! Elation tugged her spirit upward, like a kite on the wind, yet the severity of his injury yanked her back down to earth. She had dreamed of falling in love with and marrying a handsome hero, but not like this. Not when their life together might only consist of days or hours. She wanted happily ever after.

A good hard ride always cleared her head and aided her prayers; however, that was out of the question. It was dark now, and Juan had her horse. She tilted her head back to view the sky past the porch overhang. Stars peeked through the darkness, and a half-moon glowed overhead. Light in the darkness. Hope.

The chaos within her lessened.

She stepped off the porch and a gusty wind set her skirt flapping. Not sure which direction to take, Adelaide hesitated, letting the wind buffet her for a moment.

"Don't go far, miss." Miguel's voice startled her. She turned and found him in the shadows, one foot braced on the railing and the butt of his rifle balanced on his upraised thigh. "Señor Westcott no like it if something happen to you."

"Don't worry." Adelaide smiled up at him, pulling a windblown strand of hair from the corner of her mouth. "I'll stay within sight of the house. I only need a few minutes."

He nodded to her, and she continued on. Her feet led her to the corral, and a sense of rightness settled over her. Perhaps she felt at peace here because Sheba had been her confidante for so many years—through her father's death and her move to Boston, as well as the debacle with Henry Belcher. Even with Sheba away, the smell of hay and the sound of horses shifting in their stalls soothed her.

Keeping her word to Miguel, Adelaide chose a spot along the front fence line. She sat down beside a post and leaned her back against it as she hugged her knees to her chest.

"What would you have me do, Lord?" A strong breeze carried her whispered petition toward the heavens. "I love him and want to be his wife, but is that your will? Did you lead me here for more than Isabella?"

Tears pooled in her eyes, and the back of her throat began to itch. "I don't want to lose him. I don't want Isabella to lose him, either. You tell us to rest before you and wait patiently for you to act, but I fear my patience is tattered. Have mercy on me, Lord. Show me your way . . . quickly."

Adelaide lifted her head and wiped an errant tear from her cheek. She gazed at the moon, finding comfort in its brightness until a whistled signal brought her head around. Juan was riding in, the doctor's buggy behind him. Miguel must have announced their arrival, for James and Chalmers rushed out of the house to greet them. Adelaide started to stand, anxious to converse with the physician, but an inner voice told her to stay.

James could describe the wound and recount the treatment she had given. Chalmers could fetch whatever might be needed for the examination. Mrs. Chalmers was there to look after Isabella. She could afford to wait a little longer. To seek the Lord's answer. She just needed to trust God enough to be still.

Unfortunately, she didn't want to be still. She wanted to run to the house and consult with the doctor, to watch over his shoulder as he tended Gideon, to absorb everything he said and did. Paralyzed with indecision, she watched as Chalmers escorted the doctor and a second man into the house. James looked around a moment as if searching for her in the darkness, then shut the door.

Adelaide's heart demanded that she hurry and join them. Her soul urged her to be still before the Lord. The battle tossed her back and forth for several minutes before she surrendered at last to her spirit's call.

With effort, she dragged her gaze from the kitchen door and directed it once again to the moon suspended low in the sky above Westcott Cottage. The wind blew silhouetted clouds in front of the bright half circle, successively blocking and then unveiling its glow. She sat numbly for several minutes, staring heavenward, her mind unfocused. Clouds continued to breeze past.

Except for one.

Adelaide leaned forward and squinted. One cloud stubbornly refused to move. Perhaps it hung at a lower altitude, where the wind currents were different, or maybe her eyes were simply playing tricks on her, but her heart sped up just the same. Could it be that the figurative cloud the Lord had used to direct her there had become a physical signal for her to stay?

" 'And when the cloud was taken up from over the tabernacle,' " she quoted under her breath, " 'the children of Israel went onward in all their journeys: But if the cloud were not taken up, then they journeyed not till the day that it was taken up.' "

Her cloud had not been taken up.

Adelaide's heart seized upon the excuse to follow her heart's desire, while logic argued that the weather phenomenon was a coincidence of nature. Adelaide closed her eyes and looked deeper for her answers. Deeper than intelligence could take her. Further even than the depths of her emotions. She looked to her soul for confirmation. And there she found it. The Lord wanted her right where she was. With Gideon.

Doubts extinguished, she leapt to her feet and raced back to the house, nearly giddy in her eagerness to accept Gideon's proposal. She bit her lip in a futile effort to keep her smile contained, yet when she opened the door to an empty kitchen, it faded all on its own. The table was bare. Surely he hadn't . . . hadn't . . .

"Gideon!"

She pushed through the door that led to the hall and collided with Mrs. Garrett. Adelaide grabbed the older woman's arm to help steady her.

"Mabel, where's—"

"They took him upstairs to his room. Don't get your knickers in a knot. He's still breathing."

Air whooshed out of her lungs, and relief weakened her knees. Suddenly she was the one unsteady on her feet.

"Doc should be done with him pretty soon. Oh, and the preacher's in there, too. Praying, I guess. Although why he couldn't do that from town is hard to figure. It's not like the good Lord ain't already aware of what's going on."

The preacher. Adelaide's stomach fluttered. He wasn't just there to pray. She'd better tidy her appearance and throw on a clean dress. It seemed her wedding day had arrived.

Gideon had expected the luxury of his fine hair mattress and goose-feather pillows to bring him a measure of relief after spending what seemed an eternity on the unyielding kitchen table. However, being carted upstairs like a dangling deer carcass and poked and prodded by Dr. Bellows left him feeling as if he'd been moved to purgatory instead of his bedchamber. He breathed a sigh of relief when the doctor finally finished wrapping him back up and started preparing a morphine injection.

"This will help with the pain and will probably make you sleepy." Dr. Bellows walked toward his bed, a hypodermic syringe in hand.

Gideon was more than ready to have his pain eased, but he needed his mind clear for a little longer. He had to wait for Adelaide's answer.

Reluctantly, he shook his head and ignored the man's raised eyebrows. "Not yet, Dr. Bellows. I have a few matters to attend to first. In fact, I was hoping that you and the parson would witness the signing of my new will."

Understanding mixed with pity dawned in the middle-aged man's eyes. "Of course, Mr. Westcott. I would be honored." He returned to the bureau and carefully laid the syringe atop his roll of instruments.

James pushed away from the wall beside Gideon's headboard. "I'll fetch the papers," he said and strode toward the small desk situated beneath the window across the room.

He and Brother Kent had remained with Gideon during the examination, flanking him on either side of the bed. James had lent the physician a hand whenever it was required, while the minister quietly prayed in the background. Kent hadn't been too thrilled when Gideon explained his intention to marry Adelaide before knowing if he would survive. But he'd agreed to perform the rite if the lady consented. Now all they needed was the lady.

A soft knock sounded on the door. Dr. Bellows was closest, so he stepped forward and opened it. Adelaide glided into the room, a delicate blush staining her cheeks. Gideon's eyes connected with hers for only a moment before she turned back to the doctor, but the love conveyed in that brief glance stole his breath.

"You must be Miss Proctor. I've been admiring your handi-work." Dr. Bellows took her arm and led her toward Gideon.

She had changed into her sunshine calico and pinned her hair back into place. Gideon's pulse leapt as hope swelled within him. It was possible that Addie had simply tidied her appearance because they had company, but he preferred to believe another motivation had inspired the change. One that involved him and the answer to a particular question.

"You did a fine job cleaning the wound site, my dear." Dr. Bellows patted the back of her hand and grinned at her. "If you ever find yourself in need of a new position, I could use a nurse with your skills."

"Thank you, but . . ." Addie's gaze dropped to the floor, and her blush deepened. "As to positions . . . well . . . I've decided to accept one that was offered to me just this evening. A permanent position." She lifted her eyes and smiled shyly at Gideon. Joy exploded in his chest.

He swallowed hard and tried to find his voice. "Addie, do you mean . . . ?"

"Yes, Gideon. I will be your wife."

Not even the morphine waiting in the syringe across the room could make him feel better than he felt at that moment.

Adelaide let go of the doctor's arm and clutched Gideon's hand, her gaze sinking into him like warm butter into toast. "No matter what comes."

He squeezed her fingers with what strength he could muster and echoed her pledge. "No matter what comes."

A throat cleared behind them, and Adelaide pulled her gaze away from Gideon as the preacher elbowed his way between them.

"I have agreed to marry the two of you, for I know you both to be God-fearing people who would not enter into matrimony lightly. However, I have to ask you, Miss Proctor, if you are certain. Knowing the truth about Westcott's condition, are you willing to enter into this sacred union even if it is to end in sorrow?"

Gideon's wound throbbed more menacingly as he waited for

her answer. Her grip on his hand remained steady, though, as she met Brother Kent's eye. "All marriages eventually end in sorrow, do they not? The joy comes in cherishing what time you are able to share."

The minister smiled at her, all reservations erased from his features. Gideon relaxed, as well. How had he ever managed to win this incredible woman for his own? She deserved so much better than a man on his last leg, yet he couldn't imagine letting her go.

"Very well, then, we can proceed whenever you're ready," the minister proclaimed.

"Balderdash!" Dr. Bellows scowled down at them. "It's obvious the girl is caught up in some romantic fantasy about granting a dying man's request."

"A living man's request," Adelaide interrupted, her chin jutting out at a stubborn angle.

Gideon grinned. She was a fighter all right. His fighter.

The doctor went on as if he hadn't heard her. "You can't in good conscience marry them, Kent. She obviously doesn't know the truth about his condition. I haven't even talked with her yet."

"Then talk, Doctor." Adelaide crossed her arms over her chest and braced her legs apart as if facing a physical battle. The man glared down at her. Gideon's jaw tightened. James came up beside him and laid a steadying hand on his shoulder.

"Men don't recover from abdominal wounds, Miss Proctor. They die a slow, agonizing death. Are you prepared to listen to his screams? To watch him wither away from malnutrition? To endure the bruises when he lashes out at you in fevered delirium?"

"Yes."

Her quiet statement rang with assurance. Dr. Bellows's eyes widened in surprise, and for a moment, uncertainty hovered over his features before he shook his head and regained his cynicism.

"You can't possibly understand—"

"Enough, Bellows." Gideon would not allow the man to insult

Addie. Her beautiful spirit and fanciful imagination were part of what he loved about her, part of her strength. "Your professional opinion is welcome, but your cruelty . . . is not. You will address Miss Proctor with respect and courtesy or you will . . . leave my home."

"It's all right, Gideon. He's just testing me. Aren't you, Doctor?" Her face softened and her arms slid down to her sides as she tilted her head to regard the physician with a mixture of curiosity and conviction.

"You know firsthand how hard it is to watch someone die," she continued. "That's why you distance yourself. You have to in your profession. However, I'm not in your profession. If I choose to draw nearer to Gideon despite the pain it might cause, that is my right. I'm not a foolish girl whose dreams keep me from acknowledging reality. Yes, I agreed to marry him, but I also dressed his wounds. I have contemplated his mortality, Doctor. Nevertheless, I cling to hope and will dose him with it every chance I get."

Dr. Bellows ran a hand through his thinning hair and sighed. "You are right, of course. It's not my place to interfere. It's just that . . ." The man suddenly looked older than his years. "I know the pain of losing a spouse. I thought only to spare you that."

Compassion stirred in Gideon's heart. He'd forgotten the man was a widower. Now that he could see past the bluster, he recognized the grief still etched into his face. Would Addie have the same worn look in a few years? Or would her faith ease her grief?

She looked at him then, and he knew in his bones that Addie belonged to him, and he to her. Hope shone in her eyes, and he felt his own dreams awaken. Her courage bolstered his, infusing him with the will to fight. For the first time since José's bullet pierced his skin, he began to believe, truly believe, that recovery was possible.

"If you want to spare me pain, Doctor," she said, tightening her grip on his hand, "help me make him well."

Chapter 33

Her wedding looked nothing like the one in her dreams. A sickroom instead of a chapel with stained-glass windows. An everyday calico dress instead of tiers of golden satin and ivory lace. Her groom propped up in bed, lines of strain etching his face instead of the smiling man she'd imagined standing proudly at the end of an aisle. No flowers. No music. No crowd of well-wishers. Yet one element permeated the event exactly as she had envisioned it.

Love.

From Mr. and Mrs. Chalmers, who leaned into each other and nodded while the preacher expounded on the virtues of marriage, to Mabel Garrett, who dabbed her eyes with her apron every two minutes. Isabella, in her cotton nightgown and bare feet, beamed as she joined in the ceremony, placing her own small hands atop Adelaide's and Gideon's joined ones. But the strongest evidence of all lay in the intensity of emotion that glimmered in Gideon's eyes as he vowed to cherish her. His love was so raw, so transparent, so true that no chapel or dress or flowers could have improved upon the moment.

It might not have been the wedding of her dreams, but it was the wedding of her heart.

After all the necessary documents had been signed and witnessed, Adelaide began shooing people from the room. Gideon's wan complexion worried her, as did the way he slumped over his pillows at a crooked angle, too exhausted to hold his head up properly.

"Mrs. Chalmers?" Adelaide motioned the housekeeper to her side. "Please make up the guest chamber for Brother Kent. You may put Dr. Bellows in my room." A touch of heat warmed her face. "I'll be staying with my husband tonight."

My husband. The thought sent delightful little shivers dancing down her arms.

The housekeeper smiled knowingly at her. "I'll see to it at once, *Mrs. Westcott.*"

Adelaide bit back her burgeoning grin and turned to the cook.

"Mrs. Garrett, would you mind putting together a cold supper for those of us who have not eaten yet tonight? With all the excitement, I don't believe our guests have been offered any refreshment after their journey."

Mabel swiped at her eyes a final time and reclaimed her usual sour expression, hiding away the tender heart that everyone in the house knew existed behind her grumpy façade.

"The beef's probably dry as kindling by now, but I'll see if I can salvage enough for sandwiches."

"Thank you, Mrs. Garrett. I know you'll work wonders. You always do."

Isabella tugged on Adelaide's skirt. "Can I sing my song now, Miss Addie? Papa Gidyon's already in bed."

She opened her mouth to respond, but Dr. Bellows murmured in her ear, arresting the words on her tongue. "He needs a morphine injection first, ma'am. He's been battling a long time."

Adelaide wrapped her arm around her new daughter's shoulder as she glanced back toward Gideon. He'd held the pain at bay for hours and was now paying the price for his courage. His eyes were closed, yet his face was far from relaxed. Deep lines cut into his forehead and around his mouth. Her heart ached with his suffering.

"Why don't we let Dr. Bellows give him his medicine first, Izzy," she said, giving the girl's arm a squeeze. "Then you can sing. I know your papa is looking forward to it."

Dr. Bellows nodded to her and retrieved the syringe from the bureau. Adelaide steered Isabella away from the sight of the needle and moved to join James and Brother Kent by the window. Despite her concern for her husband, she plopped her best hostess smile into place and clasped the preacher's hand.

"Thank you so much for coming out to the ranch tonight, Parson. Your prayers have been a blessing. And even though our request to marry was rushed and unconventional, our vows were true, and the words you spoke over us were lovely."

"Glad to be here, my dear." He released her hand, and a boyish grin spread across his face. "Martha's going to be beside herself when I tell her." The preacher glanced sideways at James. "My wife has been speculating on the matchmaking possibilities between these two since the first Sunday Westcott brought her to services."

"I had much the same thought when she waltzed into my Fort Worth office." James winked and held out the packet of papers he had just folded up. "And now I have proof that I was right." He tucked the papers into his jacket pocket and patted his chest where they protruded. "Your wife will have to fight me for the bragging rights."

"Listen to you two." Adelaide shook her head at them in mock reproof, her mood lightened momentarily by their silly banter.

"Martha will probably take me to task for denying her the chance to do up the church for the ceremony. There's nothing she loves more than all that feminine froufrou that goes into a wedding. Perhaps after Gideon recovers, the two of you can have a second ceremony at the church so Martha and the other ladies can make a big fuss."

Her eyes burned with the tingle of oncoming tears at the hope inherent in his statement. He spoke of Gideon's recovery as if it were assured. After all the dire predictions from everyone, including Gideon, the minister's faith-filled statement served as a salve on her battered spirit. She blinked away the tears and cleared the excess emotion from her throat. "I would like that very much."

Isabella, who until then had been waiting patiently while the adults conversed, grabbed hold of Adelaide's arm and began swaying back and forth. The swaying turned into hopping, which caused Adelaide to have to catch her balance several times. Anxious to redirect the child's energy, Adelaide glanced over her shoulder to check on the doctor's progress. He was packing his bag, the injection completed.

She turned back to her guests. "Mrs. Garrett is preparing some refreshment downstairs for you, gentlemen. James, would you show Brother Kent to the dining room?"

The men accepted her not-so-subtle hint with graciousness and headed toward the door. James slowed his step for a moment, however, and drew her aside.

"Gideon asked me to post a letter to his family," he said in a low voice. "I'll hold it for a day if you would like to add a personal note."

His parents. All this time, she had been so wrapped up in her own distress, she had not spared them a single thought. How the news of Gideon's injury would grieve them. She was sure James would supply a detailed account of what had happened and explain why their son had felt compelled to marry in haste, but he couldn't assure them of her love or how she would do everything in her power to help make him well. James wouldn't think to write of Isabella and her speaking, giving Gideon's parents something to rejoice about even in the face of their worry for their son's survival.

"Yes. Thank you, James. I would like to write to them very much. I'll see to it in the morning."

Isabella jumped up and tried to hang from Adelaide's arm, but slipped off when Adelaide tipped to the side. The little monkey was driving her to distraction. She clamped her mouth shut on the snippy reprimand that tried to dart out. If Isabella didn't cease her tugging and grabbing soon . . . Adelaide inhaled a deep breath through her nose in an effort to hide her frustration. Her emotions had been seesawing for hours now, and her control was quickly reaching threadbare status.

"Now, Miss Addie? Now can I sing?"

Adelaide gladly seized the suggestion. "Yes, Izzy. This is the perfect time for you to sing."

With a grin, Isabella finally let go of Adelaide's arm and skipped over to Gideon's bedside.

"Papa Gidyon, Papa Gidyon. Are you ready for your song?"

Adelaide reached the bed at a more sedate pace, her gaze intent on Gideon's face. His brows lifted first, then his lids, too heavy to rise more than half-mast. His brown eyes were clouded. From the pain or the morphine, she didn't know.

"I'm ready, Bella mine," he slurred. He attempted a smile, but it ended up looking more like a twitch. Isabella didn't seem to mind, though. She pirouetted until her gown belled out around her ankles, then curtsied as if the impromptu dance was part of the performance. Stepping closer to the bed, she drew breath and began to sing in a clear soprano that shocked Adelaide with its purity.

> "Sleep my child and peace attend thee,
> All through the night.
> Guardian angels God will send thee,
> All through the night.

> Soft the drowsy hours are creeping
> Hill and vale in slumber sleeping,
> I my loving vigil keeping
> All through the night."

The tune of the familiar folk song pierced Adelaide's heart as she gazed upon the man she loved. Her lips didn't form the words, but her mind echoed them, praying for God to send guardian angels and vowing to keep a loving vigil throughout the long night ahead.

Isabella continued on with a verse Adelaide had not heard before. As she sang, Gideon tilted his chin up just enough to peer into Adelaide's eyes.

> "Love, to thee my thoughts are turning
> All through the night.
> All for thee my heart is yearning,
> All through the night.
> Though sad fate our lives may sever
> Parting will not last forever,
> There's a hope that leaves me never,
> All through the night."

No longer able to hold back her tears, Adelaide had to turn away. Thankfully, Isabella launched into yet another verse of the lullaby, providing Adelaide a chance to step aside and compose herself. A handkerchief swam before her, attached to the blurry arm of Dr. Bellows.

"Thank you." Adelaide took the proffered cotton square and dried her eyes. She smiled self-consciously as she handed the handkerchief back to the doctor.

"Would you like to discuss the treatment for your husband while the child is distracted with her song?"

Adelaide's nurturing instincts snapped to attention, shoving aside her more weepy emotions. She glanced back at the bed, but neither father nor daughter seemed aware of her at the moment.

"Yes, Doctor," she said, ridding herself of her melancholia with a final sniff. "Tell me what to do."

He guided her toward the door and spoke in a quiet voice so as not to be overheard. "Don't allow him any solid food for several days, and only enough water to keep him hydrated. With a puncture wound like this, the damage goes too deep for sutures, so I simply packed the wound and replaced his bandage. You will need to change the dressings twice a day. I'll leave you some laudanum to help with the pain, and I'll administer another morphine injection before I leave in the morning."

Adelaide nodded, making mental notes of his instructions.

"Do you have any questions?" the doctor asked as he grasped the handle of his bag and swung the small satchel off the bureau.

She could only think of one. "When will we know if he is going to live?"

He rubbed the back of his neck and let out an audible breath. "It's hard to say, ma'am. I've never seen a man in this condition recover. However, I have read of cases where soldiers survived similar wounds during the war. Recovery depends on how much damage the bullet does as it passes through the abdominal cavity. If it doesn't hit any major organs or cause internal hemorrhage, the patient has a chance to survive. It's not likely, but it is possible. As long as infection doesn't set in."

"So, how long until we know?" she repeated, needing something tangible to grasp.

Dr. Bellows tugged on the corner of his mustache. "I don't know for certain, Mrs. Westcott. But if your husband survives the next two or three days, I'd say his odds would be greatly improved."

Adelaide clung to the number the doctor had given her. Three days. She just had to keep him alive for three days.

She squared her shoulders and flicked a crisp nod. "Thank you, Doctor."

He collected his hat and disappeared through the doorway. She probably should have offered to escort him downstairs, but she didn't want to leave Gideon. Dr. Bellows was an intelligent man. Surely he could find the dining room by himself. His nose would lead him there if nothing else.

Suddenly the quiet in the room hit her. Isabella had finished her song. Adelaide spun around to see a little nightgown-clad angel kneeling by the side of Gideon's bed. The mattress stood too high for her to place her elbows on top, so she folded her hands in front of her and rested her forehead against the edge of the ticking.

"Dear God, you made Papa Gidyon a little better, but his hurts are still there. Did you forget to take them away? I'll keep 'minding you till they're all gone."

Adelaide smiled, her own head bowed as she listened.

"Oh, and thank you for giving me a new mama. If I can't have my old mama back, Miss Addie is the next best thing. Amen."

Contentment seeped into Adelaide's heart like warm oil, softening every hardened edge and renewing each tattered corner. She padded over to her daughter and helped her get up from the floor.

"Papa Gidyon fell asleep during my song," Isabella whispered as she regained her feet, "but I think he liked it."

Adelaide lifted the girl into her arms and braced her on a hip. "I'm sure he did, sweetheart. It was lovely."

Isabella's jaw stretched down in a wide yawn, eliciting an answering one from Adelaide. Time for bed.

After tucking Isabella in and kissing her cheek good-night, Adelaide exited the child's room and stood, unmoving, in the hall. An absurd tingle of nervousness ran through her. What did she have to be nervous about? Yes, it was her wedding night, but Gideon was certainly in no condition to perform his husbandly duties.

However, that fact did nothing to stop Adelaide's stomach from flopping around like a landed fish as she finally goaded herself down the hall.

At Gideon's door, she grasped the handle and paused. Tonight was her chance to finally be a wife—to be Gideon's wife. She didn't know how much time the Lord would grant them, so she dared not waste a moment of it. Taking a deep breath, she turned the knob and crept into the room.

With all the visitors gone, the room seemed large and a bit intimidating. Adelaide crossed halfway to the bed and stopped. She hadn't thought to get a nightgown. *Fiddlesticks.* Now what? She could sleep fully dressed, but that would be horribly uncomfortable. After the day she'd had, how could she deny herself the pleasure of finally removing her stays and relaxing in unfettered sleep? Simple. She couldn't.

She looked over at the bureau. Every bride should be wrapped in her husband's arms on her wedding night. Gideon might not be able to hold her, but she could still be wrapped up in him. A grin tugged at the corners of her lips.

Quietly sliding one drawer open after another, Adelaide finally found what she was looking for. She peeked behind her to make sure Gideon continued to sleep and dashed over to the corner farthest from the bed. The chamber had no screen to shelter her as she disrobed, so she turned her back to the room and hastily yanked the clothes from her body. Feeling scandalous, she dropped Gideon's soft flannel work shirt over her head and slipped her arms into the sleeves. Even though the hem of the shirt fell past her knees, her sense of modesty wouldn't allow her to remove her drawers. It also compelled her to button the shirt up to her chin—or collarbone, seeing as how the oversized shirt hung like a tablecloth on her petite frame.

It was his, though, and she imagined him holding her as she hugged herself and lifted the fabric to her nose. The smell of soap and sunshine was pleasant, but she wished it carried Gideon's scent. She rolled the sleeves up to her wrists and, leaving her discarded clothing heaped in the corner, tiptoed to the bed.

Careful not to wiggle the mattress too much, she lifted the sheet and crawled in next to him. *Ah.* There was the aroma she'd been craving—in the sheets and on the man himself. Adelaide closed her eyes and inhaled. After a moment, she opened her eyes again, curled onto her side to face her new husband, and watched him sleep. The rhythmic rise and fall of his chest. The gentle rumble of his breathing—not quite a snore, but loud enough that she didn't need to strain to hear him. It was comforting, peaceful.

All at once, the peace shattered as he moaned in his sleep and thrashed his arms about. Heart racing, Adelaide leaned over him and grasped his wrists.

"Shh, Gideon. It's all right. Be still." She continued to murmur soft words to him and hold him down until he relaxed. Even after he settled, she continued hovering over him, stroking his thick, dark hair and dropping occasional kisses on his forehead.

Outwardly, the peace had returned, but inwardly, Adelaide's fears began to churn once again.

"I expect you to fight for me, Gideon Westcott," she whispered, her jaw tense. "Just because I agreed to marry you doesn't mean the battle is over. I signed up to be a wife, not a widow, and I demand a happy ending to our story. It is your duty, husband."

He moaned again, and she thought she saw his lashes flutter. She ducked away and curled back onto her side, letting out a moan of her own. Stealing the man's sleep was no way to speed his recovery. Laying more burdens and foolish demands on him probably didn't help, either. She just wanted a life with him so much. So much, she ached with it.

Am I asking for too much, Lord?

She fell asleep waiting for an answer that never came.

Chapter 34

Reginald Petchey squinted at his solicitor through the dim glow of a single greasy lamp that stood atop the table between them. Hazy shadows confounded the man's features.

"Are you telling me that Westcott is still alive?"

Farnsworth's Adam's apple bulged from his scrawny neck as he swallowed long and slow. "I-I'm afraid so, my lord."

Reginald charged to his feet, sending the rickety chair flying out from under him. "It's been a week, Farnsworth. A week!"

He stalked his assistant. The coward backed away until the weathered planks of the wall halted his retreat. Reginald pounced with one vengeful strike, slamming his fist into the wood behind the man's head. Farnsworth flinched, and sweat beaded on his forehead, but he held his chin up. The show of mettle only enraged Reginald further.

"I've endured the squalor of this . . . this . . ." He gestured around at the insect-infested shell of a building he had condescended to live in.

"Line shack, sir."

Reginald's eyes snapped back to Farnsworth, and he wished he could bore into the man with something more substantial than a heated scowl. His hands itched to encircle the man's throat and squeeze just enough to . . . He gritted his teeth. Through his clenched jaw, he spat out his disgust one word at a time, his enunciation so fierce that tiny specks of saliva sprayed across Farnsworth's pinched face.

"I . . . don't . . . care . . . what . . . it's . . . called."

Could the idiot not see what was important here? Like any good hunter, he'd been prepared to wait. He'd set up the ambush and timed everything to perfection. Unfortunately, the worthless Mexican he'd hired had proven to be a flawed weapon, wounding his prey instead of killing it with a clean shot. Yet Reginald hadn't panicked. Weapons malfunctioned occasionally. One could not escape that. A good hunter must simply adjust his strategy and choose a new method for taking down his target. When José, bleeding and whining, staggered into the saloon to collect his pay last Friday, he assured Reginald that he had left Westcott with a gaping hole in his gut and a guaranteed appointment with death.

So Reginald had waited, selecting time as his new weapon of choice. He'd packed up his belongings and holed himself up in this miserable shack that sat on the western border of Westcott's property, waiting and listening for the chance to make his move. For a week! And now Farnsworth was telling him that it had all been for nothing?

A roar exploded from him, and he punched the wall again before turning away from his solicitor.

"Perhaps we should g-g-go back to England, my lord."

"And admit defeat? Out of the question." Rage grew within him until he could no longer think clearly. He wanted to strike something. Someone. But brute strength couldn't give him the results he needed. No. He required cunning, and cunning required thinking. Reginald forced himself to stop prowling around the square room like a caged beast. He straightened his cravat, brushed the lint from his brocade vest, and buttoned down the anger that seethed beneath the surface.

"I'm not like you, Farnsworth. I don't abandon my purpose at the first sign of adversity. I persevere. I look for new paths of attack, unthought-of strategies, hidden weaknesses not yet exploited. . . ."

A faint inkling tugged at his consciousness, taking nebulous shape. The energy that had fueled his rage immediately rechanneled to feed his mind. Possibilities flashed before him, almost too fast for him to keep up. But he did. A familiar rush of power surged. He loved being brilliant.

"I'm not suggesting we run away, my lord, just relocate temporarily." Farnsworth's voice buzzed like a fly in his ear. Distracting. Irritating. Making him want to swat the fellow with a giant rolled newspaper. "Our funds are nearly depleted, after all."

"And they won't be restored without the girl," Reginald barked without looking up. He paced around the tiny room and shoved Farnsworth out of his way as he circled the table. "Now, cease your bellyaching and let me think."

Westcott was still alive. And if he'd survived a week with a hole in his gut, he couldn't be counted on to succumb any time soon.

"Tell me again what the Menardville doctor said," Reginald ordered.

"It was much the same as when I traveled to town three days ago. I reiterated how thankful I was to find a doctor in the wilds of Texas who had the capability of bringing a man back from the very brink of death. This time he didn't question me about how I had heard about the case, and was more forthcoming with the particulars. Apparently tales of the rancher's recovery have spread all over town since my last visit.

"After examining my throat to ascertain if the lozenges he'd prescribed had eased the redness, Dr. Bellows updated me on

Mr. Westcott's recovery. He didn't mention Westcott's name, of course, but it's highly doubtful that he was speaking of another man with an abdominal gunshot injury." Farnsworth held his hand to his throat and stuck out his chin, as if trying to alleviate the discomfort of his feigned symptom.

Although, it hadn't been completely feigned. Reginald would never overlook such a detail. In order to avoid arousing the doctor's suspicions, Farnsworth had downed three cups of scalding-hot tea at Reginald's insistence prior to riding to town. The fellow had teared up like an infant, too. Pathetic creature.

"When I asked him if he had thought to write a paper for the medical journals on his successful treatment of the usually fatal wound," Farnsworth continued, "he became quite animated about the case. He indicated that Westcott's recovery would lend credence to something called abstentionist theory and would serve to refute a particular upstart physician named Sims who advocated an odd procedure called a laparotomy. I have no idea what he was talking about, but in the course of his rambling, he did mention that Westcott has only recently begun taking food—broths and liquids for the most part. He no longer receives morphine injections— although the wound continues to pain him substantially—and as far as the doctor knows, he has yet to leave his bed."

Reginald stopped pacing and stared without focus toward the ceiling. "So the man is weak. As one would expect. It would be better if he were dead, but in his current condition, that should be easy enough to rectify."

Farnsworth coughed, interrupting Reginald's train of thought. "Why not just snatch the girl and carry her back to England? Westcott is in no position to stop you. We should just take our leave of this blasted country before we end up on the gallows."

Reginald glared his man into silence. "As long as Westcott is alive, he threatens my claim to Isabella. You know that. Now stop being squeamish and let me figure the rest of this out."

Farnsworth slunk into the corner and, for once, kept his mouth shut.

Westcott was a noble type. Weakness. He was physically impoverished. Weakness. His men were tired from double shifts of guard duty. Weakness.

Reginald had spied out the ranch. He knew of the guards. But after a week without a single glimpse of trouble, their attentiveness and motivation would be greatly decreased. Most of them were probably grumbling about their pointless duty even now. He could use that to his advantage. And once the guard was dismantled, he could draw Westcott out with a bit of well-placed bait. Isabella would do nicely. Or that woman José had told him about, the one whose honor Westcott had defended with such gallantry. A man like Westcott could never sit back in safety while a female under his protection was in danger. He'd charge to his own death first.

Which was exactly what Reginald was counting on.

"Farnsworth, pack my bags. We're leaving this shack."

"For home, my lord?" The hope in his tone was comical. One would think that by now the man would know him better.

"No. You're going to register Mr. Edward Church and his companion at the Australian Hotel in Menardville. Westcott is sure to have eyes and ears working in town, and I plan to give them something to report. You and I will put in an appearance this afternoon. I told that sneak Bevin that I wanted to learn all I could about the town in order to report back to my dear mother's friend, so I shall. I'll visit the shops, the card tables, maybe even that doctor of yours. Then we'll pay that long overdue visit to Mr. Gideon Westcott."

"We?" his mouse of an assistant squeaked. "But w-what about his guards?"

Reginald smiled, savoring the audacity of his new plan. "We'll go in unarmed, of course. Two gentlemen come to discuss the possibility of renegotiating the current terms of guardianship."

"Westcott will never relinquish the child."

"No." Reginald flicked a piece of lint from his sleeve. "However, I imagine he knows enough about my situation at this point to expect me to try to bribe him out of his principles. And I'll oblige him. When he turns me down, I'll threaten to return to England and fight him with every last pound at my disposal to have my niece returned to the bosom of her natural family. Then we'll return to town and lament our need to leave without getting what we came for, creating a great display of disgruntled defeat. We will procure a coach, or whatever rustic conveyance the local livery can offer, and leave town, never to return."

"Only we aren't really leaving, are we?" Farnsworth asked, doom lacing his words.

Reginald grinned in answer. Gideon Westcott would soon have no say in Isabella's future.

Chapter 35

Early morning light filtered through the edges of the thick damask curtains of Gideon's bedchamber, teasing his eyelids open. The fogginess that usually plagued his mind after his drug-induced sleep was strangely absent. He pulled together fragmented memories and recalled Dr. Bellows's last visit. Two days ago, maybe three. The doctor had forgone his morphine injection, having determined that enough healing had occurred to wean him off the medication, and last night Gideon decided to go without laudanum, as well. Waking clearheaded and alert was a luxury he had taken for granted, but after struggling through a mental haze every morning for the last ten days, he'd developed a keen appreciation for the experience.

With a tentative motion, Gideon stretched an arm in the air and winced at the tightness in his midsection. It still hurt, but the severity had diminished. Of course, some of the soreness was likely due to his unsanctioned excursions. Against doctor's orders, he'd been hobbling the length of his room in the afternoons, using the furniture for support. He'd barely been able to stand the first time he attempted it four days ago, but he'd gradually worked up his endurance and yesterday made it to his desk and back. Though not up for a footrace, knowing he could putter about under his own steam soothed his pride and gave him confidence that he would regain his full strength in time. Something he thanked God for every day.

Stiff from lying in one position most of the night and a bit too warm, Gideon flung the blankets back and rolled to his left, holding the sheet aloft to ease his turn. He sucked in a sharp breath as pain shot up his torso and protectively pulled his knees up as he gingerly burrowed onto his side. Right into Adelaide.

His eyes widened, and the breath he had just inhaled hung suspended in his lungs.

Addie.

In his bed.

She puckered her face, disgruntled by his shifting, then let out a small moan and snuggled close to his chest. Her full lips parted on a satisfied sigh, and his pulse reacted as if the gentle sound were the crack of a starting pistol for the Thoroughbreds at Newmarket. It leapt forward and raced at a breakneck pace. His breath quivered while he debated for a second or two about what to do. Making up his mind, he settled his hand into the dip of her waist.

His gaze crawled over her, taking the time to absorb every detail of the woman he loved. The way her dark lashes rested against her creamy skin, flirting with the faded freckles along the tops of her cheeks. The way her unraveled braid left chestnut waves cascading over the pillow. The way the line of her neck created a hollow where it joined with her collarbone before disappearing under the fabric of . . . his work shirt?

His mouth quirked. She was wearing his shirt. For some odd reason, that fact gratified him even more than finding her in bed beside him. She could have shared his bed for convenience's sake, to make it easier to tend him during the night. But wearing his shirt?

That was personal. Possessive. She wasn't in his bed out of a sense of duty. She was in his bed because she cared. For him.

His shirt had crept to the tops of her thighs, and his eyes greedily drank in the shapely legs that lay tangled in his sheets. Even encased in drawers, their slender curves were evident.

Gideon loved Addie's beautiful spirit and godly heart, but he couldn't deny that her figure pleased him, too. Quite a lot. He suddenly found a compelling new motivation to recover his strength.

Memories tugged at the edge of his mind, leaving him fairly certain she had slept in his bed before. He remembered her discarded clothes in the corner, and the trace of her scent on the pillow next to him. He even had vague recollections of her hands on his arms and her soothing voice shushing him as he battled the pain that burned through him like a hot iron. Yet until now, she'd never been in his bed when he awakened. He vowed to change that pattern. This delight was too rich to pass up.

Like an ancient explorer charting undiscovered territory, Gideon trailed a finger out of the valley of her waist and along the rising slope of her hip. He followed the line of her thigh as far as he could reach, then turned back to retrace his steps. Tripping over the wrinkles in the oversized shirt, he continued north—onto the level plains of her arm, over the swell of her shoulder, and onto the delicate path of her neck.

Pieces of a past conversation broke into his awareness. Addie lecturing him on his duty to give her a happy ending. A sensual smile curled his lips. He was more than willing to fulfill his husbandly duties. All of them.

Unable to resist any longer, he buried his fingers in the hair at the base of her neck and angled her face upward. He leaned forward and dropped soft little kisses onto her lips, starting at the corner and working his way across until she began to stir.

Her lashes flittered. "Gid—?"

He smothered her question with his kiss. No longer playful, he took her mouth fully, holding nothing back. She was no longer Adelaide Proctor, governess. She was Adelaide Westcott, wife.

His wife.

It didn't take long for her to recover from her surprise. She clasped his shoulder for support and stretched toward him. His pulse surged, and when she finally pulled away, he refused to let her separate from him completely. He rested his forehead against hers and listened to their ragged breaths echoing in the quiet morning.

"Feeling better today, are we?" Adelaide asked as she lowered her head back down to her pillow, her face a becoming shade of pink.

Gideon grinned. "A little."

He traced the line of her hair around the perimeter of her face, tucking the loose strands he collected behind her ear. Her eyelids drifted closed, and a tremulous smile hovered over her lips. His heart hitched. How had he come to be so blessed? Not only had the Lord seen fit to spare his life, but he had given him a woman full of sunshine and love.

Sunshine. Hmm. Gideon stroked Addie's arm and fingered the blue fabric that bunched at her wrist. "I think this is the first time I've seen you wear a color other than yellow."

She opened her eyes and met his gaze. "When I selected it, I was more concerned with holding on to something of yours than coordinating it with my wardrobe." She bit her lip, and her attention dropped to a location somewhere below his chin. Her hands waved about in the small space between their two bodies as she rambled. "I hope you don't mind that I borrowed it. I forgot my sleeping gown that first night, and I found it comforting to wear your shirt, so I continued the habit even after I moved my belongings to your room. Oh, and that's another thing. I cleared out a drawer in your bureau and hung my dresses next to your coats. I hope—"

He laid his finger atop her lips to stop her nervous chatter.

"Your place is with me now, Addie. I want you here. Move whatever you like. Wear whatever you like. All I care about is having you by my side."

She dipped her chin in a nod and briefly closed her eyes, squeezing out a tear.

The droplet rolled over her temple and soaked into the sunbleached pillowcase. Gideon ached at the sight. He caressed the side of her face with his knuckles in an effort to erase the trail.

"What's wrong, Addie?"

She pressed her lips together, but not before he noticed their trembling.

"I'm just so thankful to have you living and breathing," she burst out, and relief washed over him. "I tried to believe and be brave for Isabella and the others, but deep inside I was so afraid I would lose you."

Ignoring the soreness in his abdomen, Gideon gathered her close. He tucked her head under his jaw and stroked her back.

"I'm not going anywhere, dear heart. I have a happy ending to write with you."

Addie stiffened. "You heard that?" she muttered against his chest.

Gideon chuckled, his joy too large to contain. He pulled back just enough to see her face. "Yes, I did, my little dreamer. And I plan to fulfill that duty to the best of my ability."

He sealed his pledge with a kiss filled with tender promises of all that was yet to come.

Adelaide hummed the rest of the day. She cut Isabella's lessons short because she was too distracted by thoughts of her new husband, and when Gideon insisted on being helped down to the parlor for a change of scenery that afternoon, she found one reason after another to saunter over there just to see him smile. Those glorious dimples were back in force.

The friendly, welcoming smiles she had grown to love still made her breath catch, but he'd added a new weapon to his arsenal. A secret, intimate smile that reminded her of warm kisses and strong arms. It never failed to flush her cheeks and flutter her stomach. The man was an invalid in a dressing gown convalescing amid a mound of cushions on the parlor settee; yet when he smiled at her like that, he became masculinity personified. Gideon had a dash of the rogue in him. And Adelaide adored him for it.

Now she stood at the kitchen table, cutting a slab of corn bread and crumbling it into a bowl. He'd complained earlier about not having anything to dig his teeth into. Said a man couldn't be expected to regain his health if he only consumed liquids.

He'd begged her for a chunk of beefsteak with roasted potatoes and baby onions. She'd agreed to corn bread soaked in milk. He'd pouted like a little boy. She'd laughed and promised him a treat if he was good.

Then he'd given her one of those seductive smiles and vowed to finish every last bite of his mush. Titillating images had flooded her mind at her husband's words, innocent though they were, and she'd scurried from the room to hide her blush.

How long did it take a woman to get used to her husband before she could think clearly again? Adelaide smiled at the tingles that continued to dance around inside her. Then again, perhaps thinking was overrated.

Adelaide shook her head at her foolishness and took the jug of milk firmly in hand, hoping to get a similar grip on her thoughts. She had just tipped it over the bowl of crumbled corn bread when a shot rang out from somewhere in the yard. She jumped, splashing milk on the table before yanking the jug upright.

Before she could steady herself and think what to do next, heavy footsteps thumped against the wraparound porch, nearing the kitchen door. Adelaide opened the knife drawer and closed her fingers around the hilt of a long carving blade.

The door flew open. "Señora Westcott, we have visitors."

When she recognized Miguel, Adelaide released her hold on the knife, but her heart was far from relieved. The doctor wasn't due for another day, and if it had been the preacher or another man from town, the guard would not have fired a warning shot. "Who is it?"

Her husband's foreman met her eyes, his face grim. "He gave me this." Miguel handed her a white card.

Adelaide bit her lip as she accepted it from him. She frowned at the exquisite gold engraving. The Right Honorable, the Viscount Petchey requested an audience. Adelaide glanced back up at Miguel, her spirit aching at the unfairness of it all. Just when Gideon had regained a decent grip on life, the devil showed up on their doorstep.

Chapter 36

"Petchey's here?" Gideon scowled at his foreman.

"Sí, patrón. He and his man. We check for weapons. They carry none, not even in their boots." Miguel clutched his rifle, the barrel pointing at the parlor rug, but his finger sat poised over the trigger guard. "He say he only want to talk, but I no trust him."

"Neither do I." Gideon clenched his jaw and slowly twisted his legs around until he was sitting in a more proper position. Adelaide scurried from behind Miguel to help him.

But he didn't want her help. He yanked his arm from her hold. "I'll do it."

She backed away, shock and hurt flashing across her features. He steeled himself against the guilt that tried to undermine his determination. This was no time for soft emotions. The enemy approached, and weakness could lead to disaster. It was his duty to protect his family, and her solicitous hovering only reminded him of the strength he had lost. Didn't she understand that he needed her to believe in his ability to protect her? He needed her to see him as strong. How else could he believe it himself?

"Fetch my pistol from the bureau, Addie. Load it and bring it to my study. Place it in the top desk drawer. I'll be meeting with Petchey in there. Then take Isabella up to the schoolroom and lock yourselves in. Don't come out until one of us comes to get you. Understand?"

She stared at him with big watery eyes, and he knew his abrupt manner pained her. Without a word, she nodded and turned to go.

Gideon's heart lurched. "Addie?" he called after her.

She turned but said nothing.

"I love you."

A tiny smile lifted one corner of her mouth, and the bleakness cleared from her eyes. Her chin dipped in acknowledgment a second before she pivoted and hastened from the room.

Gideon watched her yellow skirts disappear around the corner, then set his jaw and arrowed his focus back to Miguel. "Get James. You two will have to help me to the study."

By the time Juan escorted Petchey and his companion into the room, Gideon's gut was on fire from the effort required to stay upright in his chair. He'd dabbed the perspiration from his forehead only a moment ago and already felt more beading up at his temple.

He could get through this. For Addie and Bella, he *would* get through this.

The viscount strolled into the study as if arriving for afternoon tea. He sketched a bow to Gideon and smiled at James and Miguel, who flanked either side of the desk, rifles in hand, revolvers in evidence at their sides.

"Gentlemen, I assure you there is no need for weapons. We are here for civilized discussion, nothing more."

Gideon forced his lips into an answering smile. "Forgive my lack of manners, my lord, but someone recently tried to kill me. You will understand if I'm a little wary of visitors."

"Of course. Such a regrettable circumstance. I do hope you are recovering well."

Gideon gestured for Petchey to take a seat. "My doctor tells me the injury is less severe than was originally feared. It is fortunate that the man behind the incident wasn't a better strategist."

When the lines around Petchey's mouth tightened ever so slightly, Gideon knew the barb had found its mark. José was no strategist, and they both knew it.

The viscount's smile remained glued in place, however, as he lowered himself into the chair in front of the desk. "One of the many perils of making one's home in the wilds of this barbaric country. I hope you do not find yourself in such a nasty predicament again anytime soon."

Gideon nodded, taking the veiled warning to heart. In the background, he noticed Juan forcing Petchey's assistant into a chair along the wall. Juan cradled his rifle across his arm, the end of the barrel directed at the other man's chest. The fellow yanked a handkerchief from his coat pocket and blotted his neck and hairline while he edged as far from the gun as the seat would permit.

"I imagine you know why I've come." Petchey reached into his coat, and immediately three guns were cocked and pointed at his heart.

"I would recommend you extract that hand with caution, my lord," Gideon said. "I would hate for one of my men to cut your visit unnecessarily short."

"They are only papers. Nothing to cause such great concern." He did have the good sense to pull them free slowly, holding them by a single corner. James uncocked his weapon and stepped forward to retrieve the documents.

Petchey released his grip with a sardonic grin. "Good to see you again, Mr. Bevin. I would be remiss if I didn't thank you for arranging that private rail car. My journey was quite comfortable."

James unfolded the papers, barely sparing the viscount a glance. "Glad to hear it, Mr. Church. Or should I call you Lord Petchey?" He speared the man with a hard look then, but Petchey merely shrugged.

"This is a contract, Gid," James said as he stepped back into position beside the desk. "Petchey is offering you twenty thousand pounds in return for signing Isabella's guardianship over to him."

"That amount is from my own funds, not a drop from my niece's trust," Petchey said, as if he were a man of honor. "I appreciate your taking the child in, Mr. Westcott, but she belongs with her family. Her father was my brother. I owe it to him to see her raised as he would have wished, as a Petchey. After the court ruling, I came to see that you had grown attached to the girl and were reluctant to resign custody. Therefore, I thought to offer compensation. You have a lovely ranch here, one that could benefit from the capital I could provide."

He let his words hang in the air for a moment, then leaned forward and rested an arm upon the edge of Gideon's desk. "Do the right thing, Westcott. Return the girl to her family. You would be welcome to correspond with Isabella and visit her whenever you were in England. However, you must recognize how much better off she would be with me. I would see to it that she received the finest education and all the privileges a girl of her class deserves. It is more than you can offer her on this barren ranch, an ocean away from true civilization."

"Not interested." Gideon had no time for justifications or debates. Petchey's face was starting to blur before him, and he feared he'd lose consciousness if this went on much longer. He forced a strength he didn't feel into his voice. "Bella is my daughter—in the eyes of the law and in my affections. I will sign no agreement. Now I must ask you to leave my property. You are no longer welcome here."

The polite façade finally slipped from Petchey's face. "You will not even allow me to see her? To—"

"No." Gideon barked out the denial. "Miguel? Escort Lord Petchey out of my house."

"Sí, señor." Miguel stepped forward and grabbed hold of Petchey's elbow. The viscount jerked his arm out of his grasp and surged to his feet on his own accord.

"You'll regret this, Westcott. When I get back to England, I'll ruin you—you and the rest of your family. You steal my family, I'll steal yours. Your mother and father will no longer be accepted in polite company when I get through with them. I'll personally ensure that no one invests in your father's enterprises. Your mother will be shunned by her closest friends and excised from every hostess list in the country. Your brothers will find themselves unable to cultivate the business relationships they previously enjoyed. And all because of your selfishness."

Gideon cringed at the picture he painted. Was he just throwing empty threats or did he really have the influence he claimed? Gideon hated to think of his family suffering because of him, but he didn't doubt for a second that they would willingly bear the strife if they knew doing so guaranteed Bella's safety.

"Do your worst, Petchey. I'll not reconsider."

The viscount let loose with a string of curses and stormed from the room, his assistant scurrying after him.

"Follow him, Miguel—all the way to the railhead in Lampasas. I want to know for sure that he's leaving Texas."

The vaquero nodded and left.

"James?" Gideon blinked, the edges of the room fading into a gray haze.

"Yeah, Gid?"

"Don't let my head hit the desk."

As if from a long distance away, he heard his friend call his name. Then he slumped forward into the oblivion he could no longer hold at bay.

Chapter 37

A week after Miguel witnessed Petchey's departure on an east-bound train and reported back that the man's tickets had been purchased all the way through to New York, Adelaide finally felt safe to venture outside again. Gideon had slept for two days straight after the confrontation, scaring her worse than the viscount's appearance had, but her husband had improved much since then. He was eating solid food and gradually regaining the weight and strength he'd lost. He moved around the house under his own power, albeit slowly, and grumbled about not being able to check on his sheep. Adelaide concluded he was on the mend if he had sufficient energy to grouch at her and the servants.

But there was a blessing to be found in Gideon's forced conva-lescence, too. It afforded him time to reconnect with Isabella. The two spent hours together every morning, Gideon reading aloud to her or helping with her arithmetic. The girl smiled and laughed, talked and sang songs until Adelaide actually found herself hushing the little magpie on occasion.

And the evenings? Well, they were the best of all. Gideon held her snug to his chest, whispering love words in her ear and dropping kisses on her neck that sent shivers coursing through her. He had yet to fully make her his wife, but she could see in his eyes that the time would come soon. Each day he grew stronger, and each night his kisses grew more ardent.

Today, however, was a day for the girls. As a reward for Isabella's excellent work in the schoolroom, Adelaide had promised to take her riding, and they were both looking forward to the excursion. They'd been cooped up in the house too long.

"Wait, Miss Addie. You're walking too fast." Isabella's legs pumped at a furious pace, leaping every few strides to make up lost ground as they made their way across the yard.

"Sorry, sweetheart." Adelaide slowed, tempering her enthusiasm. She hadn't ridden Sheba in weeks and was more than eager to get in the saddle again.

When they entered the stables, Adelaide collected Sheba's bridle from the tack wall and a lead line for Isabella's pony. After she had both animals saddled and ready, Adelaide lifted Isabella atop the pony and led her out to the yard. Keeping hold of the lead line, she swung up onto Sheba's back and set off at a mild walk. Sheba tossed her head and strained at the bit, but Adelaide held her with a firm hand.

"I know, girl. I know." She leaned forward and patted the horse's neck. "I want to run, too, but Izzy's with us, and we have to look out for her."

Adelaide glanced over her shoulder to check on her daughter. She seemed secure in her seat, rocking gently with the pony's motion.

"Should we try a trot?" she called out.

Izzy nodded and reached for the saddle horn. Adelaide clucked to Sheba and loosened her hold on the reins. The mare shifted into a jogging gait, and the pony followed. Izzy bounced around on her saddle like a rubber ball, but her giggles proved she was enjoying it.

After a while, they returned to a walk and meandered along a trail formed by a dry creek bed. The morning sun had already turned the day quite warm, but the wind blew over them now and again, cooling their cheeks.

"Can we stop for a minute, Miss Addie? I need to use the necessary."

Adelaide hid a grin. She doubted Izzy had ever had to relieve herself without benefit of a water closet or chamber pot. But a rancher's daughter would have to learn sooner or later. Might as well be today.

She pointed toward a large live oak a short distance to the west. "That looks like a good spot. We can rest there for a while before heading back."

"All right."

At Adelaide's urging, the horses climbed out of the creek bed and ambled over to the tree that stood at the bottom of a small rise. Once there, Adelaide dismounted and helped Isabella down, leaving the animals to forage in the brown summer grass. A shallow ravine lay a few yards beyond the tree, and the two girls made their way there to tend to business.

When they returned to the tree, the shade was so inviting that Adelaide encouraged Isabella to explore while she rested against the tree's trunk.

"Look, Miss Addie! See the bird with the funny tail?"

Adelaide straightened and followed the direction of Izzy's gaze. A small cream-colored bird with dark wings and a long, skinny tail perched on the tip of an exposed branch. Adelaide picked her way across the uneven ground to join her daughter. She placed her arm around the girl's shoulders and pointed up at the bird.

"You found a scissortail," she said. "When he flies, his tail opens up in a big V, like a pair of scissors."

"I want to see! I want to see!"

Isabella's enthusiasm must have startled the bird, for he took flight and swooped over their heads as if shooing them away. Isabella ducked and giggled with delight, chasing after the bird.

Adelaide laughed, too. "Catch him, Izzy!"

She gave it a valiant attempt. She followed his erratic pattern until Adelaide decided she'd better give chase before Isabella got too far away. Finally the bird lit on a sumac bush halfway up the rise, having easily outdistanced its pursuers. Isabella plunged after it, scrambling up the slope while Adelaide massaged the stitch in her side and paused to catch her breath.

Before Isabella could reach the bush, however, the scissortail let out a shrill cry and flapped off into the sky. Something had frightened it. Perhaps a mule deer was approaching to browse on the sumac leaves. Isabella would enjoy seeing the deer up close. Adelaide set out to intercept her daughter, but drew up short when a large figure crested the rise above her. Her eyes widened. That was no deer.

A rider topped the hill and reined in his mount. He hesitated only a second before kicking his horse into a fast lope. On a path aimed directly at Isabella!

"Izzy, run!" Adelaide yanked up the fabric of her riding skirt and sprinted toward her daughter.

Isabella looked up and screamed. She stumbled as she turned to flee. Adelaide's heart pounded against her breast as she ran. *Get up, Izzy. Get up!*

Adelaide took in the form of the rider bearing down on Izzy. She'd seen him before. From the schoolroom window. Lord Petchey! But how could that be? He was on his way back to England.

The rider urged his mount closer. Adelaide sprinted as fast as her legs would carry her, but she knew she'd never make it in time. *Help me, Lord!*

Isabella pushed to her feet and started down the hill, terror etched into her face. Adelaide fought to close the gap between them. The horse's hooves ate up the ground faster.

Petchey pulled abreast of Isabella and leaned down, scooping her up with one arm.

"Noooo!" Adelaide cried.

Isabella thrashed about in an effort to free herself, but the man's hold was too tight. Adelaide continued to charge up the hill toward them, one thought dominating her mind. She had to get to Izzy.

Oddly enough, the viscount cooperated. Instead of galloping off with his prize, he pulled his horse to a stop and waited for her. She didn't care why. All she cared about was getting to her daughter.

When she was about a dozen feet away, he drew on her. Sunlight glinted off his nickel-plated revolver. Adelaide floundered to a halt. Her chest heaved. Gasping breaths moaned in and out. Her eyes fastened to the barrel of the gun; her arms inched upward.

"That's close enough, my dear." The man spoke in aristocratic tones. British tones. Much like Gideon's. But instead of moving through her like warm honey, as her husband's did, this man's accent chilled her like a bath of melted snow.

"Petchey."

"Ah. So you know who I am. Excellent." He bowed his head to her as if he were greeting her in London's Hyde Park, not holding her daughter hostage. Adelaide's fear began to recede in the wake of a rising anger. She stiffened her backbone and lowered her arms to her sides, balling her hands into fists.

"Let the child go, Petchey. You have no legal claim to her."

"Not yet. But I will." He smiled at her, and the look turned her stomach. He reeked of confidence and strength, towering above her atop his horse. But he was just a Goliath, and Goliaths had a tendency to fall when confronted with tiny people armed with stones and God's power. She was fresh out of stones, but she figured God could improvise.

Praying for the courage of David, Adelaide jutted out her chin. "Give Isabella to me. Right. Now."

"I don't think so."

Isabella sobbed and renewed her struggles. "Miss Addie, help me!" The young girl's arms reached out for her and Adelaide responded. She took one step. And another. Then Petchey's revolver clicked as he cocked the weapon and pointed it directly at her head. She stopped, her heart aching at Izzy's continued pleas for help.

"That's enough bravery for one day, Miss Addie," he said, using the name Isabella had called her. He must not know of her marriage to Gideon. Hope surged in Adelaide's breast. She could use that to her advantage.

Petchey tightened his hold on the child's middle, and Isabella's cries softened to whimpers. "Go get on that sad little mare of yours and scamper back to Westcott like a good little mouse. Tell your employer he can either sign guardianship over to me or bury the girl. His choice. I'd prefer to keep the brat alive—she is my niece, after all—but I'll let him decide. I will send my man to the ranch this evening to inquire after his decision."

Gideon would never turn Isabella over to Petchey. He would go after the man himself. And in his still-weakened condition, he would be no match for the viscount. She couldn't let that happen. Yet she was in no position to help either Gideon or Isabella. She had to play along. For now.

Adelaide met Petchey's cold, taunting eyes. "You better not lay a hand on her."

"That's up to Westcott." His mocking smile ate through her like acid.

Adelaide shifted her attention to Isabella's tear-streaked face. "Be a brave little soldier for me, Izzy. I'll come get you as soon as I can." She stared into her daughter's eyes for a long moment, trying to instill confidence and hope. Then she pivoted and strode down the hill.

"Miss Addie, don't leave me! Miss Addie!"

Isabella's tortured cries broke Adelaide's heart. Tears streamed down her cheeks, but she kept walking. She collected Isabella's pony's lead line and mounted Sheba. With back straight, she trotted off toward home, going slow enough to keep Petchey in her line of sight. She couldn't leave Isabella alone with him, not with the child's life hanging in the balance.

The moment he turned to the west and spurred his horse into motion, she unlatched the pony's lead and slapped him hard on the hindquarters to send him running back to the ranch. Then she spun Sheba in an arc that put her on a path to intercept Petchey's buckskin.

"Time to run, girl."

Chapter 38

Reginald urged his buckskin into a canter, eager to put some distance between himself and Westcott's base of operations. He'd been pleased to see that the mouse of a governess wasn't much of a horsewoman. He'd nearly chuckled aloud at his good fortune when he spied her and the brat inching their way through the trees at a laggard pace. He'd probably be halfway to the line shack before she even arrived back at the house to deliver his message. The short-legged mare she rode wasn't much bigger than his niece's pony, either, so even if she broke out of her trot, she wouldn't exactly be eating up the ground.

It was a shame he didn't have any of his hunters. With one of those sleek Thoroughbreds beneath him, he could fly over this brown wasteland.

Was nothing green in this cursed country? Even his horse was brown. His peasant horse. A cow pony, the man had called it. Reginald snorted. Noblemen didn't ride ponies. They rode horses—grand horses with lineages that could be traced for generations, not stocky animals without record of the stallion that sired them.

Disgraceful. At least this creature had decent endurance and didn't seem to labor under the additional weight of the child in his lap.

He steered his mount northwest, keeping to low ground. As he turned, a speck of black flashed at the edge of his vision. He craned his neck to get a better look and swore.

That jezebel!

Not only had she completely disregarded his instructions, but she had the audacity to ride as if she'd been born in the saddle, not at all like the straightlaced governess she pretended to be. And worse, she was gaining on him.

He dug his heels into his mount. The beast lunged forward and Isabella squealed. Reginald ignored his niece's fear and pushed his horse to a gallop. Every few strides, he stole a glance over his shoulder. The blasted woman dogged his heels, closing the distance bit by bit. His horse carried twice the weight of hers, giving her a gross advantage.

His buckskin stumbled, and Reginald turned his attention back to the front. The horse regained his stride but seemed to be tiring. Lather was forming on its neck. Reginald ground his teeth. That slip of a girl was outriding him.

Time to go on the offensive.

Reginald brought the buckskin's head around until his path ran perpendicular to his pursuer. Loosening his hold on his niece, he shifted the reins into his left hand and pulled his revolver free. He slowed to a canter as he stretched his gun arm across his body and over Isabella's head.

He squeezed the trigger. The shot sailed high. Reginald scowled. The tenacious chit didn't even veer off course. Instead, she ducked low over her mare's back, making herself an even smaller target, and continued following him. Relentless. Like a hound after a fox.

A growl rumbled in his throat. Why had the devil plagued him with such contrary females? First Lucinda escaped with his inheritance before succumbing to the poison he'd so patiently worked into her body, and now this cheeky governess thought to thwart him. But she didn't know who she was dealing with. Reginald Petchey surrendered to no one, especially not to a little American jezebel who didn't comprehend her own insignificance.

He took aim again, sighting in on her bobbing head barely visible through the mare's flowing mane. His hunting instincts rose to the fore, blocking out all else. Rhythm coursed through him, the gait of his horse overlapping hers. He had the timing. His finger tightened on the trigger. But Isabella knocked her head into his arm. She set about wiggling and screaming to such an extent he couldn't hold his aim steady.

"Be still or I'll let you fall," Reginald snapped. The girl whimpered and covered her eyes with her hands, but she stopped flailing around. He didn't trust her, though. He lowered his sight to a bigger target.

The gun fired with a loud crack. The recoil pressed his arm upward, but he felt the trueness of the shot in his bones.

The black mare crumpled, nose first, into a heap, her momentum skidding her forward several yards.

Satisfaction surged through him. He reined in and searched for a sign of the annoying governess. Nothing. Maybe she lay pinned beneath her horse. He could hope.

Reginald didn't take the time to investigate. Whether she was dead, injured, or simply unhorsed, it mattered not. She wouldn't be following him.

Gideon sat at the desk in his study composing a letter to his parents. If they hadn't yet received the letter James had posted regarding his dying request to have them care for his wife and child, they soon would, and he wanted to assure them that his health was much improved.

However, if this second letter caught up to them before they left for America, he had a favor to beg of his mother. He wished to ask her permission to present his bride with the topaz ring that had belonged to his grandmother. Anticipation filled him as he visualized slipping the delicate jewel onto Addie's finger. His mother's collection contained several costly diamond and emerald pieces which she had offered to him in the past, but the more modest gem would suit Adelaide better, a reflection of her warmth and the way she found joy in the simple things of life. Besides, it was yellow. Gideon grinned. A fitting token of love for his sunshine girl.

He lifted the top corner of his correspondence and read over what he had written. Then he picked up his fountain pen to sign his name. He had shaped no more than the G when a door slammed and heavy footfalls echoed in the hall.

"Señor . . . Señor Westcott!"

Miguel's urgent call cut through him. Gideon dropped the pen in a skid of black ink and pushed to his feet.

"In here!"

He grimaced at the dull pain that continued to plague him as he hobbled to the doorway of the study. Miguel met him there. James rushed down the stairs, not far behind.

"What is it?" James called out.

Gideon's eyes pierced his foreman, silently reiterating the question.

"The little miss's pony . . . He come back without the niña."

Gideon's gut twisted, but he tamped down his alarm. "Any sign of Adelaide or Sheba?" Addie would have brought Bella home straightaway if she'd been thrown. She'd want to tend to the child's scrapes and bruises.

"No, patrón. I ride out to see if anyone is hurt, but I no find them. I find something else." Miguel hesitated as if not wanting to impart the rest.

Gideon's neck tensed. "What?"

"Three sets of tracks."

Foreboding stabbed him. "Saddle my horse, Miguel. James, help me up the stairs to get my gun belt and boots." Already in motion, Gideon lumbered toward the banister with as much speed as he could manage while keeping his feet beneath him. James wedged his shoulder under Gideon's arm and helped him navigate the steps.

"You can't think of going after them, Gid. You're in no condition to ride. Let me and Miguel track them down."

They reached the top of the stairs and Gideon pierced his friend with a heated stare. "That's my wife and my daughter out there, James. I won't be deterred."

James shook his head and then steered them toward the bedroom. "I had a feeling you'd say something like that."

"It's Petchey, James. It has to be." Self-recrimination tore at him, torturing him with gruesome images of what could happen to his girls.

How could he have been so stupid? Gideon stomped his foot into his left boot, welcoming the pain. Petchey had hidden away for weeks. Then he suddenly decided to show up at the ranch to make a final plea? It had all been a ploy. They might have watched him leave and even followed him to the railhead, but the fiend had doubled back.

Gideon shoved his foot into the second boot and strapped on his gun belt. He would find Addie. Bella, too. They would be fine. No other option was acceptable.

Chapter 39

From her prone position beside her fallen horse, Adelaide kept her eye on Petchey's departing figure, making careful note of his direction and the landmarks he passed. It was probably safe to get up, but she continued to hold Sheba's head down anyway, playing dead a little longer. She had no doubt that her mare was injured, but hopefully it wasn't too serious.

Petchey finally faded from view, and Adelaide took her first full breath. As the immediate danger passed, the aches and pains from her fall became harder to ignore. Her left leg cramped, pinned as it was under Sheba's weight. Her arm was scraped up pretty good, too, and her back muscles protested the awkward angle she'd twisted them into in order to watch Petchey.

"All right, girl. Let's get up." Adelaide released Sheba's head. But the mare didn't move.

"Come on, Sheba. Up!" She thrust against the animal's side. No response.

Adelaide's heart thudded in her chest. "Sheba?"

She remembered the mare trying to get to her feet when they

first went down, didn't she? Yes. She was sure of it. But she had lain still for the last several minutes. Amazingly still, now that she thought about it. She'd assumed the mare had just responded to her mistress's touch, but what if more than obedience had kept her down?

"Sheba!"

Please, God, no.

Frantic now, Adelaide pushed with all her might against the horse's side. "Get up, girl! Get up!"

She had to get free so she could pull the mare to her feet. Sheba needed help. That was all. She couldn't get up on her own.

Adelaide wriggled and writhed in an attempt to free her leg, but she only extracted it a few inches. Her foot was wedged tight. She rolled to a half-sitting position and started digging the dirt out from beneath her leg. Desperation lent her speed. She had to get up. Sheba needed her. Isabella needed her.

Her nails clawed at the ground. Faster. Deeper. When she could reach no farther, she rolled back onto her side. Adelaide braced her right foot against Sheba's ribs and pressed her palms into the ground behind her. She pushed with leg and arms, grunting with the effort. Her pinned limb moved a little. She readjusted her position and tried again. The moan erupting from her lungs grew into a scream as she pushed with every ounce of her strength. All at once, her foot pulled free and she sprawled backward into the dirt.

Her head collided with the earth, sending a sharp pain into her skull, but she wasted no time rubbing the offended spot. She lurched to her feet and limped to Sheba's head. Grabbing hold of the reins, she gave a mighty tug.

"Come on, girl. Please. You have to get up!"

When Sheba failed to respond, Adelaide leaned down to grab hold of the bridle's cheek piece. Only then did she notice the blood seeping from a hole in the mare's chest.

"Noooo!" Adelaide fell to the ground. She flung her upper body across Sheba's back and pressed the side of her face into the mare's dusty coat, hugging her close. No rise and fall of breath. No movement at all—just an awful stillness that she could no longer deny.

"Oh, Sheba . . . No . . ." Her voice broke and sobs of grief poured out of her like a river plunging over a cliff.

She had no idea how long she lay there, huddled over her beloved companion, weeping her heart out. It was like losing her father all over again. The devastating heartache and pain came crashing back. She had survived his death by keeping a piece of him alive in his last gift to her—Sheba. Now that had been torn away from her, too, leaving her nothing real to hold on to, only hazy memories that were becoming harder and harder to grasp.

Petchey had stolen that from her.

Petchey!

Adelaide jerked her head up. Heaven help her. Here she was crying all over her dead horse when that madman had Izzy.

She gave a loud sniff and wiped her cheeks with the back of her wrist. Mourning would have to wait.

"You've been a good friend to me, Sheba," Adelaide said, patting the mare's neck a final time. "The best. But I can't afford to give you a proper good-bye. I have to go after Isabella."

Adelaide's legs wobbled as she pushed to her feet. She staggered for a second, then caught her balance and squared her shoulders. Gideon and the others would come looking for her soon. In the meantime, she'd head for the rise where she last saw Petchey and locate his trail. Every minute was precious. If she could save Gideon even a small amount of time in finding their daughter, the hot trek on her bruised body would be worth it.

Using the heel of her boot, she scraped a large arrow into the dirt in front of Sheba, indicating the direction she would take. Then with a deep breath, she trudged ahead, trying not to think about the friend she was leaving behind.

Gideon pulled his hat off and wiped the sweat from his forehead with his sleeve cuff as he waited impatiently for Miguel to signal that he had reestablished the trail. They'd been at it for nearly two hours now, with little to show for it. Gideon shifted his weight on Solomon's back. The creak of his saddle broke the quiet, but the change in position did nothing to relieve the tension stiffening his muscles. Then again, he hadn't really expected that it would. Not until his girls were safe.

Gideon blew out his breath and, for the hundredth time, bit back a complaint about their sluggish pace. His jaw ached nearly as much as his abdomen from the constant effort of holding his tongue. It wasn't Miguel's fault. The sheepman's only experience consisted of trailing slow, recalcitrant ewes—not racing steeds. And the man's companions were of no help whatsoever. An English gentleman and a lawyer knew blessed little about tracking.

At first, Gideon had scoured the ground, too, but he soon realized that calling Miguel over to examine meaningless scratches in the earth only slowed their progress further. So he stayed in the saddle, grinding his teeth while Miguel did the searching.

Finding the initial trail had been easy enough, since the dirt had been soft near the creek bed. Miguel quickly distinguished Sheba's smaller hoofprints from those of a larger horse and pointed them out to both Gideon and James. Gideon memorized the markings and experienced a few moments of acute relief when they seemed to lead back to the ranch. But then the tracks veered sharply off to the west. He should have known better than to think Adelaide would let Petchey make off with Bella unchallenged. She'd proven to be a fighter when it came to the people she loved, and he had no doubt she would give her life to keep Bella safe. It was one of the things that made her such a good mother. And one of the reasons he fully expected to go gray at an early age.

After their initial progress, however, tracking became more difficult. The horse's path traversed a large section of rock-hard ground, where differentiating between a partial hoofprint and a crack in the sunbaked earth became guesswork. They repeatedly lost the trail.

"This way, patrón." Miguel's focus remained pinned to the ground as he walked, leading his horse behind him.

James fell into line without a word, but Gideon held back for a moment, trying to find a shape in the dry grass that matched the template of Sheba's hoof branded on his brain. His untrained eyes found nothing. For all he knew, they were following some random game trail. His hand tightened involuntarily around Solomon's reins. He'd felt more in control when he'd been ambushed in the north pasture. Addie and Bella were somewhere out there in harm's way, and he was helpless to do anything about it.

God, I need you. You can see them. You know where they are. Show me. I beg you.

While Miguel studiously stared at the ground, Gideon raked his gaze over the land in front of them, desperately searching for a clue. However, the familiar view offered little hope. No human shape. No flash of yellow. Just scrub brush, black rocks, and crooked—

Wait.

Black rocks? Gideon stood in his stirrups to get a better look at the dark form ahead. There were plenty of limestone outcroppings on his land, but they varied in shade from gray to sandy brown. Not black.

Thank you, Lord.

"I see something!" Gideon urged Solomon into a run, his heart in his throat. The closer he came, the more certain he became. The black mass was his wife's mare.

He pulled abreast of the fallen horse and swung to the ground.

He cupped his hands around his mouth and yelled in every direction. "Addie!"

But she didn't appear.

He knew before he touched the animal that Sheba was dead. Flies buzzed around her, and the stench of spilled blood clogged his throat. Yet in a strange way, he derived comfort from the presence of the mare who had loved his Addie so well.

Gideon circled Sheba, his heart aching for Adelaide's loss. When he reached the horse's belly, he noticed a small trench. He bent down and pressed his fingers into the hole as his mind filled in the events that must have taken place.

By the time James and Miguel rode up, Gideon was pulling himself back into the saddle.

"She's this way," he said. "Follow me."

Miguel raised a doubtful brow. "Are you sure, señor?"

Gideon nodded and pointed to the carved ground in front of Sheba's head.

"She left us a marker."

Chapter 40

A distant drumroll pricked Adelaide's ears as she sat in the shade of a squatty oak. Tilting her head, she listened. The percussive sound grew louder. Closer. Anticipation speared through her chest, and she bounded to her feet. Blocking the sun's glare with the back of her hand, she squinted across the expanse of land until she made out the dark blur of approaching riders.

Finally.

She waved her arm in a wide arc to signal the men. The last hour had tortured her with dire thoughts and bleak outlooks as she contemplated what would happen to Isabella should their rescue attempt fail. She'd prayed and planned and prayed some more, hatching several ideas about how to outmaneuver Petchey and ensure that he never threatened their family again. A host of details and objectives swirled in her mind, but the moment Gideon leapt from his horse, every thought scattered. Only one notion remained. She needed her husband to hold her.

With trembling lips and tearing eyes, Adelaide limped into Gideon's open arms and clung to him.

"He killed Sheba."

It wasn't what she had meant to say, but somehow it was what she needed to say.

Gideon stroked her hair, his own voice quivering. "I know, sunshine. I know."

He rested his chin on her head and rubbed his hands over her back as she wept against his collar. Little by little, his strength seeped into her and assuaged her grief. After a minute or two, he gently gripped her arms and held her away from him, just enough to look into her face.

"Are you all right?"

She bit her lip to restrain her emotions and nodded.

"Thank God." He pulled her back into his embrace and kissed her forehead. She wanted to sink into him again, but after a tight hug, he stepped away. He was right to do so, of course. Isabella was waiting on them. Adelaide's mind picked up speed again, spinning with ideas and information she had stored up for her husband.

"I'll have Miguel take you home."

The frenzy in her brain careened to a halt.

"What?" She couldn't go home. Not now.

Gideon traced her hairline with his finger. "You've been through enough for one day, sweetheart. Let us take care of things from here."

Adelaide lifted her chin and stared hard into his eyes. "I'm not going home, Gideon."

His eyes widened for a moment and then hardened to match hers. "Yes. You are."

He wasn't going to shut her out of this. She wouldn't let him. "Be practical," she urged. "I have a few ideas about how to rescue our daughter." When he didn't interrupt her, she plunged ahead. "I know how to handle a weapon, and you need all the able-bodied people you can get to face down Petchey."

The instant the words were out of her mouth, she knew she'd

made a tactical error. Gideon's face reddened, and a muscle in his cheek twitched. He yanked off his hat and beat it against his thigh with enough force to send up a small storm of dust.

"That's exactly why I want you away from here, Addie! The man shot your horse and probably would have shot you if he'd had his way. I've been out of my head with worry all morning, and now that I have you back safe, there's no way I'm letting you anywhere near that monster."

"You're the one he wants dead, not me." Adelaide's arm flung out at him in accusation. "He already tried his hand at it once, and I don't aim to give him a second chance because you don't have enough men watching your back. Even if you don't want me around, you need Miguel." Adelaide made an effort to douse her rising temper before it blazed completely out of control. She inhaled, then continued in a calmer voice. "I can help, Gideon. I'm not a fool. I'll stay out of the way and let you handle things. But someone will need to look out for Isabella while you men are going after Petchey. Let me do that. Please."

He looked away, staring into the sky. The muscles in his jaw continued to flex and flinch as if he were physically chewing over her words. She pressed her lips together and waited.

He turned back and glared at her, pointing his hat at her as if it were a finger. "You do everything I tell you and stay out of sight when we catch up to him."

Before he could change his mind, she nodded acceptance of his terms. "I promise. Thank you, Gideon."

He grumbled something under his breath, then slapped his hat on and marched over to his horse. He mounted and walked Solomon over to her, offering her a frown as well as his arm.

Even out of sorts, he was a marvelous man. She smiled and held her hand up to him. He grasped her just above the elbow, but instead of lifting, he leaned down and whispered in her ear.

"You had better not get hurt, Addie. I couldn't live with myself if something happened to you." Love blended with anxiety in his eyes, and her heart softened.

"I'll do my best," she said, "but I need the same from you. I just got done putting you back together. I'm not ready to go through that again."

A hint of a smile played around the corners of his mouth. "It's a deal."

She braced her foot in his stirrup to relieve him of most of her weight as he swung her up onto Solomon's back and settled behind the cantle. Adelaide reached her right arm around to Gideon's front and folded it against his upper torso in order to avoid gripping his wounded stomach. His muscles gave a little leap in response, and she couldn't resist opening her palm and pressing it against his firm chest. His heart thudded just beneath her fingers.

James rode up beside them. "Did Petchey say anything when he took Isabella?"

Adelaide started. She straightened and began to pull her hand away, but Gideon reached up and held it in place. Suddenly everything seemed much brighter.

She grinned up at James. "I'll tell you on the way. Let's go."

They followed Petchey's tracks for about a mile before Gideon called a halt with a wave of his arm. They were nearing the border of his property, and he thought he remembered a run-down building somewhere in the area. He motioned the others forward and pointed toward a stand of trees ahead and to the left.

"Isn't there a small shack on the other side of those mesquite, Miguel?"

The vaquero scanned the area, squinting into the afternoon sun. "Sí. I think so, patrón."

"It would be a good place to hide out if you wanted to be close enough to keep an eye on the ranch," James said.

Gideon nodded. "Exactly what I was thinking."

Adelaide raised her head from where it had rested against his back, and a cool breeze brushed away the residual warmth. Gideon squeezed her arm against his side with his bicep to keep her from letting go. She felt so good snuggled up to him, but having her near also set him on edge. He still wanted to send her home, away from the danger, but it was too late for that now. Oh, he knew she'd keep her head. She always did. But stray bullets didn't distinguish between innocent young women and the men they were intended to kill.

God, protect her when I can't. And guard Bella through all of this, too.

Steeling himself against the fear that coursed through him, Gideon turned his attention to his foreman. "Take Addie and circle around to the back, Miguel. Keep to the trees, out of sight. I don't know if he has other men with him or not. Secure whatever horses are there and wait for James and me to make our move."

He slipped his foot out of the stirrup so Adelaide could dismount. Her body rubbed against his as she slid down to the ground. He savored the sensations her softness evoked. His gaze trailed over her face, memorizing each line and curve. She'd been his wife for little more than a fortnight, but she owned his heart. If anything happened to her, he'd be lost.

Gideon drew his rifle from its scabbard and handed it to her. "Use this if you have to, but don't wade into the fray."

Her hands closed around the weapon. "Be careful, Gideon."

He had a lifetime of living to do with this woman, and he planned to make sure they both came through this escapade unscathed.

"Petchey will no doubt be waiting for us, armed and ready, so James and I will approach through the trees, as well. We'll keep to cover and see if we can talk our way in. Then we'll have to improvise, but our first priority will be getting Bella out before any violence erupts."

Gideon looked over his tiny army, feeling much like his namesake, the reluctant biblical warrior who went into battle with a handful of soldiers to face a mighty enemy. God had brought about victory for his counterpart. Hopefully history would repeat itself.

Peering into the distance in front of him, Gideon visualized the shack and the thick grove of trees that surrounded it on two sides. He imagined where he would hide. How he would approach the building. Where Bella would likely be. Then his eyes drifted higher.

"May the Lord grant us victory and keep us safe from harm."

A chorus of somber amens sealed the prayer, and the unlikely group of warriors headed into battle.

Chapter 41

Adelaide held the rifle tight to her shoulder as Miguel crept up to the side of the shack. Her stomach cramped as she watched. He was so exposed beyond the trees. If one of the horses balked or even nickered too loudly, he'd be discovered. Then she'd have to fire at Petchey and whomever was with him to allow Miguel time to escape. She'd never shot at a human being before. The very idea made her ill.

Leaning the shoulder of her support arm heavily against the large mesquite that shielded her, Adelaide inhaled a slow breath through her nose. She held it for a minute and then blew it out through her mouth in a long, gentle stream, keeping her eyes focused on Miguel and the small window at the back of the ramshackle building.

Fortunately there were only two horses, so he would be able to gather them both in one trip. It also boded well for Gideon. If the number of men inside the shack matched the number of horses, their odds would be even. Except for the fact that Petchey had a hostage. And the advantage of a protected position. And no conscience.

Adelaide fought off a shiver. It wouldn't do to get distracted by negativity.

Miguel took hold of the first horse, then the second. Adelaide's pulse stuttered. He stroked and petted the beasts for a moment before urging them away. The smaller roan followed meekly, with no protest, but Petchey's buckskin tossed his head and snorted. The soft jangle of his bridle rang like the clattering of kitchen pans in Adelaide's ears. Miguel held his ground, only glancing toward the building for a brief second before focusing again on the horses. He scratched the buckskin behind his ears and whispered to him until he calmed. After that, both horses were content to amble along behind him.

Miguel led the animals past her. She smiled at him but kept her rifle at the ready and her attention on the shack. After securing the confiscated horses near their own mounts several yards away, he was to circle around and signal Gideon before returning to assist her. She would be the sole line of rear defense until then. A duty she didn't relish but was determined to fulfill.

Step one of their plan had been completed successfully. However, the cramping in her stomach only worsened. Step two was twice as dangerous. And Gideon was the one taking all the risks. Even as the thought flitted through her mind, she heard her husband's voice explode through the clearing.

"I got your message, Petchey."

The stirring and scrambling in the shack led Adelaide to believe Petchey had not been watching for their arrival.

"So the little governess lived to tell the tale, eh?" Petchey's words resonated from the front of the shack. "I presume you've come to make a deal."

"Yes. I will not negotiate with Bella's life," Gideon shouted. "I know what you are capable of, how you were behind the recent attack on my life. One of the men who rides with me is a lawyer. Let us in. I'm prepared to discuss the forfeiture of all rights to Isabella and her fortune."

The viscount offered no immediate response. Adelaide pressed her lips together in a tight line. So much of their plan hinged on his allowing Gideon and James into the cabin.

"You refer to Mr. Bevin, I presume," Petchey finally answered. "As I recall, he has quite a talent for twisting things to appear one way when the truth is something else entirely. A particular map comes to mind. I don't trust your man."

"You travel with a solicitor of your own," Gideon replied. "The two men can work together to compose the document to your specifications. Mr. Farnsworth can look out for your interests."

Several seconds ticked by in silence.

"Very well."

Adelaide sagged against the tree trunk in relief.

"But I need a show of good faith from you," Petchey called out. "Come into the clearing and lay your weapons on the ground where I can see them. I'm not so foolish as to let you come into my little domicile armed."

Gideon had warned her of such a demand, and she knew he and James would comply. They would do whatever it took to get into that shack, to get to Isabella. Adelaide pictured her husband in her mind's eye—unbuckling his gun belt, sliding it off his hip, and dropping it to the ground. Defenseless. It was the only way, yet listening to the scene unfold was torture. She wanted to see what was going on, to have the assurance that Gideon was safe. Without a weapon, God would be his only protection. She scrunched her eyes closed and prayed from the depths of her soul.

"The guns are down, Petchey," Gideon said. "I'm ready to work out a solution. It's not worth more bloodshed."

"Ah, but I think it is."

A gunshot exploded, and the sound cut straight through

Adelaide's heart. The rifle fell from her grasp. She moaned and covered her ears.

No!

Gideon dove to his left as pain seared his upper arm. A second shot rang out. Then a third. He rolled and crawled until the shadow of the mesquite thicket covered him once again. Scrambling backward on his heels and palms, he positioned himself behind one of the larger trunks and pressed his back into the natural shield.

He stole a quick glance around to the side. James had nearly made the tree line. Gunfire cracked again. He pulled his head back just as a bullet slammed into the tree above his shoulder.

Reginald Petchey was a good shot.

A fifth blast echoed across the clearing. James yelled out in pain. Gideon jumped to his feet, careful to keep the tree between him and the line shack while he looked for his friend. On the ground several feet away, James clutched his right leg and dragged himself with one arm to a spot behind a tree.

Thank God he was still alive. Gideon ran his fingers through his sweat-dampened hair. His hat along with his guns lay abandoned in the clearing. Inaccessible. Not that he would have returned fire anyway. He couldn't risk Bella falling victim to a stray bullet. But he missed the feeling of security his weapon afforded.

What was he supposed to do now? He'd failed to talk his way into Petchey's lair. He had no weapon. One of his men was down, and Bella was no closer to rescue.

He pounded his fist into the mesquite, but the punishment brought no new ideas. Time. He needed time to figure out what to do. He didn't yet know how to help Bella, but he could help James. In the meantime, perhaps his friend would be able to come up with a solution.

Running deeper into the trees, Gideon dodged back and forth between the cover they offered before making his way back up to

James's position. No further shots were fired, so either Petchey didn't see his movement or the viscount was content to wait for a more exposed target.

Gideon reached James just as the man tried to tie a handkerchief around his thigh.

"Did it pass through?" Gideon asked as he took over the task of wrapping the wound.

James hissed in pain and clenched a fistful of grass and soil in a white-knuckled grip. "Don't think so," he ground out. "It's not bleeding too badly, but it hurts like the very devil. I'm afraid I won't be much help to you from here on out."

Gideon tightened the knot on the handkerchief and sat back on his heels. "I need your brain more than your legs right now. We need to determine a way to get past Petchey without our weapons."

"You can have mine, patrón."

Gideon spun around in a crouch, fists at the ready.

"Miguel! Where did you come from?"

The vaquero shrugged. "I hear the shooting and make my way back."

"You were supposed to stay with Adelaide." Gideon didn't know if he wanted to embrace the man or shake him.

"She is fine. Better than the two of you." His gaze drifted down Gideon's arm.

Gideon held his elbow out and examined his upper arm. In all the excitement, he had forgotten about the injury. His shirt gaped open below the shoulder. A bright red line creased his skin and blood trickled down into his sleeve, but most of it had started to dry already.

"It's only a graze. James got the worst of it."

James grunted as he pushed his back more securely against the tree trunk. "I'll be all right. I can use Miguel's pistol to lay down cover if you want to go after the other guns."

"Not yet." Gideon shook his head. "I can't risk shooting into the building without knowing where Bella is. We need to come up with another plan."

The men fell silent. Miguel lowered himself to the ground with the others. "There is a small window in the back. I got the horses away without being noticed. I can use the window to find the girl, see where she is in the building."

Gideon scratched the stubble emerging along his chin. "Perhaps. But we would have no way of knowing if she moved before we started firing. I'm not willing to put her in jeopardy."

Miguel nodded, and conversation lulled once again. Ideas were scarce. Gideon fought the panic that rose inside him as each minute ticked by with no solution. Unable to come up with anything better, though, he finally gave the order for Miguel to follow through on his suggestion. There had to be a way to rescue Isabella. They just needed to find it.

Chapter 42

The silence pressed on Adelaide like a lead shawl, hunching her shoulders and crushing her to her knees. Gideon couldn't be dead. He just couldn't. Surely the Lord wouldn't restore his health only to have him fall prey to a madman's bullet. Yet why else would Petchey stop firing? He didn't seem the kind to grant mercy. On the other hand, she heard no evidence of celebration from within the shack, either. Maybe there was still hope.

Adelaide planted the butt of the rifle in the earth and used the barrel like a cane as she pushed to her feet. She looked around, trying to regain a sense of equilibrium in a world that was spinning out of control.

Logic slowly seeped past the chaos of her emotions and into her brain. She began to process her predicament. Miguel had not returned. He must have gone to help Gideon when the shooting broke out. Good. Her husband needed him more than she did. But what if he hadn't returned because he, too, had been shot down? What if they were all dead?

Nausea churned through her with sudden violence. She closed

her eyes and forced air into her lungs, resisting the urge to retch. A fierce desire to run through the trees until she found the men bombarded her. She needed to know how they fared. But something held her back.

Isabella.

If the men were indeed gone, she was the only one left to save Izzy. Slowly, Adelaide turned back and focused once again on the shack.

The window beckoned, sparking an idea. A crazy, illogical idea, but what else did she have? Only her faith and an ounce of courage to act upon it.

"For such a time as this." The words Mordecai spoke to Esther echoed in her mind and resonated in her spirit. She was in the right place at the right time. It had to be the Lord's will.

Adelaide took a tentative step away from the shelter of the trees. Nothing happened. She curled her fingers around the rifle and held it loosely in her fist as she stepped again, farther this time. No bullets pelted her. The earth didn't quake. She locked her eyes on the small window, grateful that there was no glass and no oilcloth, and walked. Every time the grass crunched under her feet, she prayed.

She reached the shack wall and flattened herself against the warped boards. Her heart racing at a gallop, she turned her head just enough to peer through the opening with one eye. Petchey stood near the door with his back to her, his gun hand propped against the side of the window.

Staring at his back, she found herself wishing, only for a second, that she could abandon her conscience. He'd ambushed Gideon. He wanted to exploit Izzy and steal her inheritance, maybe even kill her. Yet shooting a man in the back, even for good cause, would require her to turn her back on her beliefs. And that she wouldn't do.

Perhaps she should just threaten to shoot him and demand that he let Izzy go. But if he called her bluff, she might end up dead, and Izzy would have no one left. She would have ruined the child's one chance for escape. No, her best chance was to choose stealth over confrontation.

Another man moved into her field of vision. Petchey's accomplice. Gideon had mentioned the solicitor. Clearly not a hardened gunman, the fellow paced back and forth across the floor, wringing his hands and shaking his head.

"I want no part of this, sir. Kidnapping, attempted murder . . . It's just not right."

Attempted? A thrill bolted through her. The men must be alive.

"Stop your sniveling, Farnsworth," Petchey ground out. "You crossed the line between right and wrong years ago. You might have pretended to be blind to the fraudulent financial dealings you brokered for me, but you are no innocent. Every time you deposited one of my bank drafts, you sullied your hands."

"But that was just money," Farnsworth whined. "These are people's lives."

"You don't think financial ruin affects people's lives? Ha! You're a fool. I know of at least three suicides that resulted from your *harmless* money schemes. The only difference is that here you have to be man enough to witness death firsthand."

A whimper sounded off to Adelaide's left. Izzy? Adelaide leaned her rifle against the wall and crawled under the window ledge to the opposite side. As she stood, she searched the back corners of the room. There. Beside the crumbling hearth. Isabella lay huddled on the floor, folded into a tight ball. Her arms encircled her head while she rocked back, the same posture she adopted when awakened by a nightmare.

Tears pooled in Adelaide's eyes. She ached to pull her daughter to her breast and hold her until the nightmare vanished. But the only way to do that was to enter the nightmare herself.

For the first time in her life, she actually thanked God for making her so small. None of the men would have been able to fit through the window, but she could. The question was, could she do it without being seen?

Adelaide moved directly in front of the window before she could think too much about the answer. She monitored the men inside, waiting to be sure both had their attention focused forward. A rickety table stood between them and Isabella. It wasn't much in the way of cover, but if Adelaide hunkered down as she fetched her daughter, perhaps it would protect them from Petchey's notice.

She hopped up, bracing her arms against the ledge. Then she dragged her stomach across the opening, careful not to grunt as air whooshed from her lungs. Ducking her head, Adelaide twisted her shoulders at an angle to fit diagonally through the square space and flipped over to a sitting position. After that, pulling her legs through was a simple affair.

The men continued their grumbling vigil, unaware of her presence. Adelaide crawled along the wall toward the hearth, keeping her head below the top of the table. Thankfully, the floor was dirt and didn't squeak as she moved.

Just before reaching Izzy, she stopped, stealing a glance back at the men. Not wanting to startle the girl and alert the others to what was going on, Adelaide refrained from touching Isabella and instead whispered her name in an almost inaudible voice. The child's quivering shoulders stilled. Adelaide repeated her name. Isabella turned her head to the side, and her red rimmed eyes widened. Adelaide immediately put a finger to her lips. Izzy's gaze flew around the room, lighting briefly on her uncle before returning to Adelaide. She sat up and nodded.

Adelaide helped her daughter to her feet, took her hand, and led her back toward the window. They were nearly there when Petchey shifted.

"Farnsworth, bring me the other gun. If you're not going to use—"

He turned to gesture toward the satchel on the far side of the room and suddenly noticed Adelaide. They both froze—him in shock, her in horror. Adelaide recovered first. She scooped Isabella's legs over her arm and lunged for the window. Petchey bellowed. His footsteps pounded toward them.

Adelaide thrust her daughter feetfirst through the opening. "Run for the trees, Izzy. Miguel and Papa Gideon are in the trees."

Isabella hit the ground and looked back. "Mama!"

"Run!" Adelaide ordered. She hooked her right leg over the ledge and shoved her head through, less to escape than to prevent the man behind her from getting within reaching distance of Isabella. Petchey grabbed her around the waist and tried to tear her away. She clung to the window with all her might, her leg and shoulder blade wedged against the frame.

Petchey was too strong, though. Her hold on the wood began to slip. She watched Isabella's short legs pump across the clearing and hope soared in her heart. Then a shape emerged from the stand of mesquite. Miguel.

He sprinted out of the trees, straight for Isabella. With a last desperate surge, Adelaide reached for the rifle she had left against the wall.

"Miguel!" She flung the weapon as far toward him as she could.

Unable to hold on any longer, Adelaide was torn from the window. Her head banged into the top of the frame and her arm and leg scraped against the sides as Petchey hauled her in.

"You interfering little—" He punctuated his sentence with a slap across her face as an exclamation point.

Her neck whipped back and pain scalded her cheek. He shoved her to the floor and ducked his head out the window. He raised his pistol to take a shot, then pulled it away with a roar fierce enough to rival any lion.

The man named Farnsworth gently took hold of her arm and helped her stand. His eyes shimmered with apology but gave no encouragement. She extracted her arm from him and lifted her chin. His unwillingness to take action against his employer fueled her outrage and bolstered her courage. She stiffened her spine and pivoted to face the angry beast who towered above her. God knew how to close the mouths of lions. She just hoped he would close the muzzles of their guns, as well.

Chapter 43

Rustling brush and thudding footsteps brought Gideon to his feet with Miguel's pistol clutched in his hand. He craned his neck from side to side, searching for a clear view of what approached through the staggered tree trunks that impeded his vision. It was too soon for Miguel to have returned, and he'd just heard Petchey shouting in the shack. Could the viscount have a man on the outside?

Gideon's jaw tensed. He slid his finger into position over the trigger. Then his foreman broke out of the brush. Gideon immediately dropped his arm to his side.

"Bella?" Her name came out on a ragged breath. He had been taking aim at his own daughter.

She was clinging to Miguel's neck, her legs wrapped around his waist as the two lumbered through the vegetation. Baffled joy speared through him. He holstered his gun and ran to meet them. He pulled Bella from Miguel's arms and hugged her close. His eyes growing moist, he looked to the vaquero to explain the miracle. "How . . . ?"

Then he noticed the rifle in the man's hand. His rifle. The rifle he had given to Adelaide. Dread punched him in the gut. Miguel's somber expression confirmed his fears.

Bella leaned away from Gideon's chest and grabbed his face between her palms. "Miss Addie climbed in the window to get me, but Uncle Reg-nald caught her before she could get out. You gotta go get her, Papa Gidyon. Uncle is real mad."

Terror on Addie's behalf paralyzed him for a moment, but as fast as it came, it left, replaced by an unearthly calm. He knew what he needed to do. Gideon met Miguel's gaze. "Cover me?"

The man nodded without hesitation. "Sí."

Gideon strode over to James and handed Bella down to him. "Guard my girl."

"With my life, Gid." James slid his arm around the child's shoulder and tucked her securely into his side.

Gideon laid his hand atop Bella's head, lingering for a second or two. She looked up at him with big blue eyes. "It'll be all right, Papa Gidyon. I prayed to God for you and Miss Addie to come get me, and you did. I'll keep praying while you go get Miss Addie. God will help you."

Oh, for the faith of a child. If only he could believe as fully. *Help my unbelief, Lord. Grant us success.*

"Keep praying, Bella mine," Gideon said, his throat tight. He rubbed a lock of her golden hair between his thumb and forefinger and smiled into her eyes a final time before turning away. He strode to the edge of the clearing and drew his weapon. Miguel followed. Gideon held the revolver up, checking the chambers a final time as he laid out his plan, such as it was.

"Aim high. I'll retrieve my gun from the clearing as we advance. If we make it to the shack, I'll go after Petchey. You get Addie."

Gideon lowered his arm and looked at Miguel. "I know you have family back in California who depend on you. I'll not think less of you if you wish to lay down cover fire from the trees. You don't have to follow me to the shack. I wouldn't even ask, except that I know he'll kill her if we wait."

"I follow, patrón. Señora Westcott is a good woman. I would want someone to fight for my Rosa if she was the one in there."

Gideon nodded. "Thank you, my friend." He looked back at the small clearing that separated him from Addie. It seemed to stretch for miles, though in reality the line shack was only a good stone's throw away.

They wouldn't have time to reload. The revolver had six shots, the rifle fifteen. If he could reclaim his discarded gun, he'd have six more. It would have to be enough.

"Let's do it."

Gideon vaulted into the open and sent a shot through the upper right corner of the front window. He ran and shot and ran and shot. The report of Miguel's rifle echoed behind him as Gideon outdistanced the vaquero. He had only covered a third of the distance before Petchey started returning fire. Resisting the instinct to duck, Gideon ran on. Faster. Harder. His thighs burned. His lungs ached. He emptied his last chamber into the wood of the door, then took three more strides to where his gun belt lay abandoned in the dirt.

Miguel continued to fire. Gideon dove for the new weapon at the same time a shot blasted from the shack. He heard the whiz of the bullet zipping over his head as he collided with the dirt. He rolled toward the leather holster, pulled the gun free, and scrambled back to his feet.

The closer they came to the building, the faster they fired. Petchey got off several rounds, but his shots flew wild as he strove to keep his head protected behind the wall. A few steps from the shack, Gideon ran out of ammunition. He tossed down his gun and sprinted full-out toward the door. The old wood splintered as he kicked it in, and his momentum carried him forward into the one-room building.

"Gideon!"

He saw Addie break away from the grasp of a thin man in the back corner. In the same instant, he turned to charge Petchey before the man had time to draw a bead on him. But the viscount wasn't by the window as Gideon expected. He was lunging for Adelaide. The blackguard grabbed her by the hair and jerked her in front of him. She yelped in pain, grabbing her head and slumping in his grasp. He hauled her up, clutched her neck in the V of his left arm, and shoved the muzzle of his pistol against her temple. She stilled. So did Gideon. His heart constricted.

Miguel bounded into the room, winded but steady as he aimed his rifle at Petchey's head. Gideon didn't know if he had any rounds left, but a bluff would work nearly as well.

"Let her go." Gideon fisted his hands, keeping his eyes fixed on Petchey.

"Bring my niece to me, and we can discuss a trade."

"I don't think so."

Petchey's eyes narrowed. "Then we have nothing left to say to each other."

He shoved Adelaide at Miguel, effectively neutralizing the only weapon that could be used on him. At the same time, he extended his arm to aim his pistol at Gideon.

Like a ram defending his territory, Gideon charged. He ducked his head and crashed into Petchey's middle, driving him back into the table. The viscount grunted, and his gun fell to the ground. Gideon landed two punches to the man's stomach. Then Petchey jammed his knee into Gideon's forehead. His neck whipped backward as pain exploded in his head. The viscount pounced. He pummeled Gideon's abdomen until one jab connected fully with the site of his wound. Gideon cried out and crumpled to his knees.

As Petchey bent to retrieve his gun, a flurry of cream-colored skirts attacked. Addie launched herself onto his back and grappled for the weapon. Miguel followed her, wielding his rifle like a club.

Yet he couldn't use it for fear of hitting Adelaide. Gideon forced the agony aside and crawled to his feet. He had to get her away from the viscount.

Before he could stand, though, Petchey growled and flung Addie backward, toppling her into Gideon. Gideon closed his arms around her and cushioned her fall. But above them, the viscount brought his pistol around to point dead center at Adelaide's back. Miguel swung the rifle and Gideon rolled Addie beneath him, sheltering her with his body. The pistol fired.

Gideon flinched, but the anticipated pain didn't come. He lifted his head. Petchey lay in a heap on the floor.

Gideon moved off of Addie and looked up at his foreman. "I owe you my life, Miguel."

"Wasn't me, patrón." The man's eyebrows knit together. "He fell before I hit him."

Adelaide sat up and tugged on his hand. "Gideon, look."

He followed her gaze to the back of the room. Mr. Farnsworth stood with a revolver in his hand. His entire body trembled.

"I had to stop him," Farnsworth said, his voice hollow. "He's hurt enough people. He had to be stopped."

The gun fell from his fingers and thudded onto the packed-dirt floor.

Adelaide buried her face in Gideon's neck. He wrapped his arm around her and caressed her shoulder, her cheek, her chin, sending silent prayers of thanks to God for sparing them. He lifted her face to him. All the ugliness of what they had endured vanished in the light of her beauty. His aches faded as he gazed into her eyes, his love for her so strong it throbbed with every heartbeat.

"It's over?" she asked.

He nodded. "It's over."

Chapter 44

China cups clinked against saucers as Isabella and her grandmother shared refreshments on the veranda with the miniature tea set Lady Westcott had brought from England. Adelaide's forehead crinkled behind the book she was reading. No, not Lady Westcott. Lady *Mansfield*. Gideon's mother had explained with much patience that she was to be addressed by her husband's title, not his surname, yet Adelaide still had trouble remembering. At least Gideon had two brothers in line before him to inherit the dratted title, so hopefully she would never have to call her husband Lord Mansfield. So stiff and formal. She'd take the simple and utterly marvelous Mr. Gideon Westcott over a stuffy Lord Mansfield any day.

Although she had to admit that the current Lord Mansfield was far from stuffy. For the last two weeks, Gideon's father had acted like a man on a Wild West adventure. He actually seemed disappointed to find no warring Indian tribes nearby. Adelaide smiled as she gazed past the white porch railing at the very domesticated outbuildings surrounding the house. She'd had enough excitement since her marriage to Gideon without adding dime-novel Indian raids and masked bandits into the mix.

So much had happened since that day at the shack. Gideon testified before the circuit judge about all that had transpired, giving a favorable account of how Mr. Farnsworth's actions had saved their lives. The judge ruled the incident a justifiable homicide and released Mr. Farnsworth to return to England. James had stayed on at Westcott Cottage until his leg healed, and when he left, he carried adoption papers with him to file at the county clerk's office, making Isabella an official part of the Westcott family.

Gideon's father and mother arrived for a visit and were able to join them for the reception hosted by the Menardville church last Saturday in honor of their marriage. Mrs. Kent had outdone herself with the decorations, and the dear woman nearly fainted when an honest-to-goodness British lord and lady appeared on the church steps. However, the highlight of the evening for Adelaide was when Gideon vowed his love to her in front of all those gathered in the small clapboard building and slipped a beautiful heirloom ring onto her finger.

Adelaide held the topaz stone up to the light. The afternoon sun glistened on the golden gem and set off an answering glow in her heart. She was so blessed. She had a husband who truly cherished her and an extended family who had welcomed her into their midst despite the fact that she couldn't have been at all what they'd expected in a wife for their son. An impulsive American rancher's daughter with no family pedigree rarely made a titled gentleman's list for prospective brides. Yet their love for Gideon seemed to spill over onto her.

Tearing her gaze away from her wedding ring, she turned back to the well-worn copy of *Jane Eyre* that lay in her lap. Jane had left Thornfield and was wandering about northern England, broken-hearted. Adelaide sighed. Jane longed for her Edward much as she longed for Gideon, torn apart by the miles that separated them.

Gideon had taken his father to San Antonio five days ago on business. He needed to check on the warehouses that stored his wool clip and negotiate with the merchants who sold to the textile mills. It was part of being married to a sheepman, she supposed, but their bed felt so empty at night. How quickly she had become accustomed to his warm arms surrounding her as she drifted off to sleep.

It didn't help that she had been left to fend for herself with her mother-in-law without Gideon as a buffer between them. She wanted to make a good impression on Lady Mansfield, but she constantly felt as if she was putting the wrong foot forward. Lady Mansfield never remarked on it, however. She was always gracious and kind. Of course she was also always perfectly coifed, dressed in the latest fashion, and unerringly proper. Just a tad intimidating for a woman whose best dress looked like a rag in comparison and who was more likely to smell like a horse than the latest perfume from Paris. She didn't sense any disapproval from Lady Mansfield, though, just a slightly strained atmosphere as they both adjusted.

Thank heavens for Izzy. Equally comfortable in both worlds, she bounced between mother and grandmother throughout the day, delighting both women with her antics, and giving them at least one subject for conversation with some semblance of common ground.

Things would get better. They just needed time. And for Gideon to come home.

Shifting in her chair, Adelaide lifted her book and resumed reading. She scanned a paragraph or two, but Jane's angst was too similar to her own. She needed the happy ending. Breaking her own rule, she thumbed ahead in the story until Jane returned to Rochester, their love for one another overcoming his injuries and their differences in station. Satisfaction swept through her. That's what she needed—to flip ahead in her own tale and reunite with her love.

"Mama?" Isabella hopped up into Adelaide's lap and pulled the book away from her face. "Is that Papa riding in?"

"I don't think so, honey. It's probably just Miguel or one of the other men. Papa's not supposed to be home until tomorrow."

"But the white horse next to him looks like the one Grandfather rides."

Adelaide tossed her book aside and squeezed out from under Isabella. She lunged across the porch to the railing. Isabella was right. It did look like Gideon and his father.

Her heart fluttered. She wanted to run out to greet her husband, yet a proper English wife would never do something so undignified. But then, Gideon hadn't married a proper Englishwoman, had he?

Unable to hide her grin, Adelaide grabbed a fistful of her skirt and twirled around the spindled post at the stairway. She bounded down the steps and across the yard waving her free arm above her head. One of the riders spurred his mount forward away from the other. Solomon ate up the remaining distance, and Gideon jumped from his back a few feet from Adelaide. She ran into his embrace. He lifted her from the ground and spun her around in a dizzying circle. She laughed and clung to his neck, throwing her head back in pure joy.

As the spinning stopped, Adelaide's eyes found Gideon's, and she drank from the love flowing in her husband's gaze.

"I missed you, sunshine." His hands splayed over her back as he held her body close to his. She slid along the length of him, the feel of his firm muscles sending a shiver through her as her feet reached for the ground.

He stroked his way up her arm and cupped her face in his palm. She leaned into his touch, her eyes drifting closed for a brief moment as his thumb drew delicate lines along her cheekbone.

Adelaide tilted her chin up, longing for a kiss, but as her eyes opened, she caught a glimpse of her father-in-law grinning down at her from atop his horse. Heat flushed her face, and she tried to pull back—only Gideon had other ideas. Taking no pity on her whatsoever, he drew her even closer.

"I didn't expect you until tomorrow," she said to cover her nervousness.

"The boy made me camp out in the wilds and sleep on the ground in order to shave off a few hours from our travel time," Lord Mansfield accused with a sparkle in his eye.

"You were the one begging for an authentic Western experience. I just gave you what you asked for."

Lord Mansfield's booming laugh showered over them. "I remember what it's like to be young, son. There's no shame in hurrying home to be with your family. Now, give your bride your gift while I go greet my own wife. Love's not only for the young, you know." He waggled his eyebrows in a way that elicited a giggle from Adelaide and then nudged his mount into a walk toward the house. As he passed, he placed a lead line in Gideon's hand.

Curious, Adelaide followed the line of the rope with her eyes and discovered the most beautiful filly she'd ever seen tethered to the end. Small but with excellent form, the gleaming black animal shook her head in a show of spirit, reminding Adelaide of another horse that still lived on in her heart.

"Gideon?" Her eyes misty, she turned back to her husband.

"I named her Lily, if you approve. I know she can never replace the horse your father gave you, but I hope you will accept this gift from another man who loves you just as much."

"She's beautiful, Gideon. Perfect." Knowing they had an audience not far away, Adelaide ducked her head and stepped away from her husband to pet the black filly. Her heart nearly burst with gratitude and love for the thoughtful man who had sought to mend her aching heart with such a well-chosen gift.

Gideon came up behind her and whispered in her ear as he, too, brushed the horse's glossy coat. "You know . . . Solomon respected the queen of Sheba as a peer and fellow ruler, but in his song of songs, he called his lover a lily. 'As the lily among thorns, so is my love among the daughters.' "

His face was so close to hers as he quoted from the biblical love poem, she could feel the rasp of his whiskers and smell the manly scent that she had clung to by wrapping herself in his shirts at night. Having the man inside the shirt was ever so much better.

She turned toward him, placed her hands on his shoulders, and stretched up on her tiptoes. His head bent. His lips angled toward hers.

"Papa! Papa!"

Gideon paused. Regret glimmered in his eyes, but his mouth curved into a smile as he stepped away from Adelaide to meet his daughter. He crouched down and opened his arms to her.

"Spin me, too, Papa. Just like Mama."

Adelaide grinned, delighting in the effervescence of this little girl who had once been so quiet and somber. Gideon obliged and whirled her around, his deep chuckles mingling with girlish giggles in an enchanted symphony.

"I think you grew two inches since I left," Gideon said, measuring her generously with his hands.

"You brought Mama a new horse?" She peered around him to examine the gift.

"I brought you something, too."

Her attention jerked back to him. "You did?"

He nodded and reached into his saddlebag. "There's one for you and one for your grandmother. Yours is the one tied with the blue ribbon." Gideon handed her two small bundles. "Why don't you take these up to the house? Give the pink one to your grandmother, and then the two of you can open them together. I'll come see you after your mama and I put the horses away."

Isabella collected the two treasures and skipped back up to the house.

"That was neatly done," Adelaide teased.

Gideon winked. "Hurry. She'll come looking for us if we delay too long." He passed the filly's lead line off to her and strode ahead with Solomon, nearly at a jog.

He was serious.

Adelaide's insides danced as she scurried to keep up. Gideon disappeared into the dimness of the stable, and she followed. She moved through the entrance but didn't see her husband. Assuming he was stabling Solomon, she steered Lily into an open stall. The instant she closed the door, however, Gideon was at her side. She sucked in a startled breath as his mouth descended upon hers. His hands tangled in her hair and he pressed her gently against the stall door. Adelaide recovered from her surprise and rose up to meet him. The kiss deepened, the initial intensity softening into a tenderness that melted Adelaide from the inside out.

Finally Gideon raised his head, and Adelaide laid her cheek against his chest.

"I'm so glad you're home," she murmured.

He squeezed her arm. "I couldn't stay away another day. I have a duty to fulfill, after all."

Adelaide tipped her chin up and raised a brow at him. "A duty? Is that all I am to you?"

The kiss they had just shared made that question completely ridiculous, but her emotions were swirling around in a chaotic fashion, and a glimmer of insecurity crept in.

He smiled down at her, those dimples she adored restoring her confidence. "I owe you a happy ending, remember? I can't fulfill that duty if I'm not with you."

She laughed, the sound trilling through the rafters of the stable. "You already battled a dragon, rescued two damsels in distress, and married the fair maiden who had fallen desperately in love with you. I don't think an ending could get any happier."

"Well, I aim to keep trying anyway."

He dropped a kiss onto her forehead, and then, with his arm wrapped securely around her shoulders, Gideon led her out of the stable and back into the sunshine.

As they walked across the yard to the house, Adelaide's gaze drifted heavenward. Puffy white clouds dotted the sky, but one in particular seemed to linger over the rooftop of their home—a reminder of the One truly responsible for her happy ending. Other hardships were sure to come, but she and Gideon had a guide who would see them through.

God's way might not always be clear, but it could always be trusted.

About the Author

KAREN WITEMEYER holds a master's degree in Psychology from Abilene Christian University and is a member of ACFW, RWA, and the Texas Coalition of Authors. She has published fiction in Focus on the Family's children's magazine, and has written several articles for online publications and anthologies. *Head in the Clouds* is her second novel. Karen lives in Abilene, Texas, with her husband and three children.